JACK

Berry Knoll Publishing
Arizona, USA

ISBN 978-0-9991934-1-9

To Rock 'n' Roll.
Live long my friend.

To my parents.

To Isaac Newton.

And finally
to Jesus Christ,
my hero.

Chapter 1

It was the path and the destination. It was the race and the recovery. It was the tongue and the words that filled its mouth. It whispered, but the words were muddled and unclear, like the lyrics to a song that people hear differently depending upon the states of their minds and the thoughts that dwell there. Some are dirty and some are clean. Some are caring and some are mean. Some are shallow and some are deep, and some are very deep. The words were there to be understood, but in what way? They were voiced around each tree trunk and bend. They trickled from waterfalls and shattered in broken syllables upon the stones. There was no certainty to their meaning; there was only a feeling.

With its walls of stone and its covering of clouds, Marc's canyon home was nothing like the houses that men build which are straight, plumb, and square. Instead, it was tossed, crooked, and torn. Its floor was an upheaval of broken rocks and fallen trees. If God had carved out these walls and set this stream in its course, then he took great pains to conceal his involvement. Nothing between these ancient cliffs nor the capricious clouds that covered the sky suggested the workmanship of an intentional hand. All was chance, all was raw, all was true.

These hills and canyons were calm and empty in the winter. Marc rarely met other hikers when it was this cold. The air froze his nostrils, but he was warm from the strain of pushing on. His heavy panting left a plume of white vapor behind him. Whenever he saw a paw print in the snow, he bent down to examine it. Usually dogs accompanying other hikers left these prints, but mountain lions also occupied these canyons. During the winter, the lions descend from the tops into the warmer canyons, hunting and seeking shelter from the cold, harsh winds. Cats walk with retracted claws so their paws don't leave claw marks in the snow. This was a big print; he smiled. A male lion probably left it. They are much larger and more powerful than their female counterparts. Being alone increased the chance of an encounter.

There was no encounter, however; there never was. He reached his destination—a narrow pass where the stream spread shallow into a secluded basin. He hiked up to its sandy bed. The running water prevented the sand from freezing solid. As he walked along the faded margins of the stream, water swelled around his soles. Looking back, he saw the empty depressions in the sand slowly vanish behind him, as if shadows were tracking him. Shadows are cowards. They lurk, they mock, they taunt, and when their numbers are great, they are a dreadful sight, but when the moment of truth arrives, they sneak, they cower, or they fly away. Shadows are contemptible creatures. He waited until they cowered at his feet. Suddenly he fell to his knees. Clasping his hands, he bent to the ground.

Pressed down from the snowy tops above, water seeped from the sheer stone straining under the endless burden piled high upon it. The cliff had naught to rest its back against: no truss, no buttress, and no tie. When its beads of sweat met the cold canyon air that drifted along with the stream, they too froze against its face. Ice clung to the basin walls in pillars and pipes. Stony ledges rose in tiers upstream. Here, before an icy alter, he pounded his troubles into the sand.

As soon as he re-entered cell-service, he called his housekeeper. A hot bath in a candle lit room suggested more regarding his mental state than his physical fatigue. He drove slowly over these country roads, adjusting his speed so that other drivers could easily pass him. When he reached an intersection, his stop was deliberate and lingering. Unlike typical commutes, when he would push the limit, roll through stops, and impatiently wait for open stretches where he could bury other drivers in his contempt, this commute was supremely calm.

Today, the world resonated with the calmness that he felt. The wheels of his crossover followed every turn with the faintest nudge. The console buttons were not pressed that normally sought endlessly for affinity on the radio. There was always a cloud perfectly positioned to block the sun from his eyes while admitting a brilliant shower of light upon the landscape. If he perceived the world on the outside to be in harmony with his on the inside, then it was, for there was no experience apart from perception. There was no testimony to refute his; no evidence but his serenity. The world responded to him simply because there was no other alternative presented. There was no competing thought.

Sometimes Marc stayed in the city, especially during heavy traffic or rough weather. He kept an apartment on the eighteenth floor overlooking the financial district, but tonight he was headed to his country home, about forty minutes from the office. When he drove to the canyons, it added more than an hour to his commute. Reaching home, he keyed in the pass-code at the gate and rode through the shadows that ran and chased along the way. Twilight settled over his hillside manor with the latch-clap of the front door. The hills rested like a tired, old man whose eyes drift closed as he passes through a veil of light to an unknown world.

Marc turned down the lights in the dressing room. Leaving his clothes behind him, he walked past the full-length mirror into the bathroom, taking no notice of anything in particular. There would be no self-examination tonight, at least not eye to eye. He found his glass and ice bucket sitting on the vanity beside the tub, but he brought the decanter with him. He never allowed anyone to handle his decanter. Such things could never be replaced. As far as things go, one thing was as good as any other thing, provided it was sufficiently suited to its purpose. However, when there is more than form and substance to a thing, then it is a soul and souls are irreplaceable.

Marc's friends accused him of being cold and uncaring because he was detached from common things. He was detached from common decisions. A ball game was as good as a concert. A burger was as good as a steak. A trip was as good as staying at home. Therefore, they said that he didn't care about things. In truth, however, he was intensely attached to some things—to special souls. When he took possession of a soul, he owned it, he guarded it, and he cared for it. Some were old and some were new. Some were valued by others and some were disregarded. Nevertheless, he regarded them.

He poured a dram of Scotch into his glass and inhaled it deeply, taking a sip only after some protracted examination of its aroma and such. Dropping a few ice cubes into his glass, he raised it and said "Cheers," to the empty room. He then slid into his tub. It stood on its own legs beside its companion. The other tub was slightly shorter and narrower. The rim flared out at the top and curved elegantly from front to back with an embellished headrest at the end. It was more ornate than his. Its lion-footed legs were shorter and more slender. By contrast, his tub was plain, but complimentary. His personal tastes were rather plain, overall. He ate plain, drank plain, and with the exception of a gorgeous sports car, he lived plain. The feminine flourishes set about the house appeared more striking in contrast to their simple surroundings.

In the dressing room, opposite the bench where Marc dressed, there stood a gallery of feminine grace exhibiting photos, hats, heels, and other accessories from Lena's greatest moments. It was a stylish, floor-to-ceiling mahogany case with special lighting and inlaid upholstery. Marc had fresh cut flowers placed here daily. Marc himself took one particular shot of Lena because she refused to pose that way for a professional photographer. One of the bitterest arguments Marc and Lena ever had was in regard to keeping either the photo or the housekeeper who might perhaps post a copy of the photo to the internet in an act of disgruntled retaliation. Otherwise, Lena modestly objected each time Marc added a new article to his "shrine."

"So what if it's a shrine?" Marc asked rhetorically. "Everyone has a shrine—everyone worships something. Toby has his shrine to the Cowboys. Zachary worships wine and Carla bows every morning to the gods of tulips and daffodils."

"But that doesn't expose her girl-flower to the whole world," Lena argued.

"No, she does that just fine on her own."

"That's not true."

"Right…defending your friend. Didn't see that coming."

"I'm not defending her. I'm telling you the truth. She explained the whole thing to me."

"How do you know she didn't lie to you?" Marc grimaced slightly when he asked this question.

"Have you ever lied to me?" Lena's fear monster began to raise its head. It started as a question. Then it took on some memories which were vibrant in her recollection and faded in his. Memories—those gems of the past, a time that's dead—they filled its lungs and beat its heart; they envenomed its fangs and forked its tongue. They were the fibers to its flesh and marrow to its bone. There was an unsettled place buried deep inside of Lena that rumbled when she hurt. It was the den of her monster friend. It would hobble and pace about, foraging the morsels of fear and malice that its owner had buried there over time. During dormant times (Marc called them "good times"), its munching and moving were practically imperceptible. But the rage was swelling.

Some say that fear is the opposite of faith. That's not quite right. Fear is not the opposite of faith. Fear *is* faith— faith in powers that are evil rather than good, like a face that would turn to shadows rather than light. Under its influence, no reason, no plea, no alibi could shake Lena's suspicion that Marc was cheating on her. His defense was fodder to her fear; the more he said, the more vicious her monster friend grew. If he walked away, it binged on its own flesh until it magnified every thoughtless blunder into a calculated insult, every glance into a gaze, every mistake into a sin. He had been here before and he had handled it poorly many times. Many times he had fed it with anger. Many times he had drunk it with wine. So this time, when Lena began raging, he stood there and took his punishment like a man.

It thrashed him. It tore into him like that old back yard dog tore into Laura's vinyl doll. Laura was Marc's annoying younger sister. Her doll's long, silky hair was ripped and matted with the grime of saliva, dirt, and dead grass clippings. Most of her clothes were ripped off, two of her limbs were scattered, and her body sustained multiple stab wounds. The doll's mechanical eyes that shut while she was lying in repose never opened normally again. Laura said that it was because she was resting. She lived in her own world. Even a violent collision with "reality" was quickly resolved with a satisfying fantasy. As soon as the doll was retrieved, its limbs restored, and its clothes stitched as best she could, Laura wiped her up like a nurse tending to cuts and burns. Then she put the doll to bed. Marc tried to get her to throw the doll away, but Laura said that, "Pioneer women are menders." The Mormon pioneers were her heroes, as they were for many Utah children her age.

It started when Marc was walking home from school and he saw Laura roller-skating in the driveway. She was holding her doll outward with both arms and talking to it. He went into the house and emerged again with his basketball to shoot some hoops. He pretended to drop the ball on several drives in order to hit Laura with it. She ignored it which only made him torment her worse. "Why do you talk to your stupid doll? She can't hear you." Laura pretended not to notice him, but she protectively clasped her doll to her chest and continued in reassuring tones. He ran after her, grabbed the doll away, and threw it over the fence where the neighbor's little monster dog did the rest.

When their mother arrived home from work, she asked Laura what was bothering her. She told her mother what Marc had done to her doll. "But she's alright now. She's resting," Laura said with a sigh of relief. It was actually his mother who pressed charges against Marc. The best defense that he could offer was that he was trying to help Laura grasp "reality." His mother told him that each person's reality is different. This idea infuriated Marc.

He shouted, "There's only one reality. For example, you have brown eyes. I know that, you know that, Dad knows that, Laura knows that. Your eyes don't change color just 'cause a different person walks into the room."

"Perhaps that's true, but your dad sees my eyes differently than you do."

"No, he doesn't. He might feel differently about them but he sees the same thing I see—the same atoms and molecules that I see."

"Maybe feelings are more significant than atoms and molecules."

Marc shook his head. "Now I know where Laura gets it." This upset his mother and the conversation spiraled downward quickly. But that was a long time ago. Fifteen years of haze stood between him and those days.

Time is a ravaging fire that burns up the deadwood of the past and fills the space between with a dense smoke that makes it difficult for people to see even their own lives clearly. Despite how objectively some people claim to remember past events—learning to ride a bike, fishing a mountain stream, kissing an old lover—they often see themselves in the memory from the perspective of separate, external observers standing off and apart from the experience.

Apparently, there are ghostly stalkers who silently follow their human subjects wherever they go, who watch their actions, who hear their words, and know their thoughts. Then at night, when humans are most vulnerable, these phantoms bend over sleeping corpses and whisper counterfeit stories into defenseless ears. These faceless memory mongers take away the truth and leave plausible lies in its place. People accept anything they are told, because they are oblivious to the attrition of memory most of the time. Managing their biases is about the best that they can do because it is not a question of whether or not people lose touch with objective reality but with what bearing and distance they stray from it.

Nevertheless, the whips and lashes from Lena's monster friend were still fresh enough in memory to sting. Marc was strong—and sharp. He could lift the weight of Lena *and* her monster friend, but he was as helpless as that little doll when she turned on him. Her personality had a lot of color and texture, like a work of art. And like a work of fine art, there was a lot of contrast between light and dark. Such is the order of things in general. Time is split between day and night. For every joy, there is a sorrow and for every virtue, there is a vice.

Wound up in the guts of every person, there is a monster and there is a glory. Her monster was ugly, but her beauty was glorious indeed.

When they attended the governor's reception, she stood in her evening gown with the splendor of a goddess. The champagne colored sash with golden stitching tied around her waist repeated similar highlights in her hair. She worked hard to maintain her figure, which was apparent to the men and women stealing glances of her as she mingled with the other guests. Her satin dress freely flowed over her lean curves, only dwelling slightly upon her shoulders for support and around her waist where the sash bound it to her. It covered her chest to the collarbone, but her shoulders and arms were bare. Her back was bare also to the small of it. The color, texture, and specular shine of her gown gave her slender frame the appearance of polished stone, especially where it fell in an arching bounce from her rounded glutes toward the floor. The heels she stood on made the marble floor look like sand and her smooth legs, like sculpted marble. They set her on a pedestal that won her the love and devotion, or the envy and disgust, of nearly everyone present.

There were two women talking to each other in an arrangement that made it appear as if there was third person missing. The gap in their circle was situated toward Lena, who was standing beyond earshot but within scrutinizing proximity. Marc reciprocated the scrutiny from where he pretended to listen to a man talk about economics. One of the women was close to Lena's age, twenty-eight, and the other was about fifty. It was apparent that these two women, along with a notable number of others present, shared some kind of collective consciousness which, in spite of the variety of styles, colors, and personal interests among them, transformed them into cultural clones in uniforms. The uniform consisted of modestly designed clothing with half-length sleeves and hemlines to the knees. Their hair was short, permed, and free flowing to somewhere along the length of their necks. The older woman's hair was slightly shorter and layered in large swooping curls so that her head assumed a roughly spherical shape, like ruffled feathers which were intended to insulate the contents of her head.

Among the men present also, there were those who ascribed to a common code. Everything pertaining to their appearance was neat and tidy. They wore their hair the same, they held their jaws the same, and they smiled the same. They spoke with a hypnotizing calmness, like an overflowing wave, over exposure to which would induce one of two reactions: either the listener would be compelled to gasp for breath to save his life or he would be lulled to sleep and from sleep to death. It was better to receive a shocking dose at once.

There was a peculiar manner to these people. There is an honor and respectability in certain types of unity, but there is no virtue in unity alone, for there is a similarity in death as well as life. Decay can smell the same as well as roses can.

Lena stood on one leg with the other extending through the rather revealing slit in her gown. The two women occasionally glanced at her. The older woman was bobbing her head in a pecking motion as she spoke, like a farmyard hen, anxiously feeding on the mash mingled with the dust and dirt beneath its feet, encrusted with its own urine and excrement. The younger woman was nodding in agreement at the rate of one beat to her three. When the younger woman received her queue, she started pecking and the older woman nodded in agreement.

Finally, Marc was able to offer a credible excuse to escape his conversation. He finished it off with, "Well, my timing is my feet, so I'll be on my way now."

"Ah, you're a Bob Marley fan?"

"Yeah, his biggest," he said over his shoulder as he walked away, intently avoiding another tedious conversation.

He began nodding his head to the beat of the pecking hens:

Nah, nah, nah
My timing is my feet, so I be on my way.
Don't cry na girl. Lemme take your grief with me.
Once ya cared what others think;
Don't go back there, na, dream o' tomorrow.
There are good and there are bad,
Nah, nah, nah, don't worry 'bout that.
Turn your face to the light an' the breeze,
Where you'll see me return, girl,
Girl, when I come for you.

Marc raised his arm, dripping from the tub, shook the moisture from his hand, and pressed the "back" button on his phone to hear the song again. Even the flickering candles danced to the beat. Marc stretched out his arms on the rim of the tub like a king enthroned before his subjects—the loyal flames dancing before him and the treacherous shadows smudging the walls.

It was a small gathering, about seventy people, of some of the governor's closest friends and enemies. They all assembled for the purpose of self-adoration and mutual skepticism. Utah had recently won the bid for a major military installation. It practically guaranteed Marc's firm some high profit work. He was the president and part owner of LogicStream, a software company that had developed some advanced modeling and simulation techniques. Lena's connection to the governor through one of the state's ruling ecclesiastical families had been advantageous for them. In spite of how revolutionary Marc's computing techniques were, she was the reason that doors opened to him in business.

When Marc and Lena congratulated the governor, Marc ran his fingers along the sleek lines in the hollow of her back. Her gleaming smile in response, and the blushed glance to Marc, indicated that he had scored a point in a friendly argument.

"I'm going like this," he said in a taunting tone, trying to spark up a mild controversy. He was wearing faded jeans and a gray T-shirt.

"Oh, no you're not, Jack." Calling him "Jack" signaled her willingness to play along. Besides being a mild expletive, it also had reference to him being a "Jack Mormon," an inactive member of the church.

"Yes, I think I will." He grinned, wearing the label she put on him almost as a badge of honor.

"I think you're getting a haircut and wearing that tux I picked out."

"That would show him more regard than he deserves."

"Would it show me more regard than I deserve?" She challenged him in a crisscross stance—raised eyebrow, crooked smile, bent arm on bent hip over bent knee. It was the type of look that rips the heart out of a man—that induces him to do anything for his girl. It was an expression of the language that women speak and men understand. It was the assurance that she would offer herself as consolation for his trouble. After Lena entered into this implicit contract, Marc protested attending the governor's reception with increased intensity. The more burdened he was by attending, the more founded was his claim to a proportionate consolation prize. She cheerfully tolerated his protests. He played his part; she played hers.

It was a short drive back to their downtown apartment, but Lena was already stuffing her panties into her handbag when the two of them spilled from his black Jag into the parking garage. Lena's long hair had been meticulously styled for the reception but now it showed signs of a struggle. At first it was not apparent whether it was a struggle that had just ended or one that had just begun, but by the time they spilled again from the elevator onto the eighteenth floor, Lena's hair had suffered a full-fledged assault. It was bumps and bruises to the apartment and a tumble to the couch in the living room, but he slowed down. He slowed way down.

It wasn't a perfect landing. It wasn't a perfect evening. There is no such thing as perfection; perfection is stinting. There is only experience. An experience can only be extended or ended. If it is good, then participants hope that it lingers with their enjoyment. But if it is really good, then they stretch it out and fill it in with love. The pace of time slows down, they become hypersensitive to the experience, and even the memory mongers acquiesce to it. That's what Marc and Lena did. He kissed her lips and her toes felt it. He touched her waist and her cheeks showed it. He whispered to her skin and her body heard it. Her dappled neck and shoulders radiated like the summer sun shining through the perforated canopy of beach trees onto the moistened sand. Her breathing made the softened sound of a thousand beating wings carrying their flock upon the breeze. Her longing drew the ship to port, and though the coast was clear, it was the sort that would have flown the world and safely conveyed a ruined wreck through the reefs and tempests of hell upon a cushioned swell, had they stood between her and her seaman.

She lay upon the couch with her dress bunched beneath her breasts, where the sash that Marc had lifted out of the way still held it around her ribs. Panting from exertion, Marc fell into the seat next to Lena, stretching out his arms and legs to cool down. The spine of the couch creaked as he pressed his own against it to recline. Lena finally slipped off her dress and crossed her legs over Marc's lap. She closed her eyes and sighed. The skin's a remarkable thing. When she was excited or aroused, it would tighten and stand firmer. The tiny-pebbled texture of her skin, made by its reaching out for perception, invited the slightest stroke that would bend her body into shapes. Marc's fingertips moved her like a gliding bow moves cello strings. She arched her back and raised her breasts to him. It was an instinctive response.

The moon rose above the mountain peaks and crested Lena's with a silver glow.

That old monarch of the night steadily gained ascendancy over his twilight domain. In his stately procession, the canyon shadows flung their feeble cloak upon the land, but the higher he rose, the deeper his rivals retreated into their crevices and other hiding places. Shadows are such cowards. Marc took another sip of Scotch and saluted the shining victory by raising himself from the tub, blowing out the candle, and sinking back again. Smoke rose from the glowing wick like a troupe of silky dancers playfully tumbling over and caressing each other in the moonlight with their slender legs entwined. Marc watched intently, as if to capture every moment, aware that each dancer had but moments to give. Those players gave everything. They gave cheerfully and completely. Smiles and waves were their only gestures before they vanished into oblivion.

Chapter 2

Marc was walking through the university campus. It was one of those Salt Lake City winter days that warms one up to the thought of death, so a detour to the student union building which prolonged his exposure made no sense. They had hot soup and drinks there, but they were not good enough to warrant a trek through hell. Besides, he had soup packets and a microwave back at his office in the school of computing where he was working on his Ph.D. as a graduate research assistant. He was working under Dr. Dean Wesley on a joint venture with the physics department to simulate high energy particle collisions in order to make some recommendations on proposed changes to detectors in the CERN collider. He was fairly new to the team so they sent him on an errand to carry some imaged films between departments.

He sat down with his bowl of clam chowder and gazed at passersby through the building's exterior wall of glass. Everyone was in a hurry to get somewhere, kind of hunched over and rigid. Occasionally, students flung the union door open, as if they were on the verge of frostbite and a hasty entrance was their only escape. He assessed every pedestrian and every frosty escapist. Males were quickly dismissed and females, too, who were too short or had the wrong color of hair.

He waited. He waited longer than he should have, but she never came. He gritted his teeth and shook his head as he walked out. He had come here for two weeks since the day that he had seen her eating lunch with her girlfriends. They were laughing and bouncing out of their seats. One of them pulled out a digital camera and the others shrieked in excitement as they huddled behind it. He was in a lunch meeting with his research team when they bounced in and when they bounced out. Marc couldn't take his eyes off of one of them. She was too buoyant to notice that he was sinking. On his way out, after his meeting ended, Marc slowly walked through the residual passion field surrounding her table. It looked like a happy little boy that had managed to get more food on his face than in his belly.

After his last class, he took the downtown bus. He owned a small Nissan but it needed some work, so he had been on foot for a while. He shared a two-bedroom apartment with his roommate, Chuck, who wasn't in yet, and probably wouldn't be for an hour or so. He started up his computer and opened the project that he had been working on. It was a paltry website that would earn him a little dough. He sat facing the screen, but he was looking through it. After about ten minutes, he opened a separate browser window and clicked the top site in his favorites/girls. He browsed the updates, none from his favorite model today.

Marc found a nice set from of girl acting as yacht's first mate. The captain was away and she was playing with his things and leaving traces of herself. She had a smooth face, blonde hair, small breasts, and thin hips. She wasn't muscular, but in certain poses, the build of her calves and back showed through her softened curves. He downloaded the set and added about eight shots to a new folder. In one of the poses that he selected, she was riding a life preserver. In another, she was spreading over the steering column and stuffing herself on a knob of the captain's wheel. Marc downloaded another couple of sets and likewise selected a few from each set to add to his new folder. He started working faster; his roommate would be home soon. He had several large, loosely categorized folders of old standbys. He clicked through them and selected about sixty more shots to add to the ones he had just downloaded.

He locked his bedroom door and grabbed some lotion and a brown washcloth. The dark ones didn't stain as easily. He started the slide show on shuffle and unbuckled his belt to remove his pants and shorts. He spread some lotion over his stiff erection with bulging veins and engorged head. He tightened up, threw his head back, and groaned. He was only about two or three minutes into it when he stopped stroking and squeezed tight. He started massaging his testicles with his other hand to slow things down a bit. He would give the head a flick and a tug on the shaft occasionally, but he hadn't even made it all the way through the slide show yet. At one point, he nearly came—full stop, tight grip, closed eyes. It passed. He relaxed and secreted a little discharge from the tip. He had to back off for a few minutes. He started again—stalled again. The slide show started cycling through its second pass. He picked up the pace a little, but he was clearly saving his eruption for something special. When she finally appeared on screen, he paused the show. She was wearing a nautical cap and opening her everything to him. She gave herself with longing eyes and a pretty salute. It didn't take long; he was primed and ready to go. He sprayed the cloth with murky sorrow and translucent pain—to be washed away in time.

He unlocked the door. Chuck had a habit of bursting in on him with a single knock. Whenever his door was locked, Chuck would tease him about masturbating. Chuck was open about it, but Marc always denied it. Chuck said that's how he knew that Marc was lying. He put his shorts back on, and curled up into bed.

"Hey! Wake up! Marc! Ya coming?" Chuck was shouting at him through his open door.
"What?"
"We're goin' to grab some pizza. Wanna come?"
"Ah, yeah, I guess. Right now?"
"Yeah, five minutes. Hurry."

He had slept for a couple hours. It wasn't until he nearly finished his first beer that he completely woke up. Ben and Gary from another apartment had joined them. Chuck called Ben "chubby hubby" and he called Gary "phish." He was eccentric and had a good sense of humor. They were all graduate students at the University of Utah. Chuck came from Las Vegas and Gary came from Pennsylvania. Marc and Ben were both from Salt Lake City. They were sitting around a table in their favorite hangout. It was dark and the music was rockin', loud enough to be heard and to hear each other, too. They were talking about the usual: girls, friends, work, and classes.

Marc pulled out his phone. He spun it on the table a few times, as if he was trying to divine an answer from it. He stopped and stared at it, spun it a few more times, and stared at it again. Either it wasn't giving him the answer he wanted or it wasn't giving him an answer at all. He ordered another beer. He was perfectly willing to give the other guys advice on their girls, but he didn't put himself out there. He told them that he was trying to focus on work and school. Chuck told him that he needed to loosen up. The second beer did the job. He flipped his phone open and called Laura. She didn't answer.

Chuck and Ben were arguing about the Winter Olympics coming to Salt Lake City the following month. Their argument passed through the politics stage and escalated into a full-on attack of each other's religion. Of course, Chuck's religion was to tear down Ben's. He blasted Ben's church for being at the center of the scandal that allegedly brought the Olympics to Salt Lake. Ben emphatically denied that the church had anything to do with it.

"First of all, everyone involved in the scandal is a member of your church," Chuck barked at Ben.

"Of course they are; a majority of the state is. That doesn't mean that the church is responsible for every mistake that its members make."

"Real convenient excuse, especially when politics are dominated by you people. You won't give anyone else a chance. If anyone goes up against you, they hardly have a prayer. So, as far as I'm concerned, if you people are gonna maintain your tight fisted control of practically everything in the state, you are responsible for when it backfires."

"That's weak logic. Is the university responsible for that girl who was raped?"

"No, but the university didn't place the rapist in a situation where he had to do it or be ostracized. In fact, they cooperated with investigators and expelled him when he was caught."

"Same with the church. If those guys are found guilty, they'll most likely be excommunicated."

"Sure, choose your henchmen and then throw them under the bus if they get caught."

"You think the church controls who serves on the bidding committee and then tells them how and whom to bribe?"

"Sounds about right."

"That's ridiculous."

"Is it?"

"Yeah. If individuals make decisions contrary to the teachings of the church, it's their individual responsibility. You're trying to eliminate individual responsibility."

"No, I'm simply saying that these aren't individual decisions."

"Well, it's really easy to accuse people, especially when you have no evidence."

"No evidence? There's only one reason that the liquor laws in this state are so restrictive. If it was a matter of individual conscience, why are they being relaxed specifically for the Olympics?"

"Because there will be visitors from all over the world and they are accustomed to…"

"Bullshit! It's because the church doesn't want to look bad. They imposed their ethics on the rest of the state and then when it's convenient for them, they change them to accommodate their public image. This proves that the Olympics were just a publicity stunt for the church from the beginning."

"You want to talk scandal? How about the records being destroyed for the Nagano games? They probably bribed officials worse than SLOC did."

"That's probably true, but at least they're not hiding behind a cloak of morality."

"So you cut people more slack who are openly immoral than people who are striving to be moral, even if they make mistakes?"

"Yip, I'm from Vegas, baby—less hypocrisy."

Marc looked at the caller ID on his phone. It was Laura calling him back. He ignored the call. He was clearly enjoying the debate. Somehow they all managed to leave as they came—friends. Loneliness is awfully bland. Friendship makes everything better. Sometimes it's better to taste the bitterness than to taste nothing at all. They all had plenty of work to get back to, and it wasn't Friday yet, so they split the bill on food and each person covered his own drink tab. Chuck told Ben that it was at times like this that he envied Ben's free Coke refills. Ben smiled and said, "Yeah, membership has benefits."

Back at the apartment, Marc checked messenger to see if Laura was online. She was logged in but idle. He sent her a message to see if she was there. While he waited for her response, he started working on his website project again. However, he quickly ground to a halt like a wind-up monkey toy whose spring is spent. He was sitting in a melancholy stupor with his head tilted to one side, looking way past his screen again. Finally, messenger jolted him back by alerting him that he had received a response.

Laura: Hey, sorry I missed your call. What's up?

Marc: You know that girl you hung out with in school? I think she was on the swim team.

Laura: Yeah, Ashley, what about her?

Marc: Do you still know her?

Laura: Yeah, I was with her at a party last week. Why?

Marc: I saw her at the U a while back, there was a girl with her. Wondering, if you could help me figure out who she was.

Laura: Oh, really? ☺ Was she cute?

Marc: duh

Laura: What'd she look like?

Marc: Words are insufficient

Laura: LOL

Marc: like a goddess

Laura: LOL, it might have been Lena Brensett. Tall, blonde and beautiful. Kinda skinny. Sound like her?

Marc: Yeah, who is she?

Laura: She came with Ashley to that party. She's really pretty. She's Brother Brensett's niece. They're quite rich.
I love you, brother, but dream on. She's got about 10 RMs chasing her.

Marc: Really? Do you know her?

Laura: Never actually talked to her but she's one of Ashley's new friends at the U.

Marc: Who's brother brensett?

Laura: One of the Twelve Apostles… remember???

Marc: Oh yeah.
What was she like?

Laura: I never got a chance to talk to her. but she seemed nice

She was surrounded by people the whole time
and she didn't stay very long.

Marc: What's she majoring in?

Laura: idk, maybe business or something.
I could find out.

Marc: No, that's fine. Thanks.

Laura: np
Are you going to ask her out?

Marc: I'm considering it.

Laura: Do you ever see her at the U?

Marc: No, just that one time.

Laura: Well then, how are you going to find her?

Marc: I don't know. I can't just stalk her and then walk
up to her one day and say, "you don't know me,
but I know everything about you, would you
like to go out with me?"

Laura: You could go with me the next time I'm
partying with Ashley. Maybe she would be
there.

Marc hesitated here. He leaned back and stared at the
ceiling. The last time that Laura told him about one of her
"parties," he told her how much he respected her service to
the elderly. She pretended to be offended and hit him for
saying it. Then, she gave him a sermon on how unwholesome
his habits were and how toxic they were to his soul. He said
that he already had a mother. Laura said that he obviously
needed more than one.

Marc: ehhhhh

Laura: It will be fun, I PROMISE.

Marc: I'm sure. That piano crap you listen to really
gets the party hoppin

Laura: Hahaha. Stephen Evans? You went to school
with him.

Marc: Yeah, and I didn't like him then either.
           He would sit down at his piano like he was fuckin Chopin or something, and grind out the same damn dribble every time. Every awful piece sounded like every other awful piece.

Laura: Well, I like it.

Marc: Yeah, you and a lot of other girls. I don't get it.

Laura: LOL, Lena didn't seem to mind it.

Marc: Who knows? Maybe that's why she didn't stay long. *gun to the head, pulling the trigger*

Laura: I really don't like it when you talk that way.

Marc: ...

Laura: Well, I'll let you know if I see her again. It would be really cool if you could go out with her. She seemed really nice.

Marc: deal

Laura: Want to come to church with me this Sunday?

Marc: ...

Laura: I hate to say it, but she's not going to date a guy who doesn't even attend church. ☹

Marc rolled his eyes and sighed. He closed the chat window. Laura was working full time as a dental assistant. She said that college just wasn't her thing. Marc said that he couldn't possibly agree more. She got offended. He said, "Hey, I admire your decision. I wish more people would spare the public funds." She was living with her parents and attending the singles ward. She couldn't get a return missionary to give her a single date and Lena had ten. That's probably an exaggeration, but still sad. Laura really believed that she would find a good husband, raise some beautiful children, devote her life to the church, and live a full life. It's all she talked about whenever Marc saw her. Maybe she would, if she got lucky, but there were many women like her who couldn't find a good man in the church. If they were truly devoted, they would have to live single because the church frowned upon marrying nonmembers. The chat window popped back up. Laura was telling Marc that she loved him. He closed it without responding and logged out of messenger.

Marc didn't go on a church mission after high school. It was really hard on his family. His father, Bradley Friedman, coped with it best. He took Marc on a camping trip the summer after Marc's junior year, just the two of them, to do some male bonding and to see if Marc could be persuaded. They had spent most of the day out fishing on a small lake in a rowboat. Few words were spoken then. Bradley said that fishing recreated the soul. Engines and other noises disrupted the process. On the lake, drinks and snacks were requested by gestures and passed without verbal acknowledgements. If words were spoken, they were generally while rowing and were usually confined to the business at hand—where the fish were, it was always about where the fish were and what they were biting.

They rowed in and put up the boat for the evening, cleaned the fish, and started a fire. Bradley always roasted the fish on a spit over an open flame. He stuffed the fish with herbs and slices of lemon. Marc trussed them with cotton twine and ran them on the spit; the biggest fish went in the middle where it was the hottest. Bradley never missed an opportunity to teach. He said, "Where much is given, much is expected. Being the biggest fish means that you take the heat." He then opened a bottle of chardonnay and poured a cup for himself and a half for Marc. These were the only times that Bradley would drink. He could be disfellowshipped and lose all of his privileges in the church for drinking. Therefore, it had to be in a world set apart for a special dispensation. In interviews with his bishop and home teachers, when they asked him if he used alcohol, he told them not until he could drink it in the Kingdom of Heaven. He sat down to keep the fish turning, where the flames of the sun lit the evening clouds on fire, raised his glass to the sky and said, "Here's to heaven, son."

Marc started the conversation by saying that it was tough, figuring life out.

"So, what do you really want, son?"

"I want to change the world. I don't want to live an anonymous life."

"And you're afraid that going on a mission will prevent you from changing the world?"

"I don't know, I just, I don't think I'll be the same."

"You probably won't be the same, but you might be better."

"Better? What did it do for you, Dad? I see those medals and awards in your bookcase. It's like everything you ever accomplished was in high school. What have you done since then?"

His dad didn't take it personally. He knew that Marc was just being blunt. Bradley worked as a project coordinator for the city. He avoided speaking about his job and he never mentioned his accomplishments. He earned enough to provide a decent living, but there was no extravagance. "Well, we've raised you and Laura. I think that's a worthwhile project."

"I don't see how your mission helped you do that."

"You probably never will see how it helped, unless you experience it for yourself. But I can tell you that nothing has ever had such a profound influence in my life. It was one of the best decisions I ever made."

"I don't think it's the best decision I could make."

"Well, you've got to make your own decisions, son. No one can make them for you."

His mother, Michelle, took it much harder. She saw it as a sign that Marc was turning his back on the church and all that they had tried to teach him. She couldn't discuss it without becoming upset. It was manifested in multiple forms. On one occasion, his eternal soul was in danger. On another, she told him that nice girls marry return missionaries. Did he want a nice girl? Once she started weeping hysterically. Every prayer she uttered, she prayed for him, that he would find the path. He overheard a conversation between his parents. Michelle was crying and telling Bradley that he wasn't doing enough for Marc. He was probably the reason that Marc wouldn't go to church.

"You drink on family trips, right in front of the kids! How do you think that affects them? If the bishop found out…"

"The bishop knows."

"What do you mean?" She seemed horrified.

"Of course he knows."

"Did he cancel your recommend?"

"No, but it's obvious that he knows. It's a guy thing, I guess. I doubt that I'll be asked to do any teaching, though." He chuckled a little with his last statement, as if it was an unexpected advantage.

"Oh, this is perfect. Just perfect! Bradley, you're killing me!" She started crying.

Laura was concerned when Marc stopped going to church. She was five years younger than Marc. She asked her Sunday School teacher if he was going to hell. After church, she fell apart. She told her mother that her teacher told her that Marc was going to hell if he didn't repent. Michelle spent more than an hour trying to explain to Laura that families are forever and they were never going to give up on Marc; they would do whatever it took to save him. Ever since then, Laura always tried to help Marc. She often invited him to go to church and she always gave him a "good book" for his birthday. When Marc started dating nonmembers in college, she kept trying to set him up with "good girls" that she knew. It would be the answer to every Friedman prayer to see Marc and Lena together.

He searched the internet for Lena Brensett. The only pages that pulled up were references to her family or her uncle. He searched the university student directories, but her name did not appear on any of them. She must have set her profile to private. He searched the university website. He found a photo of the participants in a girls' summer soccer camp sponsored by the university for high school students. There were about twenty girls in the photo. He matched the names in the caption with the faces. There she was. The photo was a few years old, but it was a match. Without her student ID, he couldn't know her email address for certain. If she setup a custom address using an alias, lena.brensett@utah.edu might reach her; it was common but she might have used any derivative of her name.

Marc didn't spin his phone for an answer this time. He sent Laura an email:

Laura,

Sorry for dropping you tonight. I don't express it very well, but I love you, too. I know that you have my best interest at heart. I'm glad that you life makes you happy, but I have my own life to live and I'm no less sincere about it than you are. Trust me about that.

So, anyways, about Lena… Still want to help me meet her?

Thanks, me.

He went back, deleted the "I love you" line, and added, "I would really appreciate it" at the end. He corrected a typo, reread it several times, and clicked "Send."

He returned to the website project. He finished it that night and tested it. There were a few minor fixes that he needed to make. He noted them and jumped into bed; it was late. He lay in bed, waiting for his mind to let go. He had a smile on his face. There was a wadded up cloth buried in the laundry basket, but he was clean.

Chapter 3

The university was like a beautiful woman. She had a heart, but knowing that didn't make touching it any easier. She had a cycle, too. In the winter, she was calm, notwithstanding the expressions of icy anguish upon the students and faculty bustling from class to class. They were expressions of solidarity among fellow sufferers. "I feel ya," they were saying. In the spring, her supple flesh bloomed from the fountain of life that burst from within her. People were all over her; they would lie with her on blankets and sit with her on benches. In the summer, she was hot, too hot to handle for most, and in the fall, she bled back into the ground the sap and herbal tinctures that had painted the campus for a season.

She was impossibly complex, but that didn't keep people from trying to understand her. Researchers would dedicate their lives to uncovering some hidden gem, only to retire as bachelors emeritus, a cool title for a life of faithful devotion. They became experts in nothing, for the greater their knowledge grew, the narrower the span of ground that it covered. It was like a brain fetish—it didn't impress her and it didn't impress her friends. She led them on with coy hints and petty favors, but in the end, obscure publications are like the faded notes her suitors saved until the scent of her perfume vanished away. There's no comfort for the soul when the mind wanes and the dreams are dead.

She put up a lot of facades. They were scattered over a thousand acres. Although Marc was aware that they existed, he never walked through most of them. There were too many with too many locked doors and dim rooms behind them. Some secrets were better left tucked away. It would be easy to get lost in the vastness of them. Nevertheless, some doors she would unlock for just one man. There was no predicting whom she would give her heart to, but when she did, she would open her deepest thoughts and emotions and let him explore them to the fullest extent. Marc buried himself into it. It was good for her like it was for him.

It was a project of quite limited scope that he was working on. There would be no awards or recognitions for testing proposed changes to specialized sensors in the CERN mega-installation, but he pursued it with greater intensity than any of his prior studies. The CERN facility on the border of France and Switzerland was the largest complex of scientific instruments ever built. It was composed of a series of particle accelerators, built over a span of five decades. They hurled beams of sub-atomic particles into each other, at near-light speeds, in order to search and sift through the fallout of the blast for exotic particles. The largest accelerator, still under construction, was the large hadron collider (LHC), a ring encompassing an area 3.6 times larger than the neighboring city of Geneva. The explosions that it would contain would reach temperatures of a hundred thousand times greater than the temperature at the core of the sun, enough to melt protons and neutrons into plasma soup. The miniscule particles ejected from such collisions required creative means of detection.

Marc's work involved simulating these quantum extremes in order to help them identify the best detector design. There were three different designs under consideration. It was highly technical, so there was a lot of collaboration between the physics team and the computing team.

Quantum particles seem to evade any physical description, but they can be digitally modeled using bizarre abstractions. They abhor certainty; chance is their native law. They're like kindergarten children whose erratic behavior is loosely based on which other children are present and how intensely adults are observing them. The microscopic world is a curious dream.

Marc hopped the campus shuttle to visit the "dream weaver" in the physics department. That's what he called himself on his webpage. His office was in the "Siberian" sector, so called because it was the most remote from the main offices in the physics department. It was in an old brick building, but not like those romantic ones with stone columns and arched windows that stood on President's Circle. This one looked more like a vintage prison building. It had four stories above ground plus a basement. The windows were tinted and heavily screened, as if the designer had intended to keep the entire building as dark as the matter that its inmates were searching for. Marc walked down the dim hallway to the office in the northeast corner. The third floor seemed vacant. It was silent and there were no lights shining under the doors. Marc knocked at 307C. There was no response, but he had an appointment so he verified the office number and knocked again. This time there was a shuffle as he could hear someone stand up from a creaky chair and walk toward the door. A vague silhouette of Dr. Edberg appeared through the obscured glass in the door just before it opened.

"Hi, I'm Marc Friedman."

The old man gave him a blank stare, as if he hadn't returned yet from the mysterious place that he had been dreaming of. His white hair was combed, but messed up on one side, possibly from tugging on it in order to extract ideas from its roots or from dreaming on the palm of his hand. He was very skinny, but he looked generally healthy with good color in his face. He had an odd expression that must have jammed in its transformation from the intensity of working on a perplexing problem to the affability of greeting a stranger. His clothes were clean and pressed but the fibers in his shirt were tired and thin, like a stressed out employee coming down from a cup of weak coffee. Everything about his appearance gave the impression that he had taken an early exit on the highway of the day. In order to minimize the awkward greeting, Marc added, "I have an appointment to go over some equations with you." This seemed to work; he snapped out of his daze.

"Oh, yes, come in. Have a seat."

"Thanks."

"So you work with Dean Wesley on the computing side?"

"Yeah, I was hired in August when I started my Ph.D."

"Do you enjoy working on the project?"

"Yes, well, I didn't at first. It seemed like a mess, the math I mean, but I'm slowly getting into the groove of it."

"Life is a mess. The trick is to comprehend its underlying simplicity."

"That's what I'm here for," Marc said with a tinge of feigned excitement. "All these different particles and interactions, well, I've simulated objects using one or two forces, but this is way more complex—and strange."

"What have you done in the past?"

"Some thermodynamics, but mostly cosmology."

"What did you do in cosmology?"

"I simulated the large scale evolution of the universe."

"And now you're working on the smallest objects in the universe?"

"Yeah, I guess I'm attracted to extremes," Marc said with a mischievous smile.

It was literally true. The largest known structures in the universe are galactic filaments running billions of light-years in length. The smallest known structures in the universe are neutrinos. On the scale between these two extremes, humans stand roughly in the middle.

After noting this curiosity, Marc said, "So, in a sense, we really are the center of the universe."

Edberg ignored Marc's joke, but he seemed genuinely interested in the project that Marc had begun describing. "What were you investigating?" He asked.

A little embarrassed, Marc continued, "I was testing the idea that space isn't expanding uniformly; that matter actually acts as a sort-of mesh that holds the universe together. It was for my master's thesis."

"And, what did you find?"

"I found that it is not expanding uniformly. When we map the positions of galaxies, we see that they cluster into long, thin filaments which surround massive voids in space, like bread dough with pockets of air bubbles in it." Marc started to get enthusiastic about describing his work. "In my simulation, I found that if I treated the inflation of the universe as a separate force that was expanding space everywhere equally, these filaments didn't really form. The universe just expanded into a misty cloud with very little large-scale structure. But when I treated inflation as anti-gravity, meaning that they were two opposing sides of the same force, these filaments formed and they became denser over time while the voids in between grew larger and emptier. It became quite foamy, which is precisely what we see."

"So, did you incorporate relativity and quantum physics into your simulations?"

"I used the spacetime structure and energy calculations of relativity, but no quantum effects; it wasn't necessary under the conditions that I set for the simulations. There were two main techniques that I was working on developing," Marc enumerated them on his fingers as if to punctuate his accomplishments, "defining energy distribution maps and inflating spacetime."

"What did you use for your initial conditions?"

"The Hubble deep field and the cosmic background radiation data."

"So, nothing past the veil, huh?" Edberg gave Marc a condescending glance over the rim of his glasses. Perhaps it wasn't so much condescension as it was disappointment.

"The veil?"

"The veil."

"What do you mean?" Marc sounded a little irritated; he had evidently heard Edberg the first time.

"The universe was so dense after the big bang," Edberg started like he was explaining a difficult concept to a child, "that even though it was hotter than the sun, it took nearly 400,000 years for the first light to escape. That light became the background radiation that we see today."

"Right." Obviously, anyone who has studied the early universe understands this.

"Okay, so you didn't set your initial conditions prior to that time." Edberg said this with a tone somewhere between a question and a statement, like he was probing.

"How could I? As you said, we have no data, nothing could escape."

Edberg's interest waned. He ignored Marc's question and glanced at an email instead. "The spelling of your name is unusual. Is that short for something?"

"Yeah, short for Marcellus," Marc said, still irritated.

"Sounds Italian. Is your family Italian?"

"No."

"Ah, well, you look Italian."

There was an awkward silence. Apparently Marc didn't have anything nice to say, because he didn't say anything at all. The office was dark, hot, and stifling. There was a little heater running by Edberg's desk where it was blowing on his feet. It looked like it had come out of World War II. Its sturdy construction was characteristic of old workmanship. He had a tall, bureau style desk that partially covered the window in his office. It kept the most critical clutter in front of his face where the hidden secrets that it possessed would simmer on his mind. His desk was covered with towers of notes, papers, and journals stacked in an alternating crosswise pattern to keep the adjacent layers separated from each other. It was a nice desk, but it wasn't treated nice. There was a strip of corkboard crudely nailed to the top of the desk where papers and notes hung from thumbtacks along the length of the crown molding. The plastic heads of the tacks were all red, even though there was a box of multicolored tacks nearby. The monochromatic strip was the only thing of any apparent order in the room. The right edge of the desk ran against the wall and the left edge had papers and notes tacked directly into its wooden stile, further obstructing the window. It appeared that some of the papers had been there for years because they had a dry, fragile appearance. The computer monitor was framed by a lion's mane of white and yellow notes stuck or taped to it.

There was a coffee pot sitting on a small table. The indicator light was still on, but the room didn't have the aroma of fresh coffee. It more resembled the stale odor of coffee mugs that had been left for several days until their contents evaporated, leaving a heavy film behind. There were shelves completely covering one wall. Stuffed into the space between the rows of books and the shelves above them, there were more books, journals, and papers. Wherever there was a space, there was a something stuffed into it. A chalkboard covered the opposite wall and it, in turn, was covered with scribbles and drawings. Some were fresh and bright. Others were old and faded; their shards of chalk which had clung to the surface for years, gradually let go and fell to the chalk tray below, like a rock climber that simply couldn't hold on any longer. His bones were gathered up and placed under a headstone memorializing his final struggle and heroic endurance.

The floor initially gave the impression of being dirty because of its dull, gray color. However, it was really the cleanest thing in the room. Its dull sheen could faintly be seen by the scant light admitted through the obstructed window.

Dr. Edberg seemed to be enjoying the awkward moment, as if he was conducting an experiment to see how long Marc could take it. Marc broke. Reaching for some papers in his binder he stammered, "Well, uh, I took some classes in quantum physics when I was an undergrad, but it's been a while so I was, uh, hoping you could help me figure out these equations. I mean I understand the math, but I don't get how they fit into the overall model."

"Nobody gets how they fit into the model." Edberg chuckled.

Marc chuckled back, a little uneasy, "yeah, well, that doesn't really help me."

"It should."

"How should it?"

"It's the truth." He was definitely enjoying this. He said it in such a way that it conveyed the implied, but unspoken follow up, "Would lies be more helpful?"

"Okay, well, if they don't fit into the model somehow then why…"

"I didn't say that they don't fit in; I said nobody understands *how* they fit." He reached out for the papers that Marc was holding and examined them for a minute. The final remnants of intensity left his face and a grin pressed its way to the surface. Pointing to one of the papers he said, "You see? Where does this term come from in this equation here?"

"I don't know—that's one of the questions I had."

"It came from tampering with the equation so that it would agree with observations."

"What's wrong with that?"

"There's nothing wrong with it, as long as you're satisfied having no clue what's really going on. It wasn't based on theory; it didn't emerge as a natural consequence; it was based on brute manipulation. Where there's no theory, there's no understanding; it's that simple. I have a problem with using a model that arose from our flawed understanding and then thinking that we can use it to uncover the truth. It's the fruit of the poisonous tree."

"But the standard model has been extremely successful predicting…"

Edberg interrupted Marc with the disdain of a political analyst who was tired of hearing party pundits repeating the same old talking points. "Yip, that's what we keep telling ourselves, but the geocentric model of the universe was just as successful."

Marc huffed at this suggestion. Surely Edberg said it for shock value, and it worked. It was an insult to the scientific revolution to compare a purely modern theory to the belief that the earth was the center of the universe, even if Marc *had* joked about it. The geocentric model was developed long before the invention of the telescope at a time when mysticism provided the answers to our fundamental questions and the prime mover of the universe hid behind a black curtain in the distant sky. Pleased with the reaction that he drew from Marc, Edberg continued, "I'm serious. The quantum model that you're struggling with essentially repeats the same mistakes that ancient astronomers made when they tried to explain their observations."

Marc looked at him as if he was crazy.

"Okay, look. What did they see when they gazed up into the sky?" Dr. Edberg held his hands up to form a ball which he slowly began rotating. "It made sense. The stars appeared to be fixed to a massive sphere that rotated around the earth. They believed that everything in the heavens had to move in circles, because circles were perfect shapes. So they believed that the sun and moon also held fixed positions on smaller, nested spheres. To account for the tilting of the stars and everything, they assumed that these spheres spun on other spheres, rotating at different angles. The planets moved on circular epicycles within offset spheres to explain their meandering paths…" By this time, Edberg was twisting and waving his hands around each other in gyrating movements. He was intentionally making it look ridiculous because he started bobbing his head around in dizziness. He held his head and shook it as if to recalibrate his sense of good sense.

Edberg continued, "The model worked fairly well in terms of predicting the movement of the moon, planets and stars, but with each new discrepancy that arose from improved observation, extra epicycles and offsets had to be added to the model to account for it. All of this complexity and nonsense was added because of a few beliefs, which although they felt right, were simply wrong."

Marc flipped through his papers, slowly digesting what he had just heard. "So, essentially, you're saying that all of these equations are just elaborate epicycles that we have tweaked until they match our observations?"

"Yes, I believe that's what I'm saying," he said in a sarcastic tone.

Marc laughed off the little insult. "Well, excuse me. I've just never heard anyone make fun of it. If the model's so flawed, what's the alternative?"

"There is no alternative. Not yet, at least. We need a radically different approach. When scientists shifted their paradigms a little, they found that a few simple laws governed the motion of all heavenly bodies." He took on an intense expression again. "I don't believe that the quantum world is based on a convoluted model." He motioned to Marc's papers. "Until this beast appeared, every other theory that ever successfully described nature was elegant and simple in its final formulation. So simple, in fact, that it was only our prejudice that prevented us from finding it much earlier. It required dreamers who were so divergent in their thinking, that they were labeled lunatics or heretics at the time."

"And you're the dreamer for the job?" Marc returned the sarcasm. Edberg opened his mouth to speak, but he turned his head away without saying anything. He closed his mouth and looked at eternity. Finally, he looked back at Marc, "It doesn't appear that I am." Either this was an unguarded moment of emotion or it was a bid from one human to another to open up about a personal affliction. The polite thing to do in the first case would be to ignore it. If it was the latter, however, Dr. Edberg was inviting Marc into his life a little. It's rude to ignore an invitation.

People are generally much more perceptive than they are consciously aware. Their senses are constantly searching for signs to help them interpret incomplete clues. There is a code of nonverbal communication: eyes meet for so long, it's casual; eyes meet for so much longer, it's contact.

It was definitely contact. It would be rude to snub an invitation, but on the other hand, perhaps it was rude to offer a personal invitation to a total stranger in the first instance. Apparently, there had been enough awkwardness, because Marc said, "Well, I better get back."

Edberg recovered himself from the abrupt dismissal. "Okay. Well, let me know if you have any other questions."

"Alright, thanks." Marc checked his phone as he walked out. He had missed a call from Laura. He listened to his voice mail. She was exuberant about something that she couldn't wait to tell him. He called her back but she didn't answer and he didn't leave a message.

When Marc walked back into the project room, Amy and William from the computing team were waiting for him. They started laughing, as if his entrance was the punch line to one of their jokes. William was a year ahead of Marc; he had been working on the project from the beginning. He asked Marc, "So, how did it go?" Amy started laughing again.

"Edberg, you mean?" Marc faked a laugh to be a good sport. "Yeah, he was incredibly helpful. You could have warned me, you know?"

"And miss out on this? Never," William said.

"I have no idea why he's working on this project. All he did was tell me how messed up it is."

William and Amy erupted into laughter again. Amy started singing:

Row, row, row your boat
Gently down the stream,
Merrily, merrily, merrily,
Life is but a dream.

Marc seemed puzzled.

William asked, "Didn't he give you his reality spiel?"

"We didn't really get into it. I could see it wasn't going anywhere," Marc said.

"Oh, too bad. You'll have to go back, now," William said.

"Ha, no, I don't think so."

Amy said, "Once, he took an hour to explain to me that the universe isn't real, it's all a dream."

William said, "Well, that might be true. I dreamt once that I came to work in my underwear. It was the most real thing I've ever experienced. Do you remember that, Amy?"

"Let me see." Amy put her finger to her lips and pretended to ponder the question. "Were you wearing boxers with lipstick kisses?"

"Exactly! See, maybe Edberg's not crazy, after all."

"Maybe not."

"So then, do you remember what you did?" William asked Amy, completing his question with a gesture.

"Sick, shut up." She pushed William away.

Marc didn't seem to be entertained. He said, "Well, I need to go dig into this. One thing I realized from talking to Edberg is that I'm going to have to figure this out for myself."

"Don't get lost down the rabbit hole." William was an excellent programmer, but he didn't thirst for a deeper understanding; at least, the physics didn't seem to interest him on that level. He could write a clever algorithm to solve just about any problem that they encountered, but he was perfectly content to wait on the physics department to give him the implementation parameters. Whenever Marc would ask him why objects in the implementation interacted in a particular way, William would sarcastically say, "Great is the mystery of godliness."

Normally Marc would stay and joke around, but a weight was crushing him and he barely escaped before his countenance gave it away. His office, or closet rather, was down the hall a ways. He sat at his desk, but his eyes danced with the clock. The doodle pad cut in and it became a contest for his attention. He started sketching particles and interactions, swirling masses and exchanges. He scribbled until the pen scratched through the paper. He ripped the paper from the pad, crushed it with his fist, and sent it to hell. It was 4:55, another ten minutes; that was all. 5:05 would indicate interest without obsessive eagerness. There's nothing shameful about having an obsession as long as the obsession remains hidden.

Marc took the pad again. He sketched some particle interactions. One of them looked like a stick figure lying down with her legs spread. Marc filled her in. She looked good; he had an artistic sense.

Particle physicists, on the other hand, had a dry sense of humor. The first particles to be discovered were the electron, the proton, the neutron, and the photon. They were all aptly named, but once scientists began peering inside the proton, for example, they discovered tiny particles with unprecedented properties that required quirky, new formulations in order to describe them. These particles were named quarks by physicist Murray Gell-Mann. He took the term from a line in James Joyce's quirky novel, Finnegans Wake, "Three quarks for Muster Mark," a muddled, dream-state order for three quarts of beer for a Mr. Mark.

At first, there were three known types of quarks, as there were three types of beer (ales, lagers, and strange brews; strange brews, like strange quarks, do not appear in ordinary bars). Ultimately a six-pack of quarks appeared which were classified according to their flavors: up, down, charm, strange, truth, and beauty. Physicists did not want their model associated with truth and beauty, so eventually those quarks were renamed top and bottom. A plethora of other particles began emerging and considerable mental acuity was devoted to naming them on an order of magnitude comparable to that which discovered or hypothesized their existence in the first instance. For example, quarks were held together by exchanging sticky particles called gluons, of course.

It was 5:10; even better. He called Laura again, on speakerphone. She answered this time.

"Hi!" She hadn't lost the exuberance of her previous message.
"Hey. So, what's this thing you..."
"Oh my gosh, you're not gonna believe what happened."
"Yeah, probably not."
"Lena called me."
"B.S."
"Yeah, weird, out of the clear blue. I haven't even talked to Ashley, yet."
"What'd she say?"

"She invited me to a party at her house."

"No way."

"Way, but that's not the best part."

"K?"

"She invited you, too."

Words are powerful thoughts. Sometimes a simple phrase can cause the world to vanish away. It's a decoupling of the mind and material things. Sometimes great sorrow causes it, but in this case, great joy. It's an egocentric view, but when the fickle world reappears, there are many questions and groping for answers. Most questions do not have answers, only guesses and speculation. Guesses appear in shades of truth, which are nothing more than degrees of lies. It's a harsh way to put it, but most people simply do not have enough humility to say, "I do not know," and hence, a lie is born. It's not intended to hurt anyone, but does it help?

Whether they do it consciously or not, people generally accept the superiority of truth. They speak of "the truth" in the singular and absolute, but of lies, in the mutable plural. There is only one way to tell the truth, but myriad ways to lie. However, the nod to the truth is symbolic at best. It's impossible to establish a complete picture of anything. All of the sights and sounds are merely splinters of reality that people snag on as they skid through life. The best that they can do is to pluck them out, to gather and examine them, and to pound them into pasty tints with which to paint something surface-deep. The brush strokes are vague representations of the experiences that induced them, but they can teach people a lot about being human.

Chapter 4

Marc climbed out of the tub. He drew a towel over his back and stood in a stupor with water dripping on the bath mat. Eventually his inner reservoir gathered enough stamina from the meager trickle flowing into it that he could finish drying himself. He was well formed, lean, and muscular, but a man needs more than physical strength to carry his load. His most attractive feature was his back. He couldn't see it, but Lena could and she enjoyed touching it.

A man is what he is when he is naked – without a covering, without a friend, without a name, without a place to lay his head – stripped of all the superficial things that the world heaps upon him. A man is generally much better than he is believed to be, or much worse, but never the same. Heroes are ordinary men lifted up by strangers who want to believe that there is something grander than their own meager existence. When their heroes invariably fall, because that's what men do, their admirers feel betrayed, as if they were deceived. Their heroes were the ones deceived.

He pulled the towel tight around his waist and tucked the edge in. He picked up his phone and walked into the dressing room. He noticed that the nude photo of Lena was gone. At first his eyes grew wide, and then he shook his head. Reaching up, he massaged the back of his neck and shoulders to squeeze out the pettiness that was swelling up. He stood there like a broken god.

The gods fall into two categories, imagined and purely imagined. This is not to say that real gods do not exist, but no one of sound mind claims to see them. Hence every god is imagined. The gods have very real power, however. People trying to understand some phenomenon beyond their comprehension have invented most gods, but those gods, once conceived, become the effective means of controlling and manipulating others.

Perhaps in one of the earliest instances, a god was invented to explain some mysterious feature of nature, such as the gathering of a river from numerous, unseen sources. The river clearly possessed the power to grant or revoke life, for wherever it ran, life abounded, and where it ran not, life struggled to survive. A mother, with the purest intentions, may have told her child to avoid the river when it flooded and ran wild, explaining that the tumultuous current was angry and may strangle him. From that moment on, the imagined god of that river possessed a very real power over that child and by extension, over his children after him.

But gods fade away when those that serve them turn their backs, no more to offer up their praises and oblations. Imagine the wretched condition of King Zeus, sovereign of Mount Olympus, how miserable he must be to live in yonder loneliness, forgotten by those who once loved and feared him! Compelled to live forever, he wanders the desolate summits and crumbling temples of his former domain, a fading vagabond spirit among men of flesh and bone. To die and end his futile reign is a "consummation devoutly to be wished."

Marc meandered to his bed and turned down the covers on his side. He turned the music off and sat in a stupor again. Finally, he knelt beside the bed. For a long time, he kept his eyes open, massaging his head with the tips of his fingers, as if they instinctively knew which parts of the brain were hemorrhaging and thereby in most need of pressure to stop the bleeding. He closed his eyes and pled with the god whom he had imagined.

Life is an insolvable maze. There's no lateral exit and there's no port of re-entry, but everyone is searching in circles for the destination. Men are like mice sniffing at the edges and twitching around corners. There are arbitrary perils and rewards scattered around every turn. Few men find the big chunks of cheese, but they all find the dead end. When every path leads to a cold conclusion, the countless routes that people take seem irrelevant. There are important experiences, however, and wisdom to garner from enlightened ones. The words of the prophets echo through the streets and hallways of the tangled mess until they can't be heard over the din of daily life. Sometimes the only way to reconstruct them is either to trace them back through the impossible maze or to accept the testimony of other mice who heard them. But some mice are rats. Hence, life is a confounding march and every man must find his own way.

"Are you nervous?" Lena asked Marc, biting the corner of her lower lip.

Marc didn't answer at first. He just sat in the car, looking at the Brensett home. He was clenching the steering wheel with both hands and pressing the brake pedal with the car still in gear. Finally, he sighed, "Yeah, I guess so. Are you?"

"A little. They've never had to deal with anything like this. But we'll get through it; we'll be alright."

"Are you really willing to give up all this?"

"I'm willing to do whatever it takes. I love you, Marc. Nothing's ever going to change that." Her tenderness relaxed his rigid hold. Letting go of the steering wheel, he turned to her.

"I love you, too, Lena. If they kill me, I just want you to know that."

Lena laughed. "They're not going to kill you. Maybe just maim you." This time they both laughed.

"They're expecting us, right?"

"Yip, I talked to Daddy this morning."

Marc put the car into park and turned off the ignition. Heaving a sigh, he said, "Better let me get the door, he'll be less likely to beat a gentleman."

Marc walked around and opened the car door for Lena. She gripped his hand as they walked to the front entry. She reached out to open it, but he pulled her back and rang the bell. As if the button was a switch to the floodgate, the color drained from his face. Daniel Brensett answered the door. "Come on in, kids." He hugged Lena and shook Marc's hand. He motioned them to follow him. Surprised by their pleasant reception, Marc and Lena looked at each other in amazement. They followed him into the library.

Marc was very familiar with the library. There were three large windows in the front wall with a mammoth desk sitting in front of them. The desk had an ornate, inlaid border and two-tone wooden panels. There was a computer screen on one side and two or three picture frames on the other side. Other than a water set and a penholder, there was nothing else on the desk. It looked exquisitely elegant and completely unused.

On the opposite wall, facing the desk, there was a large painting of Jesus speaking with little children. The painting imparted a peaceful quality to the room and the recessed lighting gave the Tuscan walls a gentle glow. It was late summer, so the fireplace wasn't lit. The windows provided enough additional light that the crystal chandelier remained off as well. It was a room that needed a lot of light, however. Wooden panels and high profile moldings covered the bottom three feet of the walls. The ceiling, too, was covered with deep, wooden coffers. The carpet was a medium green with a pattern of roses and foliage. In the center of the room, there was a dark, leather sofa and two matching chairs facing the fireplace in a horseshoe arrangement around the cocoa table. It was a stunning room, but even if Jesus had channeled the fullness of his glory through that painting, there would still be enough stained panels and dark furniture to soak up the abundance of light.

The library, it would seem, was named after its least prominent feature. There was a half-height bookcase along the wall behind the sofa. Even though there were perhaps two hundred books, they appeared sparse within the shelves. The rest of the space was consumed with Brensett family paraphernalia: trophies, awards, photographs, wildlife sculptures, homemade art projects, and framed quotations. The most repeated themes within the collection of books were faith, chastity, and the love of Christ. Above the bookcase were the pictures of three men arranged in cascading order of alternating importance—the president of the church in the center, his first counselor on his lower right, and his second counselor on his lower left.

Walking into the room, Marc could see his rundown car parked in the driveway. Its condition probably cancelled any points he may have earned by acting like a gentleman. Daniel took the chair closest to his desk. Marc stood in front of the sofa, waiting for Lena to take the seat closest to her father. Once they were all seated, Daniel crossed his legs and said, "So…" with a nodding motion. He was smiling and seemed perfectly at ease. Lena looked over at Marc to see what his response would be. He didn't have one, so Daniel continued, "Well, where have you kids been?"

"Uh, well, after the wedding we spent some time in Vegas."

"But you weren't married in Vegas?"

"No, uh, we were married here, but we went to Vegas for the honeymoon?"

"Did you have a good time?"

"Yeah, we had a great time." Marc tried to be upbeat.

"What did you do there?"

"We went to some exhibits and checked out some of the architecture. Just relaxed, mostly."

"Did you play?"

"You mean did we gamble?" Marc cleared his throat. "Uh, yes, I gambled a bit."

"Do you have a, uh, problem?" Daniel asked in a fatherly, yet gentle tone.

"Daddy! He's fine. We went to Vegas because it fit into our budget."

Turning to Lena, he began to show more sincere emotion. "You know, you didn't have to take off like that. Why didn't you simply tell us that your mind was entirely made up?"

"I tried," Lena retorted. "We tried," she said more firmly.

"I know. I know you did, sweetie. It's just that, well, we never thought you'd leave the church." Her dad looked at her mournfully, as if he had been able to maintain his cheerful facade until he began speaking directly with his daughter.

"I haven't left the church, Daddy." She responded firmly but with an expression that acknowledged his sorrow.

Daniel pressed his lips and eyes together as if he was withholding an argument. Once the urge passed, he said, "Well, let me be the first to congratulate you," with a forced smile. "I hope you two will eventually be sealed in the temple," he said, glancing firmly at Marc.

She didn't respond verbally to that point, but she held his hand in a reassuring manner. Changing the subject, she asked, "How's Mom doing?"

"Your mom's not feeling well." He paused in contemplation. "It's going to take her some time, you know? But she'll be okay."

"Yeah, I hope so. I didn't want to hurt you guys. Where is she?" Lena asked.

"She's not here. She said she needed some time. Like I said, though, she'll be fine."

"Well, tell her I miss her and I love her."

Daniel said he would and then they discussed having a "proper" wedding reception. That level of acceptance seemed to improve everyone's mood until Daniel wanted them to be remarried by the stake president who was a close friend of his. By allowing everyone to attend a ceremony, it would help their friends and family to participate and rejoice in their union. Marc kept mostly quiet, but Lena felt that to be remarried would somehow signify an admission that their first marriage was wrong. She told her father that she did it with full purpose of heart; it was not a frivolous decision. He told her that it's common for couples to renew their vows. "But they're already new!" she insisted. Marc finally settled the argument by accepting Daniel's proposal and thanking him for offering to help them with a public ceremony for their friends and family. This surprised Lena, who accepted the compromise but seemed a little hurt, too.

Daniel kissed his daughter and asked her to excuse them for a minute; he had some things he needed to discuss with Marc. She left them alone and Marc's face went white again.

Marc opened his eyes and looked at the sheets on his bed. They were clean, pressed, and composed of high quality fibers. He had come a long way since those wrinkled, threadbare sheets he slept on back in college. These were small things, but there were big things, too. He had two beautiful children, a beautiful home, a kingly bed, and a successful company. But now his kids were gone, his home was quiet, and his bed was empty. As for companies, well, they're bigger than just one man. One man can't build a successful company by himself, and one man can't usually bring it down, but that naturally depends on how competently evil he is. It's like a big bridge. It takes years to build, cranes and thousands of workers, but one charge of explosive suitably placed can bring the whole thing crashing down.

Marc pulled the bath towel off from around his rugged trunk and let it fall to the floor. He pivoted around, and laid his calves and arches into bed. He snapped the covers over his naked body, and laid his scepters by his side. (For what are a man's arms, but his scepters, and what are his outstretched limbs, but his power to govern the world?) He pressed the covers tight around him; fortunately, the bite of cold sheets only stings for a moment. He usually slept with a naked chest and loungewear bottoms, and he never left towels or other things lying on the floor. Oh well.

Everything in the house was neat and tidy. The surfaces were dusted and the vacuum marks in the carpet were straight and parallel. The marble and tile floors were polished and swept. There were no spots on the dishes and the containers in the refrigerator and the pantry were clearly labeled. The home was only three years old and the occasional repair was quickly resolved.

He didn't have to look at the children's playground or their bedrooms to know that their toys were all picked up and everything was put away into their containers and stacked neatly within closets and shelves. Matilda was more of a captain in the house than a common housekeeper. Marc expected the kids to pick up after themselves and she did a great job of holding them accountable for themselves. They were doing well in school. Kimberly was in the third grade and Travis was in the first grade. An atomic engine drove Kimberly's imagination. Marc always told her that it was her secret weapon; she shouldn't let go of it at any price. Travis was into plants and animals. The mountainside in their backyard provided a rich environment in which to explore and feed his curiosity.

In short, Marc's life was perfect. It was the kind of "perfect" that friends and family eulogize at funerals. The dearly departed "always" exhibited this virtue, and "never" engaged in that vice:

> He had a loving relationship with his wife, he was a committed father, he was loved by his friends and admired by his enemies, and he loved the truth.

> She had a loving relationship with her husband, she was a tender mother, she bound the broken hearted and lifted the downtrodden, and she loved the truth.

In truth, Lena was a good mother. She could have leaned on Matilda a lot heavier than she did. She took on the education of her children and volunteered at their school. She helped them with their homework, read them bedtime stories, and took them to the park and other amusements during school breaks. If Matilda was the captain of the house, then Lena was the general. She coordinated schedules, managed Matilda's time, and set standards for her work. She even handled client relations for Marc from her own branch office in Park City which was devoted to that purpose. She spent a lot of time at the gym, probably twice as much as Marc did. She had yoga, aerobics, and kickboxing. She went jogging every morning (on the treadmill during winter). Marc often complimented her on how hard she worked to maintain her sexy figure and good health. Once he made the mistake of telling her that Matilda's salary was the best money that he ever spent.

"What do you mean?" she asked like a fierce little cat about to pounce on unsuspecting prey.

"Ah, I mean…" Marc stammered. He knew that he had committed a tactical error and his face betrayed his attempt to conceal it. If he responded before he could formulate a thoughtful answer, it would be an insult. If he took too long to respond, she would know that he was aware of the insult, which was as good as intending it. Damn! He took too long.

"You don't think that I'm capable of doing it myself?" she shot back.

"No, no, it's not that at all. I just think that Matilda makes it a lot easier for you to go to the gym… to go jogging in the morning and stuff, which I think is great!"

"Oh really? You mean that when I get up and go jogging in the morning while you're still in bed, that's because of Matilda?"

"No, but if Matilda wasn't working on breakfast, you…"

"You mean that maybe you would have to get your lazy bones out of bed and help me?"

She rehearsed the countless things that she did to keep the family afloat, while he stayed in the city, while he went on business trips, while he went golfing, skiing, hiking, or biking, or while he went out drinking with his buddies. Marc didn't have enough good sense to admit that Matilda's salary was actually for his own benefit. So instead, to prove that Lena's free time made her remarkable fitness possible, he compared Lena's domestic qualities to those of her mother. He was such an idiot. Lena's mother found time to help her children with all of those same things, plus she canned fruit, cooked for the family, and cleaned the house. Lena lashed out with comparisons between Marc and her father. He was a much more involved father than Marc was. He was home more often than Marc, he taught his family the gospel, and he took them to Sunday services. Her father never came home drunk, and furthermore, if it hadn't been for him, Marc would still be creating stupid little websites.

Daniel Brensett seemed quite upbeat when he and Marc came walking out of the Library. He kissed Lena goodbye and told her that he loved her. He patted Marc on the shoulder and said, "Think about it and let me know." Lena was anxious to quiz Marc on what he had discussed with her father. It even eclipsed the topic of being remarried. "So?" she asked with a slow crescendo as soon as Marc latched the car door shut.

"So what?" Marc returned nonchalantly.

"What did you and Daddy talk about?" she asked with upbeat enthusiasm.

"Oh, it was no big deal," he said playfully.

"Marc! Come on."

"Fine." Marc pretended to be inconvenienced by her inquiry, but he was smiling. "He said that there's a business opportunity that I may want to consider."

Lena got excited. "Really? What is it?" she asked in an eager tone.

"Well, it's kind of sensitive; he said that I really shouldn't talk about it."

"Stop it!"

"I'm serious." Marc's tone changed to reflect what he was actually saying. "It's a defense department project that would require pretty high security."

"You mean you can't even tell me?"

"Well, I don't really know much about it at this point. It seems like a really good opportunity, though. It's a lot like what I've been doing at the university."

"So, you'll be working for the government?"

"Well, not exactly. He thinks that we should start a company that would work on government contracts."

"Wow! That's incredible."

"Yeah, it is. I have the skills to do it, too, but I don't have the capital."

"So what did he say?"

"He's willing to fund the startup," Marc said. Lena shrieked for joy, but Marc plowed on through as if to cut her euphoria short. "But we haven't worked out the details. He wants seventy percent."

"Oh." Lena's enthusiasm fell, probably to sympathize with Marc's position more than to convey any real disappointment. "How much did you ask for?"

"I didn't ask for anything, I told him I'd have to think about it." Lena looked at him as if to ask for an explanation. He continued, "I own 100% of my current company. I know it's a small business, but it's doing fairly well and it's mine."

"Which one is your greatest opportunity?"

"I don't know. The dot-com bubble burst a few years ago, but a lot of my clients are solid companies seeking to establish a legitimate web presence. There's no question that the internet is the future."

"Could you do both?"

"I probably could. The downside of what I'm doing right now, though, is that there's a lot of competition." He stopped to think for a minute and Lena gave him the time to do it. "Overall there's probably more money in what your dad's suggesting, and with the capital he's willing to invest, it could really take off. I have to admit that it's a lot more interesting than building websites."

"Well, I think it's great!" Lena seemed genuinely happy for Marc.

"Yeah. It's quite different than how we were treated before we eloped, isn't it?"

"I know," she reached over and placed her hand on his leg, "but I wouldn't have changed a thing."

Marc was the renegade who stole Lena's body and then her soul. Her family had employed every method to renovate his life and to restore his faith in the church. They embraced him and showered him with love. They promised him eternal glories and a seat on the right hand of God. When that didn't produce the desired transformation, they eventually resorted to threats of everlasting punishment and gloom. There were many meetings with Daniel Brensett in the library. When that failed, however, they went to work on Lena. Her spiritual treatment was similar to his, but in reverse. Therefore, when the two of them eloped, the family recovered from the shame by conferring an artificial salvation upon their heads. Enough wealth will cover any shame and they had plenty of wealth to confer.

After visiting with the Brensetts, Marc and Lena drove to visit his family. Their reception there was similar, except that Marc's mother eventually emerged from her bedroom with a face that had been washed in an attempt to erase the evidence of tears.

Marc reached down to the floor and dried his tears with the towel that he left there. He hung it back up in the bathroom and left his decanter in the dressing room where he pulled on his typical nightclothes. The moon was hours higher in the sky and only the window sheers were lit—those and small pools of meditation where the moon spilled over the edge of the window onto the floor and the furnishings below.

Chapter 5

Marc called his sister Laura to let her know that he was swinging by to pick her up for the party that Lena had invited them to. In spite of the call, however, he waited for about ten minutes for Laura to finish getting ready. When she finally climbed into the car, she teased him, "hmmm, smells nice in here. I like what you've done with the place."

"Very funny," he said with a sneer.

"Why didn't you come inside," she asked.

"You really have to ask?"

"Mom loves you. You know that, right?"

"Yeah."

"Then why don't you give her a break?"

"Why doesn't she give me a break?"

"She's just trying to help you." Laura had an emotional bank account with Marc. A positive balance permitted her the occasional sisterly nudging and advice. However, with frequent withdrawals and few deposits, she kept the balance quite low. By this time she was overdrawn, so there was no more of that kind of talk.

On his first pass, Marc missed the Brensett residence. "Was that it?" he asked Laura. She couldn't read the number, but he could tell that he had passed it. He flipped around and approached the home more cautiously the second time.

The neighborhood was unofficially known as the diamond district because much of the real estate was originally owned by the Walker family who made their fortune in diamonds. They still owned the community's largest estate. The district sat upon the footstool of Mount Olympus, the majestic peak overlooking the Salt Lake Valley. It was named after the vacant seat of Greek deities. A beautiful alpine creek ran through the neighborhood that its residents "might have life and that [too] more abundantly." Upon every rooftop and every billowing tree, the snowy benevolence of God crowned this place.

The Brensett home was situated on a quaint little lane. Even though the surrounding city stood on the edge of a vast desert, this street possessed the character and charm of a country street that one might find in the lushland of Vermont. It was lined with stately pines and spruce trees, as well as naked oaks and sycamores which had shed their leaves for the winter. Some of the older places had white picket fences and immaculate landscapes, while the newer places were guarded by masonry walls and elaborate iron gates. If the trend toward grandeur thus continued, soon the gates of paradise would be too modest to keep the homes of the favored saints.

Salt Lake City stands on the edge of the Great Basin Desert, as if the devil had barely managed to snag it with a snap of his east-flung tail. The Great Basin is so named because it is North America's largest, contiguous and thoroughly contained watershed, with no out flowing rivers or streams. Because there are no outlets, it contains multiple salt lakes and salt flats, some exceptionally large. It is an American anomaly of extremes. The bowels of Satan himself smolder here. In the south-west corner, Death Valley plunges nearly 300 feet below sea level to the lowest point in North America and endures the hottest temperatures in the western hemisphere. In malicious proximity, God dangles glistening glaciers tantalizingly beyond the reach of his burning rival; nearby Mount Whitney, the Great Basin's border sentinel, reaches to the highest point in America where just a sip of its glacial streams might cool the devil's flaming tongue. Spanning most of Nevada and half of Utah, the Great Basin contains some of the most wicked cities in the world, and some of the most righteous.

It is bordered by the grand Sierra Nevada Mountain Range in California, the Cascade Range in Oregon, the Columbia Plateau in Idaho, and the Wasatch Range and Colorado Plateau, both in Utah. Annual precipitation levels are low. As the moist Pacific air rises over the Sierra-Nevadas on the west, it cools and condenses, dropping most of its contents before it enters the basin. The air continues to dry as it crosses the arid desert and numerous, smaller mountain ranges, like a damp cloth being wrung out against a corrugated washboard. When it rises again to pass over the eastern barrier of the basin, something magical happens; some of the driest and lightest snow in the world caps the Wasatch Mountains, producing incredible skiing conditions.

Surrounded on every side by mountainous barriers and high plateaus, the Great Basin is a gravitational pit—a black hole with respect to typical terrestrial forces. When an object falls within its boundary, there is no escape; it falls inward and downward, unless some saving transport carries it over the basin's towering containment field. Many have breached its borders from without, but their children and grandchildren remain bound within. The thing is, the mind becomes accustomed to containment. The people are happy, not knowing that they are shackled. To the few whose minds do become aware of their incarceration, the climb out is so strenuous and taxing, that they consciously accept their condition; these are the grateful dead.

"What are we doing here," Marc asked Laura with a dense injection of dismay.
"Yeah, I know. I told you she was rich."
"I can't believe we're doing this."
"Why?"
"Look!" Marc motioned to the few cars parked in the driveway. "I expected way more people than this. I'm

showing up with my *little* sister to a *little* party with *little* people I don't even know—at all!" He was nearly yelling.

With a tone of empathetic concern, she said, "I tried to call Ashley so that we could all go together…"

Marc cut off her apologetic explanation, "I've hardly spoken to Ashley in years, so what difference would it make? This is crazy!"

For a moment the two of them sat in silence, looking opaquely at the house. This two-story mansion with tall windows and a grand entry was the wail of God's alpenhorn from the little rambler in Taylorsville that they grew up in. Lena's home was finished in elaborate rockwork and smooth stucco. Its soft but pervasive lighting against the dark night gave it the contradictory features of being both welcoming and imposing.

Finally Laura said, "Well, we're here. Let's do this."
"Perhaps we should just skip it."

There's a tone that people use when they're fishing for reassurance in opposition to what they're actually saying. It's ridiculous, but it's human and it generally works among humans. The equivalent, "I want to do this, but I'm scared, I have a lot of self-doubt, and I need some reassurance," would be scorned as being unmanly. Since Laura was an empathetic human, she responded empathetically.

"Come on. There's a reason that she invited us. It'll be fine."

"No, it won't 'be fine.' Look at this place."

"Okay. Let me see," she said in a pseudo-academic voice. "I see rocks and trees. I see a front door and windows. Actually, we have all those things." She finished it off by pretending to be astonished by her startling conclusion.

"I'm not talking about that. I'm not going to go in there and 'put on my manners' for these people."

"Maybe they don't expect you to."

"I don't care what they expect."

"Okay, then don't care."

"Yeah, and make an ass of myself." He tried to use the same tone, but it wasn't working anymore.

"Dude, you're contradicting yourself. Either care or don't care, but make the decision based on who you are and not what you're afraid people will think."

Marc didn't say anything. He sat there convicted. Everything he was saying was a lie. He spent two days preparing for this party. He bought some new clothes. He shined his shoes, brushed his teeth twice, and shaved with a new razor. He expedited the needed repairs on his car. (It probably announced his arrival anyway; it made a lot of noise for having such a small engine.) He polished the exterior, which couldn't be discerned from its rusted skirt and peeling topcoat, and he even detailed the interior and replaced the air freshener to cover up the scent of vinyl protectant that was still slightly detectable. It was a lot of unnecessary work for the improbable event that he might give Lena a ride somewhere. Wishful thinking, but it doesn't hurt to be prepared.

"These people are good people. I don't know why you think that they're going to judge you."

"How do you know they're good people?" Marc couldn't let an unsubstantiated claim go without a challenge.

"Well, I know that Ashley is a good girl... And I know that Brother Brensett is a good man..." She said this as if she was standing on higher ground, with a raised tone, a raised chin, and raised eyebrows, suggesting that the natural order of things was that good people associated with good people. She didn't actually know Lena's uncle, but she had watched him deliver many sermons on television. There was no need for an individual assessment; people were either innocent by association or guilty by association.

"You don't actually know him."

"Okay, fine, but I have a testimony."

Marc rolled his eyes but didn't pursue it further. He indulged another moment of quiet contemplation. Finally, he took a deep breath and exhaled it through his pressed lips, as if he was about to negotiate a daring maneuver. When that breath was completely exhausted, he took another and said, "Okay, let's go."

When they reached the door, Marc pushed Laura ahead of him and told her to ring the bell. Soon, a woman in her late forties appeared. She was wearing a neat apron with a ruffled fringe around the shoulders. Under the apron, she wore a tan business suit with a skirt down to her knees and matching shoes. Her dark brown hair was cut to shoulder length and attractively curled out at the bottom. She wore a little make-up and looked fairly attractive for her age. However, there was a slight paleness below the surface of her skin, like the muted cry of an overwhelming exhaustion, but she hid it with a pleasant smile and a friendly greeting.

"Hello! You must be Laura; I'm Mrs. Brensett, Lena's mom."

"Hi, yes, I'm Laura and this is my brother, Marc. It's so nice to meet you."

"Hello Marc, it's nice to meet you, too. Oh shoot, come in, it's cold out here." The expression on her face said that she was scolding herself for leaving them on the porch during their greeting. Her haste only gave Marc an opportunity to nod.

"May I take your coats?"

"Oh, thanks," Laura said.

"You look lovely," she said to Laura who returned the compliment. "Nice coat," she said to Marc. She carefully laid it over her outstretched arm and laid the open palm of her other hand over it with a protective pat. She did it with such a sincere expression that it surprised him. It was not a particularly nice coat.

"You have a beautiful home," Marc said.

"Oh, well, that's kind of you to say. We've been very blessed. Thank-you. Come on in." They followed her to the end of the foyer. She took their coats to the left and motioned them in the opposite direction. "Lena and her friends are down past the kitchen there."

As they slowly walked toward the voices, Marc leaned over to Laura and whispered, "I shouldn't have listened to you." He was embarrassed. They walked into the kitchen through the first opening in the hallway. It was a stunning room with luxury cabinets, granite tops, and state-of-the-art everything. They could see a group sitting around a large table in the adjacent room. They hit reverse and continued down the hall to where it opened up into a large family room and a dining area.

Lena was the first to notice them. She hopped up, "Hi." A frostbit explorer stranded through the most relentless arctic winter could not have felt a warmer rescue than the sound of that one word. Marc's shoulders fell and a smile that could not be subdued lit up his face. She said, "I'm Lena, you must be Marc and Laura Friedman."

"Yes. It's nice to meet you," Laura said.

"Hi, yeah, how ya doin'?" Marc's words were fine, but his body language was expressed in broken grammar and stuttering hesitance. As soon as he was free to scold himself privately, he rolled his eyes and muttered a few ultimatums through his gritted teeth, like an overbearing coach that would tolerate nothing less than perfection.

Nevertheless, either Lena was unfazed by it or she was intentionally setting him at ease by ignoring his awkward manner. "I'm doing great. We're just playing a game. Ya wanna join us?" There was a board game set out.

"Yeah, absolutely."

"Okay, Laura, you be on my team and Marc, you can be on, uh, Sam's team, okay?" She introduced them to the rest of the players. There were about ten people with approximately as many guys as girls playing in mixed teams, ranging from about fifteen to twenty-five in age. Marc was one of the older ones. There were three of Lena's siblings present, an older sister named Melinda who was there with her husband, Jeremy, a younger sister named Angie, and a younger brother named Clawson. He was the youngest present.

After the introductions, Laura tentatively asked, "Is Ashley going to be here?"

"No. She couldn't make it," Lena responded with a lift and tilt of her body. "But that's okay, we'll be fine." She dismissed the subject with an easy smile and returned to vertical equilibrium.

There were two plates of home-baked cookies, one at each end of the table and glasses of milk or punch scattered around. Mrs. Brensett was working on refreshments in the kitchen. After her turn, Melinda went in to help their mother.

Lena's turn followed Melinda's. She drew a card from the deck. Clawson flipped the timer over; he was impatient that Lena had taken too long to inspect the card. It was an action word, which was typically harder to depict than an object word. The trick was to think of a related object that could be drawn in order to help her team guess the actual word. She was doing it all wrong and her team was confused, but Marc was mesmerized. She was laughing and tucking her golden glories behind her ear. When an opposing team member chided her for accidentally giving her team an illegal, verbal clue, she stopped drawing to hush herself by slapping a hand over her mouth. "Keep drawing! Keep drawing!" someone on her team shouted, but it was of no use.

Marc was trying to behave naturally in his survey of the players and the surroundings, but his eyes were settling very intensely upon Lena. While it was her turn, it was natural to watch her. Perhaps it was not so completely natural to fixate upon her face and eyes, her hair and slender frame as it would be to examine her drawings, but all the same, his momentary excuse would conclude with the last, falling grain of sand. Then he would turn away from her and behave more democratically. How strange it was that particles of sand, hanging in the narrow neck of a glass timer, could impact the world of humans so considerably—that tiny things could steer the course of men.

People exhaust an awful lot of energy trying to hide the truth from each other, even when it's the truth that one wishes he could tell and another wishes that she could hear. Instead, they both go about like radio heads, aiming their ardent dishes at each other, scanning the horizon for the faintest signs of love. They don't know whether or not their signals would be favorably received, so instead of transmitting, they search in silence and wonder why the night is so damn dark and the stars so dim. There's no lack in the number of them, only in the brightness of their shine. They faintly flicker, like sparkling eyes, but the uncertainty and vastness of space and time swallow up the little hints.

The last grain fell.

"It was 'Park!'" She exclaimed after Clawson called time.
"Why didn't you just draw a swing set and a slide?" Someone asked her in frustration.

Marc and Laura were quiet, but the group assessment had begun wherein those who were not under pressure scrutinized and advised the one who *was* under pressure.

"I was trying to draw a parking car."

"It looks like an automobile accident," one of her friends teased.

"It *felt* like an automobile accident." She played along. "Sorry, I'm not an artist."

One of her friends sketched a simple car and a row of parking stalls, "See?" Then, pointing to her drawing of a box in front of another box with arrows and X's scribbled all over it, she said, "How was anyone supposed to guess what that was?"

"I don't know; they were supposed to read my mind." She was laughing.

The game continued for a few more rounds. When it came to Marc's team, they insisted that he draw since he had not yet had a turn. He killed it. In many ways, he had an unfair advantage in this game. Drawing diagrams and representing difficult concepts in simple terms were his specialty.

Was he showing off and was Lena feigning helplessness or was their behavior all perfectly natural? Were they transmitting intended signals or was it meaningless background noise? It wasn't clear.

After the first team won, Mrs. Brensett announced that refreshments were ready. Everyone moved to the large, elegant bar between the kitchen and the dining area. There were vegetable platters, delicious sandwiches, some chips and other snacks, and a Jell-O salad with grapes and chunks of other fruit whose identity could only be determined by their size and shape since their color and flavor was thoroughly masked by the prevailing medium. It was precisely the type of spread that Marc's mother would have laid out for one of their home gatherings. The abundant wealth that the Brensetts possessed was amply apparent in the construction of their home and their furnishings, but it was utterly undetectable in relation to their food, the pictures hanging on their walls, their topics of conversation, and in the domestic disposition of Mrs. Brensett.

A few more guests arrived and the group moved into the living room. Here Marc could see the whole family. On one wall, there were individual portraits of the family's seven children—four boys and three girls. All three girls and the youngest boy were present, but the two oldest boys and the boy between Melinda and Lena were absent from the party. Even though the photos were obviously arranged in order of their ages, the middle boy's apparent youth leapt out of sequence. He seemed only eight or ten. On the opposite wall, there hung a large family portrait above a plaque that read, "Families Are Forever." The middle boy was not pictured with the rest of the family, but his photo sat on the mantel beside the plaque. Marc swallowed the lump of emotion that swelled between his jaws. Such a tender age to die.

The hair of the Brensett women peaked in length with Angie, the youngest, and diminished in length to that of Mrs. Brensett's, roughly in inverse proportion to their ages. The Brensett men, with the exception of Clawson who clearly pursued a rebellious streak, wore their hair trimmed, neat, and parted in the same place and in the same manner.

One of the guests who had recently arrived, named Brock, was a big sensation with everyone present except Clawson. Even Laura, who had never met him, was enamored. He was a little older than Lena and he donned the same distinguished hair cut as her father and brothers. He justifiably won the respect with which he was regarded, for he was polite and well spoken, with a sincere countenance and gentle deportment. Lena's family already knew him and she introduced him to the others as a returned missionary who served in India. He had been home for about two months. The typical questions followed about the mission field and what the people were like.

He told the story of an investigator whom he had managed to help. He delivered his story with genuine meekness, but with great precision, too. It was evident that he had rehearsed it many times for such parties.

"She was a widow and her son was struggling with an addiction, so she was destitute. She insisted on feeding us, but it was obvious that she was the one in need of food. We did not want to seem ungrateful or condescending, so we ate and in return, we did our best to feed her the good news that the Savior bore." Clawson was rolling his eyes behind the hair hanging in his face. Brock continued without noticing, "After we finished teaching our lesson, she clasped her hands and thanked us with tears in her eyes."

Clawson broke the somber mood. "Are you sure that it wasn't because you ate the last of her rice?" A few people laughed uncomfortably, including Lena. She tried to recover herself by pasting a stern glance over the grin on her face. "Clawson!" she snapped, more for Brock's sake than any authentic expectation of reformation.

Brock laughed, too. "It's okay." He smiled at Clawson, but he soon resumed with his more receptive audience, "No, I do not think that that was the reason she cried because when we returned for our next lesson, she had a wonderful meal prepared. It was amazing what she could do with so little. We felt terrible about imposing on her meager substance, though, so we decided to bring some rice and lentils and some other things with us to our next appointment. I know we're not supposed to do things like that, but we figured, 'What difference does it make? We buy food and eat in our apartment. Why not buy food and eat in her apartment?' Well, she refused to accept it at first. We explained to her that it was our calling to bring her the gospel message, not to eat her food. Still, the only way that we could persuade her to take it was to permit her to prepare some for us. That's how she looked at it, like we were 'permitting' her to serve us."

"Were you able to baptize her?" Someone from the group couldn't tolerate the suspense; she wanted to skip to the end of the story.

"Oh, I'm getting to that part. Be patient." He chuckled in a reassuring manner. "Well, like I was saying, she was a wonderful person—the salt of the earth, as far as I'm concerned, but she had a coffee habit, so one day we brought some herbal tea with us. She pulled out the most beautiful tea set. It was a gift from her parents, but because she had a love marriage, it was the only thing she had left to remember them by."

"A love marriage?" Angie seemed confused.

"Yes, traditional marriages in India are arranged by the parents of the couple," some girl piped up in an authoritative voice. "If the couple insists on marrying against the wishes of their parents, they call it a 'love marriage.'"

"Seriously?" Angie was shocked.

Miss trivia continued. "Yes. In fact, in a love marriage, the couple is often ostracized or cut-off by their families. It is a major social issue facing India today. It's gradually changing as a result of the entertainment industry, but it is very deeply engrained in their culture."

"Wow, I can't imagine that," Angie said.

"Can't you?" Clawson asked with a sardonic glare.

"Clawson!" his mother snapped, like a warning shot fired from the mouth of a rifle spewing flames. Ignoring the injunction, however, he turned to his mother and fired back, "It's not like we don't do the same thing." There was a brief exchange of nonverbal intimidation and defiance, but Mrs. Brensett chose not to escalate the conflict. Completely transformed, she turned to Brock and implored, "Please continue with your story. We would love to hear it." In response to his mother, Clawson shook his head. Some flames will not be so easily snuffed out; if they're swept under the rug, the whole house burns down.

Brock laughed uneasily to escape the embarrassment of his position. He was a returned missionary and Lena was the only eligible Brensett girl; Melinda was already married and Angie was still in high school. Marc aimed his receptor dish at Lena in order to capture her reaction. Whether or not she was aware of the implication of Clawson's directed remark, her glowing countenance didn't entirely say. All of her signals were at elevated levels: bright eyes, rosy cheeks, radiant smile. Clawson's shrapnel had pierced and wounded every spirit but hers. She was the queen of joy and she ruled serenely. It was as she floated above it all, rather than trudging through it like ordinary people. The strife and shame and the thousand other cares that permeated their world didn't tug on her, so she seemed lighter somehow.

Perhaps she loved Brock, though. Perhaps she really did. Love's immune to scorn. The negative opinions of family members and best friends are the exaggerated antics of opera singers on mute. To criticism, love deafens the ear, and to petty faults, it blinds the eye. Love is not blind to truth as such. Rather, it perceives the more significant truth. Why shouldn't she love him? He was a good guy and good looking, too. Obviously Clawson resented something about Brock— maybe the system he was a part of, maybe the double standard of his naïve admirers, maybe his conformity. It didn't matter. Everyone has problems, but Brock's humility could inspire a peacock to shed its pride.

Marc looked away and hung his head two notches while Brock continued with his story. He related the remainder of it in abbreviated strides which were undoubtedly intended to restore an agreeable tenor to the gathering while accommodating less interested parties. "It was the most rewarding experience of my life—to be able to participate in the development of her testimony. Her faith grew and eventually she was baptized. It was such an overwhelming experience." He smiled to indicate that he had finally answered the critical question. He switched to an instructive voice, "We need to remember, though, that baptism is only the beginning of the story, not the end." Several people nodded in agreement. "It's kind of ironic, really. When I told her that our mission was to bring her the gospel message, I didn't realize how much of the gospel I would learn from her."

"That's so inspiring." Laura chimed in with a little positive reinforcement. Marc looked at her as if to ascertain whether she intended her praise to charm Brock or to compensate for Clawson's hostile attitude.

"Yeah, that's awesome; it would be amazing to go to India." Lena started making small talk.

Stepping out of the spotlight, Brock asked Marc, "So, did you go on a mission?"

"No, no. Sounds like it would have been incredible, though."

"Yes," Brock said, nodding his head in implicit acceptance. "What do you do for a living?"

"I'm working on my Ph.D. in computing at the university and I've started my own web development company."

"That's cool. Does it keep you pretty busy?"

"Yeah, I can't keep up with it."

"That's good. I'm thinking of going for communication."

They discussed schools, programs, and job opportunities. Marc explained a little about what he was working on at the university. Someone trying to be sociable asked Marc which church ward he attended.

"Well, I uh, I'm not really attending right now. I'm kind of inactive." Marc didn't wait for the socially acceptable span of time to expire before changing the subject and shining the spotlight back on Brock. "So what did you miss most while you were on your mission?"

With a tiny smirk and a glimmer of understanding, Brock relieved Marc of the attention. "Oh, besides my friends and family, I suppose it was sports, especially skiing. I've been three times since I got back and I love it."

One of the younger guys reflected aloud, "Yeah, totally. Except with me, it's boarding." He discussed sports with Brock for a while in the spirit of a student gathering wisdom in preparation for his own mission. Brock advised him on how to prepare psychologically to forsake sports and other amusements which would only distract him from his mission.

Lena said, "All this talk of sports… Who's up for a game of foosball?"

Clawson pitched back without missing a beat, "I am! Marc's on my team, okay?"

"Sure," Marc said, a little surprised at the abrupt change of pace. It was the first time that Clawson acted happy to be there.

"Okay, Laura, you're on my team," Lena said without asking. She invited everyone to join them in the game room, but Clawson pushed the foosball players out before anyone else had a chance to respond. He took charge at the table, directing each player to his or her position. He and Lena both took forward, so Marc played goalkeeper against Lena.

Marc valiantly defended his position against Lena's assault. They both fought hard, but the signs of physical exertion appeared upon Marc's face much more than upon Lena's. His shirt darkened from the sweat rolling down his chest; his sleeves were damp where he used them to wipe his face. His jaw tightened and his eyes flickered with the pulses of her attack. He deflected most of her advances, but she beat down on him too hard. Some were bound to push through, so the score on Lena's side piled up. Marc was leaning over the table as it tilted and rocked with the thrusts and blows of their struggle. Lena stood with a cool smile and only misty beads of sweat on her face.

After the first round, when Marc played forward against Lena, he showered the fury of hell down upon her. When the ball penetrated her defenses, it didn't merely roll through and drop into the box; it hammered the back wall and thundered a resolute sound, the interpretation of which seemed to register upon Lena's face as she gasped in surprise.

Marc's team won the second round, so the next round was the tiebreaker. Clawson asked Marc what positions they should play. In a voice as determined as the sound of Marc's thundering torpedoes, Lena insisted, "Same positions." Marc couldn't hold back his grin and Lena blushed when she saw him smiling at her. It was the first time all evening that she seemed rattled by anything.

In the last round, Lena's opposition erupted from a world set apart from the worlds of men. The best man rules heaven, the worst man rules hell, and this is a "man's world," but women conceal an inner place that is a mystery to men. It's hidden from most women, too, except the strong ones. Strong men crave strong women because they know that together there is no power in heaven nor in hell that can overthrow them.

Lena was obviously accustomed to winning. She defended her goal admirably against Marc, but Laura was no match against Clawson, so the ladies' team didn't score many points. The rest of the evening passed unceremoniously. Lena remained cordial but she didn't trouble herself to speak directly to Marc except in passing and she wouldn't make eye contact with him when she did.

As they drove away, Laura burst like a happy-face balloon that couldn't take the pressure anymore. "Lena totally likes you."

"Does she?" Marc's voice fell off like a man in quicksand who knows that a struggle will only accelerate his own demise.

"What is your problem? It's obvious that she's into you."

"I'm not sure."

"Dude, did you see how nice she was to you?"

"Maybe she's just a nice person."

There were many plausible explanations for the glimmer in Lena's eyes and for the change in her disposition after foosball. However, like the clouds of interstellar dust that hide the heart of the Milky Way from view, the intervening doubts and insecurities between his mind and hers only scrambled her signals. As for his signals—well, he clearly wasn't there for the Jell-O salad.

Chapter 6

Marc stood at the exit of the computing building, looking out into the gray world. The harsh winter had driven away every cheerful color and sound. The only noises were the growls of diesel engines pulling away from the shuttle stops and the slosh of cars beating ice, salt and sand into an urban stew. There were only mounds of snow piled around the walks and the parking lots. They were speckled with gravel and grime from the streets. It was carried like grudges by the clingy treads of tires and soles into every capillary and carpet of the city. A girl dressed in black with a bright red, felt coat and matching cap walked up to the building. She smiled through her rosy face as she passed Marc, but she quickly carried her warmth away.

If the city was drab below, then it was pale as death above. A blanket covered the city, like a vapor rising from the streets that pressed against the sky. The general location of the sun could only be determined by its cool glow. Marc stood on the warm side of the glass, watching despondently as his shuttle heaved away. A minute later, maybe two, he snapped his coat up to the top and flung the door open. He pressed his arms to his side, curled his shoulders forward, and bent his head in order to minimize his exposure to the hateful wind.

As he trudged toward the physics building, Marc scanned everyone in sight. He cast his eyes about, deep field like, giving little attention to nearby pedestrians. In the distance, where he was searching, faces couldn't be discerned directly, but energy levels could be. He was searching for a bright light. Anyone who blended into the drabscape quickly fell from his attention. There, in the wintry haze, he spotted her. There was a star flying through his gaze. She filled in for the choked out sun and took the chill away.

She moved like pretty penmanship—smoothly, gracefully, and on beat. If she stopped, the earth would bloom beneath her feet, but it was not in her nature to stop, but to move, to bounce above the dreariness of an inhospitable world, and to splatter drops of summer in her wake.

Marc turned away from his path in order to intercept her. Marc's own emission paled in comparison to hers. He squeezed like a child's whole body squeezes to force a little play dough through the star shape in his plastic extruder. He floundered at first, but it worked eventually and he managed to fire up a faint glow. He opened himself up and adjusted his gait to match hers: he straightened his shoulders, allowed his arms to sway more freely, and raised his chin. As they approached each other, he stopped and she recognized him. Her face brightened by twenty degrees. It had been nearly three weeks since the party at her house. She called him by name and asked how he was doing.

"I'm fine. It's crazy cold, but I'm fine. How are you?"

"I'm doing great. Yeah, it's unreal."

They made small talk for a while. Cold weather has been an icebreaker since there have been strangers upon the earth. Small talk doesn't accomplish anything directly, but it's like the oil in an engine—the parts would seize up without it. Once Marc's tongue sufficiently loosened, he said, "So, I've been trying to get your number."

"Oh. I'll give it to you. Do you have something I can write it on?"

Marc fumbled for a notebook while she continued, "How'd you try to get it?"

"Um, I asked Laura to get it from her friend Ashley."

"Oh." It was apparent that Lena had truncated her response.

"Yeah, Ashley won't return her calls, I guess."

"Well there, you have it now." She punctuated her phone number with a burst of light that warmed her face by a few more degrees. "So," she paused as if to ensure that Marc felt the warmth from her eyes, "what do you plan on doing with it?" Her question was an invitation and Marc couldn't suppress his smile.

"Well, would you like to go out some time?"

"Yeah, sure. Sounds great."

"Okay, perfect, I'll call you. Where ya headed?"

"Just over there." She pointed to the student services building nearby.

"Alright, well, I'll talk to you later."

"Okay, looking forward to it." This caused his smile to grow even wider and brighter.

He continued to walk in the direction of the detour he had taken in order to intercept Lena. It was another one of those little lies that humans always peddle each other. It wasn't where he was headed before he saw Lena and he had no business in that direction. When she entered the building, he turned around and headed back to the physics building. By then he was quite late, so he ran.

Marc approached Edberg's office door and, as usual, it didn't appear that anyone was there. No light was shining through the obscured glass in the door, other than the soft glow of Edberg's computer screen and the pittance of natural light which wandered in from the outside. It apparently entered more from curiosity than from any sincere intent to illuminate the surroundings.

The sun is a dense cauldron of frenzied fire. The intense heat and gravitational forces within its core pummel tiny particles into each other, overcoming the massive repulsive forces that would normally send them flying apart. When a ray of light is generated by the bonding of these particles, that ray jostles and fights through billions of collisions with bully matter for the span of a hundred thousand years before finally escaping onto its blazing trail for some starving speck of somewhere in the outskirts of nature. If destined for Edberg's office, then it spends a meager eight minutes on the final leg of its journey. One might expect that it would flash a little brighter before sinking into such a paltry place.

But no; that ray with all of its lackluster friends left more of a pitiable impression entirely uncharacteristic of their animated origins within the sun. Marc knocked on the door.

Edberg burst out, "Come in Marc." He always responded immediately when he expected Marc. Marc usually volunteered when the computing team needed someone to consult with Edberg, which gave Amy and William great pleasure and ample material for teasing him about his reasons. He simply ignored them.

"I've been expecting you; you're late."

"Yeah, sorry, I missed my shuttle." Another one of those lies.

"So, what do we have here?" Edberg asked, reaching for the folder Marc was holding.

The colder it was outside, the warmer Edberg kept it inside. Heat waves might have been seen rising from the heater, if indeed there had been sufficient light to see anything clearly at all. It would take some time for Marc's eyes to adjust to the darkness. It was already a dim day, but it was dimmer by magnitudes in the corners of Edberg's office where the glow of his computer screen couldn't reach. There was a piano lamp hunched over some papers on his desk, but the bulb was so dim that Edberg had to lean over the armrest of his chair to read the papers that he took from Marc. He read them like a midnight father reads his daughter's face in the pale light shining through a crack in the bedroom door to see if she might still be awake so that he can kiss her and tell her goodnight.

The urgency to keep his appointment on time was already glistening on the surface of Marc's skin, so it didn't take long for beads of sweat to start gathering on the tips of the thousand chestnut curls in his hair. He wiped his forehead on the sleeve of his jacket, not like one does when one is ashamed of perspiring, but rather like one does when one wishes to say, "Would you turn the heat off, already?" Edberg didn't get the message, though, or he ignored it if he did.

Finally Edberg finished his initial review. "So, what is your question?"

Instead of responding immediately, Marc looked at the solid wall of books. He opened his mouth to speak but his tongue stalled, like a skydiver who approaches the open door of an aircraft, but with nothing except wispy air to break his fall and the ruthless ground to catch him, he lost his nerve. He exhaled the air that he had reserved for forming words and, instead, sat looking at the books, perplexed.

Edberg laughed. "What is it?" Turning to Edberg for the first time since handing over his folder, Marc pressed his lips together and shrugged his shoulders. "What?" Edberg pulled a little harder to extract an answer, but laughed again in reaction to Marc's strange expression. Finally, Marc began to pry open the lid to his container of secrets. "I don't know. I'm just lost. Nothing makes sense."

"That's what you're here for," Edberg responded as if he had just solved the problem entirely.

"No, I mean I'm lost." Marc pounded his chest when he said it this time.

Marc's manner caught Edberg by surprise and he traded his smile for a wave of apprehension that piled up on his forehead. "What's the matter?"

Marc burst like a valve under too much pressure, "Physics disproves everything I was taught to believe."

"Oh?" Edberg raised his eyebrows in response to the unexpected direction that Marc pursued. "What were you taught to believe?"

Marc took a second to formulate his response. "Well, like for instance that 'God has a plan.'" He took a moment to consider his own statement, as if it was the first time that he had verbally formulated a conflict between science and religion. He must have been satisfied with the sound of it, because he continued more assertively. "I was taught to believe that God controls everything. I was taught that if I lost my watch, my measly stinkin' watch, that I should pray for him to help me find it, and if I truly believed, he would help me find it. Ya know? 'Knock and it shall be opened, ask and ye shall receive.'"

"And physics disproves that God answers prayers?" Edberg probed analytically.

"Well, look at all of these equations. At the root of every one of them is uncertainty. Chance!" Marc said it like a statement, but his glance at Edberg looked like a question. Perhaps he was hoping that Edberg would refute it.

"That's right." Edberg offered no consolation and Marc wiped a little hope from his brow.

"Well, if chance is truly one of the most fundamental laws of nature, how could God have a plan for anything?"

"It depends on the scale and precision of his plan." Edberg looked at Marc to measure the impact of this idea. Edberg seemed disappointed with Marc's stoic response, but he continued, "If God had a plan for a certain particle, then his plan would have to be quite broad, or in other words, unspecific. Because chance affects it significantly. However, the larger the mass of an object, the less affected by chance it is. Like a baseball. If you can measure its speed and direction of motion, then you can predict with great certainty where it will be at a given time." Edberg again gave off an air of having solved the problem entirely.

Marc pondered Edberg's example for a while. "Yes, but suppose that I made a contraption that would release a boulder to roll down a hill." Marc enunciated the word "boulder" in imitation of its heaviness compared to a baseball. He continued, "The boulder would be released by a gate. Let's say that its latch is a switch electronically triggered by detecting the decay of a radioisotope. Now that's small *and* random! Now, how can God predict where the boulder will be at a given time if it's impossible to predict when it will start rolling?"

"Nice twist on the Schrödinger cat experiment."

"Thanks." Marc seemed pleased. "That contraption— that's me! What if free will is just an elaborate system triggered by millions of random events inside of our brains? I mean, if thoughts are merely chemical reactions in the brain, those chemicals are very small and would be subject to great uncertainty. Maybe the system is just so complex that we call it 'free will' to avoid the fact that it's hopelessly beyond our ability to comprehend."

Edberg nodded thoughtfully.

Marc continued, "So, it seems that no matter how large and stable something is, at any particular moment the tiniest thing can impact it in really significant ways, all based on chance. A person's entire life could be altered by, by…" Marc paused. "By particles of sand falling through the neck of a timer." Marc offered this example cautiously at first, but finished it with a burst. It was a thought that had suddenly ripened, like a pomegranate soaking up the milk of earth and sun until its skin ruptured from the seeds swelling within it— still shiny and moist.

"True. However, you were originally concerned with God's ability to control, not to predict."

"What's the difference? Doesn't he have to predict before he can control?" Marc asked with a concerned look.

"Possibly, but supposing that God knew about your contraption, he could perhaps initiate an intervening event that would mitigate any disruption to his plan and bring everything to within tolerable bounds."

Marc's shoulders fell perceptively; he looked dejected. Apparently the prospect that God could control everything was more troubling to him than the prospect that everything was governed by chance. "I see what you're saying, but it just doesn't make sense to me that a God who went to so much trouble to create a universe of chance would also go to such trouble to control its outcomes. People who believe that must think that God is some kind of cosmic control freak!" This description elicited a burst of laughter from Edberg. Marc asked, "Do you really believe that a universe of chance is consistent with a universe of control?"

"That's a good question, but first of all, you've made an assumption which may or may not be valid. You're assuming that God created the universe. What if he didn't? If he didn't create the universe, then there's no conflict. God would merely be on a quest to control certain outcomes, the same as our species seeks to do, only he would be much better at it."

Marc offered back a drawn out, "Okay."

Edberg continued in order not to lose his momentum, "On the other hand, if God did create the universe, then it's foolish to place limitations on his power."

"I'm not placing limitations on his power. Well, maybe, I don't know. I just don't see any evidence of divine intervention. Anywhere!" Marc's eyes widened from the expansion of another idea. He reached for his folder, as if its contents were fortuitously relevant to their conversation instead of being the very cause of their conversation. "For instance, where is it in any of these equations? Where is the God term in just one of these equations?"

"Well, as I've told you before, these equations are correlations; they do not describe the cause. They don't give a complete picture; far from it!" Edberg waved to the folder that Marc brought with a sneer of derision, "It's a loose and messy model that's been fucked with until she tells us whatever we want to hear." Marc laughed at Edberg's characterization of quantum physics as some sort of cheap prostitute.

Marc said, "So it comes down to whether God is the creator of the universe and exists external to it and independent of it, in which case he has all power, or whether he is subject to the Universe, in which case, he's just very good at mitigating disruptions to his plan."

Edberg followed up immediately, "Or there is no God."

Marc swallowed. He hadn't addressed that possibility. "Do you believe there's a God?"

"I believe that if there is a God, he doesn't want me to know it. By definition, God would be incomparably more powerful than I. Therefore, to foil his plan for keeping me in the dark would be a futile endeavor. Either there is no God, or he completely covers his tracks. Correction: he *leaves* no tracks."

"Exactly! He leaves no tracks!" Marc nearly shouted.

Edberg looked blankly at Marc, so Marc explained further, "that means that God must exist outside of—and independent of—the universe. I don't care how carefully a creature moves through the forest, it leaves traces of its presence. If God interfered with the universe as extensively as religionists claim that he does, he'd leave tracks more visible than contrails. It'd be inevitable."

"Nevertheless, some people claim that he does leave tracks, everywhere!"

"Right, I know. My sister tells me that everywhere she looks, she sees evidence that God lives. I asked her to explain how. She couldn't tell me the first thing about how stars work or why there is such a diversity of life on earth, but she insisted that they all prove the existence of God."

"That's not so strange. After all, if God created the universe, as you suggest, then everything in it is a manifestation of his existence."

"And if he didn't?" Marc asked intensely.

"Then…"

"Then there's no evidence of his existence." The words burst from Marc's mouth like steam from a pressure cooker. "You said it yourself, he leaves no tracks."

"Right. It's a precarious position to be in, for sure. If you admit any evidence, you admit all evidence."

Marc paused to consider Edberg's last statement. He said, "I suppose there's another alternative."

Edberg quipped back, "Oh! Alternatives are all that we have when we're talking God. I want to hear your idea though, but I have to go." Marc nodded in agreement, offering an expression that suitably acknowledged an insurmountable problem. Edberg continued, "What do you say to this? Come to my place tomorrow and we'll continue this discussion."

Marc agreed, but the invitation surprised him. He agreed without taking any time to consider it. "What time?"

Edberg said any time after 6:00 and gave Marc his address.

After his appointment, Marc entered the computing building, but he bypassed the project room and walked directly to his office. The place was quiet. He sat motionless at his desk. There was a knock and the door opened on him looking blankly at his computer screen. It was William. "Hey, how did it go? Can you help me out with this routine?"

"Well, we didn't really make much headway."

"Dude! What did you do? Did you get it off with Edberg? It's physics, not *physical*. Did he check your prostate? He's a physicist, man, not a physician."

"William!" Marc turned to face him. He was raging. He went from infinity to fury in about one second. "Shut your filthy mouth. I'm tired of your goddamned depravity. Is there nothing you won't lay your vulgar mouth on or slather with your stinking scum? Is nothing above being dragged through the muck? You'll never be happy until you've smeared your vile scum over every noble thought and deed. Get your mind out of the gutter. You're wallowing in shit. Just flush it, okay?"

Marc was a volcano and there was a vaporizing gust rushing from the pit, but William stood, barely ruffled, like a tree on a cool breezy day. William said, "Whoa! Dude, I didn't know that you were so homophobic."

"See what I mean?" Marc looked at William in astonishment. "It has nothing to do with homophobia. I just don't understand why every time I collaborate with Dr. Edberg you've got to turn it into a sexual encounter."

"Oh is that what they're calling it now? Collaboration? Hey, it's cool. Whatever you're into. If you're not ready to talk about it, yet, that's none of my business."

"Yet?" Marc was about to blow again.

"Hey, I'm here if you ever need to get anything off your chest."

"Thanks, I'm sure I'll manage just fine."

"So seriously, I need your breakdown on those equations."

Marc sat back in his seat. "Okay, I think I can figure it out. I just need to spend some time on it."

"Do you need any help?"

"No."

"Okay. I'll just leave this door open. Looks like you need to cool off."

Marc turned back around and resumed staring at his screen. After a few minutes, he reached behind and slammed the door. William yelled from down the hall, "You cool, bro?" Marc huffed, but he couldn't restrain from cracking a smile as he sputtered, "asshole."

He reclined in his chair and put his feet up. His leather shoes desperately needed a shine. The tips were badly scuffed and they had permanent creases along the line where his toes bent. There was a white watermark a little above the sole where his shoes got wet from walking in briny runoff from sidewalks and streets. They had carried him through two years. Even when he polished them, he couldn't conceal their heavy use. The tips turned up like mud that curls and cracks when it dries under the sun. The shoes looked so rough that they made the rest of his clothes look new by comparison. He shook his head in disgust and put his feet down. He pulled out his phone and dialed the number that Lena gave him.

"Hello?"…

Marc must have expected to leave a message. He seemed surprised to get an answer. He sat up in his chair like a solider snapping to attention. He even saluted with a sudden tilt of his phone and a tightening of his grip. One might think that a major general had walked into the room.

"Yes! Hello. This is Marc."…

"Hi. How ya doing?"…

"Great! I'm fine. Hey, I know it's kind of sudden, but I was wondering if you'd like to go out tonight."…

"Oh, okay. No problem."…

"Tomorrow? Yeah, definitely. That'd be great!"…

In spite of how nervous Marc was, he was clearly thrilled to be talking to Lena. Somehow a grin managed to percolate to the surface through the tension visible on his face.

"What time can I pick you up?"…

"Sounds good. Hey, what kind of food do you like?"…

She took her time to answer this question. There were no long pauses and the ring of her voice was energetic, as if his question had spurred other stories about her which gave her joy to relate. Through the muffled earpiece of Marc's phone, Lena's voice sounded like a music box playing the tune to a familiar song. It didn't matter whether it was a sad song or not, because the metal tines would impart a cheerful tone to any melody. There was a beat and although the words couldn't be heard, they were felt.

"Oh, I like Italian, too, and, um, Chinese; pretty much anything really."...

This was another lie, unless eating copious amounts of pizza constituted "liking Italian," and likewise for Chinese. He ate instant noodles cooked in the microwave and frozen pot-stickers or eggrolls warmed in the toaster oven. Often the lies that people tell each other are not malicious or intended to deceive. Rather, they are tales about how people would like to be, about tastes that they wish they had, motives they wish they had, or horizons that they wish to pursue. Sometimes they are merely ways of saying, "I think you're amazing and I want you to think that I'm amazing, too."

"So have you been anywhere else?"...

"Hahaha. No, I mean in Europe, or outside of the U.S."...

There was more music and it had a soothing effect on Marc. He appeared more relaxed and the tense grin that jostled for position on his face earlier was slowly replaced by a general sense of ease: smiling, laughing, and joking. Marc's eyes were wide and bright; he was listening intently to every detail that she offered.

"Okay, well, it's been really nice talking to you, Lena. I look forward to seeing you tomorrow night."...

"Alright. See you then. Oh! I almost forgot; where would you like me to pick you up?"...

"Alright, sounds good. Goodbye."

Marc hung up and leaned back in his chair. He was lit up. He began reflecting upon the conversation, because his face repeated the sequence of expressions that it exhibited during the conversation. His lips moved to mimic key phrases that he spoke. His face alternated between dismay and delight. He was beating himself up for things that he had said, for not being smoother, or for not being more clever.

Marc rehearsed the conversation several times, but the iterations of facial expressions faded into serenity and eventually a smile settled all claims. He sat there until long after the sun retreated and completely hid its face behind the Oquirrh Mountains in the west. It didn't put up much of a fight that day. At least not for the valley of the saints. While Olympic athletes were preparing to battle for the glory of sports and their homelands, the sun had surrendered the venue of the valley and the mountains to the devil and whatever humans could make of it. Humans lost on the cold front, but the devil lost on every other front. Mankind was the champion of the day. On that day, the glory of man surpassed the splendor of all nature.

From the dawning of man, ever since curiosity crept into him, he has searched the earth for wonders, looking for answers to the deep questions, and hoping to find something that would astound him. Adventurers chase the thrills that would be worth dying for, and explorers hunt for the discoveries that would change the world forever. Nevertheless, the greatest wonders of the universe are not the mysteries that people uncover, but the people who uncover them.

Man possessed something transcendent. It was forged and hammered out in the shops and in the boardrooms, in the lecture halls and in the quiet libraries, in the kitchens and in the studios, in the beauty parlors and in the weight rooms. It was refined on the ski slopes and on ice rinks where years of devotion would be rewarded with medals and tears. It was worked out between shouting husbands and wives, or between friends who met for a beer. It was vouched safe by the elderly dying for the laughter of children. The glory of man was invisible, bursting rays piercing the dark in a little office where a phone conversation between two souls left a man to sit in silence for the evening.

Chapter 7

Saturday morning. The sun was shining brightly through the windows whose blinds hadn't been drawn the night before, but it may as well have been the deep, dark night until Marc emerged from the world of hidden nightmares and dreams. Still, dreams merely spill over from that world into this, like a pot of boiling water filled too closely to the brim. The surface splashes over the flame and draws a lot of attention until the hissing stops and the steam dissipates. The deeper layers and the mysteries that they contain never meet the flame. If the world of dreams merely boils over into the conscious world, perhaps the conscious world contributes as little to dreams. It could be a very strange place. People render a third of their lives to it, like tribute paid to a despot king who offers no accounts. Whoever they become there, those characters are strangers to the consciousness.

It took some time for Marc to drift completely through the tunnel of dreams. The waters flowed more slowly than usual and the oars of his boat were tucked lazily inside. His habit was to wake himself to joy, to start each day on a positive threshold. Therefore, it didn't strike him initially that Lena had left and taken the children with her. It was evident when it did occur to him, however, from the turn of expressions upon his face. He groaned and rolled over, throwing one arm ahead of him, as if to ditch his boat and swim back from where he came. Perhaps his world of dreams was a pleasanter place.

Marc opened the gym locker and checked his texts. Laura had left several.

Laura: Hey, you remember Franceska? Jason's wife?
         I visited her this morning. She's not doing very

well, having a hard time supporting herself and
the kids now that Jason's gone.
I told her that I would see if you could offer her
a better job.
What do you think?

Marc responded and then pulled off his swimming shorts
and headed to the shower.

Marc: I've never met her, but I'm happy to help if I can.
Tell her to contact Meg in human resources. I'll
put in a word for her.

Jason Cox was Marc's long lost cousin who died overseas
of an infection resulting from a minor injury. Their mothers
were sisters. Marc never really knew Jason; they didn't do
much together when they were kids. Besides, Jason was closer
to Laura's age and she was a lot more into family than Marc
was. So nearly everything Marc knew about Jason, he learned
from Laura, who kept a detailed mental log of the affairs of
her family, extending to distant relatives as far as her parents
would tolerate her to go.

After Laura became an adult, she reached much further.
Her idea of a good time was to visit the church's family
history center to do genealogical research in order to add
deceased relatives like clay ornaments to a leafless tree. The
more figures hanging from the branches, the less obvious was
the fact that the tree was dead.

She had a little circle of friends who were as devoted to
the cause as she was. They would take turns meeting at their
homes to bake cookies and share the stories that they had
recently exhumed. Laura told about one gem of a find from
one of her girlfriends. One of her great uncles, several times
multiplied and removed, had been the grounds keeper at
Amherst Academy during the very years that Emily

Dickinson attended school there. As such, he was in the perfect position to teach the young Emily all that she knew about botany, which was extensive. Obviously she didn't get all of that knowledge from books. Surely they knew each other. After all, she attended school there for seven years. One might say that Emily derived her aesthetic sensitivities during those formative years by walking through the grounds of her school. How could reading the classics among the peonies have left anything but a marvelous impression at a time when she was most impressionable? Peonies were always a favorite in both families, you know? It couldn't be a coincidence. She was there for seven years! It's probably not a stretch to say that without the influence of that great uncle, the world would be without the poetry of Emily Dickinson.

Besides pilgrims upon the Mayflower, cousins to European nobility, and great contributors to art and science, their favorite finds were those whose lives would seem to indicate a predisposition to accept the church had it been on the earth in their lifetimes. If the dearly departed was ever on record as having performed any act of faithfulness, or having rendered any altruistic deed, it was proof positive that he or she would have accepted the church, been baptized, and lived a faithful life until the end. Therefore, it was in granting unexpressed wishes, silenced only by death, that Laura and her friends would often enter the temple to baptize their dead relatives by proxy into the church.

Marc teased Laura by saying that the only boyfriends she ever had were the poor, unsuspecting proxies she conned into helping her with temple work when no family members were willing or able to do it. He tried to ignore Laura's protracted accounts of "the family," but when he couldn't agree with her logic, he argued with her. Therefore, what he dismissed as silly, he learned by wading through it.

After Jason graduated from high school, he shot out on his own. He eventually ended up in Europe and married a Hungarian girl. When he died, Laura was the only member of the Friedman house that attended the funeral. She wiped out her savings to purchase the airfare to Hungary. She tried to get Marc to go, but he excused himself due to "pressing business." About a year later, Franceska immigrated to the United States to be with Jason's family. Laura worked tirelessly to assist Franci, as she called her, to make the preparations within the U.S.

After Marc finished dressing and packing up his things from the gym, he shot a text to Meg:

A woman named Franceska Cox will be contacting you about a job. She's a widow with two kids. Struggling. I'd appreciate it if you could help her out. Thx

In the mornings, Marc usually took the long way to his office to greet employees and to boost morale. On one occasion, as he walked past the copy room, a new woman watched him through the glass partition as he walked through the hallway. Their eyes met and he smiled back with a half wave. She was dressed in a red pencil skirt and white shirt. Her skirt held her knees together in an elegant pose with one knee bent slightly in front of the other. Her toe was turned in and resting on the tip so that the heel was raised and pointing outward. This stance made her appear to be suspended by invisible threads, as if she was not actually contacting the floor. The top of her skirt wrapped around her waist like hands about to toss her into the air. Her top was looser than her skirt, but it still managed to tug on her breasts where her nipples protruded like steel thimbles. It was a cotton shirt with a crisp collar and cuffs around her elbows.

Her brown hair, slightly lighter than Marc's, was done into a wavy up-do, but it seemed long enough to have reached the middle of her back if she let it down. It was held above her hairline in the back and fell in loose curls resting upon one cheek like a Balaton breeze. She reached up, brushed the curls aside, and looked away with an embarrassed grin that got tangled up with her eyes.

She was about Lena's age, maybe a few years younger. She wasn't wearing any make-up. Her lips were slightly pinker than her alder skin, like a dusty rose. They were not thin and they were not full, but they were far from ordinary. Her lashes were modest and her brows were fine, which neatly framed her eyes. Her cheeks were soft and brighter than most of her face, which made her eyes appear darker. Her chin was soft like her cheeks and it was softened more by an adorable plumpness underneath.

Marc gazed upon her longer than a gentleman should, like a man who looks at a pretty girl for so long that he marches headlong into a street lamp, making a comical fool of himself and doing himself considerable injury. Marc finally looked away to recover himself before he became that fool. He waved to some employees in another office. He probably didn't appear rattled, except to those who may have witnessed his awkward recovery. The whole interchange didn't last more than two or three seconds, but that was three times longer than seemed natural.

Occasionally an experience alters a man's perception of the world. Most experiences only reinforce existing paradigms, but if he's alert and prepared to receive it, some lift him to a higher understanding. It's like a flying axe that splits his consciousness from his physical senses, enabling him to perceive things that were previously hidden by his deeply rooted assumptions about the world. He takes power from it. Power is merely an attitude of expectation. Empowered ones expect to obtain a desired object by consequence of personal action and universal principle. Unempowered ones expect to obtain it by luck or special grace.

After Marc dealt with the urgent business on his desk, he called human resources.

"Hi Meg! Hey, did we hire that woman that I referred to you the other day?"...
"Okay. Where did you place her?"...
"Oh, alright."...
"No, I was just curious. What kind of qualifications did she have?"...
"Well, sounds good. Thanks for helping her out."...
"I will. Thanks."

Marc rolled back over in bed and opened his eyes. He wasn't escaping. He sighed. His crusted skin cracked and peeled as he pushed a grin to the surface for the faces that were mocking him from within the texture on the ceiling. It was a jungle up there with millions more vile things lying in wait to kill or to maim, than there were loving souls to comfort an injured man who was stumbling on the edge of a precipice. Unless someone saved him, delirium would lead to his untimely end.

Every creature must look to its own survival. Compassion is a trait of higher order among animals. Some few possess it, but not every man, and not every woman either. It seems that the more harsh the environment, the rarer it is.

Scarcity is a mindset; abundance, too. The scarcity mindset is the disposition to lust after things which are in short supply. Businesses compete for market share, co-workers compete for promotions, athletes compete for titles, and several boys compete for the attention of one girl. The pie is only so large. Therefore, one person's win is another person's loss. It's a zero-sum game because all of the wins and losses add to naught.

The abundance mindset, on the other hand, is the disposition to desire mutual growth in pursuits that have unlimited potential. Businesses innovate to create new markets undreamt of before. Coworkers collaborate for the advancement of their team. Athletes build a fan base for their sport and become legends in their own time. Men develop traits which are admired by many and sought after by exceptional women. The size of the pie increases through cumulative contribution.

In an abundance framework, the players cooperate to promote growth. It's a positive sum game because the total actually exceeds the sum of its parts. The collective body grows in power and beauty. It sits on the throne of creation; it governs the whole earth; it officiates in the realm of possibility. While weak minds squabble over infinitesimals smeared on the surface of this globe, strong minds roll worlds into view and raise up the columns of nature.

The primary difference between man and beast lies in their respective abilities to manipulate the environment. Man may choose whether to contend with greed over a crust of bread, or instead to grow a field and thereby to provide for many, to extend his influence, and to raise up friends who sustain his soul. The choice lies before him every day.

Marc raised himself from bed and pulled on his robe. He walked directly to the side door and looked outside. There was a fresh blanket of snow covering the world. He went out to the front porch and scanned the parking circle and driveway. There were no fresh tracks. He checked inside the garage. Lena's car wasn't parked anywhere. He ran bewildered fingers through his messed up hair and sighed. More from habit than from anticipation, he wandered into the kitchen, the heart of the home. The coffee pot was empty and everything was immaculately clean. Matilda had the day off; she always left it extra clean for the weekends.

Marc stood for a while in the center of the kitchen, as if he was weighing some heavy options. Finally, he walked to the freezer and pulled out a bag of coffee beans. He dispensed some into the grinder and flipped it on. While it was grinding, he returned the beans to the freezer and grabbed the portafilter from the cappuccino machine. The portafilter was of the bottomless type, which is the most difficult to operate because it offers no compensation for an improperly prepared basket of espresso grounds. The cappuccino machine itself was well built and rugged, but it only offered the essentials.

After the grinder finished he began tapping the lever to dispense grounds into the basket. "Shit!" He had forgotten to set the coarseness on the grinder. It was set for drip coffee. He threw out the grounds and adjusted the grinder for espresso. He flipped the switch again.

"Shit!" The grinder started making a higher pitched sound because it ran out of beans in the hopper. Beans stay fresher when they're kept in the freezer, so he had only dispensed enough to pull a double shot. He quickly flipped the grinder off and pulled the bag of beans out of the freezer. He added beans to the hopper and flipped the grinder on again. After it finished, he tamped another pull, but something was off; he smelled the grounds. "Shit! Shit! Fuckin' Shit!" He grabbed the bag of coffee beans. They were French roast.

"What is this shit?!" Marc asked Lena with an expression of disgusted derision as he took a whiff of the pot of coffee that she had brewed.

"It was a gift from Carla," Lena answered with a nonchalant glance over her shoulder.

"French roast?!"

"Yeah." Lena flipped the page of the fashion magazine she was reading as if she bought it for the ads.

"You like it?" Marc asked skeptically.

"Umm. Yeah, it's pretty good." Lena wasn't convincing.

"You don't really mean that."

"Yes, I do."

"Well, have you had enough?"

"What do you mean?"

"Can I dump the rest?"

"No. I think I'll have another cup."

"I can't drink this shit."

"Then can't you make yourself a cappuccino?"

Marc placed the pot back as hard as he could without breaking it.

The bag of French roast was as full as it was a year ago. "Waste of space," Marc muttered as he tossed it in the garbage. He wasn't going to give his thoughts another chance to distract him. He grabbed his keys and drove to the nearest coffee shop. While he waited in line he texted Lena.

Marc: How's it going?
          Are you going to keep ignoring me?
          I love you!
Lena: I don't think I can do this.
Marc: I understand. Let's talk about it.
          I'm not trying to rush you into anything.
Lena: I turned my back on everything to be with you.
          I believed in you. I defended you. I gave you my
          all. We promised that we would love each other

forever and I have done nothing to break that. I haven't done anything to cause you to treat me this way. I don't deserve this.

Marc: How am I treating you? I thought we were doing this together.

Lena: I thought we were together too!

Marc: We are together. I don't want that to change.

Lena: You're changing everything! I just don't understand why you're doing this.
What's wrong with me?

Marc: What do you mean?

Lena: What do you need that I'm not giving you?
What does she have that I don't have?

Marc: It's not like that.

Lena: Then what's it like?!

Marc: I've tried to explain it a thousand times. I don't really know what else to say.

Lena: Then I guess we have nothing to talk about.

"Well, at least it gave me something to do while I waited," Marc sneered as he pulled away from the coffee shop. He always ridiculed people who waited in long lines for coffee. Now he was one of them.

"What's that?" Marc asked in an interrogating tone as he pointed to Franceska's Starbucks cup.

"Coffee," she replied in a puzzled tone, somewhere between asking and telling.

"Are we out of coffee?"

"Uh, I don't believe that. Why?" Franceska asked, still puzzled. She was trying to go along with it cheerfully, but the language barrier was shaking her confidence.

Seeing that, Marc laughed to set her at ease. He said, "I'm just saying that we have great coffee here. I personally picked it out. You should try it. It's really good."

"Oh, ha." Franceska smiled back. "I have tried it, Mr. Friedman."

"Then why are you drinking that?"

"I bought it on my way to work—I like it."

"Okay," Marc said in a tone that meant, "you're not a bad person, but you do bad things." He smiled again to soften the judgment. "Well, we'll just have to see about that."

"And how will we see about that?" Franceska asked in a coy, but broken voice which was, nevertheless, coupled with body language in thrilling fluency. Marc chuckled a little nervously and continued walking down the hallway.

The next day when Marc came into the office, he asked Tara, his secretary, for two cups of coffee, one for himself and one for the new girl in the copy room. "Make it like mine," he said nonchalantly, adding by way of explanation, "She's drinking Starbucks." Tara nodded in agreement. He continued more thoughtfully, "We can't have that around here. If we let our standards down, there's no telling where they'll sink to." He laughed and entered his office.

Marc used coffee as a metaphor for work. His concern for the quality of the coffee elevated the entire work place. If he noticed a flaw, he would systematically investigate to uncover its source. Once identified, it was immediately corrected. He had tossed out bags of coffee and cartons of half-n-half. He had replaced old coffee machines and refrigerators. He had swapped out water vendors. Mediocre coffee could not be tolerated. It would undermine the entire company. Mediocrity was an insidious imp that had to be guarded against with vigilant opposition. Therefore, no one would think it odd that he sent coffee to an employee. Perhaps no one would think anything at all about it.

Later, he received an email from Franceska:

Mr. Friedman,

I would like to thank you for the coffee that I received from you. You were right, it was outstanding better. I would like also to thank you for this great job. I really appreciate it.

Thank you for everything.

♥ Franci

Marc sat in front of Franceska's email for several minutes, much longer than he would devote to any other similar correspondence. Either he was studying it intently or he was lost in thought. He eventually came back from wherever he had drifted to and composed a response.

Franci,

You are welcome for the coffee. I'm glad that you enjoyed it. ☺

It's great to have you on board. I hope that you're settling in okay. Let me know if you need anything.

BTW, you can call me Marc.

Marc.

Marc fell on the couch in the sitting room next to the kitchen. He swirled his cup of drive-through mediocrity, took a sip, and with a glance through the picture window he melded with the mountains across the valley.

"Mom, what are they drinking?" Marc asked as he pointed to a couple sitting several tables away in a family diner. Their waitress was filling their cups with a steaming hot, black liquid from a spherical, glass pot.

"Marc!" She replied in a hushed, but stern voice as she pushed his hand down to the table. "It's not nice to point," she said.

Marc made a sick face because there was syrup on the table which he had strategically avoided until then. Now his hand was sticky. "Okay, but what are they drinking?" He started licking his hand.

"That's coffee, son."

"Oh, are they gentiles?" He asked as if it was the first time he had ever seen one.

"Well, I suppose. They could be. Stop licking your hand, that's gross!" She was distracted and her answers were suffering.

"So are they going to hell?"

She hushed him. "Don't talk like that."

"Are they?" He whispered.

"Well, probably not, I mean not just for that. Heavenly Father loves them the same as he loves us."

He was puzzled. "Well, who goes to the devil, then?"

"Well, people who refuse to keep Heavenly Father's commandments."

"But isn't coffee against his commandments?"

"Yes, son. Well,... it's the law of the church." She chuckled a little at his naïve outlook.

"Well, then, doesn't that mean they're going to the devil?"

"Heavenly Father expects people to do the best they can with the knowledge and understanding that he has given them." Nodding toward the couple she said, "They don't really know better."

"So if I ever drank coffee, would I go to the devil?"

She chuckled again. "Well, it wouldn't please Heavenly Father. You would lose his spirit and that takes you away from him. Besides, he gave us the Word of Wisdom because he loves us and wants to help us keep our bodies clean and pure. Do you understand?"

"Yeah, I guess so."

"Just don't ever drink coffee, okay? You need to have Heavenly Father's spirit with you always."

"Okay." He rubbed his hand. It left a sticky residue and caused his napkin to bunch up and rip.

He made another face of disgust.

Marc got up from the couch and grabbed a napkin from the kitchen to wipe his mouth. He pulled out his phone and called Franceska.

"Hi."...

Marc's face visibly transformed from a mixed expression of vexation and dismay to one of delight, albeit slightly restrained. The tension lifted in degrees, however, like patio steps leading to a familiar, cozy place. He settled back into his spot on the couch, resting his head on the plush end.

"Well, I've been better, but it's nice to hear your voice again."...

"No, she's still gone."...

"I don't know. She won't talk to me. Sorry to drag you into this."...

"Good. I'm glad to hear you say that."...

"I know, but, well, I hoped it would be different. I wish I knew how this is going to turn out. How are you doing?"...

"This is hard. I really want to see you."...

"I don't know; she's never ignored me like this before."...

"Why don't you think it's a good idea?"...

"Well, she thought it was a good idea two weeks ago."...

"She's the one who won't talk about it."...

Marc laughed. "No, I think I better give her some time. I don't know. You're a woman! What would you want?"...

Marc laughed again. "Well, thanks, that really helps. I may as well flip a coin. Why are women so difficult to understand?"...

"Yes you are! Men are simple. Ya know?"...

"Seriously. Men are like Morse code—simple and straightforward. There are only two ciphers, the key is public, and anyone can decode a message. Lots of people do it in their head. Women are like AES."...

"It's an encryption algorithm. It's used to encode top-secret information. The key is kept private and without it, it would take a supercomputer trillions of years to decode a basic message. Actually, that's an optimistic estimate!"...

"That's right. I absolutely love you!"...

"Oh! You do, do you?" Lena screamed at Marc. She was standing in the hallway. Marc startled so severely that he flew off of the couch like a champagne cork. It took him a moment to regain his presence of mind. Lena was still shouting and he remembered that Franceska was still on the phone.

"What?!" He asked, still confused.

"You're flirting with her!"

"What? What do you mean?"

"Give me that." She tried to grab the phone out of Marc's hand. He pulled it away and shouted, "Hold on," into the mic like a runner sliding into home plate.

"No, don't hold on," she yelled at the phone.

"Settle down!"

"Give me the phone."

"No!" He placed the phone back against his cheek and she lunged for it, so he took cover behind the dining table. "I'll call you back." At that, Lena pitched the centerpiece at Marc. His head was the target, but it hit his arm below the shoulder and shattered on the floor. Marc hung up and tucked his phone into his robe pocket. "What's your problem?"

"What is *your* problem?"

"Well…" He swallowed the words he was going to say.

"You told her that you loved her."

"No I didn't."

"I heard you!"

"I told her that I loved women, at least that's what I meant!"

For several hours they hashed out the difference between Marc telling Franceska that he loved women in general and telling her that he loved her specifically. Lena didn't see a difference and Marc probably drew a larger distinction than even he truly believed existed. It was an ill-fated strategy, regardless. Lena's monster was raging and it wouldn't be quieted by an academic argument. It was an emotional issue.

Marc was slow to learn, however. He continued to build his case by offering affidavits and other exhibits for evidence. "I haven't kept anything from you. We've discussed this every step of the way. I didn't invite her. *We* invited her. You even helped me prepare dinner for her. What am I missing here?"

"You're missing how it made me feel to see my replacement walk through the door."

"Your replacement?!" Marc was perplexed and Lena broke down into sobbing. It's the arrow in a woman's quiver that men are most defenseless against. He stopped treating her like an opponent and began approaching her like a little dove that he had foolishly injured. He gathered her up and commenced mending her wing.

Chapter 8

Marc entered the apartment at about ten o'clock. Chuck was studying at the dining table. "You're late," he said.

"Yeah, I had some things that I had to get done."

Chuck looked up from his book to analyze the disparity between what Marc was saying and how he was saying it. "There's a beer in the fridge."

"That sounds great, thanks."

"So what were you really doing?"

"I told you. What do you mean?"

"I mean you don't come in here with a grin plastered on your face when you've been working late at the office."

Marc laughed. "It's true; this project is killing me. I can't seem to break through."

"Well, I don't doubt that."

Marc laughed uneasily. "What do you doubt?"

"Cut the shit, Marc. What's her name?"

The smile that was darting beneath the surface of Marc's face, like a rambunctious dolphin, vaulted into plain sight. He blushed and twisted like a child who couldn't cope with the attention. Finally he confessed, "Uh, her name is Lena."

"Okay." Chuck couldn't help but duplicate Marc's smile. "And who is this Lena?"

"She's an angel. She is the most glorious thing I've ever seen. Chuck, I can't stop thinking about her."

"Did you ask her out?"

"Yes."

"And she agreed, obviously; you act like this is your first date. So what are you going to do?"

"I don't know. I can't figure it out. It has to be perfect. I'm telling you, this girl is amazing."

"Okay, so tell me about her."

Marc's exuberance collapsed. His shoulders fell and he dropped his head. He stood there speechless for as long as the conversation could bear it. He sank into the couch and took a gulp of beer. "She's... She's... She's... Ah, shit. I don't know what to say. She's beautiful, she's smart, she's funny. But that's not all. I think about her and it feels like my chest will collapse, but when I'm with her, it feels like it will burst. I'm always looking around to see if she's there, just so that I can feel complete again."

"Wow, you've really got it bad."

Marc continued in a distant tone, as if he didn't hear Chuck. "And she's rich."

"So you think you've got to take her somewhere expensive?"

"Yeah, I mean, I can't take her to the Training Table."

"Well, if she's rich, you're not going to be able to impress her with your spending. I mean you're kinda pathetic. You should do something she wouldn't expect."

"Like what?"

"I don't know. You should do something that she's never done before. Like, you could take her to the Olympic Village."

"What?" Marc asked in confusion. "The Olympics haven't even started yet."

"I know." Chuck saw Marc's confusion and raised him some scorn. "I'm not an idiot."

"I thought you had to be an athlete to get in there."

"You do, well, unless you're an electrician." Chuck could hardly contain his excitement over the evil plan that he had concocted.

"Okay?" Marc looked puzzled.

"Look. It's something that she would never expect and Olympians...," Chuck trailed off. His smile flattened out, his eyes tightened, and his voice acquired a tone of reverent admiration before he continued, "Olympians party like rock stars."

Marc laughed, but he decided to entertain Chuck's idea. "So you're suggesting that I break into the Olympic Village with the most incredible girl I've ever met so that we can spend our first date handcuffed in the back of a squad car?"

"Only if you get caught. Besides, that would be stupid. The village is enclosed by a ten-foot wall and is under constant surveillance by a military guard. There are checkpoints scattered throughout the village and anyone without credentials is treated as a hostile intruder. Trust me, I know. I've done my research."

"Exactly. So you see the problem here," Marc said.

"Not at all."

"I don't get it."

"Look, there are almost as many volunteers in the village as there are athletes."

"I'm not a volunteer."

Chuck raised his hand with a pinching gesture and with his best Lord Vader impersonation he said, "Marc, I find your lack of imagination disturbing."

Marc laughed. "Okay, so what are you saying?"

"I know this guy. He's an electrician. He volunteers at the village as part of a support team. He says it's quite busy now but things should slow down once the games begin—they'll just be there for contingencies. His company has several slots and he thinks he can get me in."

"Wow. You've really thought this through. You're serious, aren't you?"

"Yes I am," Chuck said proudly.

"You're insane. You can't even replace a light bulb, least of all masquerade as an electrician. You'd consider this post 9/11?" Marc raised his voice. "Their security is bound to be tighter than a mason jar."

Chuck looked at Marc with an expression of bafflement. "Than a *what?*" He smirked at Marc's juvenile comparison. "It's pretty tight, alright."

"What would happen if you were caught?" Marc proceeded to answer his own question, "The electrician would probably lose his license and you'd both go to jail."

"Probably, but then again, that's only if we get caught. So what do you say? I could ask him to get you and your girl in."

"There is absolutely no way I'm doing that. Definitely not with Lena. You're insane."

"I knew you wouldn't do it." Chucked was amused by the way his experiment played out. "But I'm going to do it."

Marc looked at Chuck in amazement. "You're studying to be an attorney. Why would you risk your entire career for this?"

"Because I love the Olympics! That's why."

"I love the Olympics, too, but I'm not going to risk everything I've worked for just so that I can watch a figure skater sporting a medal around her neck. I can see that on TV."

"CTR this one, Marc," Chuck began with his favorite condescension. Marc instinctively glanced down at his hand where he once wore a ring bearing the insignia to which Chuck referred. Chuck had never seen Marc wear it, but he didn't need to. In Utah, references to it were copious and universally didactic. CTR was the acronym for "choose the right." The mantra was repeated either piously to urge others to high moral character or sarcastically, to greater tolerance. Chuck raised both arms for emphasis, "Imagine being in the village at the height of the games. Half of the athletes have finished competing. They're ready to cut loose. I mean, they've been training for years and now they're ready to *partay*! Can you imagine what kind of energy there will be?"

"It might actually help me solve some problems at work."

Chuck ignored Marc's attempt at humor. "The village gives away a hundred thousand condoms in about two weeks, Marc!"

"So you're hoping to have sex with an Olympic athlete?"

"Well, I'm not going to admire their medals. That was your lame idea."

Marc stood up and grabbed two more beers. He popped one and handed it to Chuck. He then popped his own and fell back down onto the couch. "I think you're insane and there is no possible way that this can end well, but suit yourself. It doesn't really solve my problem, anyway. My date with Lena is tomorrow night."

Chuck slammed his book shut and reeled his chair around to face Marc head on. "You asked her out tomorrow night?"

"Well, actually I asked her out tonight, but she couldn't make it."

"Are you as stupid as you sound right now?"

"What?" Marc clearly didn't understand Chuck's adverse reaction.

"You don't ask a girl out the same day."

"Why?"

"For starters, it puts her on the spot."

"It put me on the spot."

"Who cares? It's not about you. Put yourself on the spot, but give her space and options. Space and options, man, it's simple. You're lucky she didn't turn you down just for being too pushy. It's cool she accepted, but you've unwittingly communicated to her that you are more concerned about your own needs than hers."

"How did I do that?"

"Let's suppose that she's on her period. She might be interested in you, but she's probably going to turn you down. If she actually cares enough to go out with you, then she has to take on the burden of essentially putting the date together. That's your job, not hers. She should only have to select the option that best suits her. Girls don't like giving their reasons and they don't like having their reasons questioned. You want to make her comfortable. Always give her plenty of notice and offer two dates that are at least a week apart."

"Okay, but she didn't seem bothered by it. We talked for over an hour." Marc's smile returned.

"Who did most of the talking?"

"She did."

"What did she talk about?"

"Mostly vacations. Food and school. Stuff like that."

"Alright. There's still hope then. So what are you going to do?"

"I don't know. Like I said, it's gotta be great, though."

"How old is she?"

"I didn't ask, but she's a sophomore, so probably about twenty."

"And I don't suppose she's got fake I.D.?"

Marc laughed. "I doubt it. Besides, she's Mormon, so we won't be drinking anyway."

"Mormon?" Chuck threw his hands in the air. "Dude, you're fucked. If she's all you say she is, she'll never go for you."

"Maybe she will."

"Oh? Are you going to get rebaptized? Rejoin the church?"

"I don't know. Maybe."

"No way! I'll never allow it. Now who's the insane one, here?"

Marc laughed. "I'm just going to take it one step at a time."

Marc walked slowly to the front door. He had arrived early, but he waited outside of the gates until 6:01 before he crossed the line. He rang the doorbell, holding down the button until the chime stopped. The door swung open and Mrs. Brensett cordially invited him to come in and join Mr. Brensett in the library. "Lena's almost ready," she said. He knocked on the open door and a man sitting on the sofa invited him to take a seat.

"Hi. I'm Lena's dad, Daniel Brensett. You must be Marc Friedman."

Marc nodded. "Yes, it's good to meet you, sir."

"I missed you the other day. They said you came over for game night."

"Yes. I had a great time. You have a beautiful home."

"Well, thank-you; that's kind of you to say. We try, but you know, there's always room for improvement. The purpose of a home is to shelter and protect a family. Without a family, it's just an empty shell." Marc nodded and Dan continued, "How about you? Tell me a little about your family."

"Well my parent's names are Bradley and Michelle Friedman. I have one younger sister. Her name is Laura."

"So there's just the two of you? Children I mean?"

"Yes."

"Oh, I see. I was always a little jealous of small families when I was a kid. I slept in a room with three other brothers, so we were fairly crowded. Then, whenever my mother went shopping, she always bought matching sets of everything. It was a little embarrassing sometimes. It wasn't until I went on my mission that I learned to appreciate every one of my siblings."

"I guess everyone wishes for something other than what they have. I always wanted a brother. It was a little rough growing up with just a sister. All my friends in school had much larger families. I was a little jealous of them, I guess."

"I suppose you're right. That's a good point, Marc. Where did you grow up?"

"Here in Salt Lake, over in Taylorsville."

"Okay, so were you in the North Stake or the Utah Stake?" It had begun—the inevitable church interrogation. Daniel had undoubtedly been informed from game night that Marc was not active in the church. He was probably trying to assess Marc's faithfulness or lack thereof for himself.

"Ah, the North Central Stake," he answered tersely.

"Okay," Daniel paused thoughtfully. "So is Brother Kensington still the stake president down there?"

"Ah, no, he was relieved while I was still in high school."

"Oh, of course. I guess he was called a while ago. So who's serving now?"

That was the dreaded question and it surfaced in Marc's demeanor and tone of voice. "Um, I'm not sure, actually."

"Oh, of course," Daniel said apologetically. "I'm sure you're busy in your singles ward and you've probably just lost track of what's going on in your home ward. It's funny, actually. I've known kids who have moved away, who could tell me more about what's going on in my own ward than I could. Others get really involved in their new lives and move on. I suppose that's the way it should be." It was apparent in Daniel's demeanor and tone of voice that he knew that Marc was not attending either ward. However, it was equally apparent that Daniel was communicating to Marc that to date his daughter, that had to change.

Marc responded with the most noncommittal thing he could have said. "Yeah, I guess it's hard for some people to keep up with everything. That would be a lot."

"So, Lena tells me that you're working on your doctorate at the university. Physics is it?"

"Not quite. My degree is in computing, but I'm working on a physics project for CERN."

"Really? That's impressive. What exactly is it?" Dan then lowered his voice to a whisper, as if someone was spying on them. "Are you allowed to talk about it?" He asked facetiously.

Marc laughed. "Yes, I can talk about it." At that moment, Lena walked into the room. She was a distraction from which Marc couldn't recover.

Daniel let him off easy by saying, "Oh, sweetheart, there you are. We were just talking shop, but we will finish that another time. You two have a good time."

After they were both seated in the car, Marc said, "You look really nice." She thanked him as if he had complimented every detail of her appearance. She was like that, so gracious that it complimented other people's compliments.

"So where are we going?" She asked.

"I thought we could go to Log Haven. It's a really nice restaurant in Millcreek Canyon."

"Oh, that's one of my favorite places. Have you ever had their duck confit?"

"Ah, no."

"Oh, you've got to try it. What's your favorite dish?"

"Well, I've never actually been there, but it was highly recommended."

"Oh, you're going to love it," Lena said with a tidy bounce. The low roof of Marc's car wouldn't let her ascend far. He had obviously failed to create plans that involved new activities for Lena, but again her excitement complimented his attempt.

"Well, what are you planning to do for 'spring' break?" He asked.

In order to accommodate the Winter Olympics, the university was planning to take its spring break in February. It was scheduled to last for nearly the entire month, which took a substantial bite out of the semester. It was a popular topic of contention among university students. Nearly everyone had a strong opinion either way. Detractors criticized the university for allowing a sporting event to supersede scholastics. They accused officials of chasing dollars and fame. Supporters cited the importance of cooperation and sacrifice in order to stage successfully an event of international proportions. They believed that the long-term advantages for Utah outweighed the disadvantages. Few, however, were thrilled about celebrating the arrival of spring in the dead of winter.

"I'm thinking of going to Mexico with some friends during part of it, but I haven't completely decided. My parents aren't thrilled about it. How about you?"

"I'm probably going to stay and work. I like to ski, but it's probably going to be too crowded."

"Yeah, it's going to be crazy. I work for Dad's business. He wants me to stay and work as much as possible. Getting time off is very difficult. He's bound and determined to make a success out of me."

"Yeah, I know what you mean. I'm working on a project with this physicist at the university and he actually wanted to meet tonight."

"So you told him that you had to go on a date, with some annoying girl, to get out of it?"

Marc laughed. "No. No. Absolutely not." He laughed again and Lena's eyes sparkled. "Actually, I sort of agreed to meet with him before I called you. I figured you would have plans this weekend; that's why I suggested last night, but we ended up planning it for tonight and I totally forgot to cancel with him."

"So do we need to go there first?"

"Oh, no. It's fine."

"Isn't he expecting you?"

"I guess so, but honestly, it's really not a big deal."

"You have to call him, then." Her statement was laced with the question, "You're not actually going to stand him up, are you?"

"Okay. I'll call him from the restaurant." Lena turned her head back to face the road. A moment later, her torso followed, apparently indicating either satisfaction or resignation. Damn uncertainty. Marc added tentatively, "It really wasn't a big deal. It was a philosophical discussion, but we were interrupted and he wanted to finish. I don't think we even set a time."

"What was your discussion about?"

"With Edberg, the physicist?"

"Yes, your philosophical discussion that he wanted to finish."

"Oh, it was about science vs. religion. Well, sort of. We weren't really discussing the conflict; it was more like the opposite."

"What do you mean?"

"In other words, we were discussing how physics doesn't necessarily contradict the existence of a supreme being. It was actually quite interesting, but we can finish it any time. He's an old man and I think he's just lonely."

That was the tipping point. She turned to him like a child asking if she could keep the stray cat that she had adopted. "Well then let's go. Come on, besides I would find that very interesting."

"Are you serious? You'd rather listen to a couple of scientists talk about philosophy than do something fun like dinner and, and…"

"And what? That would be fun," she exclaimed. "Never mind. I'm sorry. I don't want to disrupt your plans."

"No, I just want you to enjoy yourself. If that's really what you want to do, that's fine. I just don't want you to be bored out of your mind."

"I think it would be fascinating," she said with exuberance. "But it's totally up to you."

"Okay, let's go then." Marc said it like someone dipping his toes in to test the waters.

Lena accentuated Marc's timid decision with a bounce. Suddenly the car seemed too cramped for her again.

"What?" Lena asked.

"What what?" Marc feigned confusion.

"You're grinning."

"Oh, am I?" He laughed.

"Yes, you are."

"Oh, it's nothing."

"I can see that it's not 'nothing.'"

"What can you see, exactly?" He asked with a sparkle nearly as bright as hers.

It was as if they were at the foosball table again. Each defended his or her own feelings while persuading the other to let down the guard with carefully placed lures and innuendo. Points were scored on either side, but either Lena played more skillfully or Marc played more gentlemanly.

A gentleman ultimately prefers others to himself. He places himself in danger in order to protect those he cares for. He protects the parts of a woman which keep her whole and only takes that which she freely gives him.

Therefore Marc may have risked too much, he may have disclosed too much, but he didn't compel her to compromise. Hence both contestants won, but they won at different games. His winnings were her torrents of feminine affirmations. Her reward was someone to whom she could safely direct them.

Marc had left Edberg's address in his apartment. "I'm going to run in and grab that address. Would you like to come in or wait here?"

"I'd love to come in."

When they entered the apartment, Chuck was studying at the table. Without looking up, he said, "She stood up your sorry ass, didn't she?"

Marc said, "Lena, this is my roommate, Chuck." At that Chuck flipped around and Marc and Lena both laughed at his astonishment. "I need to grab something. Try not to drive her away, okay?"

Lena and Chuck exchanged awkward greetings. Then Lena asked, "So what are you studying?"

"Law," he said, still trying to gain his composure. "It's nice to meet you. You're even lovelier than Marc said you were." She thanked him with a tilt to the tips of her toes.

"My brother is an attorney," Lena said.

"What type of law does he practice?"

"He works at a patent firm. What do you plan on doing?"

"I haven't really decided. I'm really interested in constitutional law, but there's not a lot of money in that."

"I guess you've got to pay the bills. So how do you and Marc know each other?"

"We were both placed here by housing services. I had never met him before that."

"Oh, where are you from?"

"Las Vegas."

"I love Vegas."

"When did you go?"

Lena laughed. "Well, I've never actually been there. Maybe I should have said that I love the idea of Vegas. It's kind of taboo where I come from. I guess that's made it more intriguing."

"It's a great city for…" Chuck cut himself off when Marc reemerged bearing his slip of paper.

"Well, are you ready to go?" Marc asked.

"Yeah. We were just talking about Vegas. I've always wanted to go there. Have you ever been there, Marc?"

"No. Chuck's trying to get me to go for spring break, though."

"You should totally go. I wish I could. Well, it was nice to meet you, Chuck."

When they arrived at Edberg's, Marc asked, "Are you sure you want to do this?"

"Yes, of course. I'm kind of nervous, though."

"Why?"

"Because I don't know anything about physics."

"Neither do I." With that he bolted from the car and opened the door for Lena.

Lena laughed. "You were barely asking me if I really wanted to do this."

Marc responded confidently, "I know. I didn't really mean it. We cancelled our dinner reservation, so…" He reached his hand out to take hers. She gave it and they walked together to the house. Edberg answered the door.

"Come in, it's freezing out there. Oh. Hello." Edberg was surprised to see Lena. He switched modes like a diverted train. Smiling, he said directly to Lena, "Who is this lovely girl?"

"Hi, I'm Lena Brensett, a friend of Marc's."

"Lena, this is Dr. Edberg, the physicist I'm working with at the university."

"It's nice to meet you," she said.

"It's nice to meet you. Come in. Have a seat." The only similarity between Edberg's office and his home was the temperature. The home was a renovated Queen Anne, as eclectic as the neighborhood in which it was situated. It had an updated interior with an open floor plan. It was bright and inviting with Asian artwork on the walls. The place was immaculately clean; the vacuum marks in the carpet were parallel and recently deposited. There was a delightful deli platter set out on the coffee table with cloth napkins, ceramic dishes, and an open bottle of wine with two glasses. Edberg said, "I'll get another glass."

"Oh, that's okay," said Lena. "I'm underage anyway."

"Are you sure, sweetheart?" Edberg asked.

"Yes, thank-you."

Lena and Marc sat on the couch in front of the fireplace. It was burning natural gas through a grate of polished rocks. Edberg sat in the chair at the end of the table. He poured a glass of wine and passed it to Marc. Lena was unconcerned with the wine; she was taking in the complex, yet well-balanced décor of the room instead. She seemed more pleased with her experience than Edberg was with the wine he was tasting.

"I opened this bottle two hours ago. It wasn't a minute too early, that's for sure. Well, it will continue to open up in the glass," he assured. "So, Marc, where were we?"

"We were discussing God's plan for the universe. I mean, whether or not physics contradicts the idea of a divine plan."

"That's right. You had proposed this clever contraption to show that God can't possibly control a universe that is based on chance. However, we saw that sufficient knowledge would allow him to mitigate disruption to his plan by constructing bounds for possible outcomes. You see Lena, his contraption was based on the Schrödinger cat experiment. Are you familiar with that?"

"No, it sounds kind of inhumane, though."

Edberg laughed. "No dear, it's a thought experiment which means that it's carried out in the mind. Thought experiments are useful because they enable us to test the rational extent of ideas which would be difficult to implement directly. For example, Newton discovered the law of universal gravitation by a thought experiment. He imagined firing cannonballs from the peak of a mountain so high that the atmosphere didn't interfere with their projectile paths.

"With a small charge of gunpowder, the cannonball wouldn't go far before hitting the ground. With a much larger charge of gunpowder, the cannonball would fall toward the earth, but the earth would fall way also due to its curvature. He reasoned that with a sufficiently large charge, a cannonball may be launched into orbit. It was a thought experiment because no such mountain exists and cannons capable of such blasts had not been invented. Before that, people thought that planets were held in orbit by a force more exotic than the ordinary gravity we experience here on earth."

Marc added that, "Einstein also discovered the theory of relativity through thought experiments."

"That's right, Marc; chasing a ray of light and so on." Edberg continued, "Well, in the Schrödinger experiment, a cat and a vial of poison are placed in a sealed enclosure with a sample of radioactive isotope. The isotope is just as likely to produce a radioactive event as not. When a detector measures the decay of the radioactive isotope, the vial is broken and the cat dies. So you're right, Lena, it is a little inhumane, at least in concept."

Lena said, "Yeah, I don't think I like this guy very much. What's his name again?"

"Schrödinger."

"Well, he's not a very nice person. He could have poisoned a rat or something; they're disgusting. Cats are cute."

"Exactly!" Edberg seemed delighted by Lena's disapprobation.

Lena asked, "What's the point of killing the cat anyway?"

Edberg said, "The point of the experiment is this. Quantum mechanics describes the decaying radioisotope in both decayed and un-decayed states until an actual observation is made. Schrödinger and Einstein assumed that a superposition of decayed and un-decayed states implied a corresponding superposition of states for the cat. In other words, the cat would be simultaneously alive and dead."

Lena asked, "Einstein and Shroudner believed that the cat could be dead and alive at the same time?"

Edberg said, "Well, no. They actually proposed the thought experiment to discredit the various indeterministic models being advanced in quantum physics. Schrödinger probably used a cat to make the paradox more relatable and to increase its impact. They hoped that the absurd conclusion of the experiment would convince other physicists to pursue more deterministic models. Einstein said that God doesn't play dice with the universe. But he was probably wrong. Apparently that's exactly what God does."

Marc said, "That's what I wanted to discuss when we ran out of time yesterday. It's generally accepted that Einstein was wrong about the universe being based on chance, but then you said something that made me look at it completely differently." He turned to Lena and explained, "We were discussing whether God exists inside or outside of the universe. The idea of an omniscient, omnipotent god is simply not consistent with the laws of physics, unless he's external to the universe."

Edberg broke in, "Unless he's very clever and very stealthy."

Marc responded. "No, it violates the Heisenberg uncertainty principle."

"What's that?" Lena asked.

Marc said, "It places a limit on the precision with which you can measure certain combinations of states of a particle. For example, if you measure its position very precisely, its momentum will be very uncertain. On the other hand, if you measure its momentum very precisely, its position will be very uncertain."

"Why? I thought that's what science does," Lena said.

Marc responded with zeal, "Let's say that I want to precisely measure the position of an electron. I can do so by directing a beam of photons toward it and measuring how they scatter off of the particle. I would need to use rays of light with very small wavelengths so that I can pinpoint its position." He held his fingers close together to indicate that smaller wavelengths enable greater precision. "The problem is that the shorter the wavelength of light, the more energy it possesses. Hence, when the light scatters off of the electron, it will alter the particle's momentum significantly. On the other hand, if I want to measure its momentum accurately, I must use low energy photons which have larger wavelengths. Therefore, I'll be much less certain about its position."

Lena said, "Okay, that makes a lot of sense. But eventually won't they develop better methods of measurement?"

Edberg said, "It's an inherent limitation, independent of measurement. It's been shown that the inherent limitation imposed by the laws of physics is even greater than the type of limitation that Marc is referring to, which means that there is no way to overcome it with more sophisticated measurement techniques."

Marc said, "But that's what I realized; it can be overcome—I mean by an external observer." He was getting warmed up. "In order to visualize what I'm saying, let's imagine that the universe is two-dimensional. An external observer could measure objects in the universe by shining light on them from a direction perpendicular to the space in which they are confined." He held the palm of his hand out flat and pointed downward toward it with his other hand to simulate the perpendicular rays of light. "In this way, God could measure position and momentum of particles with arbitrary precision!"

The idea surprised even Edberg. For the next two hours, the roles of student and professor were exchanged. It was an idea that Marc owned and Edberg respected it. When a man owns a thing, it becomes part of him and, like his own heart, he perceives it in ways that are clear to him but hidden to others.

After Marc and Lena drove away from Edberg's place, she said, "That was amazing."

"Are you serious?" Marc asked.

"Totally! I'm glad we decided to go."

"I was afraid that you would be bored."

"Absolutely not." She paused and turned to him. "You were awesome."

"Thanks. You made it a lot of fun."

"It felt like I was just getting in the way."

"Not at all. You had some great questions. I think you helped me to express my ideas more clearly."

"I hope so."

"Definitely." Marc offered a reassuring glance.

"There's just one thing I still don't understand. What does the uncertainty principle have to do with God's plan for the universe?"

"It has to do with whether the universe is deterministic or indeterministic. If the laws of physics do not involve chance or probability on a fundamental level, then the state of the universe throughout its entire history and future would have been completely determined at the beginning. Furthermore, if God could measure the states of all particles in the universe with infinite precision, then he could predict with infinite precision what you or I would do for the rest of our lives. Essentially there would be no free will. Chance is essential to choice."

Lena was listening, but she offered no response. Marc said, "That's enough talk about physics. Are you hungry?"

"I'm starving."

"The food he set out was pretty good."

"It looked really good, but I guess I was too interested in the conversation."

"Where would you like to go?" Marc asked.

"Training Table sounds good."

"It sure does."

Chapter 9

Most visitors waited to be admitted by Tara, but Chuck knuckled Marc's office door and swung it open without waiting for a reply, like back in the college days. "Coast clear?" He thundered out.

"Come in, Chuck." Marc rolled his eyes; some things would never change, but that didn't mean that he would accept them. "What's up?"

"I have these papers ready for you to sign. I know you wanted thirty down and eight percent, but they really squawked. I reduced it to twenty-five down, and insisted on rolling the difference into a nine percent note on a two-year term. Given their credit rating, I figured this was better than nothing."

Marc looked over the contract, signed it, thanked him, and continued to hold on to the papers while he stared blankly at the cover page. Chuck took that as a cue to elaborate on some additional details. Marc eventually looked up to find that Chuck was waiting for a response.

"I'm sorry, I missed what you said."
"I was explaining that…"
"Uh, no, it's fine. I appreciate it. Let's just go with this."

Chuck reached for the papers and Marc handed them over like Jean-Paul Marat captured in a lifeless moment that would last forever. Chuck turned to leave, but Marc stopped him.

"Hey, Chuck. Do you remember that time in Vegas, spring break?"
"You mean *winter* break? Yeah, why?"

"I was just thinking about it. Do you remember playing blackjack switch?"

"Yeah, I had a blast. What about it?"

"I think it's my favorite game. We should go back some time."

"What's this?" Marc asked as the two of them wandered down the casino aisles.

"It clearly says, 'Blackjack Switch.'"

"I know, lame ass. I can read goooood." This seemed funny to him.

Inebriation finds humor in things that sobriety dismisses offhand. The mundane becomes fascinating. To a person who drinks, there is nothing more offensive than a person who refuses to drink. The abstinent have never seen a plain woman transformed into a goddess before their eyes. They have never witnessed strangers turned to comrades, and indifference turned to love. Alcohol reveals the truth, not necessarily by bringing people closer to it, but rather by melting away the lies. For this reason, abstainers are not to be trusted; they are constipated on lies. The truth fears no substance, but lies must be wary for shadows take refuge in falsehood.

The dealer explained that the table was piloting a new game that the casino was considering. The primary difference between blackjack switch and regular blackjack was that players were dealt two hands and placed bets on both hands. Before a hit, the player had the option of switching the top cards in both hands in order to improve his odds.

They decided to play. On one round, the dealer dealt Marc a 5/10 and a 10/6. In regular blackjack, these were losing hands. The likelihood of drawing a 10 on either hand for a bust was very high. He switched the top cards resulting in hands of 10/10 and 5/6. These were exceptional hands.

126

He stood on the first hand and hit on the 5/6 hand. When he was dealt a queen, he erupted with joy. Both of his hands beat the dealer's 19. What would have resulted in two losses resulted in two wins, instead.

Marc vacantly acknowledged Chuck leaving the office. There were five or six books standing on the corner of Marc's desk. They were supported by elephant bookends which stood with their trunks raised in a majestic pose. Their skin was an opalescent glaze of amaranth inlaid with mother of pearl arranged in floral designs. The lines and creases typical of the skin of elephants were represented by ribbings of gold wire. Their feet were shod with golden bands and were studded with black pearls for toes.

"These are beautiful," Marc said.
"Thanks. They belong to my wife," Edberg said, like an auto-responder, and with as much thought.
"Where did she get them?"
"Get what?"
"The bookends."
"Oh. She brought them with her from Thailand."
"When did she go to Thailand?"
"She came from Thailand."
"I didn't know your wife was Thai."
"You didn't?"
"No. I've never met her."
"You haven't?"
"No. I didn't even know you had a wife."
"Who did you think did all of this?" Edberg asked, motioning to the spread on the table and the meticulous décor of the home.
"I thought you were just a really good house keeper."
Edberg laughed. "No. You've seen my office. And as for food, pairing wine is the extent of my gift."

Marc nodded. "I understand. I can't cook at all, but I do keep my office clean."

"Well, it's odd that you've never met my wife. How many times have you been here?"

"Like six or eight times."

"Goodness!" Edberg added apologetically, "She's quiet and usually doesn't mingle with guests. You should meet her. I'll go get her."

"Oh, I don't want to trouble her."

"Nonsense. I'll be right back."

Edberg introduced the two of them to each other. Her name was Hansa. She was as neat in her appearance as was her home. She excused herself from sitting down in order to finish her work.

Once she was out of ear shot, Marc pointed to a photo on the end table and cautiously breached the topic, "I don't see her resemblance in your children," indicating that they didn't appear to have Asian parentage.

"You don't? Neither does Hansa." Edberg laughed again. Marc was puzzled. Edberg went on to explain, "She's not their mother. Their mother died about ten years ago."

"Oh, I'm sorry."

"It's alright." Edberg cut off his response with a slight nod, slowed by the effect of wine.

"I suppose it helps when you find someone you can love and get remarried."

"Oh, I didn't get remarried."

"So you weren't married to your first wife?" Marc asked and Edberg looked at him in amusement. It was already an uncomfortable situation for Marc and his contradiction in terms embarrassed him further. "I mean, did you marry your first... Oh, you know what I mean."

Edberg was relishing Marc's uneasiness. "Yes, I married my first wife."

"How long have you been married to, uh..."

"Hansa."

"Yeah. Sorry I'm terrible with names."

"About fifteen years."

"But didn't you say your first wife died ten years ago?" Marc asked, frustrated and dumbfounded.

Edberg finally cleared up the confusion. "I married Hansa while I was still married to Mable, my first wife. We all lived here together until Mable passed away. By then the kids were grown up and had lives of their own."

"So you're a..."

"A polygamist? Yes. Well, I was until Mable died. Does that shock you?"

Marc shook his head, but his astonished eyes controverted his claim.

"I love Hansa, she's incredible, but let's just say that sharing a home wasn't her strong point. Well, it wasn't Mable's either. They never really got along. So when Hansa had the house to herself, she decided it was time to express her personality. I kind of like it. It suits me fine, but she hates this photo. Well, not because of the kids, but because it doesn't match the decorations. It's Mable's frame, you see." Edberg laughed.

Like the books neatly arranged on Marc's desk between the two elephant ends, so were the letters which were placed there each day. They were supported by two plain, cylindrical paperweights made of glass or crystal. Marc picked up the envelopes and flipped through them. He came to a stationary sized envelope. It had not been post-marked. It was simply addressed to Mr. Marcellus Friedman by an elegant hand. Inside he found an invitation to a family reunion, RSVP Laura Friedman, and so on. He rolled his eyes and tossed it aside with a sigh.

After an hour or so, he picked up the invitation again, but the item of interest was the hand written name on the front of the envelope. He studied it closely for a few moments. He smelled the envelope inside and out and set it back down with a disappointed glance to the side, as if he was looking elsewhere for clues. In every way but one, it was a typical invitation. Without being postmarked, it must have been delivered by Laura, or, possibly, perhaps even by Franceska. He obviously didn't sniff the envelope to detect Laura's scent.

He called Tara. "Did my sister drop off this invitation?"…
"The one in the unstamped envelope."…
"No, that's it. Thanks."

It was the first time that Marc ever brought home an invitation to a family gathering. Lena usually heard about them when Laura called her directly to find out if she and Marc were attending. "What's this?" Lena asked, pulling the card from behind a magnet on the refrigerator.
"An invitation," Marc said.
"Really? I thought maybe it was a subpoena."
"Would be preferable."
Lena laughed. "Oh, it's your family reunion."
"Yep."
"Well, that'll be fun."
"Will it?"
"You don't want to go?"
"I never have."
"I think you should."
"You probably think I should smash my thumb with a hammer, too."
"Oh, come on. It's not that bad. Besides, the kids are getting older and they need to get to know your side of the family."
"You could take them. Laura would make sure you felt welcome."

"They need their daddy to take them."

"I'd gladly take them, anywhere but there."

"Marc." She said this like a mother who was about to scold her child.

"What?"

"You know what."

"No, I don't. The only people crazier than your family are mine."

"What do you mean? I absolutely love your dad."

"So do I, but you can't name one other sane person. Go ahead, try it."

"Well, Laura's nice."

"Laura is batshit crazy. Are you kidding me?"

"I didn't say she wasn't crazy. I said she's nice. She's sweet."

"I get it, she's sweet. She's not ugly, either, is she? I mean she's alright, right?"

"Yeah, she's alright. Why?"

"Don't you find it strange that she'll never get married?"

"She'll find someone."

"No she won't. She has her heart set on marrying a good man in the church. There's just one problem. They're all taken. I mean they're *all* taken," he raised his voice for emphasis, "not just the good ones; all of them. She's going to get to the point where she has to start looking outside of the church and that'll never work."

"Why?"

"Because she's not compelling enough. I mean no man is going to convert for her. She's not pretty. She's not smart. She doesn't have a good job or an education. She's a monumental bore. I don't think she could entertain a critical thought if it were conferred upon her by the Almighty himself. I agree that she's sweet, but that's not enough."

"It might be enough for someone. She'll find someone. You'll see."

"I hope you're right. But if she marries a piece of shit, I'll rage. I'll rage and I don't know what I'll do."

"You'll do just what others have done for you. You'll let her make her own decisions."

"Can I make my own decisions? Great! I decide not to go to the reunion."

"Nice try, Jack. Your kids need this."

"Fine! But let it be known that I do it under protest."

Marc left his office and walked down the hallway. He hung a hard left into the development arena. This is where ideas battled for supremacy. It was an open area with a spacious lounge at one end. The couches and chairs were roughly arranged in a semicircle facing a large, transparent marker board. It was mostly covered with cartoon characters and only a few scribbles that could be reasonably associated with such technical work as the projects that they were actually engaged in. In one cartoon, a man with pointed ears and glasses victoriously raised his shiny sword to the sky while dragging a victim with a rope tied around his neck. The characters bore labels which identified them as competing solutions to a problem that the development team was working on. The victor was the fastest approach while the victim was the more versatile, robust approach. Sideline spectators were shouting praises and epithets.

In another cartoon, an old fashioned, stone well stood above an aquifer containing a jumbled mass of random terms and phrases. As the draw bucket was being raised, some of the terms were falling through holes in the bottom. Next to the well, a large barrel containing the remnants of the bucket dispensed complete sentences from a spigot which trickled downhill.

Steve and Bryan were sitting around a table debating the merits and the drawbacks of their smart phones. They continued without acknowledging Marc even though he was standing next to them. Steve's phone was more adaptable; Bryan's phone was more robust, had fewer glitches. Steve's phone had a bigger screen; Bryan's phone was easier to read outdoors. Steve's platform ran on numerous devices which offered solutions highly customized to his needs and circumstances. Bryan enjoyed a trouble-free solution that worked for him instead of one that worked him.

The discussion grew more heated and Steve turned to Marc for reinforcement, "Why'd you choose your phone, Marc?"

Marc joined them at the table and sat facing the door. "Well, as far as I can see, you've mostly been discussing features. I made my decision based mostly on ideologies. There's no question that they're both great phones and you could argue over benefits and features all day long, but I chose to support Google because it's more compatible with my values. If I had to compare them to political philosophies, Bryan, I'd say that Apple represents fascism and Google represents, um, freedom, I guess."

Steve looked vindicated and Bryan looked confused.

"What do you mean?" Bryan protested.

"First of all, Apple has a cult following. People show up in droves to purchase it without even considering the other options, as if features don't matter at all. It's a status symbol that they must have or they'll be shunned by their friends."

"That's not true; I constantly read reviews. I could probably tell you more about your phone than you could."

"I believe you, you're a brilliant engineer and you stay informed, but that's not the case with the vast majority of your cult." Bryan laughed off Marc's phlegmatic characterization of his fellow consumers as cult members. Marc responded with, "Okay, answer this question as honestly as you can. If you read several reputable reviews of a phone that offered significant advantages over yours, let's say 50% more, just to put a number on it, would you switch companies?"

Bryan thought about it for a moment. "Well, no, but…"

"I knew it! However, if Apple released that same phone, you would clamor to pay any price for it and you would praise them for their impressive innovation."

"No, I was going to say that there is more to it than reviews. There's trust in repeated satisfaction. I've used Apple for a long time. I've experienced their products and I know what to expect."

"Agreed, and with that attitude you'll never experience anything else. I guess that's my point. They totally control the user-experience. Their attitude is, 'This is how we designed it; it's the best design; if it could be designed any better, we would have designed it that way, and if you don't like it, you're not cool.'"

"Well, it must be an effective strategy; it's made them number one. Sounds like good marketing to me."

"Or good propaganda. Every fascist regime needs it."

"That's ridiculous. How can you compare a corporation that has actually done a lot to improve technology and quality of life to fascism?"

"It's easy, watch me. Fascism is a political philosophy that is characterized by statism, dictatorial authority, limited choice, suppression of opposition, and severe punishment of dissenters. Did I miss anything?"

"You said it yourself, fascism is a political philosophy," Bryan stressed.

"Right, so it doesn't fit perfectly, but it's scary how well it does fit. For instance, if you download a song for your phone, you can only play it on devices or software produced by Apple. However, if I download a song for my phone, I can play it on practically any device and on any platform."

"Lots of companies have proprietary software. It's called brand building. We do it, too."

"Yes, both companies have proprietary software. One charges a premium and the other makes theirs available for free, at least most of it. The one tries to lock you in, the other tries to fit into your life however is most convenient for you. For one, it's all about the brand, for the other, it's all about the user. There's no question in my mind which brand is going to take over the market—eventually. All chains must inevitably break." Marc instinctively stretched his neck as if the chain was wrapped around his own throat. Marc was getting worked up.

"I still think it's far-fetched. Fascism is oppressive."

"Not for people who have embraced it, who snuggle up to it, and lick its balls. They are rewarded with a sense of belonging and the feeling that they are purging the world of a great evil. And what is this great evil? Choice. Freedom. Individuality." Marc calmed himself down, but Steve finally cut in.

"Are you sure this is still about phones, Marc?"

Marc feigned a look of sincerity. "Isn't that what you guys were talking about?"

"Yes, but I'm not sure that's what *you're* talking about."

Marc laughed. "You're probably right. Sorry guys, I'll let you get back to your argument, but," changing the subject, Marc pointed to the drawings on the board and said, "I can see that you decided to go with the faster algorithm."

"Yes. We ran some initial tests. The robust solution slowed us down quite a bit."

"Okay, but doesn't it worry you that you're giving up on the safer approach?" Marc asked.

"Not exactly." Steve explained, "We can do some preconditioning to reduce the number of false projections to about twenty percent which still seems like a lot, but we determined that the bad projections are normally distributed with a mean error of only about five to ten percent when aggregated. Given the large number of trials we perform, we felt that was an acceptable error."

Marc said, "Perhaps so, if the bad projections were the only source of error, but the model itself is a significant source of error." He thought for a moment. "How much faster is the fast routine?"

"Well, under most circumstances it's about thirty percent faster."

"How much faster would it be without the preconditioning?"

"That'd give you about another five percent, maybe more, but the number of false projections would increase. The improved accuracy is well worth the tradeoff."

"Okay, what if we use both?"

"What do you mean?"

Marc explained, "The robust approach is slow but much more accurate. So, what if we use it as a filter to eliminate the false projections in the fast approach? Let's try this. Run most of the simulation using the fast routine. Then run the robust routine, going heavy where there is more 'noise' in the first pass and run it light where there is less."

"That's a great idea." Steve was excited. "We might even be able to eliminate most of the preconditioning. If this works, we would be able to generate more accurate simulations in less time."

"Sounds good," Marc added. "In fact, running the robust routine as a filter will identify areas where the model itself is injecting false projections. That will enable us to improve the model." Marc motioned to the drawing on the board where there was a clear winner and a clear loser. He said, "Looks like you need to redraw your cartoon, guys. We might need both."

Steve sighed while Bryan threw a victory punch and shouted, "Yeah, fascism!"

This caught Franceska's attention and she smiled at the three of them through the glass partitions flanking either side of the hallway between them and the copy room. Marc smiled back and as he left the development arena, they exchanged playground waves.

Marc maintained his optimistic expression and energetic bounce until he closed the office door behind him. It was as if he had suddenly entered a pensive cloud. It covered him with dew, got into his clothes, and matted his hair. He turned his chair to face the window and sprawled out into space. A vapor of thought rose above his crumpled brow like steam rising from sauna coals. Finally, with a snap of resignation, he dialed Meg. "Hey, could you come in when you get a chance?" ...

"Hi Meg. Come in."

"Hi. What can I do for you?"

"It's about Miss Cox. You know, the widow girl with two kids that we hired?"

"Yeah, I know." Of course she knew. It goes without saying that a hen knows her chicks. She grew defensive whenever her professionalism and abilities were questioned.

Marc dismissed the mild insult. "Well, I wonder if we could do a little more to help her."

"What do you have in mind?"

"I'm not sure. Where is she on the pay scale?"

"We hired her at step 3 which is our policy for someone with her qualifications."

"Can we do any better?"

"We could, but I think it's best to stay consistent with our hiring and compensation practices."

"Yes, I understand. How about a dual position?"

"What do you have in mind?" Meg asked again, like the conversation was spiraling downward, which was worse than going in circles. Exceptions made her uncomfortable.

"Maybe she could translate some of our documentation."

"Her only two languages are English and Hungarian."

"Okay, she could translate into Hungarian."

"We don't have any clients in Hungary. Do we plan on marketing there?"

"Not at present," Marc couldn't contain a guilty smile.

"I see," Meg said. "Assign her to a project and I'll take care of it."

Marc was left sitting by himself at a picnic table. He rose from the bench like an underinflated tube man. He looked at the clans scattered around at the reunion and kicked his heels toward the playground. He motioned Kimberly over to him. "Hi sweetie, you having fun?"

"Yeah."

"That's good. Do you know who that girl is?"

"No."

"She's your cousin. Do you think she's having fun, too?" Kimberly glanced over and then shrugged her shoulders.

"Well, she came all the way from Hungary."

Kimberly gave him a blank stare.

"Do you know where Hungary is?"

"Duh. It's in Europe. It's bordered by Austria, Slovakia, the Ukraine, and Romania. They speak Hungarian. Hungarian is considered a Uralic language because it is believed to have originated near the Ural Mountains. Finnish is another Uralic language. The most famous Hungarian dish is goulash and they use a lot of paprika in their cooking, like Mom does."

"Okay, I get it." Marc laughed. "How do you know so much about Hungary?"

"I wrote a paper about the satellite states in the Eastern Bloc."

"What are those?"

"They were the soviet aligned countries which were not technically part of the Soviet Union. The Warsaw Pact required that their policies be consistent with Soviet policies."

"Wow. That's impressive, sweetheart. Are you sure you're a third grader?" She stared blankly at him so he said, "I'm glad that you're learning so much. Well, I just thought that it would be nice if you would include that girl in your games."

"But she's a kid."

Marc smirked with a condescending smile.

"I mean she's a little kid."

"I know she's younger than you. That makes you a protector."

Kimberly cocked one side of her mouth a little then said, "So, what you're saying is, you want me to be a satellite of your policies?"

"No. Well, maybe. Look, Kimberly. She lost her dad. Don't you think it's a good policy to help little girls who lose their dads?"

"Yeah."

"Okay, so that's all I'm saying. Do you think you could include her and still be your same beautiful, independent, little smarty pants?"

"I guess so."

Marc found Travis playing alone in a small grove about 50 yards from the playground. "Hey son, how's it going?"

"Good."

"Whatcha building?"

"A bridge."

"What are these?" Marc asked pointing to stubby sticks in the ground.

"Soldiers."

"Are these tanks?"

"No, they're tables."

"What are tables doing in the battlefield?"

"It's not a battlefield."

"Oh, what is it?"

"A party."

"What's the occasion?"

"I don't know."

"So they're partying for no reason?"

"There's a reason."

"What is it?"

"They're happy."

"Why are they happy?"

"Because the war ended."

"Oh, that makes sense. I would be happy, too." He ruffled Travis' hair and told him to keep up the peace mission.

By the time Marc returned, Lena had joined Laura and Franceska at a different table.

"Where have you been?" Lena asked.

"Checking on the kids."

"How are they doing?"

"Good. Travis ended world wars and Kimberly told me all about them. That girl blows my mind."

Lena laughed. "Sounds about right. Are you going to talk to anyone besides your kids?"

"I'm talking to my lovely wife, right now, see?"

Lena rolled her eyes at him. "Are you going to associate with your family?"

"You and the kids *are* my family."

At this point Laura added, "We're your family, too. You can't escape it." She spoke in a blended tone of social mirth and admonishment. It was a tone that she knew wouldn't settle well with Marc, so she preemptively cut off his fiery response by turning to Franceska and saying, "Franci, you wouldn't believe how smart Kimberly is."

"Oh, I think I believe it. I see what her father has done."

Lena teased, "Oh don't believe it. Marc's not as smart as everyone thinks he is."

"That's true," Marc said. "Once I was trying to sign a client who was being extremely difficult. We needed the business badly and I was giving the deal everything I had: demos, charts, reports, everything! Our product was better than the competition and the client admitted it! He admitted that our price was reasonable. But none of our strengths were important to him, and our weaknesses were the most important issues in the universe. At least that's how it felt. Looking back, I can see how badly I handled the situation. I didn't have the confidence to realize that he was beating up on me because he actually wanted to buy. The problem was, he was taking a big risk and he was looking for someone to convince him that it'd be alright. Instead of making him feel at ease about his decision, I was continually reminding him of how big the risk was."

Lena laughed. "Yeah, I remember. We went to dinner at the end of the business trip. Tensions were running high and this guy was about to throw Marc out of the restaurant."

Marc said, "I tried pulling one of those, 'are you going to buy or not?' tactics. I was desperate and I wasn't thinking clearly. That's when Lena gathered up the reports that I brought and asked the waitress to take them away with the menus. That shocked all of us—it was like pressing the reset switch for everyone." Marc sparkled with pride. "The client immediately fell in love with Lena. From that moment on, we didn't talk about business. It was all about hunting, or fishing, or whatever."

"Hey, don't forget the slugs," Lena added, fueling the story.

"Slugs?" Laura asked with a sickened sneer.

Lena said, "Yeah. This guy was quite the survivalist. He told us all about these disgusting creatures and how to tell which ones were edible. You know? Just in case we found ourselves stranded in the wilderness."

Marc said, "You're the one that kept it going. The more squeamish you got, the more he laid it on."

"So I took one for the team—you about killed the deal."

"I know. I learned a lot that night." Marc's sudden shift from levity to sincerity preceded an awkward silence. Finally, he asked, "Who wants to play blackjack?"

"Well, you *know* I can't," Laura said.

"Oh, that's a shame."

"Marc! Be nice," Lena scolded.

"It's alright, Lena. I know he loves me. Besides, I was going to see Cousin George, actually second cousin. It's been ages since I've seen him."

Franceska was preparing to leave when she turned to Lena and said, "Well, it was nice to meet you…"

"Oh, you should stay, Franci," Laura insisted. "Blackjack is more fun with more people."

"How would you know?" Marc asked.

"Just because I can't play it, doesn't mean I don't get it."

"You mean you're not *allowed* to play it.'"

"I *choose* not to play it."

"Right," Marc said, rolling his eyes.

"Oh, come on you two," Lena scolded, "you're worse than the kids." She quickly shifted to an inviting tone when she turned to Franceska and said, "Yes, Franci, we'd love to have you stay."

"Okay, that sounds fun. Yes, I would like to," Franceska said.

"Actually, let's play blackjack switch," Marc said.

"What's that?" Lena asked.

"It's fun; I'll show you."

Chapter 10

If Salt Lake City was the capital of the saints, then Park City was the capital of the sinners. The two cities had enjoyed a colorful rivalry. Brigham Young founded Salt Lake City as a refuge for the people of God, to be a place where righteousness would prevail. In the valleys of the mountains, far from the mobs and corrupt politicians who had plagued their tumultuous beginnings in New York, Ohio, Missouri, and Illinois, the saints established a utopian society based on high moral values, industry, and economic cooperation.

The thing about utopia, however, was that one man's heaven was another man's hell. To assist those who didn't fully appreciate the heaven that had been created for them, an extensive organization grew up among the saints to redirect the wayward back toward the straight and narrow. They were gently brought along until they developed a character capable of enduring such great light. The process was similar to how one might imagine cattle being led through chutes to their eternal salvation, the pearly gates of the immaculate meat processing plant.

Park City sprung up as a mining town. The miners and fortune seekers who poured into the area represented the antithesis of Mormon values. They drank liquor and chewed tobacco. They kept whores and lived in squalor. Every man pursued his own way, as long as the way pointed to personal riches.

Silver and gold mining, with its attendant influences, was a bur under Brigham Young's saddle that had to be expurgated lest it infect the saints with loose morals. Legends persist wherein Brigham implored the Lord who miraculously relocated known veins of precious metals in order to hide them from the gentiles and the saints. The gentiles would only consume them upon their lusts and the saints were not yet prepared to enjoy such riches in righteousness.

Church approved mining was a different matter altogether. When the church could ensure that proper conditions prevailed and that the proceeds flowed through proper channels, small-scale mining operations were conducted for the sake of self-sufficiency. The church was mainly interested in iron and other essential raw materials. The limited gold and silver that they obtained through their iron mines provided some means to trade for the things that were not practical for them to produce themselves.

To the gentile miners, the rankling over morals was all quite humorous. They accused the Mormons of living in glass houses and casting stones. What was the difference between Mormon temples where polygamous unions were solemnized and Park City saloons and brothels? Miners had left their wives hundreds of miles away, they worked hard, and they were lonely. Whose business was it if they exchanged a few pieces of silver for some comfort in the arms of a woman?

The Mormons rebutted that there was a world of difference between their holy practice of plural marriage and the whoredoms of the miners. The saints were building families in the service of God with eternal value. Theirs was a sacred commitment to maintain the honor and virtue of their wives, to care for them, and to protect them. They argued that when the veins of silver and gold ran dry, the miners would leave nothing behind but ruin—the ruin of land and the ruin of women.

After suffering several economic setbacks, Park City mining eventually died out and the city crumbled, fulfilling various prophecies of the saints that the Lord would strike down sin and error. The Lord didn't forsake the city entirely, however. Instead he rebuilt it into a world-class destination—not exactly what the saints had in mind when they prayed for its destruction. Travelers from around the world would come to enjoy its skiing, its scenic accommodations, and its artistic flare. Apparently there was a cultural advantage in being rebellious reprobates.

Utah revived mining operations in Park City, except this time tourists *brought* their gold and silver, already refined, and exchanged it for a few paltry drinks and trinkets purchased from boutique art galleries. It was brilliant. With only eight thousand permanent residents, the vast majority of the population were travelers looking for a cool place. Park City made them feel like patrons of the arts, and it was fun.

From art galleries to renowned festivals, Park City's reputation grew. Under the wing of Robert Redford, the Sundance Film Festival drew big names and big bar tabs to the area. Utah, a state largely controlled by churchgoers, was known for its oppressive liquor laws. However, unlike the ore extracted from Zion's hillside by whoremongers, golden greenbacks were heaven sent; at least state lawmakers didn't seem to complain about the revenue as their former prophet did. Park City was like a special dispensation revealed to Utah in order to foster a more suitable environment for trade. The laws were relaxed and liberal liquor licenses were issued. A plethora of secondary festivals emerged from the Sundance underbrush. Headlining bands played for small crowds in intimate venues. If ever a fan wanted to take shots of Jack with Ke$ha, this was the place where it could happen. In Park City it was easy to forget that you were in Utah.

Marc and Lena moved there during the off-season—the time between the melting snow and the emergence of firm mountain trails (which brought the next wave of tourists). It was a time when the locals could briefly reclaim their inheritance from the hordes of visitors. It was their opportunity to take measures and to enact ordinances that would shape their community through the upcoming year.

Park City led the state in green reform. If any religion bound this city together, it was the worship of the earth. In this theology, nearby Salt Lake City was perceived as the resident evil. It was the headquarters of the church. Mormons had large families. Large families consumed natural resources, produced mounds of waste, and built sprawling suburbs. They were also a burden on public funds since they rarely produced as much in taxes as it cost to educate their little brats or to provide healthcare assistance.

In Park City, the earth was their god and recycling was their principal sacrament. On Wednesdays, bins of different colors cluttered the street for collecting aluminum, glass, paper, and general waste. When Marc and Lena moved to Park City to raise their family, Lena became ardently devoted to saving the earth, also. In Salt Lake, ward houses were as common as gas stations, but in Park City, they were as rare as pubic hair on bikini models. Lena was looking for something new to fill the vacancy that the church left in her life.

Lena bought organic produce and she composted everything possible. She kept a box of worms in the backyard that she used to consume cardboard and other paper products. For instance, when she made lemonade for the children, she used fresh lemons. The rinds went to the compost pile and the paper bag (which contained the sugar) went to the worms. She used refillable containers for household cleaners, and so on. Consequently the Friedman family produced very little waste. They could easily fit all of their garbage into one can each week.

Early one morning she welcomed a neighbor who was knocking at their door. The neighbor had been out jogging and noticed that the Friedman garbage was not separated into recycling bins. Apparently, she had found some glass containers mixed in with the general waste. She recognized that the Friedmans were new to the community and, in spite of the interruption it was to her jog, she wanted to let them know how things were done in Park City. Lena thanked her kindly for the information and assured her that she would correct the problem. Every Wednesday for the next 3 months, Marc heard Lena venting about how the neighbors' four recycling bins were overflowing, practically falling onto the street, while her four bins were nearly empty.

Marc sat watching the wrath of winter through the patio door. It was the kind of day when Sunday morning coffee could start early at the fireplace and stretch into afternoon wine. Inside, it was unusually serene since the children were with Lena's parents. They would be going to church with their grandparents. It was unavoidable at this point. After the shouting had died down and the vases were cleaned up that Lena had thrown at Marc when she walked in on his phone conversation with Franceska, Lena assured him that Kimberly and Travis didn't know the reason that they were staying with their grandparents. He told her that kids aren't stupid. They could put two and two together. They had to know that their parents were struggling. Marc told Lena that he didn't need them finding religion over a temporary squabble.

"Religion didn't hurt me," Lena said.
"You know what I mean," Marc said.
"Do I?"

It was ironic that the weather on Saturday had been so peaceful when Marc and Lena were fighting. Sunday was a fray outside and Marc had left Lena sleeping peacefully in their bed. He heard the bathroom door shut, so he hustled into the kitchen and cooked up a cup of cappuccino. Lena soon floated in, rubbing the dreams from her eyes. The sun was merely a candle to her face and tossed up hair. Marc finished just in time to say, "Here you go, gorgeous. God, you're more beautiful than on the day I met you."

The wind was stirring up snow and bending pines, but Lena, of course, answered lusciously, like fountain grass answers a summer's breeze—with a curtsy and a wave. The grass doesn't exactly have a choice. It is involuntarily actuated, either to dancing and joy or to wrath and rage. When the tumult comes, the grass will flail and angrily shake its head, but to no avail. Women, though, are greater than grass. They're greater than the wind. Come fury, come hell, but the girl will prevail.

She raised the cup from Marc's hand with open palms as if she was accepting an offering. "I had a lot of fun with you last night," she said.

Marc smiled. "Yeah, I did too. You were a rock star."

"Well, you kind of made me want to show off a little."

"And it was one hell of a show."

Lena acknowledged the compliment with a sway again. Marc took it in and then looked away and continued nonchalantly, "Speaking of a show, I noticed that your picture was missing."

"It's in the car."

"Oh, good."

"What do you mean?" She was assessing the meaning of Marc's tone of voice.

"Well, as long as it's intact, you won't have to pose for another one."

"I think I proved last night that I have overcome a lot of those fears."

Marc laughed. "Yes, but how about for a real photographer?"

"I think I would."

"I love it when your eyes do that."

"Do what?" Lena feigned indifference like a sunflower that turns its face imperceptibly, but always toward the glowing sun.

"Ah, like when you make these little leaps in life, your eyes light up. It's like a flash and then all of the sudden, you're willing to do things that you never would before."

"Such as?" The sunflower would accept the rays if the rays must come.

"Well, like posing nude. I fought with you for like two years to get you to do it. You finally did it, but you wouldn't do it for a photographer. You were paranoid about showing too much pussy, then you were paranoid about having it on display. Now you're saying you would bear it all for a stranger."

"It's scary. You wouldn't do it."

"I'm not supposed to do it. I'm not a chick."

"Girls like a little eye candy, too, you know."

"Maybe, but whatever. You're my little dolly." He spoke as if he was teetering on a decision, like whether to brush her cheek and kiss her somewhere tender or to grab her hair and bite her lip. Without moving to do either, he continued in a resolute tone, "I'll dress you or undress you. I'll peek under your panties or rip the damn things off." His eyes widened as if to capture fully her reaction, "That's just the way it's going to be."

"Yes, sir. I like being pretty and showing off for you. Do you have any other examples?" The sunflower was reaching again.

Marc thought for a moment. "Well, it was a struggle to get you to take on client relations. You were obviously very good at it, but you were reluctant to take it on as a formal position. I think you liked being the hero that could swoop in and save the company from a disaster, but you also liked being able to avoid a situation if it was hopeless."

"That's probably true. I was afraid of failure and I was afraid of disappointing you."

"I've never been disappointed, Lena. Quite the opposite. I watch you in admiration. Remember that time on the Wilkes account? You damn near resigned, but you decided to see it through. You figured out how to address the customer's concerns and by the end, you had them eating out of your hand. It was one of the most dazzling things I'd ever seen. The next time we were deciding on a challenging account, your eyes did that same thing. You were like 'don't worry, I got this,' and you were right."

"I know. It takes me some time. But I love that you push me to grow."

"Growing pains," Marc said, tossing his eyes.

"Hey, I didn't get a degree in this, Mr. Programmer."

"Ah, yeah you did!" Marc gawked at her incredulously.

"Well, yes in business, but I didn't focus on that aspect of it."

"I didn't focus on what I'm doing either. Is that the best you've got?"

"I just don't think you appreciate the struggle I deal with. Change is really hard for me."

"And it's easy for me?"

"I'm not saying that, but yes, actually. You adjust much easier than I do. Sometimes I wonder where you come from. I mean, it's like... I don't know. It's like you can slip out of one skin and slide into another. I can't do that. For instance, I was raised to believe that pornography is a sin..."

Marc shouted, "It's not pornography! Besides, I was raised to believe that drinking cappuccino is a sin."

"Quit dismissing me. You're not the one who had to explain to the kids why Daddy had a naked picture of Mommy on display."

"Heaven forbid that they know how much I adore their mother. It's bound to screw them up for life. Besides, I told them to stay out of there, so that's on them."

"Seriously? That's just a challenge, especially for *your* kids. Where do you think they get that from?"

"You're welcome! Would you rather they were more like Melinda's kids? I think her worst fear is that her kids might have a thought of their own."

"You just think that she's controlling because she believes in teaching her kids."

"Ah, correction: I know she's controlling."

"You don't know anything about her. You've talked to her, what, like three times? You don't understand her reasons and you don't know what she's thinking."

"You're right; I don't know what she's thinking, but I suspect very little if anything at all."

Lena shook her head. She knew there was no reconciliation between Marc and Melinda. For either one, accepting the other would have been an act of psychological suicide. It could be done, but it would require a complete dissolution and reconstruction of their core principles and values. Defending her sister was not intended to change Marc's mind. In defending his position, he showed her a world that fascinated her—being so very different from that which she had previously known. In trying to understand it, she vigorously engaged him in conversation, like a pivotal battle. Lena usually fought harder than Marc, as if she alone had something dear to lose. That was the cruel deception; she struggled to capture his world, oblivious to the fact that she *was* his world.

"Just because Melinda's quiet and reserved doesn't mean that she's unthinking."

"No, you're right. The thing that means she's unthinking is that she accepts everything she's been told without any evidence, without any analysis, without any...thought! Okay? Being quiet and reserved is the result of the fact that she's so damn judgmental of other people. At least she has the decency to keep it to herself."

"She's not judgmental. She's actually really nice. She just has 'bitchy resting face.'"

"That's funny, but I don't believe in it. When a person is happy, it shows. It's called 'ev•i•dence,' a novel concept to people like her, I know."

Lena laughed. "People like her?" she asked, raising her eyebrows. She continued without waiting for an answer. "You're no better. You accept things without 'ev•i•dence' all the time."

"Take that back this instant," Marc shouted pretending to be hurt.

"No! You mock other people for accepting their religion without proof. Isn't that what religion is? Something you accept without proof? So really you're saying that there should be no religion."

"Wow! You've convinced me," Marc said throwing his hands into the air like there was nothing more to say.

Lena laughed as to acknowledge that Marc scored a point. "What about you wanting to marry Franceska? Are you saying that you don't have religious reasons for that?"

"Well…"

"I knew it--thinking with your joy stick again. So typical."

"I thought you were as committed to it as I was." Marc's weak comeback signaled a point for Lena.

"The difference between you and me is that you can't question my motives."

"And you question mine?"

"You're the one who wants to fuck her."

"Then sex is the ultimate evil? I'm not being deceitful; I'm not sneaking around behind your back and making up stories. I…"

"How would you feel if I had sex with another man?"

"Ah, yeah, that will never do." He paused. "I will have you to myself."

"What's the difference? I ought to just so that you know how it feels."

"First of all," Marc said calmly then erupted with, "I haven't had sex with her!" He continued Socratic-like, "Nevertheless, all I ask is that before you do, you discuss it with me and give me a chance to fully express myself...as I did with you."

"You used my religion to get what you wanted."

"No I didn't. I said nothing of religion. You're the one who brought your grandfather and religion into it..."

"My great-grandfather!"

"Whatever! You told me what a noble and great man he was, how he would never do anything immoral. It was the hardest thing he ever did, but he reluctantly entered into plural marriage in order to be obedient to the revelations of Joseph Smith. I don't give a shit about any of that."

"Maybe you should."

Marc laughed. "Okay! If you insist, I claim religion."

"Sure, I know you'll do and say anything to get what you want."

Marc set his coffee cup down and put his arm around the small of Lena's back. Drawing her in, she instinctively wrapped her arm around his shoulder and he lowered his voice. "Do you know how I know that you will never have sex with another man?"

"How?" She swallowed half of her word.

"Because you love me. Because you know that you can't get this, what we have, anywhere else. I'm tired of dancing around the truth. If you need a revelation, here it is. The truth is that I love you, Lena. I love you! And you know that we have something special, I mean cosmically rare, and you won't put that at risk. Deep down you know that I have more to give; we both do, and that's why you entertained the idea of Franceska. It didn't have a goddamn thing to do with your great granddaddy or his beliefs. This is about you and me. You're as curious as I am to see what we can achieve. I want to live big. I can't settle for the confines of a coffin while I'm still alive. You know that there is more capacity in this family. I want to pursue it and I need your help, Lena. I need you."

Lena took some time to consider what he said. "What if you're wrong?" She asked looking at the floor.

"Wrong?"

"Yeah, it can happen; you're not infallible, you know." She spat venom back, but it was an act, like someone playing the devil's advocate.

"No, it's you people that believe in infallibility."

"You people?" She let go of his shoulder.

"Stop it, babe."

"Don't tell me what to do."

"I wasn't telling you what to do. I was gently inviting you to make better choices." Marc smiled.

Lena pushed away from him. "I'm sick of you criticizing my family. Just because you don't agree with them, that doesn't give you the right to continually belittle them."

"I don't always criticize them. I think Clawson is awesome!"

"Very funny."

"I'm not joking. I will prove that I think your family is amazing." He pretended to pause for dramatic effect. Then he dropped the bombshell, "They produced you and Clawson. See?"

"You know perfectly well they've done more than that. Your company exists because of Daddy."

Marc looked like a fish that nearly took the bait, but decided to swim away instead. Marc poured some wine and they moved to the living room where he lit the fireplace. It cost a small fortune to replace the gas-fired insert with a wood-fired one. Marc preferred the flame and the glow of natural embers. Lena wanted to keep the original fireplace because it was cleaner and more efficient. Marc insisted that, "this feels more like the sun."

The sun, it gleamed through the leaves of a massive tree. Its branches spread over a few sparsely placed picnic tables like the hen that oft would have gathered her chicks but they would not. Marc and Lena had purchased a few sandwiches and spreads from the winery's deli. They were laughing about something, it didn't matter what. Neither one could remember what it was when they discussed it several days later.

"Oh, you're out of wine. Would you like some more, me lady?" Laughing. Lots of laughing.

"I don't know. I think I've had enough."

"Enough of this?" Marc flung his arms around, like the branches of the tree, pointing to sky, the hillside, and the vineyard.

"No." Her eyes glistened like wine in the sun. "I'm quite tipsy."

"Tipsy?" Laughing. "Tipsy?" More laughing. "Don't you like it?"

"No. I like it."

"Then have some more."

"Okay, maybe a little." Marc poured a plentiful portion to which she protested. This was at least the second time that he had ignored her pouring instructions, yet she would drink the whole glass, as she had each time before. It was a dance that all classy women must trot, choreographed long before their time.

Exaggerating the behavior of a wine snob, he said, "I think it's a fine bottle. Let's see… It's from Linda's Vineyard. Ha. Linda's Vineyard." He laughed as if he had stumbled upon something truly profound.

"What's so humorous?"

"Would you like some more wine, me Linda?" Hysterical laughing.

"What?" Lena looked puzzled.

"MeeeLinda."

155

"Oh. Very funny," she said unimpressed.

Marc offered some clever insults. Lena took offense. She was rather sensitive, after all. She said something about not ruining their vacation. Marc would never allow someone as stupid as Melinda to ruin their vacation. That's not what she was talking about. He would fight for Lena's honor. Honor? What did honor have to do with it? Couldn't she see what honor had to do with it? She was better than Melinda. People are not better than other people; they're just different. She wasn't better than her mother. What did her mother have to do with it? "I didn't say anything about your goddamned mother." Marc would still be working freelance if it weren't for Daddy. Daddy. Daddy! Daddy can go to hell with the rest of them. Freelance? Free isn't bad. Free is good. Freedom is free. Freedom is good. "Of course I want to be free." What did he have against her family? The branches were blocking the sun. "What we really need is to shed some light on the subject." "You're not listening to me. You never listen to me." "Listening is all I do. I can't do anything else." "You won't let me explain." "Go ahead. Explain away." "My family means more to me than anything." "You don't think I listen because you keep saying the same thing." "You keep interrupting me." "Okay, no more interruptions." "Well, I forgot what I was going to say, but…" They were out of wine. "You can't let me get through one sentence." "That wasn't me, it was the wine. It interrupted you. Damn stuff always runs out in the middle of a conversation and makes a scene." Marc laughed. "You've had enough wine." "I feel like we're making some real progress here." "No, we're not." "Then we need more wine." Marc laughed. Lena laughed, too; no, she probably didn't laugh. It's very unlikely that she laughed. Short steps. No hurry. Too short. Walk naturally. For the love of God, walk naturally! First stop: restroom. Tile clean, grout dirty. It's not that dirty, just needs steam cleaned. For the price of this wine, they could hire someone to steam clean every grout line individually. Gush, trickle, drip. Squeeze, pull, tap. Squeeze, pull, tap. Squeeze, pull, tap. Tap, tap, tap. Wait. Zip. Glance around, glance around again, all alone, leave without washing. No piss on the fingers. Pussy doesn't offend anyone. Being thorough has its advantages. Piss on everything, nothing matters anyway. Walk. No, walk upright, upright into the deli shop. Smile. Look around for a minute. These soaps. Exfoliating. Made with grape skins and seeds. Merlot. Zinfandel. Cabernet. Syrah. Smirk. All natural. We'll see about that. Ingredients? Whatever. It's all made in the belly of a star. Grab one of each. Counter. Wait in line. Keep hips from swaying. Elvis is dead. Elvis is really dead. "I'll have a bottle of the Linda Cab." "Which year?" "The first…I mean the oldest." Keep sentences short, payment at hand. Walk back to the picnic table as naturally as possible. Twenty layers of paint. "Are you going to finish that?" "No." "What's the matter, babe?" "I'm fine." "Let's talk about it." "I don't want to talk about it." Family. Religion. Wine. Listen. Family. Tyranny. Listen. Wine. Listen. Tyranny. Listen. Listen. Listen.

Marc sat under the sun. The sky. The clouds. The hen. Above the grass reaching for light through the fallen leaves. Decaying bark. Footsteps long gone whose effects remain. Beside the trellises and vines. The hillside. The pride of husbands that hung in the air; the pride that let them tell their women to go. "Go then." Marc sat facing the hillside. He wouldn't turn to see if the limo was still there. He sipped at his wine. He was going to finish that goddamn wine. Sip. It was taking a long time. He stretched this way and that. Stole a glimpse of the limo. No, he didn't; it wasn't there. Maybe it moved. No, it wasn't there. He was not going to finish that goddamn wine, no way! He flung it from his glass. It left a trail like a man pissing blood. He picked up the bottle and poured its belly onto the ground. There they were, both sexes and their worthless pride spilled on the land. Puddles are not good for grass. Would probably be a barren spot.

"Marc!" His mother nearly shouted in astonishment. He didn't come around often.

"Hi. Where's Dad?"

"He's outside, out back. Can I get you something? Do you want a cookie?"

"No thanks. I just need to talk to Dad real quick."

"Hi, son. How are you doing?" His dad asked.

"I've been better."

"What's the matter?"

"Well, I'm wondering if you've seen Lena."

"No. Why?" There was obviously a problem and Bradley's voice reflected it.

"Ah, well, I haven't seen her since Saturday."

"Weren't you in California?"

"Yes, she left a day early."

"Oh, I see." He continued with his yard work, spreading the tension a little thinner, over more time. He had a manner in doing it. Without saying anything, it was apparent that he was working on his response. Finally, after he reached the end of the flowerbed, he said, "Have you asked her parents?"

"No. I thought I would ask you first."

Bradley chuckled. "You thought you'd preserve your pride."

"No, I got back last night and headed home first. She wasn't there and I had work all day today."

"Son." That was a complete sentence, which, depending on its context, had one of a whole range of meanings, but was never ambiguous. "Get back in your car and drive, don't call first, drive to her parents' house, knock on their door, and ask to see their lovely daughter."

Marc looked at his dad as if he had inhaled some of the fertilizer with which he had been working. He stumbled over his words but managed to cough out, "You don't even know what happened."

"It doesn't matter," his dad snapped back.

"How can you say that?"

"Do you love her?"

"Yeah, of course I do."

"That's how I can say that. I know there are two sides to every story, and I'm sure that your side is very important to you. Her side is very important to her. Maybe neither one of you will ever understand the other person's position entirely, but you have something more important than that and it must be nurtured."

"Exactly! Why did she walk out on me, then? She didn't feel like nurturing it."

"It's not her job! That's your job. She's a great mother. She's a great wife. She works *and* keeps the house, and most impressively, she puts up with your bullshit."

Marc looked convicted. "I agree."

"So what are you going to do?"

"I don't know," Marc said, nearly whispering. Bradley started on the rose bushes. Finally Marc asked, "What if she's not there. I don't see why I shouldn't call first."

"You know your wife better than anyone. Go where she will be; make the gesture. Who do you want to take the first step?" Marc didn't respond, so Bradley continued, "It's hard, I know. Maybe she'll call you and apologize, but maybe she won't. Everyone wants to save face, but that's not what leaders do. If your family has a problem, you have a problem."

Chapter 11

Even in the summer Edberg kept his office hot. Marc was sweating as usual while Edberg was soaking up the heat like a passive solar collector. He had his eyes fixed upon the papers that Marc brought for review. To read from the top of the page to the bottom, he slouched in the chair such that his arms remained resting on the same spot and his eyes, head, and torso remained rigid. It was like watching a mummy whose joints were greatly restricted. When he reached the bottom of the page, with pains he would raise himself in the chair again and repeat the process.

Marc observed the scene for several pages. His amusement was escaping in little nasal bursts. Finally, he said, "I guess I should have emailed it. It would have been easier to read."

"Oh, you're making fun of me," Edberg said.

"Uh, no. Okay, maybe a little." Marc laughed. "Are you okay?"

"I'm exhausted."

"What's the matter?"

"My body is falling apart," Edberg said. Marc responded with a concerned look which conveyed something between "should I call 911" and "stop being so dramatic." Edberg continued with resignation, "I have diabetes. I've been dying for a long time. Of course everyone spends a long time dying, but I was supposed to be dead ten years ago. I've been living on sheer determination. Science has kept me alive and I don't mean the medicine."

"I didn't know you had diabetes." Marc somehow missed the most important part of Edberg's announcement.

"Very few people do."

"You don't *look* like you have diabetes. Two of my grandparents had diabetes."

"You mean because I'm not obese and I can still walk spryly. I have a strong heart and good nerves. At least I hope I have good nerves. The dilemma is that if they were bad, I would be too impaired to know it." Edberg pointed to his head, suggesting that they were the nerves he was most concerned about.

"Uh, you're a leading scientist on a world class experiment. I think it's safe to say they're fine."

"Well, it's always nice to get a confirmation." Edberg sighed like someone who dodged a bullet to the head. Only survivors realized how lucky they were.

"So if you were supposed to be dead ten years ago, how have you survived so long?"

"I have observed a starvation diet for about thirty years as an alternative to insulin therapy. All of my doctors advised against it, but I did my own research and felt that it was my best option."

"So you don't take insulin?" Marc asked in amazement.

"Oh, I take it but only when I absolutely must, about one fifth as much as others in a comparable condition. My strategy seems to have worked since my doctor is always telling me how healthy I am for someone with a case as severe as mine. Nonetheless, I can tell that the end is near."

There was an awkward silence. Marc eventually filled it with, "What about the wine? You seem to really like your wine."

"I said I was dying, not dead. Not yet, anyway."

"That's what I mean. I thought wine was kryptonite to diabetics."

"I suppose it is, but I'm not your typical diabetic. I seem to do okay with wine; it's Scotch that is my nemesis. I have to be really careful with the hard stuff."

"Does it scare you, the thought of dying?" Marc asked with apprehension.

"Yes and no. I'm tired of living; it's a lot of work and as I said, I'm exhausted. It's a lot of pain, too, but there's a lot of joy mixed in with it to make it tolerable. You and I have talked extensively about the existence of God, but one thing we haven't talked much about is the afterlife."

Marc squinted. "You're right. I kind of think of them as the same."

"They're not."

"No, you're right, obviously. I just hadn't really thought of it that way."

Edberg continued, "Personally, I believe in God. I know that I've entertained the opposite view in our discussions, but I really do believe in God. I'm very concerned with him; what I'm unclear about is whether or not he's concerned with me. Other than the human backlash to the idea of a final end, I have found no direct evidence of a life after death. Many have claimed to know, but I'm a scientist. If an experiment cannot be repeated, then it's merely a curiosity, at best, or possibly a downright lie. I'm not keen on taking people's word for things, but I can't entirely rule out the possibility that they are right, either."

"Do you believe that Joseph Smith was right?"

"I hope so. He taught some very compelling doctrines. Who doesn't want to believe that they can be gods? Joseph Smith was an interesting man. First of all, he was a believer, through and through. He took it as a given that God was our Father. He took scripture at face value. He was also a first rate thinker and a philosopher in his own right. He simply asked, 'Cannot a son become like his father?'" Edberg laughed and his body shook as much as his spine would permit. "When you put it that way, you kind of have to admit that he can; a son, I mean, can become like his father. I'm willing to concede that if the Bible is true, then Joseph Smith is, too." Edberg paused to take a drink of water.

"For my part, however," Edberg continued, shifting to a more academic tone, "I have found nothing but the testimony of so-called prophets to suggest that we are anything more than a mere statistical incident in the vastness of space—a chance occurrence—a bubble in a sea of confusion. Given billions of worlds, there is bound to emerge an intelligent creature, here and there. Well, not intelligent, not really. Unless there's something divine in man, we're just concentrated lumps of whatever stuff space and time are made of. There are laws that govern the universe and we exist because those laws spit out a pattern, here and there. It's no wonder that we struggle to understand the secrets of the universe. It's like a domino trying to comprehend its own existence—where it came from and why it behaves as it does. That we have learned anything at all is stunning, but it should also cause us to be highly suspect of what we think we know."

Marc interjected, "The only problem I have with your analogy is that dominoes are created objects. If we're statistical incidents, then…"

"Oh, I don't get hung up on things like that. Creationists think that the only way that God could create man was for him to roll up his sleeves and wallow in the mud and the mire. They object to evolution. Idiots! It's a much more elegant way to make a man."

"Particularly if you're not in any rush," Marc chimed in.

Edberg laughed, "Yes, don't claim to be a god if you don't have plenty of time. Evolution is the most sublime explanation. It suggests that we've been fourteen billion years in the making. Now that's divine, if I've seen anything divine at all, but some people would rather believe that we were made with a lump of clay and a dash of magic in one day. Preposterous!"

"This doesn't settle the creation issue though. You can't use a created thing as an analogy for something that wasn't created." Marc seemed determined to pursue his objection.

"True, but you're getting hung up on the definition of 'creation.' I say that if God decreed the laws of the universe then, by extension, he created everything which those laws give rise to. One of the most fundamental laws of nature is entropy. 'In the beginning,'" Edberg framed the biblical phrase with air quotes without raising his arms from the chair rests, "the universe was incredibly dense and highly uniform. If it had been perfectly homogeneous, however, no stars or galaxies would have formed. The universe would have simply expanded and cooled, uniformly and indefinitely, into a vacuous cloud of near nothingness. It was the tiny inconsistencies, the random jostling, that gave rise to galaxies and stars and planets and, ultimately, to us. Organization from disorganization. Order from chaos. It's like the universe is having a massive identity crisis," Edberg concluded with a triumphant crescendo.

"Okay, so you're saying that you *are* afraid to die?" Marc's lack of tact never seemed to bother Edberg. In fact he seemed to thrive on it.

"Oh perhaps, but not because of that."

"Then because of what?" Marc asked.

"It's simple. Either there is life after death or there isn't. If there isn't, then this is as good as it gets and it ends in a numbing silence. If there is life after death, then I doubt that the life there beats the life here."

"So you're afraid of dying because there *might* be life after death?" Marc asked perplexed.

Edberg left the question hanging. "Enough about me. Let's speak of life, not the end of it. How are things with you and Lena?"

"Good."

"Good? That's it?"

"Good. Really good." Marc's face gave him away like a child who knows the contents of a gift and is so excited to see it that he blurts it out before the recipient has a chance to unwrap it.

Marc returned to the computing building.

"I hope you got something good," William said, visibly stressed.

"Wesley was just here." Amy seemed depressed.

William said, "Yeah, while you were shooting the breeze with Edberg, Wesley ripped us apart for not being finished with the micro DLL."

"Oh, is he suddenly interested?" Marc asked sarcastically.

"We're a month overdue," William retorted.

"Relax, Man. Shit's easy," Marc said.

"If it's so easy, what took so long with Edberg?" William asked.

"You wouldn't appreciate it if I told you."

"Try me."

"Okay," Marc shot back defiantly, "we were talking about life after death."

"Oh my god!" William erupted.

"Exactly!" Marc laughed and Amy seemed amused, too. Marc concluded, "I knew you wouldn't appreciate it."

"Why would I? We're running behind and you're jacking off to Bible quotes."

"Actually, I've learned more about the laws of physics by discussing the existence of God than I did in all my physics courses combined."

"For example?"

"Well, it's more of an approach to physics than anything else. It causes you to look at possibilities that you wouldn't normally..."

"It causes you to look at nothing," William cut in. "It causes ignorance!"

"I agree. But I'm not talking about being religious, okay? I'm talking about having a reverence for creation. For instance, if God created the universe, then you have to ask, 'Why like this? Why not some other way?'"

"It's called the anthropic principle," Amy said. "If the universe were significantly different than it is, we would not be here to ask, 'Why is it like this?'"

"Apparently Marc is not familiar with it." William was rolling out the insults.

"Thank-you Amy." Marc stressed her name, as if to say that at least she was contributing something to the discussion. He continued in response to her mention of the anthropic principle, "That's exactly what I'm talking about. So maybe there are countless universes, but only those capable of sustaining intelligent life lead to anyone asking questions. So think about the equations that we use to describe our universe. They are merely the coincidences that we have observed." William and Amy seemed puzzled, so he elaborated. "If every circle were exactly ten square centimeters, then our equation for the area of a circle would look like this…"

He wrote $A = 10 \text{ cm}^2$ on the board.

"It's only because we have experience with circles of every imaginable size that we know the correct equation."

He wrote $A = \pi r^2$.

Marc threw his papers on the table and shouted, "What do you see on these pages?"

"Your man-seed," William said.

"You're such an idiot," Marc said. He turned to Amy and continued, "Here's the upshot. We live in a universe where every proton is the same size, every electron, quark, and so on. Consequently, our equations for describing them are full of constants based on measurement rather than theory. It's a mess. What they are really telling us is that we haven't even begun to understanding what's really going on."

William interrupted, "I understand that we're about to get fired. We have a job to do and you're spending all of your time questioning the meaning of life."

Amy blurted out, "Get off it, William. Hear him out." She caught them both by surprise.

"Fine! I don't care! I'm going to get some work done," he said as he stormed out.

Marc looked at Amy. "What's his problem?"

"I don't know," she said. "I guess Dr. Wesley upset him pretty bad."

"I guess so."

Marc returned to his office and sat at his desk, looking intensely at some drawings he had made on a sketchpad. They weren't telling him what he was looking for. He wrote some equations in the margin. Solved and substituted. Solved again. Zero equals zero. Useless. He ripped the paper out and tossed it away.

There was a knock at the door. It was Amy. "Hey, I just wanted to say that I was really interested in what you were saying back there. I was wondering if you would finish explaining it." She was wearing cut-off jeans and a tank top—a comfortable way of communicating uncomfortable messages.

"Uh, sure. Have a seat." Marc motioned to a seat beside his desk.

She crossed her legs and bounced the upper one. They were smooth and evenly tanned. She clasped her hands and leaned forward with obvious interest. Marc reciprocated with interest also; he noticed those silky legs and all that her top revealed.

"Well, where were we?" He asked.

"You were comparing the fundamental particles to circles. Like what if all circles were the same size?"

"Right." Marc flashed a smile, the kind that flashes from the eyes, too. "I was saying that our equations are telling us that we don't really have a clue what's going on."

"So what's going on?" She asked. Physics couldn't account for her smile.

"That's a great question." He attempted to be clever, but it only encouraged her.

"That's what I came for."

"Well, Amy, I think that you may be asking questions that I don't have answers for."

Amy sat back in her chair. "I'm sorry; I really want to know more about what you were saying."

"It's okay."

"I should probably go," she said somewhat embarrassed.

"No it's okay. Seriously. Discussing it would help, a lot actually."

"Okay. Sure. I really am interested."

"Alright, great. Here's the thing that fascinates me—let's compare general relativity to quantum physics. Both theories reflect our experience, but relativity describes gravitational fields and velocities, and so forth. We have experience with a broad range of values for parameters in this realm: small, large, and everything in between. Consequently, our equations involve continuous variables and are quite elegant. By contrast, when it comes to quantum particles, almost everything about them is discrete and static. Their size, mass, charge, and spin are all constant. Consequently, our theory for quantum physics is fraught with discrete variables and arbitrary constants... At least I think they're arbitrary. The result is that quantum physics is messy and complicated, almost the opposite of relativistic physics."

"Yes, but it has been shown, over and over again, that if you change the fundamental constants of the universe, even slightly, life as we know it wouldn't be possible."

"Holy shit! You just gave me an idea." Marc turned to his notebook and began feverishly scribbling notes as if he was attempting to outpace the memory mongers, to prevent them from stealing his idea. His fingers moved like foxes bolting away from hungry hounds. His eyes darted like flashlights searching in the darkness for a suspect.

The memory mongers are more patient than men, however. It's impossible to jot down a flash of insight faster than the time it takes to begin to fade. Amy was apparently aware of this. She waited. When Marc waged war with the ceiling, she waited. When he pulled on his hair in despair, she waited. When he shouted for glee or groaned in anguish, she waited. She waited until he set the pen down and sighed.

"What was it?" She asked.

"Oh. I thought I had something. No, I *know* I had something."

"Tell me about it; maybe it will come back to you."

"It was when you said you can't change the fundamental constants of nature; I realized that in my analogy with the area of circles, the formula $A = \pi r^2$ still has a constant in it—π. I realized that I've been trying to find a system where the constants disappear. I've been trying to eliminate the constants from the model. Do you see?"

Amy looked at him as if she desperately wished that she could see what he was trying to say. She said, "Of course you can't eliminate π from the equation."

"Right. Circles are mathematical objects, not physical objects. That was the insight. Not every circle is the same size. Not every circle has ten square centimeters, but every circle has a *3.14ness* to it."

"Ah, I see what you're saying. Some constants are coincidental—others are inherent."

"Exactly! I'm still convinced that the constants in the standard model are coincidental; they're mere occurrences of the underlying laws, but how do you uncover the grand principle when all you have is a skimpy sampling?"

"You need a theory."

"Precisely. That's what I was working on."

"May I look at it?" She leaned over the desk. Marc leaned toward her with the notebook; he happened to brush her arm with his hand as he turned the notebook to face her. Her eyes shot up, but his as quickly turned toward the page. She perused the page for a few moments and then said, "I gotta say, Marc, this makes utterly no sense." She laughed and he acknowledged the critique in like manner.

"The essence of it is that I'm postulating many universes with radically different conditions. Like you said, most of those will not be capable of supporting life, but the thing that really interests me is the space between them."

"What do you mean?"

"Well, there's nothing new about the idea of multiple universes, but can you imagine what could be done if you could view our universe from the space outside of it? I mean from the space where the universe was created?" Marc regained his excitement with an extra dose.

"Uh, amazing shit."

"Come on, I'm being serious. Take for instance the uncertainty principle. It places a limit on how accurately we can measure momentum and position."

"I know what the uncertainty principle is."

"Well, that's a big deal because if we can't make accurate measurements, we can't make accurate predictions!"

"Is that how this all ties into the micro DLL we're working on?" Amy asked.

It took Marc a moment to register her question. "Oh, I don't know. I guess so, but I haven't thought about that. This is way bigger than that."

One supreme idea gives a man supreme confidence. It endows him with the power to ignore criticism and to break the shackles of oppression. He can bypass the angels who guard the gates of heaven. He knows that the judges who stand between him and God have nothing on him. They may render a judgment, but he does not fear it. They will have their day of reckoning, too, so they had better walk gently. Those in power want to stay there. Hence, they brand new ideas as crazy or heretical because those ideas disrupt the establishment and threaten the control of the ruling class.

Within the week, Marc was clearing out his desk. Apparently employers expect their employees to focus on work, not to pursue their own personal interests. There were deadlines so figuring out the universe could wait. CERNshmern. There was a knock at his door. Amy stood there with tears in her eyes. "Hi, come in Amy," Marc said.

"I'm going to miss you," she said.

"I'll miss you guys, too."

Amy started crying again. "That's not what I mean and you know it. Why do you have to be such a jackass?"

Marc set his things down and reached to put his arms around Amy who was still standing in the doorway. He said, "I'm sorry. I know what you meant. I mean it, too."

"Can I come in?" She fought off the deluge of tears.

"Sure," Marc said. She closed the door behind her.

"William is such a jerk."

"Why, what do you mean?"

"He got you fired."

"Are you sure?"

"Obviously. I mean, I don't know, but how else would you explain…"

"It doesn't matter, Amy."

"What do you mean? Of course it matters."

"I'm not going to worry about the things I can't control. I'm going to focus on this." He tapped his notebook.

Amy wrapped herself around him and held on for maybe ten minutes or so. He tried to assure her that he would be fine. He told her that she shouldn't fight with William or Dr. Wesley over this; it would only makes things worse for her. His nonchalance about working there and all of the time that they had spent working together must have upset her because she finally burst out of the office.

Marc carried his things out to the car. As he drove away, something thumped the window hard and he slammed on the brakes. It was Amy; she had run to catch him. He rolled the window down and she stooped down and kissed him. She didn't give him a chance to object or to avoid it. It was clear that she ached for him. "If things don't work out with Lena…"

Marc said, "I know, Amy. You're awesome; I really mean that. Let's stay in touch."

He didn't stay in touch, though. He sent Amy an invitation to his reception and wedding reenactment after the elopement, but she didn't show and he never called to verify that she received the invitation. The CERN project at the university was eventually completed and the old team dissipated into space and time.

Marc opened the lower desk drawer. Neatly stacked inside were five notebooks. He picked up the bottom one and thumbed through the pages. In the margin where he stopped was written, "This is very impressive. ♥ Amy." He read through several of her comments; they were scattered over about forty or fifty pages and ended as abruptly as they began. He then picked up the notebook on the top of the stack and continued working where he had left off previously. Eventually he received a text from Chuck.

Chuck: What are you doing?
Marc: Working. Why?
Chuck: We're over at Zack's if you want to come over.
Marc: Okay, I'll see you a little later.

When he arrived, the music was a little louder than usual. He knocked on the door and three guys answered.

"What happened here?" Marc asked.
"Carla happened," Chuck shouted.

There were several wine bottles scattered around on the table. "I've never seen you drink wine from Solo cups before," Marc said.

"She took my glasses, well she took everything," Zack said.

"Not this!" Chuck was sitting on one side of a bench seat with his legs crossed over the length of it, imitating the famous reclining-nude pose of renaissance paintings. The house was mostly bare. The bench and the table where they were sitting were the only remaining pieces of furniture. A portrait of Zack's grandfather and some potted plants were the only decorations. The floor was dirty where feet had carried off the vestiges of a civil union. Debris cluttered the floor where it fell from drawers and couch cushions. "They tried to take this but I just looked at them, like 'You're going to have to carry me with it.'" Everyone laughed.

"Who? Was she here?" Marc asked.

"No. She sent her brothers with instructions to take everything," Toby said. "Me and Zack were sprawling over the table and chairs or they would be gone, too."

"Good. I love this table. I don't know what Chuck sees in that bench, but I really like this table," Marc said.

"It's not about the bench," Chuck shouted.

"What's it about?" Marc asked.

"It's about not kicking a man when he's down. This was just shitty."

"Regardless, you look lovely on it. Apparently, you've found yourself," Marc said.

"Thanks. I've been working on it."

"How did you guys tie down all of these plants?"

"We didn't. Her brothers didn't want to stack them on top of each other, so they're coming back for the rest of the stuff tomorrow."

Chuck looked at Zack and shook his head. "Are you going to lie down and let them walk over you, too?"

Zack laughed. "No, I made a deal with Carla. I didn't want to drag this out in court."

"Did it involve giving up your manhood, too?" Chuck moved to the table. "Does she have your nuts in a packing box?"

Zack said, "I don't want to be on bad terms with her. To be honest, I never stopped loving her and I need to think about my kids in all of this. Besides, you're one to talk; you've never even been married."

"And now you can see why," Chuck said. "Marriage is expensive."

"You mean divorce is expensive," Toby said.

"Same thing," Chuck said with a mordant glare.

"They're not the same thing. Not all marriages end in divorce."

"Then they end in misery which is worse."

"My parents are still happily married."

"Good actors, aren't they?"

"Who spit in your cup, Chuck?" Toby asked. "Your chuck-up-cup?" Laughing around.

"No one, but it irritates me what Carla's doing here."

"Dude, I'm fine with it." Zack tried to quell the rising anger.

"No, you're not!"

"Okay, I'm not '*fine*' with it, but I'm dealing with more important issues."

"Do you think you're getting her back or something?" Chuck asked.

Zack looked like he had been caught, tried, and convicted. "Ah, possibly."

Chuck erupted. "You're divorced. I'm sorry, dude, but what part of that don't you understand? It's over. She's gone. Accept it and move on."

"I don't believe it's over. It's never over until it's really over and it's not really over. I don't think it's over."

"Yes, it is. Let me show you." Chuck grabbed one of the potted plants and ejected it from the front door. By this time the wine bottles had multiplied and the voices were contending louder than the music which had eventually been turned up until it was playing at its max.

Marc had remained silent through most of the discussion, but seeing Chuck's treatment of the plant, he shot from his seat, marched out of the house, and picked up the stems and leaves which had been smeared over the sidewalk and the front lawn. It was an imitation plant, so he knelt down to reassemble it as best he could. Before he could reattach the final limb that had been ripped off, he was hit in the back by another plant. "Take that," Chuck shouted. Standing up, Marc nearly lost his balance. He stammered back into the house and set the plant back where it had been.

"What the fuck are you doing, Marc?"

Marc didn't respond to Chuck, he simply marched out to gather up the second plant. Again, before he could reattach its leaves, the first plant came skidding along again. Marc yelled at Chuck, "Damn you. These are not easy to fix."

Chuck hollered back, "Then stop fixing them, you moron."

"Stop destroying them or I will destroy you."

Before long, it was a full-blown war. The ground forces were marching munitions into the house only to have them ejected back like missiles into the front yard. With each round of fire, the poor plants became more ragged and torn. Eventually Marc resigned the field of carnage. There were broken limbs and foliage lying from the back wall of the house to the middle of the street. There was one plant, however, that Chuck would not abandon. It was a beautiful reddish-pink orchid. It had already been ejected and retrieved several times, but somehow it still possessed a flare. Marc picked it up and carried it toward the house. He set it down and stood guard over it.

"What's your problem?" Chuck asked.

"Whatever you do to this plant, I'll do to you," Marc challenged.

"You can't stand there forever."

"I want this plant saved."

"It's not going to be."

"Zack, do you want this plant saved?" Marc asked.

"I don't care," he said.

"Oh, I thought you cared. I'm sorry." Marc sat back down.

Chuck picked the orchid up and tossed it in the garbage can outside. They opened another bottle of wine and burned through some more tunes. Carla was going to be angry. There were some leftovers in the refrigerator. They would replace Carla's plants. "Pass the crackers, please." "We won't be replacing the orchid." "You're a jackass." "You're a jackass." "See you later." "Goodnight." "Love ya, man."

Marc was stammering again. As he left, he surveyed the carnage over the front yard and picked up the foliage in the street. He dropped it into the garbage can and raised the orchid out. He set it by the front door and started his trek home. Without his car it would only take about thirty minutes, maybe forty walking like this. It was time to think and mumble to oneself.

Chapter 12

The Brensett family referred to this occasion as "the bloom" because spring had prodigiously arrayed their yard in flowering orchids. There were still a few remaining snow-filled crevices in the jutting peaks of the Wasatch Mountains and the gangly trees were budding out. It was a fine day for family gatherings in the diamond district. The Friedmans were cruising with the windows rolled down; Lena was beaming and bouncing in her seat to the sound of the music, singing along and turning to Marc and the kids to pour her heart out on her favorite lines.

"Look kids," she said with overflowing enthusiasm, pointing to the flowers as they approached her parents' house. She was like that. She didn't want to miss a thing and she didn't want those she loved to miss anything either. It didn't matter if it was dolphins or whales, fireworks or falling stars, she made everything seem more amazing—bigger than it really was—even this place. "These are my favorite flowers. We always had so many that no one ever got mad at me for picking them. You can pick some, too. I just have a little advice... Pick the ones farthest from the house and always say to Grandma, 'Look what we got you.' She will smell them and then let you keep them."

Marc smiled. Kimberly ran for the house and Travis ran for the dirt. "Stay out of the mud!" Marc yelled. Travis shifted slightly in his angle of attack, pretending not to hear his dad's injunction.

They approached the front door. Marc put his hand on the handle but rang the bell instead.

"Oh Marc, stop it," Lena said.

"Too late." He laughed.

"I'm serious." She tried to pull his hand off.

"Do you want them to see us fighting when they open the door?"

"Do you want to be pulling on the handle when they try to open the door?"

"Good point," he admitted. He let go and she entered without waiting for someone to answer.

Mrs. Brensett and Melinda were baking in the kitchen. After her mother greeted Lena, she hugged Marc and said, "I'm so glad you could make it. As I recall, you missed last year. Everyone's outside. Help yourself to the refreshments and let me know if there's anything at all that you need," she said with a warm smile. She would make an excellent TV show hostess.

The rest of the family was gathered in the backyard, except the missing boy in the family pictures and Clawson. Angie had recently been married and she was showing off her catch. She was dragging him from sibling to sibling and droning on about her fabulous life in response to their polite questions.

"Here she comes. She's coming, she's coming. Watch out." Marc narrated her approach.

"Be nice, Jack. I mean it, be nice." Lena raised her eyebrow enough to be seen above the rims of her sunglasses.

"I'll be nice, of course, but she won't."

"She's excited, give her this."

Marc didn't have a chance to respond to Lena's last warning, as Angie had already dragged her husband into his bubble. As she and Lena began to catch up, Marc shook her husband's hand. He called Marc by name, but Marc could never get his name to let go of his tongue. They talked about work. If men are talking about work, either they don't care about each other or they don't know enough about each other to discuss anything else. It would be a brighter world indeed if there were a social grace that required that when strangers meet, they are required to take shots together or to ignore each other entirely. Since the former was not an option at such gatherings, nor in any circumstance where more than two Mormons were present, Marc said, "Well, I'm going to get some more lemonade; would you like to come over." Angie's husband politely refused with a pathetic glance to his bride who still held his hand firmly. Marc must have known this, which made it a perfect escape.

As Marc stood next to the lemonade bar, sipping and grazing on cookie crumbs, he was startled by a voice behind him, "Hey man." Clawson was leaning against the wall with one foot resting against the stucco and his hands folded behind him.

"Oh, hi. I was wondering where you were. Back from Europe, I see."

"Yeah. I've just been upstairs."

"What's the matter? Don't you like hanging out with your family?"

"About as much as you do," Clawson answered with a half-smile.

"What do you mean? I adore your family."

"You don't need to lie to me. I know you can't stand them."

Marc laughed. "What do you mean? I've never said anything."

"You don't need to. I'm not stupid, bro. You came over here to avoid talking to my sister. You obviously weren't looking for lemonade and cookies. Frankly, I don't blame you. I've been upstairs avoiding these hypocrites, too."

Marc laughed again. "Well, I guess I'm not so fortunate. I'm kind of expected to be here."

"Okay, but you don't have to be miserable. Should we spike that lemonade?"

Marc laughed. When he could see that Clawson wasn't laughing, he stopped. "Okay, yeah, sure. I'd love something. What do you have?"

"Vodka."

Marc's laughter was becoming cyclical. "Okay, sure. I'd have some."

"Then come upstairs."

"No way, dude, I was just kidding."

"So, you don't want any?"

"Of course I want some."

"Okay, it'd probably be less obvious if you came upstairs to get it."

"Look, I want some, who wouldn't? But I was just calling your bluff."

"I wasn't bluffing."

"Your parents would hate me."

"They already do."

That was all Marc needed to follow Clawson upstairs. "It doesn't smell like Vodka in here." Marc stated the obvious as he entered Clawson's room.

"Oh, I wasn't drinking," Clawson said as a matter-of-fact. He reached into his closet and pulled a bottle out. "I was smoking. I know you prefer whiskey, but this is all I have. Would you rather smoke pot?"

"Absolutely not. This is great, thanks. So, uh, your parents know that you smoke?"

"Oh, they know. I don't hide it, bro."

"How did you know that I prefer whiskey? I don't think we've ever talked about it."

"I know a lot about you. Lena talks to Melinda; Melinda talks to Mom; Mom talks to Dad, and Dad is always ragging on me."

"Ah, I see," Marc said contemplatively. "So you were saying that your parents hate me."

"Oh, for sure."

"They always treat me well," Marc said somewhat puzzled.

"That's for Lena."

"I see. So is it because of my drinking?"

"They don't like that, but no, that's not the main reason."

"Okay, spill the beans, Cloak and Dagger."

"No, I don't think so. I'm curious if you know the reason that they hate you."

"No idea. I mean other than I stole their daughter away and have introduced her to the vices of life."

"That was a fairly minor problem. You work for Dad so it makes him feel like Lena is still under his wing."

"Actually I work *with* your dad. So what then is the major problem?"

"That's what I'm asking you. I didn't take you for a coward…"

"I'm a coward am I?"

"Let's see."

Marc laughed. "Let's see, do they hate me for loving Lena with my heart and soul?"

"Not exactly."

"How do I know that you know anything? You're high, possibly paranoid, and you're using some supposed offense that I've committed to get me to confess something that's none of your business."

"Stay cool, bro. I know it's none of my business. You can do whatever you want." Now Clawson was laughing. "Lena's just my sister, that's all. But you know what?"

"What?" Marc asked a little irritated.

"You're my brother."

"And you're my brother. I just don't care for people meddling in my business, especially when Lena and my family are involved."

181

"I know, man. That's what I love about you. I guess you have good reasons for doing what you're doing."

"What is it exactly that I'm doing?" Marc asked, still a little irritated.

Clawson decided to end the guessing game. "Man, you're seeing another woman."

"Like hell I am," Marc said with fury in his eyes.

"No need to get worked up."

"I'm not worked up…" Marc paused. "Okay, maybe a little, but the fact that I'm still talking to you means that I respect you, not your accusation."

"I get that, bro. So, you're saying that it's a lie?"

"Of course it's a lie. I guess there's a kernel of truth to it, but no I'm not seeing anyone, not like that."

"Then like what?" Clawson asked.

It was several weeks before the bloom. The days were warming up, but the nights were still cold. The moon had gained its ascendency over the shadows and the silvery snow pack on the mountain peaks. Marc was sitting on the couch in his downtown apartment scanning through some documents. It was obvious how much he regarded something by how quickly he read it. If it was inconsequential, he would read forty pages in two minutes. If it was really important, he might take forty minutes to read two pages. There was a knock at the door; it was Franceska. She was the vision of loveliness and the scent of emerging spring which she carried indoors with her from the crisp night outside.

"Oh, hello."

"Hello, Mr. Friedman."

"What can I do for you?"

"I have some papers you wanted to see."

"What papers?"

"Well…" She opened her carrier and reached to pull them out.

"Go ahead and bring them in," he said. He motioned for her to take a seat in the chair next to the couch where he had been sitting. "Sorry about the mess. I've been working. Glamorous, I know. There are a thousand things I'd rather be doing."

"Oh, well, I can deliver these tomorrow."

"No, that's not what I meant. I appreciate you bringing them by."

"You were not expecting them, sir?"

Marc chuckled with a tinge of uncharacteristic embarrassment, possibly intended to set Franceska at ease. "Possibly, let's look at them." She handed them to him. He looked them over for a minute and added, "Thanks. I appreciate you bringing these by."

"You're welcome, sir. Is there anything else I can do for you?"

"I can't think of anything. I appreciate it. May I offer you a drink before you brave the cold?"

"That would be very nice, thank-you."

"I'm drinking Scotch but you'd probably like something else. Do you have a preference?"

"What you're drinking sounds good."

They discussed her girlhood and how she met Marc's cousin, Jason. She grew up in the country near the expansive Lake Balaton. It's a fresh water lake and the largest in Hungary, although only a fraction of the size of the Great Salt Lake. When she came of age she moved to Budapest to take advantage of improving economic conditions. She found, however, that it was much more challenging than she had expected. The country was struggling to recover from the communist policies that had governed them until about 1990. Political jostling led to instability.

The best paying positions were taken by people who were better connected than she. To offset her living expenses, she started as a hostess at a hostel in exchange for room and board. She shared a room with the day hostess. It wasn't anything special, but they became good friends. The living conditions were poor, but the wonderful thing about the hostel was that it offered a sense of community. Travelers would often stay for weeks or months because it was so cheap, and sometimes they would return from visiting other cities. It gave her an opportunity to get to know people really well. For some travelers, she was happy to see them leave, for others she was sad. She had a preference for the Americans. They had an air of possibility about them.

"It looks like you're struggling with that drink," Marc said.

"Oh, yes." She covered her face for a moment. "It's very strong."

"I kind of figured it would be. Would you like something a little more... subtle?"

"That sounds nice. Thank-you."

"Do you have a preference? I feel like I've asked that before."

Franci laughed. "I like vodka."

"Oh, I'm sorry, I don't have any vodka."

"You don't? Okay, anything is fine."

"I'm kidding. I have vodka; I'm just not going to make you a vodka drink."

Franci giggled. "I'll gladly drink anything, sir."

"How about bourbon?"

"I don't know about that, but anything you want, sir. I'll do anything you want."

Marc's eyes surged like small waves as he assessed her intent. "Okay, anything?"

"Yes, anything." Her whole body made her meaning perfectly clear.

"Okay. Do you like strawberries? I just got a package of produce from my farming cooperative in California. The strawberries are delicious."

"Yes, I love strawberries. Do you own a farm in California?"

"Not exactly. I own a share and it pays dividends in produce. It's great. You're welcome to join me at the bar if you'd like."

"That sounds nice. Do you mind if I take my jacket off?" Franceska asked.

"No. I'm sorry, I should have offered. Let me take it for you." Her arms and shoulders were completely bare and the tops of her breasts also to about the height where, no matter how many times a man sees it in the movies, it's always exhilarating when a woman bares them to him. "Make yourself at home," he said.

She followed him to the bar and he set her jacket on the stool next to her.

"You look really nice, Franci. I like the way your lipstick matches your dress."

"Thank-you, Mr. Friedman."

"I told you, call me Marc."

"Yes, sir."

Marc smiled. He pulled the strawberries out of one of three cardboard boxes that were sitting on the counter. Without looking up, he said, "I really like your shoes, too. I've always been a fan of black on black."

"I didn't know you noticed."

Marc then looked into her eyes as far as they invited him to penetrate. "I notice everything." He then tossed some strawberries into the air. "Look at these babies. You have to try one." He washed and dried it and held it out until she took it from his hand. He then proceeded to wash about twelve more. "What do you think?"

"You're right. They're delicious."

He cut the tops off and placed the strawberries in the blender. "Sorry, this thing makes a lot of noise." After he pureed them and scraped the sides several times, he added a little Blanton's and further liquefied them. "I never add water to a puree. I don't like how it dilutes the flavors." He then strained the puree, dipped a spoon in, and handed it to her. "Do you think it needs sugar?"

"Yes, maybe a little," she said as she handed her spoon back to Marc. It had lines on it where the natural crevices of her lips left behind streak of puree on the surface.

"Mind if I check?" She shook her head. He dipped her spoon back into the blender and scraped some of the remaining puree from the side. He licked the spoon clean. "I agree; it needs a little." He shook a little sugar into the mixture and stirred it in with a clean spoon until dissolved. He handed her another taste. "What do you think now?"

"I like it."

He scraped the upper edge of the bowl with her same spoon again and taste-tested it. "Yip, I think so, too." He looked around the kitchen. There were some herbs growing in the window. He muddled a little basil in the bottom of his shaker, filled a rock glass with ice, and dumped it into the shaker. He added 1.5 oz. each of Blanton's bourbon, Cointreau orange liqueur, and strawberry puree. He added a couple dashes of Angostura orange bitters and shook it. He strained it over some fresh ice into the rock glass. "Now for a garnish." He cut off a sprig of the basil and topped the drink with that. "Do you mind if I taste it?" He asked.

"Please do."

"Okay, I might adjust the proportions for the next one, but let me know what you think."

"The next one? Are you inviting me to stay for another drink, Mr. Friedman?"

"It's Marc. Maybe, let's see how it goes."

"It's delicious Mr. Marc." She giggled and he responded with a momentary glare. "What is it called?" She asked.

"I don't know. I just made it up. I thought it would be nice to use some of these fresh ingredients."

"You should give it a name," she said.

"I made it for you; you should name it." He poured himself some bourbon straight. "Let's sit back down."

One day Jason came into the hostel. At first she wasn't attracted to him. There was a small kitchen and combined dining area in the hostel where guests could bring their meals from the nearby shops and markets to eat. Jason seemed to be content with the modest meals which the hostesses ate and he always paid extra to cover the cost. He stayed for about two weeks, so they spoke a lot about America and the world. He had no interest in returning to America, but he was still the most American of all the Americans, whatever that meant. The time came for him to leave. He went around saying goodbye to the other community members. He reached out to shake her hand, but she threw her arms around him, kissed him, and cried. He proposed to stay longer which delighted her. He never left. They were married in Budapest and that's where they stayed until he died.

"Would you like another drink?"

"Yes, Marc. Please." While he was in the kitchen making another drink, she asked, "Where is Mrs. Friedman?"

"She's out of town, but I suspect that you knew that already." Marc handed her the drink and sat back down.

"Yes, I knew."

"I suppose it's not hard to discover her work schedule," he said.

"I was talking with Laura. She told me that you believe in marrying more than one wife."

Marc laughed. "What? No. No. I think what Laura was explaining is that Mormons used to believe that." Marc paused then added, "But not anymore."

"Have I offended you, Mr. Marc, by coming here?"

"No. No, dear Franci. You're a lovely girl; you have not offended me at all—quite the opposite."

"You have been so kind to me. I thought maybe... I thought Laura..." She sat on the verge of tears.

"Come here, Franci." He motioned for her to sit beside him. "I don't know what Laura told you, but it's true that there's a history of this among us. To be honest, I would love to enter into a relationship like this with you. I have grown quite fond of you. I think you're wonderful."

Franci kicked off her shoes and wrapped her arms around him.

He pulled her closer and laid his hand on her knee. "It would require Lena to be in agreement. Do you understand that?" She nodded. He lifted her chin so that he could see into her eyes. "I'm serious. Do you understand?"

"Yes, sir. I love Lena. I don't want to hurt her in any way. I would be blessed to live beside her."

The moon was descending to its resting place, and the city was beginning to stir. Franci was resting in Marc's lap and he was stroking her hair. The bourbon had fulfilled the purpose of its creation and the night had changed them forever.

"Are you awake?" Marc asked.

"Yes."

"Can I make you a coffee? I hate to see you leave, but..." He cut himself off and paused to think. "I knew a professor at the university once who lived polygamy. He's dead now, but his wife might be willing to explain the process to me. I need to talk to Lena, too. There's a lot that needs to be done."

"Thank you, Marc."

"No. Thank *you*." He carried her to the kitchen and set her upon one of the stools. "I'm in the mood for espresso. How about you?"

He narrated the process as he did with the cocktail. The machine was identical to the one he had in Park City. There was so much technique involved that he didn't want the trouble of mastering two different machines. He explained the difficulties associated with using the bottomless type portafilter, how it exposed flaws in the process such as grind coarseness, tamping, and clumping. A pressurized portafilter, by contrast, keeps water in the grounds for the right amount of time to help compensate for flaws and inconsistencies. Franceska yawned.

"Am I boring you?" He asked.

"No, not at all. I never knew there was so much to it. If it's so hard to use, why don't you use a different type?"

"Well, let's see if I can show you. Watch carefully." They were nearly cheek-to-cheek, peering at the machine where the black velvet poured out. "See that? See how the espresso is coming out evenly around the edge? And how it forms a cone? If I don't get that, I can tell what's wrong by simply looking at it. Check out that crema. There's nothing like it." He tamped another shot and hit the switch. "Now see this, it's not coming out evenly. Let's taste them. Do you see how mine is less robust?"

He continued to explain the nuances of temperature, pressure, acidity, and bitterness, but she was crashing. He helped her on with her jacket and embraced her. "How are you getting home?"

"I have a car."

"No. You should take our shuttle. I'll walk you down. Hopefully my nosey neighbors are still in. Where are your kids?" Marc asked apprehensively, possibly ashamed that he had not inquired earlier.

"Laura has them. She wanted to give me a night off."

"So they're at Dad's?"

"No, my place."

"So she was expecting you to be gone all night."

"She told me to take as long as I needed."

"Wow, I'm a little mind-blown right now."

"It's all right. She suggested it. Please don't be mad Mr. Marc."

"I'm not mad, Franci. I'm glad you came."

He escorted her to the front desk. She carried one of the boxes of produce and he carried the other two. "Would you please deliver these with my guest to her residence?" He tipped the driver and thanked him for his discretion.

"Wow, that's freaky," Clawson said. "What did Lena say?"

"She took it surprisingly well. I mean after the initial shock, anyway. I think she's kind of excited, actually."

"Have you talked to the professor's wife, yet?"

"I called her. She didn't want to give me the name of the man who married them until she could talk to all three of us. Edberg told me that she wasn't very happy living in a plural relationship, so I think she's worried about Franci and Lena getting into a situation that they don't really want."

"Dude, she's probably going to try to talk them out of it."

"Maybe."

"Aren't you worried?"

"I wouldn't call it that. I agree with her. We shouldn't do it if we're not really committed to it. I think she just wants to make sure that I'm not pressuring them into it."

"Well, I hope it works out for you. Sounds awesome to me. Crazy awesome."

Marc pulled up behind another car and switched off the ignition. He sat in the driveway for a few minutes taking it all in. The yard was immaculately kept. Fountains of color burst from perennial beds and the grass was cut and tucked in around the edges. "I'm pretty sure she does all of the work around here on her own," Marc told Lena and Franceska.

"She does a really good job," Franceska said.

"Well, are we going to go in?" Lena asked boldly.

"Of course. That's what we're here for," Marc said.

"You don't act like it," Lena said, prodding him to move forward.

"How about you two? Are you ready?" He asked. They both affirmed that they were, so he opened the door and walked toward the front door. Lena and Franceska followed.

"Hello there," Hansa said. "I'm glad you all could make it. Come in and have a seat. I'll be right back."

Marc took his usual seat on the couch next to Edberg's old chair. Lena sat next to him and Franceska took the chair opposite Edberg's. Marc was silent, staring into the cold, dark fireplace. Lena and Franceska were giving off a nervous energy, like two kids on their first date.

Eventually Hansa appeared with tea and homemade morsels of heavenly glory. She served each person according to his or her preference. She then brought another chair from the dining table and sat at the corner of the coffee table, leaving Edberg's seat open.

"I'm sorry. Is this your seat?" Marc asked, sliding to the edge of the couch. He had never been there when Hansa sat down.

"No, not at all. Please be comfortable." She assured him, "This makes it easier for me to serve my guests."

"It's so nice of you to go to all of this trouble," Lena said indicating the tea and refreshments.

"I'm glad you enjoy it. So you are Lena," Hansa said, and turning to Franceska, she said, "You must be Franceska. I'm glad to make your acquaintance. Lena has been here before, but this is the first time that I have met you." She then turned to Marc and continued, "Bobby always spoke so highly of you and your lovely wife. I understand that you are now interested in adding another lady to your family."

Marc looked toward them. Lena said, "Yes," and passed the baton on. Franceska nodded. It was as if the three of them were on trial before an empress; such was her deportment.

"May I ask, was this the first time the three of you have ridden together?" Hansa asked.

"Yes," Marc responded.

"I thought so. Lena, does Marc usually open the door for you when you exit the car?"

"Yes."

"I thought so; I remember it, but he didn't today. I was watching from the window. You waited until Marc had begun walking toward the house to open your own door. Do you know why he did this?"

"He's nervous I suppose."

"Yes, he is, but not because of me. He didn't want to show a preference by opening your door and not Franceska's, or by opening one door before the other. Do you understand, dear?"

"I think so."

"Are you prepared for everything to change?"

"I know there will be a lot of changes."

"Yes, changes that will cause you to question his love, your existence, everything about your life. Actually, these are changes that you can't possibly be prepared for because you've never experienced anything quite so dramatic." She then turned to Franceska. "You're in love. I can see that. I can see that Lena loves you, too. I can see that you have not been with Marc intimately. Do you know how I know this?"

"I don't know, but it's true. We have not been together like that."

"Yes, because Lena still looks at you like a friend. Are you prepared for that to change?"

"I hope it doesn't."

"Oh, it will. You are excited about commencing a life with a man that you love and admire, and you will be very surprised when the woman that you thought was your friend becomes your greatest enemy. You will work very hard to prove your love and devotion to her and you will receive nothing but suspicion and scorn in return. Can you possibly be prepared for that?"

Franceska's face was reddening. She responded in a respectful tone, "Difficulties are part of life, but I believe that Lena and I will always be friends."

"Oh my dear children." Hansa wiped her eyes. "I can see that you are very determined. I will give Marc the information that he requested." She handed Marc a piece of paper that was sitting on the mantel. "Now let us rejoice." She brought a case of wine from the kitchen. She hadn't seen Marc for several years and she wanted him to have it. It was a selection of some of Edberg's favorite wines. He resisted such an extravagant gift, but she insisted that he have it. She also handed him the elephant bookends, saying that she knew how much he liked them. He tried to refuse, but again it was no use, so he asked if they could open one of the bottles of wine to enjoy together.

"Yes, but not one of these. I have a bottle of champagne for such an occasion." She poured out four flutes and offered a toast "to love and courage and unfailing devotion."

Marc also offered a toast "to one of the dearest friends I've ever had, Professor Edberg." They continued through another bottle, asking and answering questions, giving and taking advice. On the way out, Marc said, "Let me open your doors, ladies." They laughed.

Chapter 13

The wintry night fell fast against the western slopes of the Wasatch Range. The tumultuous weather died down and hearthside decorations cast their gauzy-gray puppet friends onto the floor and furniture in rhythm to the voracious flames consuming tinder and coals. Marc seemed mesmerized by these shadows dancing around the room. They were the cheery, playful type, for none could harbor demons when a light like Lena surrounded him. Nevertheless, the grace of Sunday was ending, yielding to the grind of Monday with its cares and woes.

Lena shattered Marc's contemplation. "Well, I better go."

"Why so soon?"

Lena laughed, "It's not 'so soon.' I've been here much longer than I intended. I told Mom I would be back three hours ago."

"I'm surprised she hasn't called. Should we just go pick up the kids and bring them home together?"

Lena pretended to consider the question, but her answer came quickly enough that it was apparent that she had already made up her mind. "I think I need more time."

"Time for what?" Marc asked as if he didn't already know the answer. "Do you realize it's been nearly a year since we visited Hansa?"

"We've already discussed this, Marc."

"Lena. Don't do this, babe."

"You're the one doing this," she snapped back. Her tone turned pleasant again just as quickly. "I love you. I really do, but I need to consider whether I really want this or not. At least you can finish your conversation with Franci without me getting in the way."

"Oh, you're going to be okay with that?"

"I don't know what I'm okay with, but I know I can't stop you."

"How do you know that?"

"I know you, that's how I know."

"Do you know that I love you?"

"I've got to go, Marc."

"Okay, just give me one more kiss."

"Marc."

"What?"

"You know what."

"It's just a kiss."

"And then what?"

"Then nothing. A kiss."

She rolled her eyes at him, but nonetheless she reached up and gave him a peck.

"What was that?" He asked.

"A kiss."

"No it wasn't. This is a kiss." Marc took her in his arms as a blacksmith takes an iron and the hotter he gets it, the more it bends to him. He had an audience in the fireplace, which clapped and cheered for him. Lena was malleable and responded with a subtle glow and sighs. Marc's hands carried his promise of "just a kiss" as far as they could without turning it into an outright lie.

He picked up her bags, walked her to the car, and opened her door. He swept his fingers over the nape of her neck and dug them into her hair. Lena kissed him back, but whatever he was hoping for, she didn't allow him to take it there.

"See you soon," he said. She smiled back; she wasn't making any promises. He opened the garage door and she drove away.

"Hey!" He shouted and whistled. She stopped and he ran after her. "I forgot my photograph," he said with a mischievous grin. If the dove which bore an olive leaf back to Noah had fully understood how it cheered Noah's heart, it couldn't have produced a greater sense of hope than the expression on Lena's face did when she clicked the rear door open. Marc retrieved the photo and closed the door. "Thanks," he said.

"You're welcome. See you soon," she said and then drove off.

Marc placed the photo back in his display case within the walk-in closet. Lena hadn't brought any bags back with her the day before, which meant that she left in a rush or she fully intended to return for her things. He looked through the drawers and hangers on her side. There were still so many articles left behind that it would require a perfect memory of the contents of her closet in order to determine what she packed into those bags that he carried out for her. He looked into the hamper and found the underwear and clothes that she was wearing when she returned. What did that mean, or did it mean anything at all? He had a puzzled look on his face.

He sat back on the couch where he was when Lena burst in the previous day. He called Franceska.

"Hello."...

"No, she's gone; she went back to her parents' place."...

"Yes and no. We had a big blowout, but we were able to work some things out. We actually had a good time after the... the freaking volcano, or whatever. I think she'll come around, I really do."...

"Absolutely not! Do you?"...

"Okay, then don't worry about it. Let me work this thing through. We're not going to wait forever. As long as we're progressing, then I'll keep working with her, but if she's dead set against it, we'll just go ahead."...

"It's not what anybody wants. I wish we all could be one happy family, but I'm not the same man that I was. This—

you and this whole experience has changed me forever; I'm never going back to what I was before."...

"It's just that I felt blind. Well, I didn't feel blind at the time, but looking back on it, I see things so much more clearly now. It's one of those things that I will always appreciate about Lena; she saw something in me before I could see it myself. She believed in me when no else did."...

"She was incredibly courageous; she would challenge norms with impunity."...

"I mean she didn't worry about what other people thought and she couldn't be accused of being rebellious or mean because she did everything with so much intelligence and love and,... I don't know. It's like this date I took her on."...

Lena came skipping out of her parents' home and landed into Marc's car. She knew that he hated coming to the door, so she saved him the trouble of enduring the hospitality and concomitant scrutiny of her family by watching for him at the window. Her animation and enthusiasm at being with him raised his spirits. She only witnessed the upper echelons of his mood because it began improving before he pulled into her driveway and accelerated upward when she emerged from the house before he even came to a complete stop.

"Where are we going?" She asked.

"It's a surprise," he said.

"Oh, I love surprises."

"It's going to take a little while to get there. That's why I wanted to leave early, he said. Is it okay with your parents if we're gone a little longer than usual?"

"I asked if I could leave early, so I'm assuming so."

After he pulled onto the serpentine route along the base of the mountains, he said. "There's something I've been meaning to ask you." She looked at him with eyes as wide as any subject, so he continued, "I've been wondering why you invited Laura and me over to your place that night, the foosball night. I mean, Laura said that you two were at a party together, but you never really met, and I assume you had no idea who I was."

Lena started laughing. "Yeah. I didn't know either of you before that night."

"Well, it makes sense that Laura would be invited, because you're both friends of Ashley, but I have no idea why I was invited. I don't think Ashley even likes me."

"Yeah, she definitely doesn't like you. I guess she doesn't think you deserve me, or whatever. She's such a snob. She said that you were staring at me in the student union building. It irritated her, but I thought it was cute."

"Well, that's embarrassing. You knew that I was watching you? We never made eye contact!"

"I know, but Ashley was describing you the entire time."

"So you all were laughing at me?"

"Kind of. Well, not exactly. We were arguing about whether to wave at you or not. Ashley wanted to, like to make fun of you or whatever, and I said 'let's just go talk to him.' When I decided to invite you to that party, Ashley refused to come."

"Really? Well, like I said, I didn't think she liked me."

"And like I said, she's a snob so I don't think we're going to be friends anymore. All she cares about is status. The only thing that she could say about you was that you don't go to church."

"Speaking of church," Marc said as if he had been waiting for an opportunity to breach a particular subject, "it was pretty obvious that that return-missionary-what's-his-name was intended for you. Everyone but Clawson was encouraging him."

"Oh, Brock? Yeah, he was nice, but not really my type. I didn't invite him."

"What's your type?"

"I don't know how to describe it, really. I guess it's not a type, it's a person—a particular person. I can't really explain it, but I'll know him when I see him."

Marc left it there; he didn't press his bet. They drove through Park City and began climbing the mountainside past the end of a paved road onto a graveled surface. Aspen trees were quaking in the breeze. The snow had disappeared from the peaks and ski slopes, but there was only about an hour of daylight left, so it was a little chilly.

"What's that?" Lena asked pointing to an old dilapidated building. It was quite large and with its nine or ten levels of tiered ruins that were piled upon a receding hillside, it resembled the bones of a fallen dinosaur, suspended forever as it stretched to reach for salvation from an impending doom. The roof was rusted and large sections of it had caved in. There were a few remaining panes of glass clinging to their frames, but there were many more that had succumbed to the ravages of time or to shooters who had shattered them for target practice.

"It's an abandoned mine," Marc said.

"Is that where we're going?" Lena asked with a tinge of reluctance, as if Marc had asked her to touch some dubious creature, not knowing if it was venomous or not.

"No, but we can if you want."

"Oh, no, that's fine."

Marc laughed at Lena's air of relief. "I've been there before. It's mostly just a garbled mess of junk metal and glass. There wouldn't really be anywhere to set up our picnic."

"Oh, we're having a picnic?" Lena asked with glee.

"Yes, and here we are." Marc parked the car in a grove of trees, where it was barely visible from the road. "It's just a little hike down from here." Marc opened the trunk to pull out their provisions. He had a small cooler, some blankets, a backpack, two helmets, and two long ropes.

"What are those for?" Lena asked pointing to the ropes.

"Don't worry; I'm not going to tie you up."

"I didn't think so," Lena said with a sparkle in her eye.

"They're for rappelling," Marc answered nonchalantly.

"Rappelling? You didn't tell me we were rappelling!"

"I know; I said it was a surprise."

"Well I'm certainly surprised."

"Good, it worked then."

"I've never done this before."

"I was hoping you hadn't. I wanted to treat you to something that you've never done before, and don't worry, I'll make sure you're safe," Marc said deeply into her eyes.

"I'm not even dressed for this," Lena gently protested.

"Oh, you'll be fine. Besides, it's not long."

"Where are we rappelling? I don't see anywhere."

"Just down this small ravine, there's a mineshaft."

"A mineshaft?!"

"Yeah, stop worrying. I'll show you how. Are you ready?" He asked.

"I guess so. I trust you," she said.

"You should," he said into her eyes again. "Do you mind if I strap you in?" He asked.

"Please do."

Marc wrapped the belt of her harness around her waist and adjusted the length for a snug fit. He then said, "I need to gather your skirt around your thighs, okay?" She consented. She gasped, though, when his hands brushed the inside of her thigh as he strapped and adjusted the leg loops. "Okay is that comfortable?" He asked. She nodded affirmatively as she bit her lip. He showed her how to control her descent and finished off with, "Okay, we better get going, it's going to be dark soon." They hiked down the ravine to a large rock leaning against another rock. Between them was an opening into darkness. It was a naturally formed cavity into the mineshaft below. Marc explained that all of the man-made entrances were sealed off. He laughed it off when Lena asked him if he didn't think that they were sealed for a good reason.

Marc tied off the tops of their ropes and strapped on their headlamps. They tied the cooler and blankets to the bottom ends and lowered them into the shaft. When the provisions came to a rest at the bottom, he said, "Looks like about forty feet. I'll go first; it's pretty tight at the beginning." He descended about eight or ten feet and then said, "Okay, I'll wait for you here. Go ahead."

"I'm not going to lie, this is kinda scary," she said.

"Don't worry, just take your time. I'm right here and I have plenty of traction so I can catch you if anything goes wrong."

"Alright, I'm trusting you."

"You should." He coached her on. "You're doing great. Take it easy. Watch your head. A little to your right." Eventually she nestled into his arms. He held her tight. "Do you feel safe?"

"Yes," she said.

"Okay. You got past the bravest part, which is getting started, but this part is going to feel scarier because there's less to hold on to. The opening is going to widen until we reach the full mining shaft. Eventually we'll be side-by-side. Just do what I do. Are you ready?"

"Well, I came this far, didn't I?"

"Yes, you did. Alright here we go. We're almost to the mining shaft where we'll rappel side by side." The cavity opened up into smooth surfaces where miners had chased a vein of silver ore many years prior. The sky, though dimming from the falling sun, seemed brilliant from below the earth's surface. Light from the narrow opening above illuminated floating dust in glowing ribbons. Lena shrieked with nervous delight. They descended about another thirty feet to the bottom of an intersecting horizontal tunnel. It was considerably larger and exhibited intricate mineral patterns on the walls.

"This is so cool," Lena shrieked again.

"I'm glad you like it," Marc said. "A little more fun than sitting and listening to Edberg and me drone on about the cosmos, isn't it?"

"That was fun, but yes, this is utterly unbelievable."

Marc removed Lena's harness as she continued to search her surroundings by darting her headlamp around. He found a smooth spot and laid down the blankets between two rusty old rails, "By now we probably still have about 40 minutes of light left, right?"

"I guess so; do we have time to eat?" Lena asked.

"Oh, I'm not afraid of eating in the dark. There's something else I wanted to show you."

She followed him down the tunnel. It was in good shape with very little collapse. They came to an intersection and followed to the left down a timbered tunnel. To this point, the tunneling had sheer rock surfaces in good solid condition. The timbering was also in good condition, but it signified less stable rock formation. The last twenty feet contained some broken timbers and beyond that was some heavy collapse. Marc stopped Lena about twenty feet before the first broken timber, where it was still solid and safe.

Marc said, "About ten years ago, I carved all of my sins on one of those timbers down there. Well, my worst sins anyway, the ones I was really ashamed of. It was kind of a confession. I wanted to get it as close to the rubble as possible; I wanted it to be buried deep in the earth when the mine eventually collapsed. At the time, it seemed significant that I was risking my life to put it there. It just seems stupid now."

"It doesn't seem stupid to me," Lena said, shining her headlamp onto his face.

"Well, if it's still there, you can read it. The only problem is, I promised I would keep you safe, so I'll go first to see if it's buried, yet."

Lena took Marc's hand. "I don't want to know your sins, but I'll go wherever you go."

He explained that he had carved it on the last unbroken lintel, just above eye level, while standing on rubble from the collapsing tunnel. With trepidation, they approached the last unbroken beam. His confession wasn't there, which meant that either they had taken the wrong tunnel, or the earth already had claimed his shame.

"Well, there you go, it's buried, past and gone," Lena said in a reassuring tone, as if narrating the end of a story that she didn't want to pursue any further.

"Or we took the wrong tunnel," he said.

"I don't think we should go searching for it. It's late and this looks dangerous."

"I agree, besides, I'm pretty sure this is the right spot. I wonder how far buried it is." He stood there for a moment looking into the rubble as if he could see into a stone.

"What are you doing?" Lena asked in alarm after Marc approached the collapsing section and began climbing up onto the rubble.

"I'm just going to look around. It might be just below the surface."

"Let it go, Marc. You got what you wanted; it's gone."

"I know. I just have to make sure. I don't know why."

"You're scaring me."

Marc didn't respond, but continued lifting rocks away. "Here it is." Marc retrieved a splintered piece of timber about five or six inches square and about twice as long. He rubbed off the debris and blew away the dust which obscured his carved words. Some of the words were indecipherable and some were missing where they had run past the end of the board. For several minutes, he sat on a pile of silver ore and reviewed his dark deeds. He smirked at some and grimaced at others. Finally he asked, "So do you want to see it?"

"Yes," Lena said urgently without moving any closer to the heap he was sitting on. Marc chuckled as he climbed down and handed her the timber. She tucked it under her arm without looking at it and said, "Can we go back now?"

"Back home?" He asked bewildered.

"No, to our picnic. You're not getting rid of me that easily."

"What are you doing?" Marc asked.

"Oh you can rummage through rocks, but I can't gather a little fire wood?" She asked playfully. "I'm cold and I assume that you packed s'mores."

"Actually, I didn't but I do have matches and a hatchet in my pack."

"Well, I guess a girl can't have everything."

"I'm willing to test that theory," he said. They both laughed.

She took his hatchet and built a fire under the shaft they rappelled through. Once she had it lit, she placed Marc's confession face down into the fire. "So did you even look at it?" Marc asked.

"No. I told you, it's in the past. All I care about is where we're going from here." Lena used the plural pronoun. Perhaps it was an invitation to Marc to press his bet. Perhaps it was a condescension, instead. Blasted uncertainty.

Marc continued cautiously. "Reading that timber, I realized that what I once thought was sin was really just nature and naiveté. It felt weird seeing it. Like, I was seriously face-palming myself."

"No need to worry about it anymore. It's soon to be ashes and dust," she said.

"When I wrote it, I was really struggling with doubts about my faith. I guess I'm still struggling, but I'm a lot less concerned about what I'm doing wrong now and a lot more concerned about what I'm doing right."

"What do you think is right?"

"Right is whatever leads to happiness, to love, to growth and advancement and prosperity, for ourselves and for others, now and forever." Marc answered with certainty, as if he had thought about it before and had already arrived at a conclusion.

"That's something I believe in," Lena said. "I could be part of that."

"So yip, that was the first time we made love," Marc summarized the rest of the date for Franceska. "She had more confidence in me than any person I had ever known. She made me feel like I could do anything. That's the remarkable power and influence that a good woman can have on a man."...

"See, that's what I mean. I can never go back to what I was before. Going through this process with you and Lena has expanded my life and my thinking in ways that, uh... Well, it's like this. For a long time I was a dot, just a single point—with no dimension. Then I met Lena and she extended me. When you extend a point, it makes a line segment, which is one-dimensional. She made me feel like I had become infinitely more than I was before. Then *you* came into our lives and you're nudging us sideways into another direction. When you move a line sideways, you get two dimensions, like a square. A square can't revert to a line segment without diminishing to comparatively nothing. You see, squares have area, but line segments don't. Shit. I'm sorry for always explaining things so mathematically. I'm probably boring you."...

"Oh my darling, you move me. You move me into... into existence. That sounds lame, but..."...

"Well, to lose that I'd be sinking into oblivion, and I just can't do that. I'm fighting for survival. I need Lena *and* I need you. Without you both, I can't feel whole. I will not give up on this soul, this flesh and bone that we're creating, that's emerging from..." Marc paused. He was straining to put a word to an idea—an idea that was growing. "That's emerging from intangibles!" He seemed satisfied with that term. "It's the most incredible thing that I've ever experienced."...

"I agree. Franci, I hope you'll continue this process with me. I feel like a little bird, a chick that's peeking out of its shell for the first time, that's hearing unmuffled sounds and seeing distinct shapes for the first time. I want to explore! I want to taste the full spread, the worm and the seed. I want to fly and see the bright new world. I want to build something and perch on top. I know that there will be pain along the way, just like Hansa said, but sometimes pain makes me feel alive!"...

Marc laughed. "I know. I'm a mess, an ambitious, tossed up mess. Will you clean me up, sweet Franci?"...

"Good. It melts me to hear you say that."...

Marc laughed again. "I guess we can be a puddled up mess together then."...

Marc launched back into his comparison of plural marriage and projective geometry. If a square is lifted, it sweeps out a three dimensional cube. Considering the reverse, however, if a light shines on a cube, it projects a square. In every instance, the lower dimensional shape is merely the shadow of the larger shape: a square is the shadow of a cube, a line the shadow of a square, and a point the shadow of a line. A shadow of something is nothing compared to the thing itself. In essence, then, a solid was born from points and intangibles.

The idea excited Marc and he zealously labored to convey his vision to Franceska. Each person in the relationship was a point and the reaching toward other points with intangibles, such as love, created a solid object, a transcendent soul, and souls are precious.

"What?"...

"Oh, yeah." Marc laughed. "We got out of the mine safely enough. She was so freaking cute. I sent her up first and followed closely behind for backup. I confessed that I could see up her skirt a little. She said that she wasn't in a position to do anything about it at the moment and she invited me to enjoy the show. We were definitely different people who came out of that mine than who went into it."...

Lena's clothes were wrinkled and dirty and her hair was all messed up from the equipment and from climbing through narrow openings. "What are you going to tell your parents?" Marc asked. She was an adult, but in her culture, unmarried children were closely accountable to their parents regardless of their age, and they were strictly expected to marry within the faith, too.

Heber J. Grant, seventh president of the church, whose tenure spanned the twenty-six years prior to the invention of the atomic bomb, taught that any true church believer would "rather bury a son or a daughter than to have him or her lose his or her chastity." It was a two millennia old idea, however, tracing back to at least as early as Plutarch's description of Spartan women telling their sons to "come back with [their] shield - or on it." Indeed, the greatest virtue for a Spartan man was to die in battle and for a Spartan woman, to bury her heroically fallen son. The sentiment is probably as old as values that must be forcefully thrust onto children in order to ensure their continuation in the earth. In a letter to his son circa 1800, William Fey, an English surgeon, wrote, "My fond wishes would fain see an amendment in your sister's health, but her removal hence will only be the speedier possession of eternal glory. I would rather bury all my children, than see them departing from the way of truth and righteousness." Once this idea reached America, it appeared mainly in the pitiable expression of a parent's sincere desire to see his or her child avoid a fate worse than death, such as marrying into wretched conditions or enduring a harsh subsistence or occupation.

Heber J. Grant may have intended it in a similar tone, but once it became fully assimilated into the Mormon collective, the expression lost all fondness as it took on a threat-like fierceness as a deterrent to children dabbling in unsanctioned relationships. It became the mantra of the most pious parents, who embellished it with morbid frills and codicils intended to compel their children to lives of faithfulness and sexual purity, even after the parent's own departure from this life. It succeeded in convincing some that their parents might actually kill them, either from this side of the veil or beyond, in order to prove the sincerity of their holy injunctions.

Lena looked down, brushed some wrinkles and dirt out of her skirt, and straightened her hair in the passenger side mirror. Then she said, "I'll tell them the truth, of course...that we did a little hiking."

Marc said, "The younger generation never lies to the older generation as much as the older generation lies to the younger."

"Lying less didn't make it right, but it didn't entitle them to the truth, either," Marc told Franceska. "It's hard to dismiss their methods entirely, though. Mormon kids are some of the finest specimens of innocence and virtue I've ever known. Lena managed to make it to the age of twenty as a virgin and she was one of the most beautiful girls in the valley. I told her that as far as I'm concerned, she was still a virgin. She didn't lose anything that she gave to me. I'll always keep it and cherish it.".....

"No. I guess what I'm saying is that virginity is an intangible. If a person cares for it, then it can't be taken away. Rape doesn't take it away. Judgment doesn't. Nothing does as long as it's regarded by the person to whom it belongs. It can be shared, though, and used to fill in the gaps between people. I'm all about filling in the gaps.".....

Franceska needed to take care of one of the kids so they ended their conversation. He told her that he couldn't wait to see her in the morning; he was in no condition to drive to the valley that night. It was late, but Marc wasn't tired. He had drunk enough wine that it was calling the shots. Going to bed would be the prudent thing to do, but prudence is overrated. Insight, understanding, and the extraordinary—these are the gems that wine dangles before the eyes of the inebriated. He'd be alright in the morning, but if not, Monday could go to hell.

Chapter 14

Marc awoke to his phone vibrating on the stand next to him. He ignored it. His ears perceived the morning before his eyes could. He resisted the tug of the wakeful world for about twenty minutes or so, but the frequent interruption of his phone made it increasingly unlikely that he would win. Finally, he grabbed it like he was wrapping his fist around the neck of a snake and confronting it face to face. He had missed his alarm and there was a mix of texts and missed calls from Franceska, from Tara, and even from Chuck. What in hell had raised its head? He was able to ascertain that there was an armed security guard in the office.

Marc didn't bolt from bed. Being in a rush wouldn't change anything. He sat up and massaged his shoulders and neck instead. The glass on the stand still held wine from the previous night. A maroon ring like a devil's halo had formed above the surface of the wine where some had evaporated. The drips which had dried from his lips around the rim looked something like wrath raining from above. Marc rolled his eyes and scoffed at it. He dragged himself into the kitchen, filled a large glass with ice water, and washed some ibuprofen down his dry throat. He then buried his face into cupped hands where he collected some cold grace from the running faucet.

Nature is always on standby like that to ease the suffering of bad decisions. Nature is unquenchable love—not the rocks and the trees particularly, nor the oceans and the covering of the great blue sky, but rather the elements and the forces which constitute the mundane everything. Nature does not punish nor does it hate. It does not judge. Gravity does not punish those who fall and break their bones. It simply keeps them planted on the earth where they can prosper and grow.

He retreated to the closet where he unclothed himself and engaged in a brief but scathing face-off in the mirror. He was obviously not pleased with the consequences of his excessive drinking. He stepped into a tiled surround and turned the knob. It was that effortless, but the elements of nature generously responded with bursting streams and a torrent of comfort washed over him. Nature was kind.

It was rude of him to leave the people hanging for so long who were anxious to get into contact with him, but he clearly needed this time. It was going to be a rough day and rough days require ample preparation. It wasn't until he had taken a long shower, fully dressed, eaten breakfast, and inhaled the frigid mountain air from the back patio with a cup of joe, that he finally returned his first text: "I'm coming in." It was a terse reply but probably sufficient for those who were concerned.

The sky was clear and the sun brightly illuminated the newly laid cover of snow. It was going to be a great day for skiers and snowboarders. Marc was late and the slopes were already spotted with enthusiasts trying to carve up some unsullied terrain before their competition did.

There was a strip of interstate between Summit County and the Salt Lake Valley where travelers transitioned between looking down onto the atmospheric inversion and being smothered by it. If it was really bad, then one could not see the city below until one had descended below the layer of dismal, smoggy haze. Often a snowstorm would cleanse the air by pulling the filth into the streets and streams below. It wasn't good for the streams but they all eventually emptied into the Great Salt Lake where nothing could live anyway. Therefore, of all places to pollute, this was the place. The inversion was still dense and gray, indicating that the snowstorm had mainly dumped on the boundary of the basin and left the inhabitants of the valley to see the light another day.

Marc was intercepted in the main lobby by an attorney and two armed men. "Good morning, Mr. Friedman. My name is Jeff Greenwald. I'm representing the board of directors. They sent me to execute security measure…"

"Let's discuss this in private, shall we?"

"Of course," Jeff replied.

The three of them followed Marc into the elevator. After exiting, he took the most direct route to his office. Tara, his secretary, was visibly shaken, but she seemed relieved to see Marc approaching. There were two additional armed men flanking his office door. Marc was stunned to see the woman who was sitting beside them in the reception area, and he nearly came to a complete halt. Chuck was waiting impatiently and he jumped up to meet the approaching party; it was a good cover for Marc's astonishment at seeing the woman. "This is my attorney," Marc told Jeff. They shook hands.

The woman stood up and approached the group. "This is Ms. Albrecht," Jeff said to Marc. "She works with our firm doing information and systems audits."

"Hello Ms. Albrecht, it's nice to meet you," Marc said calmly, having recovered from the initial shock of seeing her.

"Nice to meet you, too," she replied. Neither she nor Marc acknowledged that they had previously met or had known each other. This was Amy Albrecht, Marc's doctoral research colleague from the university.

"I didn't realize that systems audits were accompanied with guns." Marc directed his response to Jeff by turning in his direction, while keeping his eyes on Amy until finished with his sentence.

"I thought you wanted to discuss it in private," Jeff said.

"Yes, right." Marc motioned the group into his office. He, Amy, the two attorneys, and the two armed men from the lobby entered together while the two men who flanked the door remained at guard.

"Please remain standing," Jeff told Marc who was approaching his desk.

"I'll just go ahead and sit at my desk," Marc said.

"I'm afraid you won't," Jeff said as he motioned one of the security guards. "As I'm sure you are aware, as a private contractor for the defense department, this company operates under approved security measures in order to facilitate the safety of its assets and the peaceful removal of any officer deemed," he read from some papers he was carrying, "of any officer deemed a security threat to the company, or if deemed hostile to the United States or any state, or to the American people."

"I'm a threat?" Marc asked skeptically.

"The board held an emergency hearing last night. An initial statement of their reasons is given here; a follow-up statement will be issued within ten days." Jeff handed some papers to Marc who glanced at them and passed them to Chuck.

"This doesn't say anything other than the board, 'believes that a credible concern exists.'" Chuck baulked. "That's a bunch of bullshit. You may as well say he's being disciplined for the length of his hair."

"The board isn't required to give any further details until the follow-up statement," Jeff said. He turned to Marc and continued, "You are permitted to gather your personal items. The board's representation has the right to inspect any items or information removed from this office or the premises during this procedure. You are not being permanently dismissed at this time; you are being placed on administrative leave with full pay and benefits. A permanent decision, if deemed necessary, will be pending. You should know within ten days, as I said, but there's no deadline for dismissal."

"May I sit now?" Marc asked with a tinge of defiance.

"Yes, I'm sorry. I simply needed to put you on notice before you touched anything or accessed any information networks. Ms. Albrecht and I will be observing until you have finished collecting anything you need. Do you have any questions?"

"Do I?" Marc asked Chuck.

"It's a very heavy handed way of dealing with someone," Chuck said.

"I apologize," Jeff said. "We're simply following the protocol."

"I understand," Marc said. "Well, let's get started." He seemed to be in higher spirits than he had been since he spoke with Franceska over the telephone the previous night. He collected his books, his elephant bookends, some magazines, some notebooks, some artwork and photos, and some other miscellaneous items. With each item, Jeff picked it up and looked under it, over it, and through it for anything that may have constituted a security breach. When he came to the notebooks, he was extra cautious since they were really the only items that could have possessed proprietary information.

"What are these?" Jeff asked.

"Notes from college," Marc said.

"What are they here for?" Jeff asked.

"Don't you think that it would be useful to occasionally refer to my notes in work as technical as what we do here?" Marc asked.

Jeff flipped through them. "It's 'Greek to me.'" He handed them to Amy. "What do you make of them?" He asked. She inspected them thoroughly. At one point, she allowed an unguarded smile to surface. "What is it?" Jeff asked.

Amy seemed flustered, almost imperceptibly. "Oh, I just noticed where, ah, where he got really frustrated with a problem he was working on and started scribbling."

"May I see it?" Jeff wasn't taking anything for granted. Amy folded the notebook in half so that only one page was showing. "Ah, I see. I would be frustrated, too. Math was never my thing," Jeff said as he handed the notebook back to Amy. Scattered throughout its pages were notes and comments from Amy when they worked together in college. More than just a few were flirtatious. With as thoroughly as she was inspecting the notebook, it was certain that she would find them. It must have been the real reason that she smiled.

"They look like typical grad-level notes to me. I don't see anything proprietary here," Amy said.

Marc responded, "Alrighty, then. I guess I need to collect my personal files now. Is it okay to login?"

"Protocol requires that you keep personal files on a personal computer," Jeff said.

Marc said, "Yes, I know, but let's face it, everyone uses work computers for personal use. Don't tell me that you've never downloaded a family photo or typed a personal document on your work computer."

"I'm not telling you that I haven't and I'm not telling you that I have." Jeff maintained his unflinching persona.

"Look, I kept all of my personal files in something like five local folders. I don't even need to access the network. You two can look over my shoulder and check everything I do."

"Alright. Login and locate the files you wish to take. Save them on a separate flash drive. We will analyze the files and if there's nothing out of sorts, we'll turn them over. Be advised that your network security clearance has already been suspended and the IT department keeps records of all network access requests to classified information."

"You got it. Thanks." Marc called Tara and requested a clean flash drive. He copied the contents of several folders to the flash drive and handed it to Jeff. Jeff then handed it to Amy.

Marc thanked Tara for everything and expressed his desire to return soon. "Batten down the hatches," he told her reassuringly. He carried his things into the elevator and emerged again from the elevator on the eighteenth floor outside of his apartment. Sometimes a person can travel between two points and have no recollection of anything in between. Intense mental focus often accompanies the condition. It is as if the space and time between the two points were wadded up tight, and lit like a paper used to start a flame. It could lead a person to question the sovereignty of nature, for there is no evidence that anything but that all-consuming thought existed between A and B.

Marc walked to the apartment door, set the box containing his personal items down, and pulled his key card out. When the door was open, he slid the box inside with his leg, kicked it to the side, and then fell onto the couch. After some more space and time were wadded up and burned, he called Franceska.

"Hey, gorgeous."…

"Sorry about that. Yeah, I'm alright."…

"I've been put on administrative leave."…

"I didn't want to go traipsing through the office with security guards."…

"Can you come up for lunch? I'll explain then."…

"Okay, see you soon. Just relax. Everything will be alright."…

There was a knock at the door. Marc checked the peephole and opened the door. Chuck stormed in.

"So what was that all about?" Chuck demanded.

"Just what they said; you know as much as I do," Marc said nonchalantly.

"I'm sure I don't. What did you do?"

"Nothing."

"Four armed guards, an attorney, and an IT forensic don't descend all at once for nothing."

"Fine." Marc paused. "As you know, my father-in-law, Daniel Brensett, and his cronies have a controlling interest in LogicStream. This is nothing other than a tactic to manipulate me into…" Marc cut himself off.

"Into what?" Chuck insisted.

"I don't want to tell you," Marc laughed.

"This is no laughing matter. I'm your attorney. How can I help you if you don't tell me what's going on?"

"You can't help me, Chuck. Daniel's just trying to put my balls in a vice. Nothing short of handing over my gonads will satisfy him."

Chuck looked at him as if he was losing his patience.

Marc burst out, "He thinks I'm cheating on Lena. And he's giving me ten days to abdicate my manhood."

"Are you? Cheating on Lena, I mean. We all know you abdicated your manhood years ago." Chuck smiled. Even in an intense situation, he couldn't refrain from talking shit.

"No. Not really. Well, in his mind, maybe. I'm sort of involved with another girl, like I'm trying to marry her."

"How is that not cheating?" Chuck was visibly irritated.

"Because I haven't had sex with her." Marc paused. "And I'm not leaving Lena," he said intensely.

"So you're a goddamned polygamist?"

"Not yet, but I'm working on it."

"Oh, this is worse than I thought. It'd be easier to defend you against fraud or embezzlement."

"Yeah, you see my problem?"

"Polygamy is a felony, you idiot! And because of your security measures, you don't have to actually be guilty; you only have to be considered susceptible to guilt."

"Exactly," Marc said with a tone of finality. "You seem disappointed that I'm not a fraud."

Chuck ignored Marc's jest. "How long has this been going on?" He asked bewildered.

"I met her a little over a year ago."

"How have I not known this? I'm your best friend."

"Like you said, it's a felony, and I knew you wouldn't approve."

"Damn right I don't approve! It was a bad idea to get married in the first place and now you want to compound your mistake by doing it again—simultaneously!"

"See what I mean?" Marc rolled his eyes.

"What did you expect?" Chuck thundered back. "This is the dumbest damn thing you've ever done. You're going to lose Lena. You know that, right?"

"No. I don't think that's a foregone conclusion. She's been with me every step of the way."

"Utah's new anti-polygamy law makes the women felons, too. Not just the men. There's no way that her family is going to tolerate this. They're gonna crucify you, man!" Chuck said imploringly.

"Perhaps," Marc said thoughtfully. "We've survived their meddling in the past."

"This is nothing like the past, Marc. This is suicide. Besides, I thought you gave up on all of that Mormon shit."

"I'm not doing this as a Mormon. They don't do polygamy anymore," Marc said.

"Right, but they hate it worse now than their own enemies hated it before."

"That's why Daniel's squeezing me, treating me like a scoundrel for doing something that his grandfather did openly and honorably."

"If you're not doing it as a Mormon, then what are you doing it as?"

Marc pulled into a suburban driveway. It wasn't far from Edberg's home. "What is this, a polygamous neighborhood?" Marc asked himself aloud. The style of the home was similar to Edberg's, but in its condition, it needed some repair and the landscaping wasn't as neatly kept. He opened up the slip of paper that Hansa had given him when he, Lena, and Franceska visited her together. It bore the name Joe Bower with phone number and street address. He compared the house numbers. He took a deep breath and approached the home. A man in his seventies, possibly in his sixties considering his apparent good health, answered the door. He was wearing dark, pleated suit pants with a crisp white full-length shirt and black suspenders.

"Hello, my name is Marcellus Friedman."

"Yes, come in. I've been expecting you. I'm Brother Bower. Have a seat, please."

The interior was dated but clean and tidy. The entry was large enough for formal entertaining; it had two doors leading into other areas but they were closed. There were photos of men and women hanging on the walls, most of them in black and white. One considerably large matted frame displayed a series of men, about a dozen in all, arranged neatly in rows, and all in black and white.

The only electric light was a six-foot floor lamp next to the chair in which Brother Bower sat. Beside it also stood a small reading stand with several stacks of books and pamphlets. In spite of the lack of indoor lighting, the room was well lit by the south facing windows which, although they were heavily draped on both sides and covered with sheers in the middle, admitted considerable light owing to their size and the summer months which had arrived.

Two walls were covered with white-on-white wallpaper exhibiting an intricate leaf-and-vine pattern. The only trim was a four-inch, white crown molding with golden accents. The shag carpet was from a bygone decade. It was brown and gold in undulating colors and it appeared to be clean even though it showed signs of heavy wear. The house was quiet and Marc didn't do anything to disturb the peace.

Brother Bower didn't seem to mind the silence. He didn't behave as if he was waiting for Marc to begin the conversation. He was looking at one of the photos on the wall in a blank stare, like it was merely a point upon which to rest his eyes; his mind seemed to be somewhere else.

Finally Brother Bower turned to Marc and said, "So you know Sister Edberg?"

"Yes. You mean Hansa? Yes. Well, not very well, but I knew her husband quite well."

"Oh, how did you know him?"

"I worked with him for about year at the university, but I maintained a friendship with him until he died. He was a great mentor. Hansa was quite reserved, so I never really had much to do with her."

Brother Bower chuckled, "Yes, that's Hansa alright. I've known her since she first came here from Asia, I don't remember which part." He paused as he was trying to recall the name of the country.

"Thailand," Marc said.

"Yes, Thailand. That's right. Dr. Edberg asked me to help with her. I recall that he had a little trouble convincing her to join his family, but she's been a faithful member of the group since she gained her testimony of the principle. She's a good woman."

"May I ask what you mean by 'the group' and 'the principle'?" Marc inquired.

"How much about us do you know already? I presume that Dr. Edberg told you something."

"We talked a lot about God and the creation and such. I knew that he was a polygamist, but we didn't talk much about that. I never met his first wife because she died before I became acquainted with him and I didn't pry much into his personal life, if that makes any sense."

Brother Bower said, "Yes, it makes perfect sense. Good friends respect good boundaries. To answer your question, 'the principle' refers to the principle of plural or celestial marriage. It became known as 'the principle' because of its importance and how much controversy there was surrounding it. It was spoken of so frequently that the name of it was shortened to avoid mentioning sacred things too often and to make it easier to say."

"I understand," Marc said. "What is the group?"

Marc learned that there were multiple fundamentalist Mormon groups who were unaffiliated with the mainstream church. They were mainly defined by which subset of doctrines they clung to which had been abandoned by the church. These groups differed widely from each other but most of them held two things in common: they claimed to be the only true believers in Joseph Smith and they professed polygamy. Joe Bower explained that the primary thing that set his offshoot apart from the others was that they were the only group that held a legitimate claim to priesthood authority. It had been handed down to the present day through an unbroken chain of ordinations from John Taylor, the third president of the church. In 1886, he gave authority to several men and placed them under covenant to ensure that polygamy would continue in spite of intense opposition from their enemies, especially the federal government.

The Morrill Act was the first federal anti-bigamy legislation in the United States. Congress passed it in 1862 and Abraham Lincoln signed it into law; he ran for president on a platform, two major planks of which were abolishing the "twin relics of barbarism"—slavery and polygamy. Slavery divided the union, while polygamy united the union in hatred against the Mormon people. Nevertheless, fighting the battle against slavery and the ensuing cessation of southern states consumed the resources of the federal government. More of necessity than of forbearance, this chiefly led Abraham Lincoln to ignore the "Mormon problem."

Beside the lack of funding, the Morrill Act was difficult to enforce for another reason. The legal definition for bigamy required that one person entered into two or more simultaneously, legally valid marriages. Few Mormon men entered into multiple civil marriages and for those who did, the court couldn't compel their wives to testify against them. Consequently the Mormon people were largely left for another two decades to practice their system of holy matrimony until more stringent amendments to the Morrill Act were enacted—the Edmunds Act of 1882 and the Edmunds-Tucker Act of 1887. These two laws broadened the punitive scope beyond bigamy to include "unlawful cohabitation." Under this legal maneuver, it was no longer necessary to prove that a man entered into multiple marriages. It was merely sufficient to prove that he lived with more than one woman.

Of course, nineteenth century lawmakers left the term "unlawful cohabitation" intentionally vague in order to render it easier to prosecute. The most obvious proof of cohabitation was the existence of children. Unlawful cohabitation was punishable by up to three hundred dollars and six months imprisonment. Courts considered each day as a separate count. So if a man unlawfully fathered five children by a woman other than his legal wife and it could be proved by witnesses or other means that he had spent an additional five days with the mother, he faced five years in prison. If he committed the egregious act of also marrying her, he had committed a felony and an additional five hundred dollars and five years could be added to his sentence. Thus, this hypothetical man with two wives and five children through his second marriage faced a $3500 fine and ten years imprisonment.

Furthermore, the Edmunds Act stacked juries against polygamists by incorporating a test oath which precluded anyone from serving on a jury who merely professed a belief in polygamy. Because the church adopted the principle of plural marriage as a tenant in 1852, this effectively barred believing Mormons from serving on juries. Consequently, it was nearly impossible for an accused polygamist to obtain a fair trial. The jury was entirely composed of those who denied or denounced a belief in plural marriage. Since the issue of polygamy had a way of stirring up hatred against the church, juries were hardly impartial.

The law also vacated all registered and elected offices and filled them with new federal appointees who often hated Mormonism. Additionally, polygamists were disqualified from voting. Thus in a nation founded on democratic representation, the federal government imposed an oligarchy upon the inhabitants of the Utah territory.

The Edmunds Act was a heavy blow to the saints. It turned fathers into criminals, beloved children into illegitimates, and honored wives into single mothers. The saints howled about the unjust treatment but the federal government would not ease off. Smugly, federal marshals never applied the law to men who participated in illicit affairs or to men who impregnated women and abandoned their offspring. In a day before DNA testing had been invented, the only way to prove that a man was the father of a child was that he claimed and cared for his son or daughter. The gentiles (as non-Mormons were known) were very smug about it, particularly the miners in Park City who engaged in similar behaviors but never claimed any divine justification, never bestowed the title of wife upon their women, and avoided offspring like hot irons. Even if a gentile claimed children from other women, he was under no threat of prosecution; it was well known that the law was intended to abolish Mormon polygamy, not other forms of cohabitation.

Officials in Washington felt that they had been too lenient with the Mormons. They had levied heavy penalties on individuals, but there was still a glaring hole in their attack. The church, to which all of these individuals looked for guidance, was left unmarred. In spite of the woeful condition of those who were caught living the "fullness of the gospel," the church itself continued to advocate and solemnize plural marriages free from the threat of prosecution.

Congress addressed this obvious defect with the Edmunds-Tucker Act. It levied a slew of additional penalties upon the church itself and intensified pressure upon individuals. It dissolved the legal entity of the church and confiscated its property. It extended the test oath beyond jurors to voters as well. Therefore, a conviction was not required to disenfranchise a polygamist. Instead, a mere belief in polygamy was sufficient to disenfranchise any voter, regardless of whether or not he actually practiced plural marriage. The law barred children of polygamous wives from inheriting their father's estates. It also revoked common law spousal privilege for plural wives so that the court could compel them to testify against their husbands. Finally, among other provisions, the law abolished the right of women to vote which had been granted by the 1870 Utah territorial legislature.

Therefore, a law whose declared purpose was to free women from what was perceived as the degrading condition of polygamy ultimately disenfranchised them and thrust them and their children into a condition of destitution. Women's suffrage was finally instituted nationally in 1920 through the ratification of the nineteenth amendment. Hence, it took an additional fifty years of struggle for America to grant women the dignity that Mormonism did as a matter of principle.

In 1890, the Supreme Court upheld the anti-polygamy legislation and within a few months the church released an official declaration stating that it had abandoned the practice of plural marriage. This was the death knell of mainstream Mormon polygamy. Apparently the church could suffer its members being subject to imprisonment and all manner of persecution and abuse of federal power, but the church had grown wealthy and the one assault that brought it to its knees was the escheatment of its property to the federal government. Wealth was more important than principle.

"I can't believe it," Marc said.

"Can't believe what?" Chuck asked.

"I can't believe the Supreme Court would uphold a law so obviously unconstitutional."

"Why do you say it's unconstitutional?" Chuck asked.

"Well, for one it's an ex post facto law."

"How so?"

"It retroactively applied to marriages entered into prior to the passage of the law."

"Well look at who's become a law expert," Chuck smirked.

Marc confidently ignored Chuck's snide remark. "It also violated the free exercise of religion clause and," Marc had been building up to this part like it was the bombshell, "it was a bill of attainder which means..."

"I know what it means." Chuck didn't give him the satisfaction of showing off his newly acquired prowess at law. "Of course it targeted Mormons, although I can't say it was done unjustly. Mormondom wasn't exactly a small set—it was an enormous cult—and polygamists weren't declared guilty without a trial."

"But the right to an impartial jury was denied without a trial, the right to vote was denied without a trial, and the property of the church was confiscated without a trial."

"The first two were rights—there were no criminal consequences—and the last pertained to a corporation, not a person," Chuck said in a dismissive tone.

"I think you're splitting hairs," Marc said a little deflated. "I'm not an attorney, but I've done a lot of research and I believe it was a horrible abuse of power."

"Perhaps it was, but the Supreme Court considers a lot of case law that you're not familiar with."

"Let's face it. There's no justification. It was compelling interest," Marc declared.

"Oh, for sure. The Supreme Court is not immune to societal movements, but it is what it is and we have to deal with it."

"I don't," Marc said.

"Then you'll suffer the consequences. And let me be perfectly clear, the consequences *will* be dire. If you were a regular guy, living somewhat anonymously, maybe you could get away with it. Thousands do. But *you* won't get away with it. You could lose everything, Marc. The church is fighting the war against polygamy now, socially and economically. Your wife's family is well connected. History repeats itself; the persecuted become the persecutors."

"Yes, I know."

Chapter 15

There was a knock at the door. "That's probably Franceska. You can finally meet her," Marc told Chuck.

"Oh, happy day," Chuck sneered.

"You'll love her," Marc said as he opened the door. "Hello Angel. You're a mighty fine sight for sore eyes. I've been visiting with this ugly son-of-a-bitch." He introduced the two of them.

Chuck said, "It's nice to finally meet you. I'm going to see what I can do about this mess, and I don't mean you, Franceska. I can clearly see that you make Marc happy. He's been keeping you a secret. I don't know why, though, unless it's because he's afraid of some competition."

"Competition? Please. I just wanted to spare the lady from your bad manners," Marc said.

"That may be true," Chuck admitted. "But I'm well-mannered enough to know when I've out-stayed my welcome. I'll leave you two lovebirds alone. Again, it was nice to meet you. We should go to dinner sometime, my treat."

"If I lose my job, it'll have to be your treat," Marc said.

Chuck left and Marc wrapped Franceska up in a hug. "It's really good to see you," he whispered into her ear.

"I've been worried about you," Franceska said almost quivering. "Everyone at work is talking about it. The HR department announced that it was a routine security drill, but nobody believes it."

"They shouldn't; I didn't hire dummies."

"What are you going to do?" She asked, getting gradually more emotional.

"Ignore it."

"Ignore it? Why? I don't understand."

"I'm going to ignore their threat. I'll lose my job, but that's okay. It's a good time for a change, anyway. I'll need to cut expenses, but we'll be fine."

"What can I do to help you?" Franceska seemed to be buoyed up by the thought that she could do something to help Marc in a time of need.

"I don't know, yet, but I'm sure I'll be leaning on you a lot."

"I hope so. I want to help you Marc," she said with eyes that would melt any man.

"Thank-you, Angel." He kissed her on the temple of her forehead. "I suppose I'll need to let this apartment go, and I'll need to let my housekeeper go, too. That's too bad. Matilda has been a god-send."

"I'm sorry, but I can take her place. I would love to."

"That's very kind of you, thank-you. This is sort of exciting, Franci. I think you should keep your job for now, but after the wedding, I'll move you and the kids to Park City. I don't want the kids thinking that we're living together before we're married."

"That sounds wonderful," she said, visibly recovering from her anxiety.

"Great. Now let's go have lunch. Where do you want to go?"

After lunch Marc dropped Franceska off at the office and headed straight to the Brensett home. He rang the bell and waited for an answer. Mrs. Brensett opened the door with an angry look already on her face. This was an entirely new experience for Marc. She had always received him with politeness, although forced at times.

"What can I help you with?" She asked.

"Good afternoon. I'm here to see Lena."

"Marc," she grew irritable and her voice trembled, "you made your choice and she has made hers. I would appreciate it if you would respect that and not come here again to harass her and pressure her."

"I'm not here to harass her. She's my wife," he said as if he couldn't believe that he had to explain this to the mother of his bride.

"Be that as it may, this is our home and I would appreciate it if you would respect our wishes. If Lena wants to see you, she has your number. Goodbye, Marc." She closed the door without waiting for a reply.

Several days passed unceremoniously. Without a job, Marc spent a lot of time lying on the bed or the couch, staring at the shapes in the ceiling texture. He placed the apartment on the market for rent. He told the agent that he wasn't ready to sell. She said that it wouldn't take long to find a renter, so he halfheartedly began packing things up.

One day he was staring out the window with boxes and stacks of books piled around. Amy had suggested meeting in Wendover. The town of Wendover is a small hellhole in a big hellhole. It sits on the border of Utah and Nevada on the western edge of the Bonneville Salt Flats, about two hours west of Salt Lake City. There is a stretch of interstate highway, straight as an arrow, extending over forty miles that varies in elevation by only about fifteen feet. It's one of the flattest places on earth, and, due to the salinity of its soil, it's one of the most barren, also. Passage is an exercise in mind over monotony.

The only plant capable of enduring such salty conditions is a concrete sculpture titled *Metaphor: Tree of Utah* by Swedish artist Karl Momen. It stands eighty-seven feet above the plain, whose salty crust reaches a thickness of sixty inches in some places. The tree looks like celestial orbs and a giant tennis ball suspended by a concrete column. Perhaps as a joke, perhaps as wishful thinking, or perhaps as an allusion to

Lehi's vision in the Book of Mormon, the sculpture is often referred to as the tree of life. Truly, the only visible life are the tourists stopping to take selfies with the artwork.

The Great Salt Lake Desert is the size of a small country and receives an accumulated wintertime precipitation of a little over an inch. The briny broth never freezes and when temperatures are low, evaporation is minimal. Hence, driving through portions of the desert is like hovering over an expansive inch-deep lake.

On the Nevada side of Wendover Boulevard, there are two casinos, one on each side of the street. Their parking lots are on the Utah side and their east walls stand on the Nevada border. This brings the vices of freedom as close to the inhabitants of Salt Lake as legally possible. There is an unspoken agreement among Mormons to "play it cool" if they notice fellow parishioners there. It's not uncommon to witness close acquaintances pretending to be complete strangers if they accidentally encounter each other in Wendover. They will literally trek, "through the valley of the shadow of death" for a latte or a long island ice tea that they can enjoy without looking over their shoulders.

Marc was overlooking Salt Lake City from his downtown apartment. He finished his cappuccino and left the apartment. He walked one block west to the City Creek shopping center. The church bought two downtown malls which occupied the better portion of two adjacent blocks. It demolished them and renovated the space into a first rate shopping and residential center. It included Marc's apartment building, fine restaurants, and pedestrian areas where residents and visitors could enjoy the creek flowing through the city from a nearby canyon. There were several heirloom buildings owned by other entities which survived the massive reconstruction project. Marc walked into one of them, a coffee shop located at street level. It was the only coffee shop for blocks around. Third party restaurants in the City Creek Center were allowed to serve coffee, but no dedicated coffee shops were permitted to occupy church space. Church-owned restaurants served sodas containing four or five times the caffeine and a cocktail of other carcinogenic chemicals, but they refused to serve coffee. Not even so much as a mocha flavored dessert or candy could be found in the church-owned shops.

"Why did you want to meet here?" Amy asked a little annoyed. "I thought Wendover would be a safe place."

"Are you kidding?" Marc said. "A coffee shop one block from the temple is the safest place in Utah. My enemies would never be caught dead in here."

"That's a good point. I hadn't thought of that," she said with a chuckle.

"I've had a lot of experience. Dad liked Wendover. He would go there to escape the bullshit, but he would also run into a lot of other Mormons. You wouldn't believe some of the stories."

"Makes sense. By the way, I already ordered. I didn't know what you wanted."

"Oh, I've already had coffee; I'll probably just have a muffin." Marc continued in a brighter tone, "So, Amy, it's been a long time. It's nice to see you again. I kind of lost track of you. I'll confess that I've tried to stalk you on Facebook several times, but I couldn't find you anywhere."

"In my line of work, it's best to stay hidden."

"Your line of work?" Marc asked probingly.

"You know—forensics, private investigation. I'm pretty good at what I do and I've made some enemies of my own."

"I'm sure," Marc said confidently. Then he quickly added, "That you're good at what you do, I mean."

Amy laughed.

"What kind of enemies are we talking about?" Marc asked.

"The kind that I don't want to find me," she said.

"Fair enough. So what did you want to discuss with me?"

"Do you remember that day you got fired from the university?"

"Yeah. I think about it a lot, actually."

"Well, as you know, in this investigation, my job was to analyze your personal files: emails, documents, photos, … There was quite a bit to keep me entertained, umm, employed, I mean. That's what I meant to say." She smirked.

"Yes, I know. You've got to do your job," Marc said as if he was trying to calculate the direction that Amy was taking.

"Apparently, you're seeing a girl named Franceska and Lena doesn't like it."

Marc looked silently at Amy, still calculating.

"Well, when you got fired from the university, I suggested that if things didn't work out between you and Lena…" She cut herself off, to allow Marc to form the conclusion.

"So you wanted to talk about you and me?"

Amy smiled. She was cute and the years hadn't hurt her at all. She still rocked the grunge look although she had matured in her execution of it to be slightly more conducive to the profession that she had chosen. She wasn't shy just like she wasn't shy in college, and she was perfectly comfortable leaving Marc to stew in his thoughts.

Amy turned up the heat. "Polygamy, huh? I would never have guessed. Religion didn't seem to suit you."

Marc smiled as he took the bait. There were some triggers that he couldn't guard himself against. "Religion? Why does everyone assume that polygamy has anything to do with religion? It's possible, you know, for a man and a woman to love each other for their own sakes."

"So none of this has anything to do with religion?" Amy asked.

"I didn't say that." Marc chuckled. "I'm still figuring that part out."

"There were some pics of Franceska in your files. She's beautiful. I'm sure a revelation is forthcoming," Amy said tauntingly.

"I'm not like that. I don't put words in God's mouth. I have a profound respect for the creator of this universe." Marc paused and then he smirked and added, "I don't even know if he exists, but I hope he does. I don't claim to speak with him, but I wish that I could. 'I will not cease to call upon God, I have other things to inquire of him.'" Marc's levity left him as he quoted a line from the Book of Moses in Mormon scripture.

"I don't know about that, either, but I seem to remember some vibes coming from you back in college."

Marc said, "It's true, I liked you, and if I knew then what I know now... Oh, never mind. Lena would never have gone for it. If it's hard for her now, it would have been impossible back then."

"But I'm not talking about back then."

Marc's eyes widened. "What are you talking about, then?"

Amy laughed. "I'm just having fun. I really liked you, too. I think I made that clear."

"Yes, you did," Marc confirmed with a smile.

"But that was a long time ago. Besides, can you see me as a wife, much less as a polygamous wife?" Amy threw her head back laughing.

"Actually, I can see it."

Amy stopped laughing. "Oh, you're hilarious. Um, anyway, to the reason I wanted to meet... those files that we confiscated."

"Yeah, I didn't think you wanted to meet in Wendover to talk romance. It's not a very romantic place. What about them?"

"You're stealing from LogicStream."

"Oh, really? And what exactly am I stealing."

"You tell me," Amy said in a commanding tone.

Marc laughed. "There's nothing to tell."

"Marc," she said in the tone of a school teacher who had caught her student cheating, "I extracted copious quantities of hidden data invisibly embedded within photos, videos, and sound files. I have to tell you, it was quite clever how you did it, but like I said, I'm pretty good at what I do."

"Wow, really? And what did these hidden files contain?" Marc asked innocently.

"I can't say," Amy said disappointed. "They were encrypted with an algorithm I've never seen before."

"Then why do you say I'm stealing? Maybe it's just background noise. Files get corrupted; happens all the time. It must be that damn internet connection; I've been on IT for months to get it fixed," Marc said deviously.

"Nice try," she said with an incredulous scowl. "These were not 'corrupted' files," Amy said with air quotes. "They were perfectly viewable files which would look totally normal, to most people. I'm not 'most people.'"

"Indeed, you're not."

She ignored Marc's ambiguous compliment. "You were hoping to remove them without anyone suspecting them. Besides some of those porn vids? Really, Marc? I know those girls aren't your type. That is, unless you've been hiding a kinky streak."

Marc raised his eyebrows, but held his silence.

Amy continued to build her case, "It wasn't the internet connection. The odds of readable files being corrupted from random processes is something like 1 in a 100 trillion."

"Wow! That's remarkable. I've always maintained that given enough space and time, any event, no matter how improbable, is bound to occur. I just can't believe it happened to me. I must be the luckiest guy in the universe."

Amy wasn't amused. "I handed over the extracted files to the law firm. I'm sorry, but I had to. There are other people working on the case and if they found out that I let this pass by, it would destroy my career. I could even be prosecuted."

"I understand, Amy. You have to do your job."

"Why are you taking this so lightly? This is serious. You could go to prison for this. With LogicStream's defense contracts, you could get your ass kicked."

Marc didn't respond.

Amy continued in an abrupt manner. "I made copies of everything, Marc, but I'm not giving them to you unless you talk to me."

"You'd give them to me?"

"I want to help you, Marc. I know you're a good man, but you've got to give me something to go on. Since Lena's dad is the chairman of the board and a major stock holder, it's not hard to imagine that you're being unfairly targeted."

"He's just trying to bully me into giving up Franceska."

"Then give her up! It's not worth it, Marc. You can't afford to call his bluff."

"Oh, I don't think he's bluffing. I know him and his type too well. He'll destroy me if he can. It was a major embarrassment when Lena married me outside of the church. He recovered by getting us remarried by the stake president and setting me up with a great business opportunity. That's how he looks at it! I provide comfortably for his daughter and he thinks it's all his doing. I own a decent portion of LogicStream and I earned it. I built this thing. I'm being accused of stealing? Stealing what? Shit that I created, that's what. He didn't build it; he can hardly find the power button on his computer.

"He tells everyone that I'm 'inactive' in the church. Inactive! Can you believe it? He can't face the truth. The truth is, I don't have any desire to be in the church and neither does Lena. But he thinks he can keep her by lying and throwing money around. Well, I'm sick of it. He doesn't get to define me.

"Now he thinks that he can manipulate me into leaving Franceska. He's resorting to threats, just as he did when I was dating Lena. Except, he knows he can't use religion this time so he's using money. Well, he's not going to win. He didn't win then and he's not going to win now. I am going to keep his daughter *and* marry Franceska."

Amy was emotionally impacted by what she heard. She asked, "Why does she mean so much to you? You were willing to give me up."

"Like you said, Amy, that was a long time ago. Things would be different now, I assure you of that."

Amy reached into her bag and slammed a flash drive down on the table. It wasn't hard enough to break the drive, but it was hard enough to communicate a level of frustration. "I don't know if you really mean that, but I choose to believe you, I've always believed in you. If it gets out that I gave this to you, it would destroy me."

Marc took the flash drive. "Thank you, Amy. I understand and I did mean it," he said with intensity. "Do you work exclusively for that firm or are you freelance?"

"Freelance, why?"

"I could really use someone like you to help me with a little project I'm working on."

"Involving those files, I presume?"

"Yes."

"Aren't you at all worried about possessing stolen property?"

Marc looked at Amy with a peculiar expression, obviously holding back from saying something.

"What?" She asked.

Marc exhaled tension and paused, apparently weighing his options. "Don't take this the wrong way, but it sort of feels like you're trying to get me to admit that I stole something."

"'Don't take this the wrong way?'" Amy asked in disbelief. "You don't trust me. I just handed over your files." Amy seemed to be fighting back a wave of anger.

"I want to trust you, I honestly do, but I don't technically know what's on this drive. It might not contain anything at all."

"I can't believe this!"

"Look at this from my point of view. I haven't seen you for years and then suddenly you show up at precisely the time I'm being investigated by my father-in-law. I want to trust you, but it feels a little suspicious. For all I know, you're wearing a wire."

"I'd offer to let you pat me down, but you're being a total jerk."

Marc smiled, "I'd love to pat you down, actually."

"See what I mean," Amy was fuming.

"I'm sorry, but if there were a subtle way to approach this subject, I would have taken it. I guess I'm just…"

"A total jackass. I put my neck on the line for you. I'm a forensic investigator; when else would you expect to see me? I didn't bring this upon you—you did—and I don't need it. I'm sorry I helped you at all. Try not to screw me over. Bye."

Marc seemed alarmed. He had until she walked out that door to make a grand gesture of trust. Perhaps he had already blown that opportunity. If what she said was true, then she had taken a huge risk for his sake; it was impossible to know before she reached the door. Oh, confounding uncertainty— it makes everyone white-knuckled, gripping at every branch or twig, tuft of grass or crumbling crag, anything at all that one hopes might be firmly planted in solid ground. Nevertheless, life takes everyone for a ride. There is nowhere to stand—only wafting clouds, sinking sands, and reeling seas. Jesus wasn't the first to walk on water, only the most graceful. Most people pass through life like reeling dancers on a skateboard that's getting away from them. Many people simply sink until they reach their belated deaths.

Amy was a friend and a gifted collaborator. Friends are hard to come by. They're treasured above all things. Hence, the scales of justice demand that betrayal should be the hardest thing to recover from because betrayal belongs exclusively to the domain of love, of friendship.

Marc drove past the driveway shadows running to hide behind rocks and trees. They put on quite a show, waving their arms above their heads. Whom were they kidding? Marc smirked. If they were truly frightful, they'd take their show on the road—test their talent on Broadway or something. Instead they loitered around their hometown like they had nowhere to go. Amateurs—content to be big actors on a small stage. Marc may have been out of his league, but at least he wasn't settling for cozy mediocrity.

The garage door opened before him. It was common but regal. The kings of the past never enjoyed such reverence and convenience. They never carried fifty rock bands around, with soaring vocals and full orchestral accompaniment. They didn't ride in coaches carried upon springs and cushions of air. They never controlled temperatures as Marc did. It was cold outside, but he was warm. Explosions fired within precision-cut cylinders powered his drive and his jam. The smoke was exhausted without a nuisance while glass and mirrors kept the world in his view. Everything was common yet astonishingly regal. It was a day when any man could be a king, but instead most settle for drudgery and an employer-matched 401k so that they could die in comfortable chains.

Marc pulled up beside Lena's wagon. Entering the home, he found the kitchen clean, the lights dimmed, and Lena sitting at the table with her back to him. She was listening to somber music and drinking wine. She had set the table beautifully for dinner and lit candles, too.

"I'm not late, am I? I didn't know you were planning dinner."

Something this nice suggested that Lena was either in a really good mood or really foul. If she were somewhere in between, she likely would have prepared something simple or suggested going out. This didn't bode well. She often put her anger into something gourmet. The fury drove her to finish early. If she were happy instead, she would be dancing in the kitchen and dinner would be late; Marc would be helping with food prep and swaying with her even though it wasn't his kind of music. She had that effect on him, somehow.

"No, you're not late. I was just waiting for you," she said.

He washed his hands in the kitchen sink while she sat motionless facing the wall. He sat down at the table and she stood up. He watched her serving his plate. He must have felt like a man facing a desert sand storm rolling in—running was futile. His best chance of survival was to cover his airways and calmly wait. He might enjoy the beauty of impending doom before everything went dark.

"What's the matter?" He asked the storm.
"Franceska spent the night with you."

The color drained from Lena's face, like a flower smothered by strangleweed, a pale-colored parasite that slowly spreads tendrils over its host plant, piercing its stems, and sapping its strength. Travis called it an "alien spider web" because of its otherworldly appearance. He was out exploring once and came frantically rushing into the house to tell his dad that alien spiders were attacking the earth. Marc tried to calm Travis as he tried to calm Lena, by gently removing the suffocating net and dissecting it with facts.

Marc ran his fingers through his hair and squeezed his neck and shoulders in preparation for a protracted conflict. "Yes, that's true, but nothing happened."

"Oh, 'nothing happened?' You expect me to believe that?"

"I hope you'll believe it; it's true."

"What was she doing there?" Lena added with a burst, "All night?"

Marc meticulously explained the circumstances surrounding that night: Franceska brought some papers over; he invited her to stay for a drink; she was a new employee and he wanted her to feel welcome; somehow they delved into the subject of religion; that led to a discussion on polygamy; polygamy was in both Lena's and Marc's family history; Franceska expressed an interest in joining Marc's family; she admired Marc and she loved Lena, thought Lena was the greatest; he explained to Franceska that polygamy is not a current practice; he told her that he couldn't do anything without discussing it with Lena first; he loved Lena and wouldn't hurt her, and so on.

Lena argued that Franceska was not very new to the company; Franceska had been working there since before the family reunion. Staying all night was completely inappropriate, regardless of how long she had worked for Marc. Franceska hadn't really associated with Lena enough to love her. Franceska might be playing on Marc's emotions for financial gain, and so on.

Lena seemed to accept Marc's oaths that he hadn't had sex with Franceska, at least for the time being. However, it was a fear that would feed her monster friend for months to come. It didn't seem consistent with her experience that he would stay up all night discussing religion. She knew how he behaved in the abandoned mine. When the two of them were in close quarters, things heated up and passions flew high. What was to keep that from happening with Franceska? He tried to explain that things were different back then; he wasn't already married when he met Lena. Apparently marriage didn't mean anything to him anyway. "That's not true, goddammit! I have not had sex with Franceska or any other woman, for that matter." Even his love for Lena kept coming back to bite him in the ass. Why couldn't she believe that he had pure motives? Why couldn't anyone believe? Was there any good in him at all?

Interestingly, Lena didn't contend over polygamy, or reciprocating Franceska's love, or permitting her to join their family. It seemed that Lena was more concerned about Franceska's possible motives than the idea of her joining their family. It was a subtlety that didn't escape Marc's attention for he seemed to exploit it even more subtly over the next several hours.

Marc told fragments of the truth. It may have been generously intended to portray Franceska more virtuously. Perhaps he was protecting Franceska from Lena's suspicion and scrutiny, a genuine instinct that men have toward the women they love. He left out details that he supplied when he told Clawson the same story, and he filled in other details that he omitted from Clawson's rendition. For example, when telling Lena the story, he didn't mention the dress that Franceska was wearing or anything about her physical appearance. When telling Clawson the story, he omitted key aspects of the religious discussion.

He omitted from both renditions that he requested the documents to be delivered that evening, knowing that Lena had a commitment in Park City and that Franceska worked in the copy room, making her an obvious choice for the assignment. He didn't tell Lena about the flirtatious glances they exchanged in the hallway whenever he passed by. He didn't mention the interoffice emails and the little notes she left with copy work routed for his desk. There was a multitude of omissions that would keep Lena's sleuthing powers busy for weeks and months to come.

Marc lied simply by not telling the whole truth. It's impossible to tell the truth anyway. Lying is the inescapable condition of human life. Memories fade and motives color every word. The brain fills in missing information with what it perceives *should be*. This requires judgments to be formed on partial evidence, which undermines the truth because "what should be" and "what is" are seldom the same thing. Oh, the memory mongers clap with glee. One should get everything in ink, because that's the hardest thing to rape.

Anyone who has ever wished to have his or her brains fucked out needs only cling to one creed. The greater his or her fidelity to the truth, the harder the erection of the memory monger grows, jutting through those drab, gray robes. The libidinous little beast patiently waits beyond notice, always present but rarely seen. It floats about, developing a ravenous appetite for the ears, the eyes, the nose, the mouth; being faceless, it has none of its own so it lusts after his and hers. Its desire grows throughout the day like pressure in a hose about to burst. When its helpless prey surrenders to the paralysis of sleep, it squats above the bed and dips its thick long rod into the wax, tears, mucous, and spit. It feverishly plunges into the features and contents of the head, without consent. It jumbles the brains and spews its seed into a fucked up mess. Such is the fate of those who most fervently declare to know a truth. As the nearest approximation to the truth, silence provides little lube and less enticement.

Regardless of the motives behind Marc's omissions, it was anecdotal evidence that everyone lies. Some lie with the intent to deceive, some to protect, and some to help others believe. In that sense, there is little distinction between deceiving and evangelizing. No one knows the truth; it's beyond the scope of human reach. Preachers claiming to know something that they don't are some of the vilest creatures on earth. Fervently believing a delusion only makes it a stronger delusion. They would do well to shut their face holes, but that doesn't win converts and it doesn't deposit tithing checks.

Amy had made a big enough scene that the barista was shaking her head and looking scornfully at Marc. He jumped up and ran to the door. "Amy," he called down the street. She turned around long enough to flip him the bird.

Chapter 16

Marc stumbled into the kitchen, massaging his face and prying away the dried up remains of dreams with serrated edges from the corners of his eyes. It was an ungodly hour for a man to rise, but the sun didn't think so. It shone brightly through the windows in the opposite room, causing last night's dreams to pierce him once again when he squinted. He had responsibilities and no one to pass them on to. He hadn't closed the blinds and tucked the house in for the evening as Lena was accustomed to doing. Therefore, the house had a frazzled look, too, and it didn't greet Marc cheerfully, as *it* was accustomed to doing. Instead, it pouted and frowned at him like a child who had awakened from a rough night, blaming its parent for its distress.

After sufficiently ridding himself of dream crystals and acclimating to the light, he peered out at the opposite mountains overlooking Park City. He noticed Kimberly lying on the couch reading. "Good morning, sweetheart," he said.

"Morning."

"Whatcha reading?"

"*A Separate Peace*," she said without looking up.

"What's it about?"

"Two boys in a private school during World War II," still not looking up.

"For school?"

"No."

"Just interested in learning more about World War II?"

"No."

"What then?" Marc asked a little irritated.

"Trying to understand boys. They're so stupid." Kimberly finally looked up.

"Oh. I suppose you're right. Keep thinking that way."

"Haven't seen anything to change my mind, yet."
Kimberly glared at her dad. She was only nine years old but
smart enough to insult like an adult.

"Okay." He hadn't had coffee, yet, so a father-and-
daughter talk would have to wait. "Speaking of boys, where's
your brother?"

"Playing outside." She was back into her book.

"Are you hungry?"

"Not really."

"How do pancakes sound?"

"Fine."

Marc wrapped his bathrobe tightly around him and
stepped out onto the back patio. He walked to the corner
where the patio, the grass, and the playground met. The
sandbox was crusted over with frost. The grass was green but
frosted over also where it was shaded by the house and trees.
Footprints zigzagged through the frost where Travis had
created trails. Marc found him playing in the dirt where the
sun shone over the ridge of the roof.

"Good morning, son."

Travis jumped up and ran to his dad. "Good morning,
Daddy," he said as he wrapped his arms around Marc's legs.

"Already building something, huh?"

"No, I'm mining."

"What are you mining?"

"Gold."

"That's good, son. That's exactly what I'm doing, too."

Travis looked up at him with a proud smile and rolled his
shoulders up.

"Hey, do you want to help me make pancakes for
breakfast?" Marc asked.

"Yeah."

"Okay, let's go, bud. By the way, don't go outside of the
house until I'm awake, alright?"

"Alright."

Marc started the coffee and then pulled out two mixing bowls, a measuring cup, flour, baking powder, baking soda, eggs, milk, and sugar. He dispensed the flour, baking powder, and baking soda together into one bowl. He cracked some eggs and poured the milk and sugar together into the other bowl. Travis whisked them together. Marc then took a pinch of the dry ingredients, tasted it, dipped his finger into the bowl of wet ingredients, and tasted that also.

"That's gross," Travis wrinkled his nose as he grimaced.
"What's gross?" Marc asked.
"You're eating raw eggs."
"How else am I to know if I have the right proportions?" He asked.
"You could follow a recipe," Kimberly piped up from the living room. "Besides you can get salmonella from eating raw eggs."
"Momma and 'Tilda always follow a recipe," Travis said.
"Well, I don't know any recipes," Marc explained, "but I know what it's supposed to taste like. See, I can tell that the dry ingredients need more baking soda and the wet ingredients need more sugar."
"Sugar isn't wet," Travis shook his head, thrilled that he caught his dad making such a silly mistake.
"I know, you goof," Marc laughed, "but it's considered a wet ingredient for two reasons. It dissolves quickly in wet ingredients, and if you mix it into the dry ingredients, it makes it harder to tell if the dry ingredients have the right amount of baking soda and salt."
"You put salt in pancakes?" Travis asked, confused.
"Oh, for sure, but we save that for last. Salt is one of the most important ingredients. A little salt makes all of the other flavors blend together."

"Daddy, why don't we just mix it all together in one bowl?" Travis asked.

"That's a good question, son. Wheat flour has a protein called gluten. When you mix the pancake batter together, the gluten forms longs strings. It's what traps all of those bubbles in your pancakes and makes them rise instead of just spreading out. But the more you mix it, the longer and tougher those strands become. So, if you mix it too much, your pancakes will be hard. Does that make sense?"

"Yeah," Travis said.

"Right. Nobody likes hard pancakes. By keeping the ingredients separate, I can make all of the adjustments I need to before I begin building those gluten strands."

Marc tasted everything again. He noticed the lack of vanilla and added it. He then showed Travis how to mix the wet and dry ingredients together. "Okay, it's your turn." Marc handed the mixing spoon over to Travis and continued coaching him, "Mix from the bottom, and take long, easy strokes so that you don't mix it any more than necessary. Okay, good. We're done."

"But it still has lumps in it." Travis felt that it needed more mixing.

"That's okay." Marc reassured him, "You won't notice when you eat them. We'll just set the batter aside while we heat the pan and get the rest of breakfast ready. That will give those gluten strands some time to relax before we cook them. These pancakes are going to be amazing!"

Marc asked Kimberly to mix the orange juice and heat the syrup, and so on. Travis set the table. Marc cut some fruit.

"It's time to cook the pancakes," Marc announced. "Look at all those bubbles," he said leaning over the bowl, rapping his fingers together like a witch pleased with the contents of her bubbling cauldron. By this time, even Kimberly seemed interested. He continued to instruct Travis on the art of fluffy pancakes. "When you spoon the batter into the pan, scoop it out like you're lifting all of those bubbles with it. Don't smash them. If you push the ladle down, you'll smash them; you gotta scoop along the surface. Okay, good job."

While they were waiting on the pancakes, Marc poured his second cup of coffee and delved deeper into the art. "You see, son, building pancakes is a lot like building a marriage. You've got to be gentle and keep it light. Sometimes you separate the ingredients so that you can make adjustments. You don't worry too much about the lumps, because overworking the batter only hurts it. But sometimes you stir it a little too hard and you've got to give it time to relax."

"And sometimes, it takes both salt and sugar," Kimberly added with smile that nearly split her head in half.

"That's right, sweetheart," Marc said as he wrapped his arm around her. "How'd you get to be so smart? You must have gotten it from your mother along with your good looks. Well, let's eat."

They served up the pancakes with fruit and juice. Marc anointed his pancake with syrup and praised Travis' crafty work.

"Well, let's get ready to go," Marc said. "Your mother's going to be waiting for you. Today's the big day."

"Are you coming?" Kimberly asked her dad.

"I'm afraid not. I'm not exactly the most popular person with your grandparents these days."

"But it's a tradition," Kimberly said.

"I know, sweetie, but it's not my tradition; if I'm not wanted there…" Marc cut himself off.

"You'd probably just rather be with Franceska's kids," Kimberly said.

"That's not true. That's not true at all. I love you with all my heart and I'm working hard to get us all back together again. I love Benny and Kira, too, but that doesn't make me love you any less. Nothing will change that. I love your mother; I love her dearly; I always have and I always will. I'll never stop fighting for her and for this family."

Hearing their dad declare his undying love for their mother restored their smiles. As they rode to their grandparents' home, they sang along to some of the family's favorite songs. It was warmer in the valley, so once they reached the Wasatch Bench, they rolled the windows down and turned the music up. Marc hollered, "This is *our* tradition. Never gets old does it?"

"Nope," Kimberly yelled back. "I wish Mom were here."

"I do, too, Kimmy, I do, too. Let's rock out and show her how much fun we had. Put her song on."

They were late getting there. The driveway was full, as were the orchids in bloom. "You coming in, Daddy?"

"Absolutely. I've never missed it. Why would I miss it now?" He feigned a reassuring tone.

The kids got super excited and ran into the house. Marc's smile disappeared when the kids disappeared. He approached the front door in a meditative stroll. He reached out and rang the bell. It chimed as it had a hundred times before. There was an awkward wait, unlike any time before; awkward times are always unique. Marc looked down at the porch. This is where Lena would normally have stood—where she would have fought over entering instead of waiting for an answer. He looked through the obscured glass in the door—where Mrs. Brensett might receive him lukewarm, or where an amiable Mr. Brensett surprised them both after their elopement, or where any of the siblings of impertinent indifference might leave him to close the door behind himself. This door was like a confessional screen with a reluctant priest on the other side who assigned a menial penance, but always ended with "may God have mercy on your soul." A figure appeared through the door. She moved like the breeze and smiled like the orchids when she said, "Hello."

"Hello, Lena," Marc said. Strangely, this was the first time she had ever answered the door to him.

"It's good to see you," she said.

"It's really good to see you," Marc said with intensity. "May I come in?" He asked, faking a sense of equanimity.

"I don't think that's a good idea," she said.

"Come on, Lena."

"Don't start with me, Marc. This is not the place and not the time." Lena's mood changed quickly.

"I just think it would mean a lot to the kids to see us together for a bit."

"Don't drag the kids into this," Lena snapped back.

"Nothing can prevent that. It's inevitable at this point. I'm just trying to… Can we discuss this out here?"

Lena stepped out and closed the door behind her. She looked at him as if she was already impatient.

"What?" Marc asked.

"You were about to say…" Lena prodded.

"The kids didn't ask for this," Marc said.

"I didn't ask for this, either."

"Okay. All I'm saying is that we should do this for the sake of the kids," Marc said.

"I'm not going to make this any harder for them than it has to be. Giving them a false sense of hope…"

"It's not a false sense of hope," Marc shot back.

"It's *your* hope, not mine. I can't pretend to something I don't believe. I won't."

"I wouldn't ask you to. That's one of the things I love about you, Lena. I don't know what I believe either, but I believe in us."

"You have a strange way of showing it," she said.

"So it's strange. That doesn't make it any less real. Maybe the truth is strange, stranger than either one of us is prepared to believe."

"Look who's suddenly talking about the truth," Lena said with a glare.

"It's not sudden. The truth is all I care about. It's all I've ever cared about. I yearn for it. It's the opus magnus of my entire existence—the guiding light…"

"Do you mean 'magnum opus'?" Lena cut him off with her signature move: a raised eye, a hand on her hip, and a lovely tilt of her body. It didn't bother Marc much to be corrected; it amused her and that was a better sign than he had received since her luscious smile upon opening the door.

Marc defended himself sheepishly, "Whatever! I like the sound of it."

"Sound and sense," Lena said, exaggerating the move even more.

That shut Marc down for a moment, but his grin gradually conquered his face. "God, I love you. Now that's the truth! I don't know the whole truth; I may never find it, but I'll search till the end of my days. I'll look for it like…" Marc was searching for a metaphor and Lena was willing to give him all the time he needed. It must have been important for both of them to get it right, to put precisely in words the dilemma that had impinged so dreadfully upon their lives. So, when he struggled to find the words, she didn't interfere. She didn't mock or rush him. He stuttered, "like, like, like a, a, like a… Shit I don't know! But it's what I yearn for and I'll never cease searching for it. I'm sorry that it eludes me. I don't have the answers, but one thing I'm fairly confident about is that together…"

At that, the door flung open and Melinda stood there with an irritated look on her face. She said, "Oh, there you are. Sorry, I didn't mean to interrupt. I was just wondering what happened to you."

Lena said, "Oh, just finishing up. I'll be in soon," and then she pulled the door shut in Melinda's face, another good sign.

"That was a bunch of bullshit. She knew damn good and well that we were talking out here," Marc said.

"I need to be getting back," she said impatiently.

"Okay. I'm taking Franceska to meeting. I know you won't go, but I just wanted you to know. I wish you could come."

"I still can't get used to you going to church," Lena said looking hurt, "but have a nice time." She turned to go back into the house.

"Wait, there's more, Lena. Brother Bower is trying to get us to set a date for the wedding."

Lena opened the door and slowly turned to go back into the house.

"Tell the kids I love them. I'm sorry that we couldn't...," Marc finished the sentence to a closed door, "hang out together." Marc turned and slumped back to his car. He heard someone whistling. He turned around to find Clawson waving at him to stop.

"What's up?" Marc asked.

The Brensetts had invited a widower to the house. He was about Marc's age, athletic, and wealthy. It was obvious that they intended him for Lena. Clawson just wanted to give Marc a "heads up."

"What's his name?" Marc asked.

"I'm not sure, actually. He's an ass-wad, though."

"Why?"

"He's not really, he's okay, it just pisses me off that they're doing this."

"Well, text me his name, would ya?"

"Sure thing. Take care, man."

"I will, thanks. I appreciate your help, Clawson. Keep an eye on the kids."

Marc went over to pick Franceska up. This was her first time attending a polygamist church service. She was in her bedroom getting ready and Laura was watching the kids. They were excited to see Marc, but they quickly reverted to the TV show they were watching. Marc asked Laura, "So, how much do you know about what's going on here?"

"Quite a bit," Laura said beaming.

"Do Mom and Dad know?"

"Yeah."

"Why do you seem to be so happy about it?"

"Do you know how long I've been praying that you'll find religion?"

"Easy with that shit!" Marc exaggerated the act of looking around to make sure no one heard.

Laura laughed.

"Besides, it's not the same religion."

"You should talk to Dad about it."

"What do Mom and Dad think?"

"To be honest, Mom's not very thrilled about it, but like I said, you should talk to Dad. He's helped me quite a bit to sort things out."

"Sort things out? More like chewing the cud on my life."

"It's not like that. We're all trying to help you."

"Mom will never be happy as long as I'm making my own decisions."

"She's just worried about you, that's all."

"Bullshit. She's worried about how her friends in the church will perceive her. She hates defending me to them. My becoming a polygamist would be the final blow."

"Mom will be fine. She'll work through it, she always does."

Franceska came out of the bedroom. Even the children were distracted by her appearance. "Mommy, you look beautiful," Benjamin said. Everyone complimented

Franceska in his or her own way except Marc. For that, he waited until they were alone in the car.

"You really do look stunning," he said.

"Thanks." She smiled back.

"How do you expect me to listen to anything being said with such a beautiful woman by my side?"

"Do you think I'll blend in?" She asked. It was apparent that she was nervous.

"In all the right ways, and in none of the wrong ways," he said.

"Wrong ways?"

"You'll see what I mean," he said with a smile.

Marc had attended several of these meetings since his initial introduction to Joe Bower, so he was wearing the standard men's apparel for such occasions: a simple dark suit, a long-sleeved white shirt, polished leather shoes, and a tie. The women, however, exhibited a much greater range in fashion than did the men. Some women wore make-up; some did not. Some wore their hair down; some wore it up. The styles and lengths of their hair varied almost as much as their fashions, except that there was a clear preference for long hair.

In many ways, the congregation resembled an audience that one might find attending an elegant theater performance except for two obvious distinctions. First, the dress here was generally more conservative and modest, and second, the older members of the congregation made little or no attempt to be as fashionable as their younger counterparts. Because the fashions and the styles of the women varied more than those of the men, the distinction between the older and the younger women was more obvious than the distinction between the older and younger men.

It wasn't necessary for a new convert (or investigator) to make these observations independently. One of the most common topics that speakers hammered on was modesty. They particularly beat on the young people, which essentially meant that the older people wanted the younger people to dress like them. The younger people looked at the older people and revolted with disgust. It would have been humorous to observe had it not been so abundantly clear that they were alienating their children. It was like a vine poisoning its own fruit. When the vine withered, there would be no seed to grow in its place.

They called this meeting a cottage meeting because it was held in a residential home. It was decorated similar to Brother Bower's home, as if there was an approved mode of interior design among these polygamists: the wallpaper, the affinity for white and gold, the lighting, and even the portraits on the walls—they all bore a remarkable similarity to the Bower residence. A profound silence prevailed prior to the start of meeting. If anyone spoke, it was brief and in a hushed whisper. It was a good time for meditation. The quietude made a noteworthy impression especially considering that a few hundred people crowded into the living room, kitchen and dining room, hallways, and bedrooms. They sat on folding chairs and some even sat on the stairs.

They were meeting in the neighborhood of Sugar House bordering several large shopping areas. The people were expected to park in these areas to avoid filling up the residential streets with cars and attracting undue attention from the neighbors. Only their leaders (whom they called "The Brethren") and the elderly parked on the premises. This didn't stop the neighbors from noticing hundreds of people parading down the sidewalks dressed in suits and Sunday dresses, however.

"We're going to church in a grocery store?" Franceska asked facetiously.

"No," Marc laughed. "They've asked us to park here and walk to church."

"Where is it?"

"See those really tall spruce trees down there? That's it."

Privacy was of upmost importance. At about the time of the last police raid, these spruce trees were planted close together along the entire frontage of the home and were immaculately kept and groomed in order to provide a forty or fifty foot tall, year-round visual barrier against gawkers. There was also a solid white fence about six feet tall. Both the pedestrian entrance and the driveway were guarded by large men who may as well have been speaking into their cuffs and taking orders through earbuds. They were not, of course; instead they seemed to be taking cues from the spirit as to whether those entering were friends or foes. As Marc and Franceska approached the entrance, he turned to her and said, "Act natural." He seemed to be entertained by the whole display.

He learned in one of the sermons that day, however, why the polygamists were so guarded against intruders and outsiders. A middle-aged man was called on to speak. He related his father's experiences surrounding the 1944 raid. He said that the church hired spies to gather information about the fundamentalists as part of its agreement to assist state authorities in their investigation to put the polygamists behind bars. These spies, whom he called "snoops," would write down the license plate numbers of those who were attending cottage meetings. They would sneak around and hunch below open windows to gather evidence. There was no air conditioning in those days, so windows were kept open to ventilate the house, making it an easy target for eavesdroppers. The speaker described his father being arrested, convicted, and sentenced to spend five years in prison. He served his time in the former Sugar House State Penitentiary which once stood not far from where they were then meeting.

State investigators were able to gather enough evidence to indict twelve women and fifteen men. Much of the ensuing media coverage portrayed the court action as a debacle and the state grew more and more embarrassed with the proceedings. Eventually officials offered a deal to those who were convicted: in exchange for a commuted sentence they would renounce polygamy, abandon their polygamous families, and never teach or advocate polygamy again, or, if they refused to accept the deal, serve their full sentence and be subject to further scrutiny in the future. Some of the brethren accepted the deal and got out early, others refused, saying that it violated their conscience. None of the men who got out early kept their promise to the state. They viewed the state's deal as a manifestation of God's hand to clear the way before them to fulfill their sacred responsibilities.

The incarcerated brethren received a warning from a counterspy working within the church of a plot to stage an explosion in the section of the prison where they were detained. The prisoners held a prayer circle asking the Lord to intervene and spare their lives. Within days, a member of the Twelve Apostles who had led the charge against the polygamists and who had been in perfect health by all indications suddenly fell sick and died. The speaker told this story to the congregation with an air of Mosaic exoneration—the Lord had clearly chosen his favorites and had fought their battles at a time when they were incapable of doing it themselves. The Lord protected his people with a "pillar of cloud by day, and a pillar of fire by night."

The Lord didn't send a pillar of cloud that day to shade the home where Marc, Franceska, and three hundred faithful followers sat in sweltering heat, however. In Park City, the days were still cool but in the valley, it was hot. The residentially scaled air conditioning system was no match for 30,000 watts of body heat and sweat. It quickly turned into a sauna.

The pattern for conducting these meetings was to call on several members from the congregation to give extemporaneous speeches prior to the brethren giving their own sermons. Because speakers from the audience seldom knew when they would talk, they were usually unprepared; hence the quality of their speeches varied immensely. One speaker occupied two or three minutes, which nevertheless seemed like an eternity, waiting for a subject to strike him from heaven. He eventually expressed his gratitude for the gospel and the priesthood and sat down. Another speaker hammered on the lack of dedication and faithfulness of the young people. "Here we go," Marc whispered into Franceska's ear. The speaker was alarmed and fervently dismayed at the manner in which they dressed. Marc leaned over again and said, "They don't look frumpy enough." Franceska smiled.

The third speaker nearly put the congregation into a coma. He opened and closed with a sentence of his own and otherwise occupied his time at the pulpit reading a lengthy sermon from one of the former priesthood leaders. The fourth speaker related the aforementioned history of his father's time spent in prison for the sake of the principle.

The brethren commenced giving their sermons, which by contrast to the anecdotal discourses of the previous speakers, were generally more focused on teaching and expounding principles of the gospel. Nevertheless, the audience seemed spent about an hour before the meeting ended. Women and children were fanning their faces with anything they could find: pamphlets, hymn books, or Asian fans which they brought with them for that purpose. Men sat stoic so it wasn't clear if they were praying for understanding or for the meeting to end.

After the closing prayer, the people formed long serpentine lines where they slowly made their way to the front to shake hands and greet the brethren. There was a visible reverence for the brethren notwithstanding the scathing sermons which some of them had just delivered. When Marc and Franceska made their way to the front, Brother Bower was elated to see them. He told Franceska that he was happy to meet her finally. He told Marc that he would like to visit with him briefly after meeting. Marc and Franceska waited outside by strolling through the gardens.

"So what did you think?" He asked Franceska.

"It was interesting. Really long."

"Yeah. You can say that again."

"Do women ever talk in church?" She asked.

Marc laughed. "Are you worried about talking?"

"No!" She said adamantly enough to call into question her honesty. "I was just curious."

"Well, I've been here four times, and there was only one meeting when they called on women. I really enjoyed it actually. I think they're more interesting than the men."

"Do you think it's true? That story about the bomb and the men in prison?" She asked.

"Who knows?" Marc asked, rolling his eyes. "Every time I ask any of these people where I can go to verify their stories... I mean, I don't say it like that. But every time I ask where I can go to learn more about a certain story, they usually tell me that it's just something that they've always heard. Nothing's written! They say that it's because they can't keep written records; they would be used as evidence against them in court."

"Well, I believe it," she said.

Marc looked at her in amazement. "What do you mean? You believe what?"

"I believe what we heard in church. Don't you?"

Marc's reaction suggested that he was dreading that question. He looked away and thought for a long time. Finally, he said, "I don't know." He looked pitiful, like a wounded dog.

Franceska didn't question him further. She put her arms around Marc's arm and leaned on his shoulder. Brother Bower finally came out and Marc walked over to meet him on the edge of the garden.

"Are you ready to move forward?" Brother Bower asked.

"I think so. I just need to get Lena on board. She's struggling with…"

Brother Bower cut him off. "If you're ready to move forward and Franceska is ready to move forward, let's go ahead. We're not going to wait for Lena. Whatever you lose will be made up to you a hundred-fold; that's the promise of our savior and trust me, he'll do it."

"I, I don't know," Marc stuttered.

"I do know," Brother Bower said. "How does next Saturday sound?"

"Okay," Marc responded.

Chapter 17

Marc found himself standing outside of a door, again, ringing a bell or knocking, again. It was the story of his life. Perhaps if he knocked at enough doors, something significant might open to him. If he sought enough, he might find. That was the promise; what are promises good for except to be tested? The trouble with promises is that the greatest ones are the hardest to give up on. One never knows when one has tested them long enough. The big payoff may be lying behind the next door. "Hello, Marc. Come in," Brother Bower said, welcoming him into his home.

"Thank-you for seeing me. I hate to take up so much of your time."

"No problem. It's my calling and my pleasure," he said cheerfully. He continued in a scriptural tone, paraphrasing John, "How can a man claim to love God whom he has not seen, if he doesn't love his brother whom he has seen?"

"That's a good point."

"How can I help you?" Brother Bower asked as he motioned Marc to take a seat.

Marc sat down like a convict on death row. The priest was there to hear his final confession. All of his appeals were spent and the governor had been elected on promises of cracking down on crime. There was no hope left in any earthly tribunal. Further denial of the truth would only hurt his chances for final absolution, if indeed there were any such thing. It was probably a bunch of bullshit, but he'd indulge in the ritual for the remote possibility that there was any virtue in it.

"I wanted to tell you the truth about me."

"Okay," Brother Bower said hesitantly, not knowing what Marc was about to reveal. Depending on what Marc said, Brother Bower may need to rededicate the house. It was a Mormon belief inherited from the Mosaic tradition that unclean things desecrate holy places. Verbal filthiness required verbal rededication; with enacted filthiness, the place may as well be burned to the ground. Neither God nor his Spirit would ever enter into that place again. These were the holy places of polygamy. Ever since polygamists were hunted and excommunicated by the church, their houses became their temples and their barns, their tabernacles. A spiritual leader couldn't take careless chances with his own home. "Should we take this outside?" Brother Bower asked.

"No, it's not like that," Marc said.

Filthiness was the opposite of holiness. It was good that Moses laid down the law before the days of microwaves and memory chips. Nowadays, filthiness was transmitted on every frequency and carried into every place where circuits went. Pulsing airwaves excited the very molecules of Brother Bower's white walls and gold trim. It was good that God's Spirit didn't understand physics or it would have blushed to see how those atoms were writhing about. Filthiness printed on magazines and centerfolds would offend the angels and drive them out. It was good then that they couldn't read the binary brail printed on tiny wafer boards with transistor ink. God's holiness, it would seem, was determined by the understanding of an illiterate hominid. In that scheme, wickedness was anything natural.

And it was good that Moses determined the chosen race before DNA tests. It's much easier to establish a claim when there is no mechanism to refute it. Claims. Claims. Claims. Kings claim to be gods or sons of gods and the people are willing to have it so as long as they, the kings, provide bread and beer like gods. Moses taught that there was but one god. Consequently, his god provided bread from heaven. It also conveniently turned to beer (except on Sabbath days when it would not ferment). The scripture said that if the Israelites gathered too much, it rotted, but that was merely the view of primitive prohibitionists.

With the advent of genetic technologies and the creation of the state of Israel as a Jewish refuge, peoples from around the world began seeking to prove their Jewish genealogy. Many have successfully demonstrated that they possess genes regarded as Jewish. However, the one ancestor that they can't substantiate, and yet the most critical, is Abraham. If John the Baptist lived today, he might say, "Ye no more have Abraham to your father than these stones." Joseph Smith hit the scene in a time and a location when and where no one could make a credible claim of ancient ancestry. Therefore, his doctrine centered on the principle of divine adoption. For him, the children of Abraham were those who did the works of Abraham.

"Are you willing to do the works of Abraham?" Brother Bower asked.

"I hope to do better than that," Marc scoffed. "Abraham couldn't keep Sarah from running Hagar off." Brother Bower raised his eyebrow and Marc immediately began back peddling. Marc said, "Come to think of it, I don't know if I'll keep more than one wife, either."

Brother Bower said, "Already, you have gained a little humility. That's good. It's one of the advantages of this principle. You'll find that it's mighty hard to be proud."

Marc said, "I love good principles, but I guess I'm saying that I don't believe in religion. I think it's a joke, a farce. I've attended several meetings, but most of the time I'm shaking my head."

"Oh? I haven't noticed that," Brother Bower said with a smirk.

"I'm shaking my head inside of my head. Okay, I know how that sounds, but I don't believe the things that I've heard. I don't believe that God is a cosmic control freak—that he dictates the minutia of people's lives. I don't believe in a god that is threatened by people exercising a little free will. We call him 'Father,' don't we? Fathers don't stifle their children—they develop them. I'm afraid that the kind of saints you're looking for are mindless sheep. People sheeple. At least sheep do what they are conditioned for."

"You seem quite upset, Marc."

"I'm not upset; I'm being honest. I can't live under a false pretense. I had to get this out before the wedding. I guess there won't be a wedding, now."

"You've told me a lot about what you don't believe. Can you tell me what you *do* believe?" Brother Bower asked.

"I believe in science." Marc paused and started over. "I believe in God. Science is merely a way of understanding his creations. I don't know what he's like, really, but I believe that his character should resonate with good sense and reason. After all, he endowed us with those things. I believe that God is expansive in his thinking. He's supremely invisible, too. I take that to mean that he's made us free to imitate good in our own ways, without excessive control or interference. I see people placing limitations and boundaries on being good. I don't see God doing that."

Marc paused as if to consider his own beliefs. With no response from Brother Bower, he continued, "I love God. I love him the only way I know how—through my own experiences and reflections. I love this life; I love the mystery of it—the suspense of it—not knowing how anything will turn out, but believing that I can affect it somehow. I love the richness of it—the heights and the depths of it—the marvels of the universe and the beauty of the earth. It's stunning!" Marc was growing in excitement. His eyes were wide and focused on objects far beyond the ceiling and the walls.

"I love man. I love the faculty of his mind—its ability to reach far beyond his own grasp. We glimpse the stars and describe them in figures and models. We probe the boundaries of the universe where light and matter slip forever beyond our view—like drift wood approaching the edge of a water fall—and we dream of things on the other side. What can't be seen is imagined, like parallel universes and alternate dimensions.

"We argue and debate about whose theory of the impossible is best. It's like building a bridge that reaches into eternity, supported on only our side. It's really a game and the winner is the one with the most elegant play. There are poor losers, as in any game, but most players are decent people who have devoted their lives to advancing human knowledge and they respect other people engaged in the same cause. Consequently, we know more about distant galaxies than we know about our own hearts.

"I'm grateful for that, too, for the mystery of our own beings. The nearest I've ever come to finding God was in that tiny space between Lena's body and mine—a space that I can't squeeze tight enough. I'm grateful for that, too; it keeps me searching for ways to merge with her, and it deepens my appreciation of God even more. I love being inside of a woman and wrapped around her at the same time; it's Holy-Ghost-like." Marc paused. Brother Bower didn't escort him out. Instead, he seemed to be perfectly at ease so Marc continued.

"If you want to talk about the mysteries of God, this is the mystery as far as I'm concerned: I'm wrapped around her, but somehow she shields me. She surrounds me with a love that pushes out the nastiness of the world. I'm physically stronger, I guess, but she's a thousand times more powerful. And yet she submits to me—wow! She gives me everything—puts it all in my hands. It's like she hangs on my word. I don't know why. I guess because she wants to build me up—help me climb higher.

"That's why I believe in God. I don't even care whether he really exists or not. I mean I care, obviously, but I don't need proof. I will spend the rest of my days searching for him.

I will serve the God of man-and-woman with all my might—the creator of this beautiful, stunning world."

Brother Bower said, "Well, that's sufficient for me, Marc. If those dear women of yours were here, I would seal you right now. Those angels that you were afraid of offending with your silly cell phone—well, they're actually thrilled."

"See, that's what I mean," Marc said. "I don't give a shit if you talk to angels. All that religious nonsense drives me crazy. I'm not sure you want someone like me in your group."

Brother Bower continued, seemingly ignoring Marc's outburst, "I think you should keep our date for this Saturday. If Lena is willing, I would seal her first, but don't put it off because of her. Franceska has as much of a right to the blessings of her Father as Lena does."

They soon wrapped up their conversation. After they said their good-byes, and Marc was walking down the steps of the front porch toward his car, Brother Bower teased him, saying, "By the way, you're not the first scientist that I have dealt with. I can see why Dr. Edberg loved you so much."

If there was any such thing, Marc drove away in high spirits. He gave the command and his car phone called Chuck. It fetched him faster than any servant ever fetched a king's friend.

Chuck answered, "Hello?"

"Get your ass over to Tonio's," Marc said.

"I'm working."

"Not anymore. I'm fifteen minutes away and if I get more than one beer ahead of you, well, that will suck for you."

"Okay, I'll see what I can do."

"'See,' madam? Nay. Be. I know not 'see,'" Marc said, slaughtering a line from Hamlet.

"Are you sure you're not already several beers ahead of me?"

Marc laughed. "I'm driving there now. Hurry."

There were a few students hanging out in the restaurant, but it was mostly empty, being mid-afternoon. Music was playing just like back in college, except that it included newer tracks. Marc looked at the menu; it hadn't changed much—didn't need to. Pizza was one of those things that would be served during the millennial reign of Christ. He ordered a tall beer and a combo to share with Chuck when he arrived. He sat at their old table, staring blankly at an empty table against the opposite wall.

"Look at that old couple over there," Marc said to those sitting with him which consisted of their regular college pack: Chuck, Ben, and Gary. It was noisy. The restaurant was crowded with students letting loose on a Friday night after a week of exams. There was that one piece of pizza left which didn't have the right proportion of toppings; someone would eventually eat it out of boredom rather than hunger. They had consumed several beers, except Ben; he always drank soda.

"What about them?" One of them asked.

"Do you think that'll be us someday?"

"I have no intention of ever marrying you," Chuck said.

"I mean do you think we'll be coming back here at the end? Back to where it all started?" Marc asked irritated that Chuck had to make a joke of everything.

"What started here?" Ben asked.

"You wouldn't understand," Chuck said scathingly.

"Oh boy, here we go again," Ben said.

Chuck indulged himself in attempting to derail Marc's points at any time, but if Ben ever attempted it, Chuck dismissed him as a brainwashed "moron"—a juvenile term for a Mormon—too stupid to grasp what Marc was saying. While they fought it out, Marc turned his attention back to the old couple. For some inexplicable reason, he couldn't take his eyes off of them. It was awkward when they made eye contact and Marc would glance away, pretending to be disinterested.

Eventually the couple broke up the argument between Chuck and Ben by asking if they could join them at their table. They were doing a little reminiscing; said that the group seemed like a lively bunch—reminded the old man of himself. The guys learned that the couple had met while attending the university. Ben excused himself saying that he had a lot of work to do. Chuck apologized for him, saying that Ben always had an aversion to fun. After Ben left, they took turns telling a little about their academic backgrounds and what they wanted to do after graduation. The guys were mesmerized for a couple of hours listening to the couple's stories about the old university, the poverty that they had suffered while they were young, jobs that they had held, special accomplishments, how they had achieved financial success, and what their three kids were doing, and so on. After they had visited a good long time and things were winding down, Marc asked them to offer some parting advice for students about to commence in life.

The old man said, "I'm reluctant to give you boys advice. I will, since you asked, but don't take anything I say too seriously." After an awkward silence, Marc asked him to relinquish the advice. The old man said, "That's it. That was my advice. Just because something worked for me, doesn't mean that it will work for you."

He then told another story. The landlord at one of their first apartments required a security deposit. It was exorbitant and completely unfair since the apartment was in terrible condition to begin with. However, since the rent was affordable, the couple sucked it up, withdrew their savings, and went hungry for a month or so to cover the deposit. The landlord ignored all of their repair requests, but since the location was good and they couldn't afford rent at any of the nearby places, they scrubbed the carpets and patched the walls at their own expense. They also repainted and repaired some of the appliances. After a couple of years they had the place looking pretty good, no thanks to the landlord. They finished their degrees and decided to move away. The landlord refused to return their deposit on the grounds that the kitchen countertops needed to be replaced.

"They needed to be replaced when we took the apartment in the first place!" The old man exclaimed. "It was piracy; he was stealing food from out of our mouths."

"That sucks," someone commiserated.

The old man said, "Oh, he paid for it. He didn't pay me, but he paid. I wasn't very good at waiting on karma in those days." He explained how he took vengeance on the landlord. He graduated as a chemist so he knew exactly what to do. He snuck into the utility room. The landlord always left it unlocked because he was too cheap to pay a maintenance worker, so renters did a lot of the upkeep themselves such as replacing filters, adding salt to the softener, shoveling snow, resetting breakers, and so on.

He made a bomb out of tissue paper, oil, sodium and other household compounds. He washed it down the utility drain and waited for the explosion. He then made an anonymous call to the health department. The landlord was required to replace the sewer main and many of the plumbing fixtures and drains which were damaged by the explosion.

"Wow! That must have cost a fortune," someone said.

The old man said, "True, but they were repairs which needed to be made anyway. The plumbing was always a problem. Some of the lower apartments were even flooded with raw sewage while we were living there. When the health department found some of the violations, they forced him to make the repairs without raising rents for three years or they would fine him."

The beer had made Marc bold, because he grew more demanding. He said, "I know you've got more than that. Give me something that I can sink my teeth into."

The man said, "You really want some advice, huh?"

Marc yelled, "Yeah!"

"Relax," Chuck said.

The man replied calmly, as if he knew that it was just the beer yelling and not a personal assault. "It's okay. I've learned a few things that I can share with you boys. Experiment— experiment a lot. Let's face it; no one knows what he's doing anyway. Break the rules; they didn't get other people very far. Make a lot of mistakes, but don't injure others; let that be your guiding star. Look to your own concerns; look to the needs of your own people, people whose lives you can actually touch in meaningful ways. The faults and failings of your people are a window to your own stinting temperament. If you want to be a leader, act like it. Be generous. I told the story of my landlord because it was his gross selfishness and my severe impoverishment that led me to desperation. I'm not proud of it, but I decided that generosity was going to be the basis of my life after that, and I haven't regretted it."

"Why did you want to meet here?" Chuck asked when he finally arrived two beers later. "Feeling nostalgic?"

"I like it," Marc said, still looking blankly at the empty table where the old couple sat that night.

"I haven't been here in years. There are better choices, you know."

"Better for what?" Marc asked rhetorically. "I didn't order you a beer because I didn't want it to get warm."

"I'll probably have wine," Chuck said.

"Suit yourself. I'm sure they keep some garbage under the counter for people like you."

"Wow, what got into you? You were chipper on the phone."

"I don't know. I'm frustrated, I guess. I'm marrying Franceska this weekend and Lena won't respond 'yea' or 'nay' about joining us. I can't get a commitment from her. I'm afraid she's going to leave me, Chuck." He paused to check his emotions. "I can't live plural marriage with one wife."

Chuck laughed restrained-like. "That's true. I'll be right back." He went up and ordered himself a glass of wine. When he returned to the table he said, "That's a tough decision, you've got there. 'Do I stay with the beautiful Lena or do I abandon Lena to be with the beautiful Franceska?'"

"I'm not abandoning Lena. You're as bad as a woman, Chuck. A man can love more than one woman. Can't you see that?"

"Sure I can see that. The only difference between you and me is that I am a serial polygamist and you're a parallel polygamist. Oh, and I don't marry them; I like to keep things simple."

"There's a lot bigger difference between us than that. I have kids. I go into these relationships with the intention of taking responsibility for the consequences; you run for the hills whenever things heat up. You're missing out on life's greatest moments, Chuck. You're going to die cold and alone. You'll be found from the stench of your corpse."

"I'll always have you, Marc. You'll smell my stinking corpse."

"Perhaps, but I won't be keeping your bed warm. Ya know, with the fire of..." Marc cut himself off and laughed.

"What's so amusing?" Chuck asked.

"I always thought it was interesting that Moses saw a bush that burned with fire and wasn't consumed. I've experienced better than that—I've burned with fire myself and been nearly consumed. Have you ever felt that, Chuck?

Probably not. You're afraid. You avoid the fire because the girl wants a wedding ring and a kid."

"Oh, there's passion, I can guarantee that. Heat? I got heat, son. I can melt a woman into a puddle of tears."

"I don't doubt that, because women are trusting, and each one probably thinks that she'll be the one that changes you. But have you personally ever felt it?"

Avoiding Marc's question, Chuck said, "This is exactly what I was afraid of. You've found religion and now it's all burning bushes and holy spirits."

"Found religion? I don't think so, but I've always revered God. I've found something that gives me purpose."

"There is no God," Chuck emphatically stated.

"Maybe not. That doesn't concern me."

Chuck looked confused. "What do you mean, that doesn't concern you?"

"I can carry on without a knowledge of whether God exists or not."

"Do you believe that he exists?"

"I hope that he exists," Marc said.

"Do you hope that God is evil?"

"No. What are you talking about?"

"God is evil. He supposedly has all power, all knowledge, and he does absolutely nothing to prevent evil. What kind of a God is that?"

"Please tell me you're not using that logic," Marc said with disgust.

"It's perfectly good logic."

"How's your wine?"

"It's okay. Why?"

"It must be puckering your brain." Marc motioned to the guy at the counter for refills to their drinks.

"Objection your Honor, ad hominem attack," Chuck said looking up into vacant space where his imaginary judge sat at the bench.

Also looking at the imaginary judge, Marc said, "I'm only demonstrating the nature of the prosecution's own argument."

"Explain yourself," Chuck said, assuming the role of the judge.

Marc explained. "The prosecution is slandering the defendant's character based on circumstantial evidence and the actions of evil-doers, with whom the defendant, God Almighty, is only loosely associated. Hence the nature of the defendant's character cannot be determined by their actions."

"How about natural disasters?" Chuck asked, abandoning his courtroom persona.

"You mean like earthquakes and hurricanes?" Marc asked.

"Yeah, and volcanos, tsunamis, fires, landslides, 'the heartache, and the thousand natural shocks that flesh is heir to.'"

"Wow, I'm impressed," Marc said in a patronizing tone.

"You're not the only one that reads Shakespeare, you dipshit," Chuck said with a tongue dipped in wine.

Marc laughed. "No. Indeed not, but I would expect someone who *did* to employ better arguments. Let's address these so-called evils by type: natural disasters including accidents, illness, animal attacks, and so on, and human abuses including murder, rape, assault, and so on.

"To disallow natural disasters, God would have to create a world without forces, without potency, without cycles, and without contrast. There would be no hot and cold. There would be no calm and no ferocious. There would be no turnover of land and sea. These cycles produce potency and fertility. Without them, the earth would be a barren wasteland.

"Contrast creates beauty. How would you like the sea if it never rolled with waves? How would you like the earth without a moon to drive its tides? With the ability of the sea to churn also comes its ability to kill. If the sea didn't have tides, it wouldn't incorporate much oxygen and couldn't sustain life. So with life comes death. It's an essential, unavoidable consequence.

"On the other hand, God could allow all of those forces of nature, and the beautiful cycles that result, without any adverse effect on man if he surrounded every person in a shroud of protection, like a shell. Then we humans could go running, swimming, and flying about without any fear of injury. We would be miraculously protected from disease, starvation, and harm. If we fell from the sky, we would bounce like a beach ball on the ground. If we sank, we would carry with us a bubble of air sufficient to survive until we reached the shore. It would be some kind of miraculous force field, permeable enough to allow two people close enough to kiss but strong enough to stop a boulder in midair if it was about to fall on a little girl.

"Everyone would live until a ripe old age until an appointed time when an angel capable of piercing the veil would come take life away. We'd long for it, too, because without risk there would be no adventure. Without danger there would be no thrill. We would live like spoiled brats that can't value a treasure because they've never had to struggle for anything. Death would be the *only* gift, but I wouldn't want to live like that. I don't think I could be happy without wonder and the greatest wonder is that I'm alive today.

"Then there's human abuse. That's the nasty one. If you can get close enough to kiss someone… You know? Close enough to evoke joy in someone, then you can get close enough to hurt that someone, too. Shielding people from harm doesn't produce happiness or joy, so in this case God would have to exercise control and prevent people from inflicting harm on each other. If I slapped you on the back, my hand would make contact, but if I slapped you on the face, I'd be restrained somehow.

"I'd be nothing but a puppet, though. God would read my thoughts, judge my intent, and interfere with all of my actions. I would never be permitted to test an idea to see if it led to good consequences or to evil. I would only ever be faced with two choices: to do or not to do." Chuck rolled his eyes at Marc's allusion to Hamlet again. He was growing tired of Marc's protracted response. Marc said, "I'm sorry, I couldn't help myself."

"I knew you couldn't. I saw it coming from a mile away. Are you done yet?" Chuck asked impatiently.

"Almost," Marc said. "Give me a minute."

"Oh, no problem. I've had plenty of practice," Chuck said.

Marc took a deep breath and, with a tone of closure, he marched through Chucks less-than-subtle insult. "So, in this state of affairs, we would have no freedom to love. We would be compelled to love or compelled to do nothing at all. If I know that someone loves me because there is no alternative emotion, it destroys the magic of it. If I love because I have no viable alternative, it douses the fire of it. Hence happiness is curtailed again. Ultimately, life is dangerous, life is sad, life kicks you in the balls and rips your heart out, but there is no other way to have it as far as I'm concerned. It's designed for our greatest happiness. That is not evidence that God is evil. Rather it is the strongest evidence that God is good."

Chuck started slow clapping. Even the attendant behind the bar was gawking to witness the shame. "That was beautiful, Marc. I have to tell you, I'm truly touched. There's just one problem."

"What's that?"

"I was being sarcastic about God being evil," Chuck said.

"I hope so, because that's the lamest argument I've ever heard. Only the lowest in intellectual stature would stoop to such logic," Marc said.

"My actual point was that God doesn't exist."

"Oh," Marc said in a nasal burst, as if he missed an obvious point and didn't want to prolong the embarrassment of it. "Well, that's no problem. I already addressed that."

"Remind me how; it was quite a while ago."

"It wasn't that long ago. Relax. You act like I took you away from something important."

"You did," Chuck insisted.

"Quit pretending to be important, Chuck. We all know that you're a glorified ambulance chaser."

Chuck laughed. "Alright. Is that why I negotiate all of your business deals?"

"Not all. I save the important ones for other attorneys." That shut Chuck up as if he was actually hurt. Maybe he just didn't have a good comeback, but Marc laughed it off and said, "I'm kidding. You know my business better than I do."

"That was never in question." Chuck seemed to be back to his normal vim and vigor.

Marc continued with the original point. "For a long time, I was troubled by the existence of God, or the lack thereof. I finally realized—I was letting other people frame the issue for me. I was worrying about the existence of *their* god. Of course *their* god doesn't exist." Marc laughed.

"So you've merely created a god in your own image," Chuck said.

"Maybe. Who knows? But I don't think so."

"Why not?" Chuck asked.

"Because my God is based on observing his works— silently, reverently. I've tried to set aside the dogmatic drivel and formulate a conclusion about his nature and character as objectively as possible. Have I suffered from an observation bias? I'm sure I have, but it's impossible to escape that entirely."

"What conclusion have you come to? What god have you found at the end of your rabbit hole?" Chuck asked.

"I haven't found a god, per se. I've found a *theory* of God."

"A *theory* of God?" Chuck asked incredulously.

"Yeah, I don't know what else to call it. It's crude, but I'm working on it. It's kind of like black holes. Long before we found one, we knew that they existed by investigating certain conditions within Einstein's equations. We can't observe them directly, but we can detect the invisible little suckers by observing the indirect consequences of their presence, such as space-time geometry, radiation, and so on."

"So you're saying that God is a black hole?" Chuck asked, thrilled that Marc had given him that gem of an insult. "Finally, I'm inclined to agree with you."

"Very funny," Marc said, rolling his eyes. "I'm saying that God is an idea. He is an idea that radiates through space and time like the rays of the sun. Consider this! The sun is ninety-three million miles away, yet it gives off enough radiation to burn you if you're exposed to it for more than a few minutes. With a tiny lens, you can start campfires. And it does that in every direction, continuously, without bias, without judgment, and without malice. The entire earth receives less than a billionth of the sun's energy. Yet, what we *do* receive is more than enough to sustain seven billion of God's children and all plant and animal life on the planet.

"As I said, God is an idea. He is abundance. He is happiness. He is love. I'm hopelessly devoted to the idea of God. When I say that I hope he exists, I really don't doubt him; I just hope that he exists in bodily form. If he turns out to be a god of 'body, parts, and passions,' as Joseph Smith taught, I will leap for joy. I'd love to throw my arms around him. I tell you, Chuck, that would be a cosmic hug." Marc swallowed the lump that was beginning to crush his voice and fought back the tears welling up in his eyes.

Finally, when he conquered his emotions, he continued. "Yes, I'm hopelessly devoted to that God. It's also why I can't be satisfied being married to only one woman. I adore this God so much that I yearn to be like him. I want to shine like he shines. I want radiate in the lives of many more." A strange look crept up on Marc's face.

"What?" Chuck asked.

"You're the first person that I've explained that to. I don't think I was completely aware of my own reasons until now."

"Lucky me," said Chuck.

277

Chapter 18

Marc was working at his desk. He was alternatively sitting in a stupor, scribbling in notebooks, and pounding out some technical program. The house was quiet except for the clicking of his keyboard and the occasional blowing of the air conditioner. There were still some boxes lying around from moving his things out of the downtown apartment. The kids had been with their mother all week, so he had nothing to do but to prepare for the wedding and pour his fury into his computer. He looked like he was creating something that should come to life, but he was doing it without a star to wish upon.

There was a ring at the front door. Marc answered it. There was a stranger in his mid-to-late twenties dressed in a suit.

"Hello," Marc said.

"Hi. Is Marcellus Friedman home by chance?" The stranger asked.

"Yes, he is."

"May I speak to him please?"

"May I tell him who is inquiring?" Marc asked.

"Yes. This is Max Planck."

"Really? It's an honor, sir, to make your acquaintance," Marc said gleefully. The man looked confused, so Marc clarified. "You said you were Max Planck, no?"

"Yes."

"The renowned physicist?"

The man laughed. "No, Max Plank: P-L-A-N-K. It's spelled differently."

"Oh. How disappointing. Is Marc expecting you?"

"No. I don't believe so."

"Then would you like to make an appointment?" Marc asked.

"No, that's okay. I'll catch up with him later."

Marc decided to take pity on the clueless man. "I'm Marcellus Friedman. Sorry to lead you on. I've actually been expecting you."

"You have?" The man asked puzzled.

"Yes, you're obviously not a salesman. By the way you're dressed, I assume you're a paralegal and you're probably here to serve me papers."

The man looked embarrassed and handed Marc an envelope. "Yes. Here you go." He asked Marc to sign a receipt and turned to leave.

"Why are you leaving so soon?" Marc asked.

"Uh, that's all I needed."

"What about my needs?"

"Excuse me?"

"Would you like a beer?" Marc asked.

The man looked more embarrassed. "Uh, no thanks. I better be getting back."

"Okay, that's too bad. Are you sure?"

"Yes," the man said, nearly to his car.

Marc went back inside with a smirk on his face. He verified that they were divorce papers and went back to work until it grew dark and the computer screen blinded him to the shadows prowling about the room. He then went into the closet and took down the erotic photo of Lena. He started packing up the trinkets and charms of Lena's past which he had collected into his shrine. There was a story behind each one. Some of the stories were small—just fragments of the larger story of their lives together. The story was that he adored her; he cherished her; he worshipped her, but none of that was sufficient to keep her. She was like an exotic bird without a cage. She could come and go on a whim and now was the time for her to go.

Most of the items were woven, coated, extruded, embroidered, grown, or cut from an enigmatic substance, which regardless of the color, form, or texture of each item, required that they be handled delicately. Some items were strong while others were fragile, but it was the substance of them, not their fragility, that stimulated his gentle touch. It was the substance of femininity. It emitted perfume and light which were perceived by senses other than the five.

There was a drawer that contained some visually unappealing items which would have clashed with the open display, but they meant no less to Marc, for he spent as much or more time reminiscing upon them as the others. He packed away some rappelling gear: a harness, interlocked carabiners, and a fragment of rope. The tears flowed. Out went the drumsticks and guitar picks. The corks and travel stubs, tossed. He slowly strolled through a shoebox of notes. He flipped through some photos. After the memories of Lena were buried in cardboard sarcophagi, he sat down on the floor and lost himself in the kids' drawers. He clenched the hospital bands of Baby Girl and Baby Boy. He opened their homemade envelopes and studied their drawings and precious words. They said that he was the best dad. They said that he was loved very much. Kimberly wished that he didn't have to leave her to work. Travis hoped that he liked this leaf.

They grow too fast. In making the trade, the tooth fairy didn't kiss and hold the child. Operating at a loss.

Finally, after Marc had tormented himself enough, he stood up. He took up the vase containing yesterday's flowers. They were daisies. Matilda had continued placing fresh cut flowers here until her last day. She had been a member of the family and a wonderful worker. Marc wept when he let her go, but he had lost his job and needed to reduce expenses. Matilda was sad to leave, but she understood. She probably didn't understand, actually. It was a form of betrayal and that's hard to comprehend. He smashed the vase and tucked Lena's things into the garage. He set out his clothes for the next morning and went to bed.

He didn't sleep much, though. After gazing into darkness for an hour or so, he went back into the garage and placed the nude picture of Lena back in its usual place. He went back to bed, but after about another hour, he retrieved the boxes containing Lena's items and placed them back into the case, packing them a little tighter, apparently leaving room for additional items.

The next morning, he picked up Franceska.

"Good morning," she said as she climbed into the car.

"Good morning," Marc said. "You look like an angel. I guess they exist after all."

Franceska laughed. "It's good that you come to this conclusion before your baptism."

"Yeah, it feels weird. I never thought I'd be doing this."

"It feels right to me." Franceska was gleaming. She came from a family that considered themselves Christian with loose ties to the Lutheran church, but they didn't really practice. "I wish that Kira could join us."

"She'll be able to next year."

"Yes, she said that she can't wait 'til she turns eight."

"The age of accountability," Marc said pensively. "Too bad that accountability and wisdom don't come as a package deal."

Franceska didn't know how to take that so she changed the subject. "I guess that Lena and Kimberly will not be joining us?"

"No, they won't be. I didn't want to tell you until later, but there's no good time to say it. Lena has filed for divorce."

"Oh, Marc, I'm so sorry." She reached up and placed her hand on Marc's shoulder. "This is my fault."

"No, Franceska. This is not your fault. It's nobody's fault. It's not what anyone wanted, but we don't always get what we want."

"This makes me sad, Marc."

"I know, but we saw it coming. Let's do our best to enjoy our time together. We're getting married, it's intended to be a joyous occasion," Marc said with a forced smile. He changed the subject. "How was your last day at work?"

"It was okay. I think Meg has been looking for excuses to get rid of me. She never liked me. When I gave her my notice, it was the happiest I've ever seen her."

"Oh, I'm sorry, babe. That's too bad."

"It's fine. I can't wait to move in with you and be your housewife," she said brightly.

Marc's face lit up. "Will you wear a short, little maid costume?"

"Of course, sir, however you like it."

"Will you bend over when you dust the furniture?"

"As low as I can."

"Will you make it very hard for me to concentrate when I'm reading?"

"Impossible."

Marc laughed with delight. "If we're not careful, we'll have to be baptized twice."

They arrived at the meetinghouse. There was a baptismal font in the garage. They were baptized in the morning and, after they went home to change and get ready for the wedding, they returned in the evening and were sealed in the main meeting room as husband and wife. It was a simple matrimonial ceremony. A few of the leading brethren were there and some women that Marc recognized as their wives from the church meetings he had attended. There were none of Marc's or Franceska's friends or family in attendance. It was treated as a highly sacred and secretive affair with no "outsiders" being invited.

Prior to the wedding, Laura doted on Franceska as if she was her mother, sister, and friend, all-in-one, helping her with her hair, makeup, dress, and so on. She started to cry when Franceska left. It wasn't apparent whether her tears were caused by pride in Franceska's bridal makeover, sorrow that she wouldn't be permitted to witness the ceremony, or jealousy that she herself wasn't the one getting married. Perhaps some of all. Franceska looked stunning. She wore a white dress that covered her completely from ankles to wrists. It buttoned up along the length of her back with beads and loops, elegantly fitting her frame above the waist with a subtle embroidered pattern, and loosely flowing to the floor, below. Her hair was done up and woven with flowers.

After the ceremony, there was no reception, no one to celebrate with. No toasts, no dancing, and no compliments. They were alone in their joy and alone in their shame. If it had to be kept secret, perhaps it was wrong. Perhaps, but perhaps the world was wrong, instead. There was a solemn silence in the car. Laura was keeping the kids, so they drove directly to the Park City house where they spent their first night together. Marc carried Franceska over the threshold and gave her a tour of her new home.

Marc tried to compensate for the lack of mirth by opening some champagne and giving his bride a toast. "Franceska, you are incredibly beautiful and you possess many other qualities, too. I feel more blessed than any man has a right, or a hope, to be. You are courageous, you are kind, and you are a dear friend. You have this uncanny ability to remain serenely calm in a terrible storm. Sometimes I feel like my life is a storm and you're a haven where I can leave all my worry behind. I love you and I always will. No matter what happens, I will never give up on us. I know it won't always be easy, but I will never forsake you. I wanted to say something witty, something to make you laugh, but the thought of you brings tears to my eyes. You've brought so much talent and beauty into my life. I feel truly honored to stand beside you. I can't wait to see what kind of life we can create together. Cheers, my love."

She told him how much she appreciated those sentiments and how much she admired him, too. He had a charcuterie platter already prepared in the fridge to accompany the wine, and gradually the laughter returned. They talked about the food and the childhood memories that it brought back. They discussed the lack of photographs they had to document their relationship. Marc said that he preferred to enjoy experiences without the distraction of cameras, that he preferred to let experiences live in his memory. She asked why. He said, "Because I feel that my privacy is being violated. I despise cameras, cunning little bitches, poking around, capturing moments that don't belong to them and then multiplying counterfeits for strangers who were not there. It's offensive!" Franceska laughed. He asked if she was ready to make a special memory with him. She nodded with excitement.

He took her into the bedroom, seated her upon a queenly throne, knelt at her feet, and buried his face in her lap. Finally, he looked up and after probing glances and eager smiles, he slipped off her shoes and kissed her feet. He removed her stockings and stroked her thighs. He pulled down her panties and licked her clit. He lifted her dress and ran his fingers along the surprises and frills which she had planted for him underneath. He caressed with nose and lips. He worshipped at the gate and pilgrimmed at the cleavage of chin and peaks. He told her that she was deliciously wet and she responded with an affirmative heave and moan. He took her in his arms and handled her like overripe fruit. He moved her ribs and bent her hips. He thrust himself into her, like a reamer into citrusy pith. He juiced her and left her filled, too. It was a glorious exchange that made them both the richer for it. At the end, he thanked her for giving herself to him with such grace and she thanked him for taking her with such "életerő." She didn't know the English word, so after they cooled down a bit, he translated it in bed. Vigor—she loved his vigor.

"I have this stupid thing that I need you to see," Marc said.

"What is it?" Franceska asked.

"It's uh... I don't know; it's really stupid, but I... I'll show you. I just about trashed it, but I decided instead to leave it and expand upon it." He showed her the closet case with Lena's things. He was embarrassed but she told him that it wasn't stupid; whether or not she truly believed it, it set Marc at ease. He said that he wanted to add some of her wedding attire to it.

"What do you want?" She asked.

"How 'bout your shoes and that lacy band?"

"Okay," she agreed. Then she said with a sly grin, "This is a beautiful photo of Lena. I thought you didn't like photographs."

Marc laughed a little nervously, like she had caught him in a lie. He recovered with the excuse, "Yes, but I love beauty; I love art."

"It's really too bad that she isn't here," Franceska said.

"Yeah, she..." Marc trailed off as if he wanted to say more but couldn't.

She continued, "I have so much gratitude for what she's done for me. Do you think it would be okay to text her?"

Marc thought for a moment. "I wouldn't recommend it. I think we should give her some space. Maybe tomorrow."

They didn't have elaborate honeymoon plans. There hadn't been a lot of time to make arrangements. It had only been a week since they were given a wedding date and only several days since Marc's manifesto of scientific faith which he confessed to Brother Bower, thinking that it would kill the deal. They stopped by Franceska's place to check on Laura, to pick up some things, and to kiss the kids before they took five days in San Diego. There were some nice dinners, a little sightseeing, some sailing, and plenty of time spent lounging on the beach. They returned from the honeymoon to a strange sight. Amy was waiting on the front porch. Marc introduced Amy as a colleague and Franceska as his wife. Franceska offered to go ahead with the unpacking while they talked.

"She's even more beautiful in person," Amy said.

"Thanks," Marc said fondly. "I think so, too."

"Getting back from your honeymoon?"

"I'm not going to ask how you know that. I've tried calling and texting you several times at the number that you used to contact me. It was an internet number, so I didn't know if you were receiving them."

"I received them."

"I'm glad. I had no other way of contacting you. I certainly couldn't call the law firm. Look Amy, I'm sorry for what I said in the coffee shop, basically for not trusting you. All of my files were there, just like you said."

"It would have meant more, you know, if you could have said that before you saw the contents of the drive."

"I tried, remember? You were too pissed to stick around after our conversation."

"You were a jerk."

"I know. I'm sorry. So why are you here?"

"Are you ready to level with me?"

"Yes, I am."

"Okay, start by telling me what those files contained."

"Come in," Marc said as he opened the front door. He took her into his home office and showed her the project that he was working on.

"Are these the files that you took from LogicStream?" Amy asked.

"Partly. I've put a lot of work into them since then. I could really use your help, Amy."

"What are you trying to do?"

"This is classified," Marc said tentatively.

"I understand. You can trust me," Amy said.

"We were working on a system to gather intelligence for counter-terrorism. It was kind of like a smart reader. It would digest the contents of newspapers, blogs, stock prices, mergers, real estate transactions, YouTube videos, Facebook posts, Twitter, porn accounts, you name it—and it would spit out webs which showed connections among various entities."

"Okay, sounds pretty basic. Why did you take it?"

"It's the best in the world; I didn't want to recreate it," Marc said defensively. "I'm going to take it to a whole new level. I didn't think the government wanted it for exactly what they said. There are obvious extensions beyond that. I think they were plugging our work into a larger project."

"Like what?"

"Prediction."

"Prediction?" Amy asked as if she didn't see what the big deal was.

"Yeah, it's like a crystal ball." He saw Amy roll her eyes and retorted, "I'm serious. We think that people are so unpredictable, but they're really not. They form habits and patterns. If people persist in a pattern long enough, they leave footprints—physical remains of their behavior. The difficulty is that there is so much activity that doesn't relate to anything of importance; it needs to be filtered out."

"I agree, but what are you doing with it?"

"I'm looking for conspiracies."

"Conspiracies?" Amy asked alarmed. "You're a conspiracy theorist?"

"I guess you could say that, but not like you're supposing."

"Conspiracies?!" Amy asked even more alarmed, like she wasn't listening to his defense.

"Hear me out. I'm not trying to prove that 9/11 was a government plot or anything like that. The question isn't whether or not conspiracies exist, they do. You and I formed a conspiracy to remove files from LogicStream. The reason that conspiracy theories set off people's insane-o-meters is that they are usually so farfetched. Any paranoid freak can retroactively validate a conspiracy theory. It literally doesn't matter what it is. There's always a plethora of coincidences to support it and a vacuum of actual facts which makes it appear that evidence has been covered up. It hasn't been covered up! It never existed in the first place. Uncertainty is the nature of existence. Nature itself hates a vacuum so it fills it up with random fluctuations and we humans, who love patterns, try to make sense of it."

"So you're looking for conspiracies proactively instead of retroactively?" Amy asked.

"Kind of, but not exactly. A predictive theory doesn't necessarily refer to the future. It suggests that the theory applies to events never before seen. You can't look at the data with an actual event in mind, or you'll always find what you're looking for. To be useful, a conspiracy theory has to be determined before the event is observed. For example, if I roll a die and write down the list of numbers, it's not hard to find patterns in the data, but if I try to predict the sequence of numbers beforehand, I'm most likely going to be way off. That's the problem with conspiracy theories: for the most part, they're just looking for patterns in existing data."

"Let's try it," Amy said. "Do you have a die?"

Marc handed her a die. She rolled it multiple times and wrote down the sequence of results:

5, 5, 1, 6, 3, 1, 4, 5, 6, 5, 3, 4.

Marc said, "Look! The first three digits of pi—3.14. What are the chances of that?" Marc asked facetiously. "But there should be a one between the four and the five. That's proof of a cover-up!"

Amy laughed. "Look at this: six and three add to nine. That's the next digit in pi, but this five has been planted to throw us off the trail."

Marc laughed, too. He said, "Exactly. Now roll the die again. Let's see if pi will raise its evil head again."

She wrote down the next dozen numbers:

6, 1, 4, 3, 5, 4, 5, 1, 6, 1, 6, 6.

She said, "There it is again, but it's jumbled this time."

Marc added, "Sure evidence that the sequence has been tampered with. Look at this, though, if we take half of six," he said pointing to the first digit, "we get 3.14 again. This three has undoubtedly been planted to throw us off, and the next two digits add to nine."

Amy said, "I get your point."

"That's just how ridiculous most conspiracy theories are. Instead, I want to formulate a scientific approach. I don't care about conspiracy theories for the common reasons. I care about predicting human behavior."

"So how are you going to make predictions if bogus patterns can be found so easily?"

"Do you remember that problem I was working on in college?"

"The one that got you fired?" Amy asked scornfully.

"Yeah, that one," Marc said in a manner as to acknowledge something trivial.

"It's not funny, Marc. You left me standing in the street."

"I know. I was stupid; I'm going to do better, Amy, much better," he said directly into her eyes.

"So what about the problem from college?" Amy asked getting back to the subject. "I could see that you continued working on it when I inspected your notebooks in the office."

"I've never solved the problem, but yes, I've been working on it. If you'll recall, my hypothesis was that our Standard Model for the elementary particles, interactions, and so forth, is extremely convoluted because we've built a theory around circumstances rather than developing a theory that elegantly predicts the state of the universe."

"So it's like conspiracy theories."

"Precisely. If you build a theory around circumstantial evidence, it tends to be convoluted. It might accurately describe what is happening, but it doesn't lead to a deep, fundamental understanding."

"Then you're trying to develop a conspiracy theory of all conspiracy theories."

Marc laughed. "Well, I've never thought of it like that, but basically, yes. It's based on these concepts." Marc flipped to a page in his notebook. There were sets of definitions and axioms which Marc had used to develop a rudimentary theory for conspiracies. One of his concepts was that, all things being equal, the severity and duration of a conspiracy would diminish with its size. He explained that the more people there are involved, the harder it is to keep it covered up. He also explained that with greater commitment of resources, such as investment of time and money, the severity increases.

Amy took some time to read it over and contemplate what Marc was saying. Finally, she asked, "What about terrorist attacks? It seems like someone can do a lot of damage with very little investment."

Marc said, "That's true, but rare. This is based on probabilities. Think of it like an electron. Its position is given by a probability distribution. It's impossible to predict with absolute certainty, but you can say where it is most likely and where it most likely isn't. Besides, terrorist attacks are broadly known at the time of execution, which significantly limits their duration. I think we'll find that there are many more conspiracies that are unknown, particularly political and economic conspiracies. It's harder to hide a dead body than a bank account." Marc thought for a moment and then added, "If the severity of a conspiracy is much larger or smaller than expected, I think it's likely caused by chance effects. Either that or there's a lot of missing information. Don't forget, though, that even with isolated acts of terrorism, there is usually a tremendous amount of intellectual capital, time, or association with other extremists that are invested into the project."

Amy bluntly raised a topic which she evidently felt driven to discuss with Marc. "I disclosed the hidden files that I extracted, remember? Marc, they know that you were stealing information."

"But they don't know that you gave them to me?"

"No."

"Then don't worry about it. They'll never find out."

"How can you be so certain? I'm honestly scared, Marc. Maybe I've destroyed my life. What if the courts force you to disclose your encryption key?"

"I'm counting on it," Marc said nonchalantly. He could see that this alarmed Amy, so he continued, "The files are triply encrypted. Well, to be more precise, they're doubly encrypted with a filter between."

"What do you mean?" Amy asked.

"I encrypted the files with an initial algorithm that they'll never break. It's essentially impossible," Marc said, proud of his work. "I then passed the encrypted files through a shuffling filter which paired bit segments with bit segments in existing videos, photos and several financial reports. Finally, I encrypted the filtered files with a basic routine that any idiot could decrypt."

"Thanks," Amy said pretending to be offended because she was unable to decrypt them.

"I mean any idiot with the key. I'll give it to you if you want. I don't mind giving them the key to decrypt the final pass. I'm just waiting for the court order."

"Why? What do the filtered files contain?" Amy asked suspiciously.

Marc's grin nearly dislocated his jaw. "Certain misdeeds by members of the board. Let's just say that they won't be anxious to have prostitution, adultery, and tax evasion made public."

"Wow," Amy said. "I'm impressed."

"You're not the only one who's good at your job." Marc smiled.

"I know. We're made for each other," Amy said bashfully.

"Palease, Amy, I just got back from my honeymoon."

"I meant professionally, Marc," she said in a scandalizing tone.

"Marc, could I visit with you?" Daniel Brensett asked, standing in the doorway of his library. Marc was there to pick up Lena and the kids. Daniel closed the door behind them.

"I've spoken to Lena. She's pretty upset."

Marc returned a blank look.

"She says that you're getting involved with another woman—talking about polygamy."

Marc returned the same blank look.

"Is that true?" Daniel asked.

Marc nodded.

Daniel's voice began to grow with indignation. "I know that you're not keen on the church, but you know that polygamy is not sanctioned."

"Yes, I'm aware of it," Marc said with defiant tranquility.

"It's terribly wrong," Daniel said, as if he was stating the obvious.

"Oh, is it?"

"Yes!"

"Didn't the church endorse it prior to 1890?"

"Well, yes."

"Was it wrong then?" Marc asked.

"No. It served its purpose, but that's in the past."

"Oh. What was its purpose?"

"To care for the excess pioneer women and to help populate the territory," Daniel said as if he was repeating a line memorized from a script.

"Care? Excess? Populate?" Marc asked in a crescendo of skepticism. "Are those things wrong?"

"No, it's how you go about it," Daniel said. "Things have changed since then. We have church programs for those people."

"So putting a woman on the public dole and church welfare for her support, filling her life up with society meetings, and consigning her to a life of celibacy is better than bringing her under my roof, loving her—body and soul—and giving her the opportunity of raising children with a husband and a father?"

"You're making it sound ridiculous, Marc. A woman can't be fulfilled in polygamy. It's impossible. The relationship that I have with Patty is sacred and fulfilling for both of us. She's my life companion, bone of my bone and flesh of my flesh. It reduces the status of a woman to stuff her into a harem for your sexual pleasure." Daniel was upset. He never spoke like that. It required a holy crusade to justify him in using the word *sex* or any of its derivatives and synonyms. It was taboo above all terms. Usually, euphemisms such as *relations, intimacy, touching, sleeping,* or *fooling around* were used to hint at what couldn't be said.

"I'm making it sound ridiculous? Am I?" Marc asked, more like an accusation. "You've referred to women as 'those people'—an excess—suitable for populating a wasteland but only worthy of menial activity in the modern church. I'm not making it sound ridiculous, you are! By the way, that's the life of my sister. It's real."

293

Daniel's tone changed. "That's really unfortunate, Marc. The church goes to great lengths to help unmarried people find their mates. Sometimes a girl's faithfulness… I mean that sometimes the girl needs to involve herself a little more. My girls…"

Marc laughed contemptuously over Daniel's boasting. "Laura's one of the most faithful girls you'll ever know. She's more involved than your girls ever dreamed of being. Her problem isn't lack of faithfulness. Her problem is that there are more women in the church than men and she lacks of sex appeal." Marc added in a burst, "Oh, and political connections within the church."

"Your connections certainly haven't hurt you, Marc."

"I don't deny that," Marc said, "but my work has certainly benefitted you, too. Hasn't it?"

Daniel ignored the question as his tone changed to one of resignation. "Marc, you're obviously suffering from a lot of anger. You sound like a typical detractor. You get disgruntled and suddenly the church and its leaders are to blame for everything that's gone sour. I tried to warn you about this when you first started dating Lena. I wasn't able to work through your hate then and I obviously can't now. I thought I would give it one more shot, but it's time to move on."

Marc looked at him inquisitively, not sure what he meant.

Seeing Marc's confusion, Daniel inhaled a breath of fortitude, and said, "We've discussed it as a family. Lena and the kids are staying here. They're not going home with you."

"You discussed it as a family?" Marc's ears turned red and his face began to burn.

"Yes. We're not willing to allow our daughter to become a victim of polygamy. We're not going to expose our grandchildren to sexual avarice."

"This is *my* family," Marc snarled.

"Then you should treat it with greater care."

"I care about nothing more."

"This is not under debate. The boys are here," Daniel said, referring to his older sons. He added, "I don't recommend making a scene. If you need to, take some time to think about it. This isn't what I want, Marc, but I'll do what I must to protect *my* family."

Marc thanked him for his concern and excused himself. The boys were standing in the foyer. He cordially shook their hands. He calmly left, but his inner rage drove him to the canyons, to challenge the hungry cats, to kneel before an icy alter in the snow where he pounded his troubles into the sand. He moved from rage to solace and a moonlit bath. It was a turning point.

"So when was that?" Amy asked.

"Let's see," Marc said, thinking back. "The security siege—actually, the security sham—was on a Monday. You were there. This happened the Friday before that."

"So you knew the whole time?"

"Yeah, while my father-in-law was lecturing me on the virtues of monogamy, I had evidence of his extramarital affairs. Some wonderful monogamy he has going on there."

"How did you get the evidence?" Amy asked.

"It wasn't hard. I knew how polygamy would go over, kind of like a lead balloon, so I wanted to be prepared. I hired a private investigator." Marc chuckled. "He told me that it was one of the easiest cases that he ever put together."

"Why didn't you expose him?"

"I didn't want that to be the basis of my relationship with Lena. If I get her back, I don't want it to be because I destroyed her family. However, I can't let them destroy my family, either."

After the honeymoon, Marc moved Franceska and her kids into the house. Kira shared her bedroom with Kimberly and Benjamin shared his bedroom with Travis, but they had their own rooms when Kimberly and Travis were gone, which was most of the time. After the wedding and after the divorce proceedings had begun, it became harder to arrange visitation with Lena. The Brensetts put up smoke screens and mirrors to foil Marc's efforts to see them.

The days rolled on. Amy became a regular collaborator on Marc's project. In further explaining it, he started calling it "relationship theory." Predicting conspiracies was merely an example of what it could do. He hoped that it would help him to understand human interactions and relationships, somewhat like other theories helped physicists understand interactions among fundamental particles and forces in nature. He said that humans were the real mystery and also the most significant objects in nature.

Marc moved a desk into his home office for Amy. He remodeled a little to create a more collaborative environment with marker boards and such to improve brainstorming. They worked well together. She helped Marc clarify his ideas and she was a better programmer than he for many aspects of the project. As a freelancer, her work with the law firm had slowed significantly after she disclosed the stolen files. She told Marc that she feared that they were preparing a lawsuit against him. He said, "Bring it on."

"You want them to decrypt the files, don't you?"

"Uh, maybe. It would certainly be interesting," he said.

Franceska took care of the kids and the house. She seemed to thrive in her new role as homemaker. She considered it a luxury which she had never enjoyed—she had always worked to help Jason provide for the family. When he died, she carried the burden of it herself. She had never learned to cook, so Marc helped with meals and taught her the basics. She buried herself into culinary books and cooking shows. Eventually Amy started staying for lunch, then she started staying for dinner, then she started helping with the cooking, too.

One day Franceska came into the office where Marc and Amy were working. She proposed that they go out for lunch. Marc said, "Sounds good. You coming, Amy?"

"No, I'm not really hungry. I'll watch the kids. You guys go have a nice time."

"Are you sure?" He asked.

"Yeah, I'm sure."

Franceska said, "Thanks, Amy. The kids have eaten. They're playing and there's a bagel sandwich in the kitchen if you get hungry.

When they came back from lunch, Amy asked Marc, "So how was it?"

"It was good," Marc said distantly, as if his mind was on something else. Franceska was glowing.

"Well?" Amy asked.

"Well, what?" Marc asked back.

Amy turned to Franceska. "Did you tell him?" She asked bluntly, yet enthusiastically. Franceska nodded with excitement.

Marc's eyes widened. "You knew that she was pregnant?" He asked Amy, shocked.

"Of course," Amy said as a matter of fact.

"How did you know?" He asked.

"Men are so clueless," Amy said, rolling her eyes.

"Yes, they are," Marc said.

Chapter 19

Marc parked in a downtown lot, paid cash for his spot at the kiosk, and made his way toward LogicStream in sunglasses, a pea coat with turned up collar, and a visor beanie cap. It was autumn and there was a chill in the air, but not much sun due to the overcast sky. Therefore, except for the sunglasses, he fit in with typical workers who were getting off of their shifts. As he approached the building, he pulled his cap down to hide more of his face. He knew where the security cameras were and as he approached them, he lowered his head. He passed the side alley where security would more likely spot a suspicious person, and opted instead for the more crowded, front approach. Walking among the other pedestrians, he finally darted sharply into the parking garage.

He lurked among the shadows, creeping from car to car to avoid being seen by people leaving work. The garage was emptying out, leaving fewer places to hide from the cameras. Eventually Lena appeared, strutting and bouncing with blonde hair as if she was carrying the sun upon her shoulders. Her charisma was instinctual; she was not aware that she was being observed. She was wearing a dark suit with a short skirt and a cream shirt with matching heels.

He was on the passenger side of her car hiding behind a large truck, fortuitously parked. She reached for her remote. Pushing the remote once would open the driver side only, but pushing twice would open both. She often pushed buttons twice; she was a double-checker. She would push "off" on the oven twice, she would check twice that the iron was off, sometimes thrice if leaving the house, and she would double-click the mouse when a single click would suffice. She clicked the car remote two times, and once she was inside, he jumped into the passenger side.

She screamed a scream, and then she screamed, "Marc!" She looked terrified, then relieved, and then irate. "What are you doing here?" She demanded.

"I needed to see you and I'm sick of your family interfering."

"You scared the hell out of me!"

"I'm sorry."

"How would you like it if a stranger did that?"

"Oh, I'd probably kill him," he said.

"Then why would you do it?"

"I'm not a stranger," he said, stating the obvious. "Can we talk?"

"Sure, talk!" She said, still rattled.

"Can you settle down?"

"No, I can't settle down."

"Let's go somewhere."

"Where?"

"Sushi."

"Fine!"

After they were seated, she said, "So, was that all part of your plan?"

"What?" He asked.

"To ask me out when I was too freaked out to realize what a bad idea it was."

Marc smiled. "Now a man needs a plan just to ask his wife out?"

"Wife? Not for long, we're getting a divorce."

Marc changed the subject. "I hear you took my old job."

"Yeah," Lena said somewhat defensively.

"Mrs. President," he said in a slow tempo to add weight to the title. "I'm very impressed. It's the smartest thing they've ever done; I should have done it."

"Thanks," she said tentatively, as if she was trying to determine whether or not he was being sincere. The combination of his starry eyes and admiring smile, however, seemed to convince her of his earnestness. She added, "It's hard."

"You can do it. I've never doubted you."

"Thanks," she said again with a bashful tilt while tucking a sunny lock behind her ear. She was finally coming down off of her anger ledge.

"I wonder if you have an opening for a software engineer," he said lightheartedly.

Lena laughed. "If we could hide it from the board, I'd be willing to hire you. Everyone still loves you. It's like they're always comparing me to the old boss, waiting for me to fail."

"Does the president still love me?" He asked.

"The president loves you, but she needs to do what's best for her this time."

Marc smiled at Lena's heartfelt confession. "You'll do incredibly well; you'll blow their mind holes."

"Well, I don't have the programming expertise that you do," she said in a self-deprecating tone.

"You have something far better. You always compensated for my shortcomings. I miss that, Lena."

She looked at him pitiably. "Marc, what's this really about? What did you bring me here for?"

"I hear you have your own place. Is it nice?"

"Yeah, I like it. Stop avoiding. What do you want?"

"I want you. Come back."

She looked at him, waiting for him to add reasons to his plight.

"I carry no hard feelings, Lena."

"You carry no hard feelings? You still don't get it, do you?"

"Okay, that was a stupid way of saying it. I do get it, Lena. You feel that I've betrayed you, but I want you to know—what I meant to say is—I love you. I always have and I always will. I have never betrayed you in my heart. I never took any steps without also taking pains to include you as much as you would. I've been an open book. That's how you knew when to serve the divorce papers—one day before the wedding."

Lena looked embarrassed. She said, "That wasn't my intention, it just happened that way."

"Okay, but I'm sure your dad got a kick out of it. He's orchestrated this whole thing, hasn't he? Probably set you up with the meanest attorney in the state."

"I didn't want this," Lena said emphatically, "I wanted us, but I'm not going into this new life with you. I've made that perfectly clear. It wasn't a trifling decision."

"Okay, what about the kids?"

"What about them?" She asked.

"Are you really going to take them—sever them from their dad?"

"What do you mean?"

"I mean the case that you're mounting—sole custody."

"I'm just following the advice of my attorney."

"And he's following the advice of your dad, no doubt."

"Quit making this about him, Marc. This is *my* decision. I can allow them to visit you; sole custody doesn't prevent that."

"You can *allow* them to visit?" Marc asked in a tone of mounting anger, pain, and frustration. "I have rights, too, Lena. I'm their dad!"

"Settle down. There's no guarantee that the judge will even grant my request. It's just a negotiating tactic."

"I'm trying to settle down, but I'm in a hopeless situation and you're exploiting it," Marc said in a strained whisper. "Is that what the attorney told you? It's just a 'negotiating tactic?' Think about it, Lena. A polygamist has no rights in this state. The judge is going to grant you full custody strictly because I'm a polygamist." Marc laughed sardonically and added, "And I'm not even a polygamist if you divorce me. I'd have a better shot at this hearing if I were a serial killer with a meth addiction."

Lena laughed, but contained as much of it as she could. Still trying to contain her amusement, she added, "Just imagine how much worse it will be when the judge hears that you car-napped me."

"I hope that remains between us," he said.

"Of course. I'm not evil, Marc. I'm just looking out for the best interest of our kids."

"Then let them come home with me."

"I don't know," Lena said tentatively. "I don't think it's a good idea."

"They haven't visited since you initiated the divorce," Marc said. "I've tried to avoid creating a scene—heaven knows that I don't need any more going against me—but I have as much of a right to see them as you do. You know that they need me. They need their dad."

Lena took plenty of time to consider her decision. "Okay, next weekend."

Marc smiled. "Great, but why not this weekend."

Lena hesitantly said, "Daddy will be out of town."

"What does your dad have to do with any of this?" Marc asked defensively.

"Nothing, I just think it would go over smoother for everyone involved."

"As far as I'm concerned this only involves us and the kids."

"Marc, I don't want to fight about it."

"Okay. You're right, no fighting, but if the kids are coming next weekend, you'll have to bring them."

"Why?"

A smile bubbled to the surface of Marc's face. "Oh, I don't know. There's someone who would really like to see you."

"Who?" Lena asked with a puzzled look.

"Franceska."

Lena rolled her eyes.

"What?" Marc asked. "She loves you. She's never stopped talking about you."

"Like she's screwing my husband, sleeping in my bed, and cooking in my kitchen?"

"No, not like that. You know that she adores you. She wants to make peace with you."

"My problem isn't with Franceska. It's with you, Marc."

"I know, but we should be adults about this. There's this dust cloud that's been looming over our family for months. We need to clear the air. It's best for everyone, especially the kids."

"The kids?" Lena asked with a sneer.

"Yes, the kids. She's going to be a significant person in their lives."

Lena shook her head and turned away.

"Lena, this is important. Unless you're really considering taking the kids away from me, we should learn to work together. If we can't be married, we should at least be friends."

Lena sat quietly, still turned away.

Marc's face turned white. He covered his mouth like one does when one receives news of a tragedy. "Lena?" He asked in a discreet but urgent tone. "Lena, the kids?" He asked more forcefully.

She ran out of the restaurant. Marc sat motionless like a marble statue, no blood flow to his face. He was like a man tied to his chair, sinking in an ocean of fears. All of the normal thoughts undoubtedly flew through his head. Most of them led to jail. Fear promotes dreadful decisions. What could a man do, but stand by and let the court take his children away? How many crimes would he add to polygamy to keep his little ones? Running from AMBER alerts is no life, not for a man and not for a child.

He had difficulty responding to the vibrating vocal chords of his server. His mind fought through the foamy numbness that had replaced his flesh to ask for the check. He wandered the streets back to his car. He hadn't even finished one glass of wine, but he walked like ten. Once he came sufficiently to his wits, his texted Lena but received no response.

When the weekend came that she agreed to allow the kids to visit, she made excuses, instead. The custody hearing was set for the following week. He was working with the best divorce attorney that Chuck could recommend. Marc hadn't seen his kids for several months and his attorney advised him to use the fact that Lena had deprived him of his parental rights to fight her claim. He initially refused, telling his attorney that if he brought that up, she would tell the court that he forced his entry into her car. The attorney yelled at him for being stupid: stupid to force himself into her car while he was fighting a custody battle, stupid to think that she would not use that fact regardless of her promise not to, and stupid to dabble in polygamy in the first place. It was Marc's stupid decisions that led to his predicament; he needed to give the attorney free rein to fight in a manner that would give Marc a fair shake.

The attorney said, "If you would screw your side gigs like a normal man, discreetly in a hotel room, you might still be getting a divorce, but at least you would fare infinitely better in court."

Marc spit fire when he told the attorney that he had better refer to Franceska with greater respect. He gave the attorney permission to use whatever tactics would best serve their case, but Marc would not tolerate personal attacks on Lena. During the hearing, Lena's attorney had no such hesitation. Therefore, it was a one-sided blood bath. Lena looked embarrassed, but she accepted sole custody when the judge granted it. Marc's attorney was upset. He told Marc that if it hadn't been for Chuck, he would never have agreed to represent him.

After the judge granted the divorce and all of the paperwork was wrapped up, Lena sent Marc a text.

Lena: I'm really sorry about that. That was awful.
        You probably hate me. I don't blame you.
Marc: I don't hate you. I told you that I love you.
        Always have... always will.
Lena: I didn't want it to be like that.
Marc: I know.
Lena: What do you mean?
Marc: I don't think you would have done that on your own accord.
Lena: I didn't. I was under a lot of pressure.
Marc: I understand.
Lena: I've been thinking about what you said.
Marc: About what?
Lena: About working together for the sake of the kids.
        They really want to see you.
Marc: They've wanted to see me for months, Lena!
Lena: I know, I'm sorry. I never thought that this
        would turn so sour.
        I was shocked at the hearing. That wasn't me,
        Marc.
Marc: Like I said, I know.
        So are you willing to let me see the kids?
Lena: Yes. I'll bring them this weekend.
Marc: Until your dad objects...
Lena: No. I'm serious. I'll be there Friday around 2:00.
Marc: Okay, I'm looking forward to it!
        BTW, Franceska is pregnant.
Lena: Congratulations

Marc: I hope that doesn't affect your decision.
Lena: It doesn't. I'm happy for you both.
Marc: Thanks. See you then.

On Thursday, when Marc and Amy were wrapping up for the day, he said, "Let's take tomorrow off."

"Why, what's going on?" She asked.

"Lena's bringing the kids to visit."

"Wow," she said. "How did you pull that off?"

Marc shrugged, but he was smiling.

"And Lena's bringing them? Wow, wow! That's exciting, Marc. I guess you just don't want me around when Lena gets here."

"No, not at all," Marc protested.

"I don't believe you, but I don't blame you, either. You've got enough to worry about."

"Thanks," he said.

It was 1:30 Friday afternoon and Marc was watching the driveway like a school kid waiting for his crush to walk by. He had finished early. Everything was in order, or at least in some kind of engineered harmony, contained within reasonable bounds and margins of error. For the amount of preparation that went into this occasion, Marc should have been serene, but he wasn't. There was an anxious cloud over his head, like an old cathode ray TV tube playing static. Franceska was biting her fingernails.

There was a bottle of champagne chilling. Marc and Franceska had a beautiful spread laid out and the kitchen was shiny clean. The whole house was clean, cleaner than Matilda had ever made it, though she was really good at what she did. Marc did the menu planning and shopping for the occasion because, as Franceska said, he knew better what Lena and the kids liked. It was Fall Recess at school and Kira and Benny were entertained by a movie in the family room. Lena's music was playing in the background.

"What is this shit?" Marc asked.

"It's not 'shit.'" Lena said. She was relaxing on the couch with a bottle of wine listening to some bluesy-soulsy-jazzy stuff. "There's a glass on the counter," she said, "if you'd like to join me for a little cultural education."

"I'd love to," Marc said with a guilty smile. He sat beside her and said, "I'm ready, teacher," as he poured himself a glass of wine. "Pinot? Seriously? You're really stretching me, you know?"

"It's good for you, babe. Always do your stretches before any heavy lifting," she teased.

"You call this heavy lifting? It's more like watered down zinfandel augmented with a splash of rubbing alcohol."

She laughed. "I was talking about the music. It's a wonder that I like you so much. For someone who pretends to be so smart, you're really dumb, sometimes."

"Then you'll just have to educate me," he said as he attempted to kiss her on the neck.

"I'm trying," she said, pushing him away, "but you've got to have an open mind."

"Show me how," he said, spreading her legs.

"Marc! I said an open mind."

"I heard you."

"That's not the mind. Now listen you brute! She's brilliant."

"Fine!" He said, folding his arms. "Who is it?"

"Amy Winehouse. She's a British singer."

Marc listened for a while. Finally he said, "Okay, I admit she's not bad, but would a little rock and roll kill you?"

Lena rolled her eyes and shook her head. On another day, maybe two years later, Marc walked in on a similar scene, but Lena was crying. It was a Saturday, about noon; and the music was playing much louder. Marc asked her what the matter was. "She's dead," Lena sobbed. "Amy's dead."

"Amy Winehouse?" Marc asked.

"Yeah!"

Marc held her but there was nothing really to say. The circumstances of life inevitably change, sometimes abruptly and it rips the heart out, and sometimes slowly, like a whittling knife, when it's the reminiscing that finally reveals the loss of something weighty. The heart always grows back, though, but scarred and less supple, less able to bounce back, until eventually it breaks for good.

It was 2:10 and Lena's car drove in. She had kept her word. He met her in the driveway. The kids were really excited to see him, even Kimberly. He kissed and hugged them and told them to meet him inside.

"Come on in," he told Lena, who remained in the car.

"I just came to drop off the kids," she said.

"May I have a seat?" He asked with a sly smile.

"You're not going to force your way in?" She asked with the same sly look.

"Not a chance."

"Then, since you asked nicely, please do."

Marc sat down. "I thought we were going to work together… You know, like friends."

"I want to, I really do. It's just not a good time. I have a lot to do."

"If it's not a good time, it'll never be a good time."

"I'll make time. I promise."

"Franceska really wants to see you. I told her you'd be coming in for a while."

"Why'd you tell her that?"

"I thought that's what we were doing," Marc said raising his voice defensively.

"That's not what my text said." She picked up her phone as to start looking for proof.

"No. Look, I don't care what the text says. We'd just really like to visit with you. Franceska's been working on a little snack."

"I think I see what you're doing here, Marc," she said with probing eyes, "and I'm not interested in this lifestyle. I came today for the sake of the kids."

"I understand. For the sake of the kids. Come in and have a snack for the sake of the kids."

"Fine," Lena said frustrated, "but I can't stay long."

Lena walked into the house and Franceska gave her a big hug. "It's nice to see you," Franceska said with nervous vivacity.

"It's nice to see you, too. Congratulations," Lena said to Franceska whose pregnancy was beginning to show. "The place looks nice. Nice music," she said turning to Marc.

"Amy Winehouse," he said smiling. "Someone educated me. Let's grab a plate of food."

"This is quite a bit more than a 'little snack,'" Lena said.

"I hope you like it," Franceska said.

"So, I was able to get in with the same key code," Lena said referring to the driveway gate.

"There's no reason to change it. You're always welcome here," Marc said.

The small talk was underwhelming and there was an awkward silence. Just before it appeared that the conversation would turn to the weather, Marc popped the champagne which immediately helped. Within ten minutes the three of them were laughing and conversing on a broad range of topics: work, finding an apartment, pregnancy, and what it's like to be married to Marc. Lena and Franceska took turns roasting him. They would laugh hilariously at his quirks.

Lena said, "He's a cute nerd."

Franceska said, "He always ties everything into science, even how many legs a table has."

Lena added, "But he can't understand how a woman can be too tired to make peanut butter sandwiches and yet has plenty of energy to go shopping for six hours."

Franceska said, "And two days later, she has nothing to wear."

Lena said, "That's because he would wear blue jeans to the governor's ball."

Franceska said, "No way!"

Lena said, "I kid you not."

Finally, Marc changed the subject by asking how the kids were doing in school. Lena said that she preferred the Park City schools. Franceska said that it would be fun to have all of the kids attending the same school. She would be happy to watch them until Lena could pick them up if Lena wanted to switch schools. Addressing the business at hand, Lena asked how they would be spending the weekend. Marc said that he was planning a fishing trip on Saturday and the alpine park on Sunday. Lena asked where all of the kids would be sleeping. Marc said, "Same as their old rooms." The girls would be sleeping in Kimberly's old room and the boys in Travis' old room. Franceska showed Lena the kids' rooms. She said that she hoped Kimberly and Travis would like their rooms. Lena complimented her on the decorating.

"Oh, my! I've spent much longer than I intended," Lena said. She wished everyone a good weekend. She and Franceska hugged again and Marc walked her to the car.

"Thanks for coming," he said.

Lena said, "I had a good time. I'm glad you convinced me to stay. Keep an eye on Kimberly, she's being really emotional."

"I will. Hey, Lena."

"What?" She asked.

"It was really nice to see you."

"It was good to see you, too," she said.

"I hear that you've been spending some time with a guy. Someone that your parents approve of," Marc said.

"Who told you that?" She asked.

"Clawson."

"Oh, right. Clawson doesn't like him. He never likes anyone."

"He liked me."

"Yeah, he liked you. You're the only one."

"So is it serious, your relationship with this guy?" Marc asked.

"No. I wouldn't really call it a relationship. You know my parents. They just want me to be happy."

"I want you to be happy, too. I want to make you happy, Lena. I know I can."

Lena didn't respond. Eventually she kissed Marc on the cheek and said that she had to go. Marc was obviously hoping for more. It was nice of her to kiss him, but when a naturally warm person is cool instead, it cools the world.

"Okay," Marc said. "I'll drop the kids off Sunday night. I'd like to see your new place, if that's alright."

He walked back to the house like a warrior whose friends left him to fight alone. He couldn't rely on Lena forever. He was a man and a man is strong, right? It was time that he found his own source of warmth and light.

They played board games. Kimberly didn't want to play. Marc told her that she liked this game. "Not anymore, Dad. Besides, 'those mind tricks don't work on me,'" she said, quoting Watto from Star Wars.

"'Dad?' You call me 'dad' now?"

"Yip."

"That's fine, sweetheart. What do you want to play?"

"I don't want to play anything. I'm reading."

The others went on without her. They switched to a movie in the evening, but Marc insisted that everyone went to bed early so that they could rise early to go fishing. He went into their bedrooms to tell each child goodnight. He started in the boys' room. He kissed Benjamin goodnight and told him that he loved him.

"Goodnight, Daddy, I love you, too," Benjamin said.

"Are you looking forward to fishing in the morning?"

"Yes," he said with a big smile.

"This is your first time, that's a big deal," Marc said. He then asked Travis how he liked the room.

"I like it," Travis said.

"It's a little different than when you were here last, isn't it?" Marc asked.

"Yeah."

"How do you feel about things being different?"

Travis shrugged.

Marc said, "Things change. When a seed grows, it changes, doesn't it?"

Travis nodded.

"Sometimes change is hard, but sometimes a seed grows into a big, beautiful tree that you can climb. That can be a good thing, right, Travis?"

Travis nodded again. Marc kissed him goodnight and told him that he loved him.

Travis said, "Daddy?"

"Yes, son?"

"Benny called you 'Daddy.'"

"That's right. You're brothers now, son. Our family is growing."

"Okay. I love you, Daddy."

The girls were both older and less talkative. Kira returned Marc's love, but when he told Kimberly that he loved her, she wrapped her arms around him and said, "I love you too, Daddy." After several minutes of clinging to him, she added, "I'm sorry, Daddy."

"That's okay, sweetheart. I understand. We'll talk more in the morning."

"Okay, I'm looking forward to it."

"I am too, Kimmy. I am, too."

Fishing went great. Everyone caught at least one fish, with Travis capturing the largest. Franceska's was the smallest and she released it. Kimberly tried to pout, but there's absolutely no way to be angry when reeling in a fish. It's impossible, like frowning while blowing bubbles. She scowled when Travis referred to Benny and Kira as their brother and sister, but she smiled when Kira caught a nice big one. On the way home, they stopped at the market for some produce to complement their fish, which they planned to grill. There was something about enjoying the tangible benefits of wild effort that refreshed everyone. Marc conducted their first ever family prayer. Everyone linked hands as he uttered:

Dear God,
Our ultimate role model and most generous friend.
Thank-you for this day. Thank-you for our family.
We love each other very much and Lena who
      couldn't be with us.
Thank-you for this food. Thank-you for these
      sacred fish.
We want you to know that they didn't live in vain.
We have had a really good time enjoying your
      wondrous universe and the creations of this
      beautiful earth.
We will use all that you have placed in our care to
      perpetuate your grace in the earth.

Thanks again for everything you've done for us,
We humbly pray in the name of the best we know,
Jesus Christ.

Kimberly seemed to appreciate the special mention of her mother, and Franceska looked like she wanted to jump on him, which she did once they reached the bedroom.

The next day, they visited the alpine park. Marc left them enjoying some concessions at a picnic table while he stood in line for tickets to some of the attractions. When he returned, Franceska was visibly upset.

"What's the matter?" He asked.
"I'll tell you later," she said.

While the kids were later engaged in their activities, he asked her what had her so upset. Franceska explained that while she sat at the picnic table, a woman, about sixty years old, engaged her in conversation. The woman asked Franceska about her due date and how the pregnancy was progressing. The woman thought the kids were really cute. She asked Franceska whose children she was tending. Franceska proudly stated that they were all hers. The woman became angry and wanted to talk in private. She told Franceska that she was having too many kids; it was a disgrace; four kids with another on the way! What was she thinking? The woman knew a good doctor and urged Franceska to terminate the pregnancy. When Franceska refused, saying that she wanted the baby, the woman stormed off, muttering something about selfish women over-populating the planet. Marc apologized for such people, and told Franceska not to allow it to ruin her day.

That night, Marc drove the kids to Lena's condo. It was a stylish place in a trendy complex. Lena opened the door and welcomed him into the entry. She thanked him for bringing the children, but she made excuses for not admitting him farther. He played the part of a subtly disappointed gentleman and left the flowers that he brought.

When Amy came to work the next day, she asked how the visit with the kids went. Marc told her that they had a great time. He talked a little about fishing and said that Franceska had a rattling experience at the alpine park. Amy wanted to know about it, but he suggested that she ask Franceska about it personally, which she did at lunch.

Amy grew irate at hearing the story. She said, "It's none of that bitch's business whose kids they are, anyway. Next time you take the kids out, I'll go with you. We can split them fifty-fifty, but if any shriveled up cunt tries to make you feel like a criminal for having kids again, I'll wrap a cable around her neck and dangle her from the Ferris wheel as an example for people who want to mess with polygamists."

Franceska laughed.

Marc laughed, too. He said, "Technically I'm not a polygamist."

Amy said, "Technicalities, technicalities," and all three of them blushed.

The kids came to visit four times over the next two months. Each time Lena dropped the kids off, Marc urged her to stay, but she never spent more than a few minutes, and he only extracted one kiss. The activities eventually turned to boarding and skiing. Marc and Amy delved into their project between visits. Marc said it gave him something to channel his frustration into. Amy remained true to her word; she accompanied the children on their outings and pampered Franceska as her pregnancy ripened.

One Monday morning Amy came to work and Marc was sitting at his desk in Saturday's shirt. His hair was a mess and he looked like he hadn't slept. She asked what the matter was.

"It's a failure," Marc said.

"What's a failure?" Amy asked.

"The project, it doesn't work. I've been running tests all weekend. It doesn't work."

"What are you talking about? It should work great. Show me."

"I haven't showered for a while."

"I can handle it. You're no rose, anyway."

Marc showed her the results of his tests. There was a graphical interface which displayed clusters of data and entities on multiple flying layers which could be rearranged, flipped, and morphed in size and shape. Events had their own layer, as did people, publications, social profiles, organizations, web searches, and so on. Their web crawler associated dots on each layer with any other dots where a connection could be established. It even crawled the deep dark web, the hidden majority of the internet. Their method targeted domains and addresses based on activity which they mined from the existing content.

Associations between entities were strengthened with multiple passes and each connecting segment of the multi-layered map contained parameters describing the nature of each encounter. However, it wasn't the strongest connections that interested Marc and Amy most. Rather, the nucleus of their theory focused on weak or non-established connections where entities with strong, robust connections to various layers seemed to cluster around hidden attractors. It was like pit bulls being held by threads or invisible leashes; it didn't make sense unless there was a lot of hidden activity. It required massive computing power to uncover this clustering, and a lot could be determined about these hidden entities from their context.

Marc had isolated some strong clustering involving conflicts of interest, submarket transfer of state assets, and criminal manipulation of state and federal bids. He showed Amy the context surrounding the hidden attractors. It strongly implicated the Brensett family, certain leaders in the church, state officials, and the governor.

"What is your problem, Marc? It looks like it's working perfectly," Amy said alarmed.

"That's the problem. That's it precisely. It's working *perfectly*," Marc said facetiously.

"I don't understand," Amy said.

He threw his arms in the air, saying, "It's like finding flies on the pile of shit. That doesn't require much power of prediction."

"But this is exactly what you need," Amy said.

"This was never about blackmail. It was about science, about finding the truth! Besides, this could be nothing more than a colossal coincidence, like finding pi in a sequence of random numbers. I struggled all weekend to run a successful test, but it wasn't until I started looking for something specific that all of this came out. I already knew there was massive corruption; everyone in the state knows it. But this isn't evidence; it's worthless."

Amy said, "You know, Marc? I was wrong. You really should go shower. Besides, I want try this for myself."

Chapter 20

Life has a way of laying everyone low at some point. Sometimes one must acquire the power to pull oneself out of the depths from external sources. There's a place where one can always go for refuge and a person to whom one can always turn for comfort. The place is home and the person is Mother. Apparently Marc hadn't hit rock bottom because instead he called his father and suggested a day of ice fishing. He told his dad that he needed some advice. Bradley couldn't get off work, so they agreed to meet on Saturday at their old spot. It wasn't far from Marc's Park City home.

He received a text from Amy.

Amy: I won't be able to come into work this week. Have a lot of catchup to do.

Marc: That's fine. We're done with that project anyway.
Is there anything I can do to help you with your shit?

Amy: We're not done.

Marc: May as well be. Let's face it... It didn't work.

Amy: Marc, you're an incredible man.
I really admire you. You're one of the smartest people I know.
You're not done, and we're not done.

Marc: I admire you, too, Amy. I've loved working with you.
But since the project didn't work out (just go with me on this one) what can I do to help you?

Amy: I'm a one woman show. It's just the nature of my work.
I'll see you on Monday, most likely. You're not getting off that easy.

Marc: I'll miss you until I see you on Monday, most
          definitely. ☺
Amy: ☺

Marc loafed around the house, waiting for Saturday, waiting for Monday, waiting for something to happen that wasn't happening now. He was getting up late and drinking extra coffee. With the kids in school and no project to sink himself into, he tried sinking himself into Franceska.

"Would you like some coffee cake with that?" She asked as he poured himself another cup.

"Is that what we call your pussy, now?" He asked.

"I'm starting my third trimester, Marc."

"I'll be careful," he said.

"Benjamin was born premature. I can't take any risks."

"Okay. What about your ass? What about your mouth?"

Franceska laughed.

"Why are you laughing?" Marc asked straight faced.

Franceska laughed again.

"This is not helping," he said.

"It's not helping me, either," she said. "I'm sorry, Marc. Those options create more strain than when you pound me in the pussy."

"Okay, I'll accept bids for your hand."

"I will later." She saw his reaction and said, "Does it have to be right now? I'm trying to finish the laundry."

"How about now *and* after the laundry?"

Franceska sighed. She said, "I'm really not in the mood. Why don't you get me some help?"

"What do you mean? I could use my computer but that's not as fun."

"I don't mind if you use your computer, but that's not what I meant."

"What do you mean, then?"

"You know what I mean, Marc. Amy really likes you."

"I really like her, too," Marc said like he was confessing something that no one knew.

"Then why don't you propose?"

"I don't know. Sometimes I think she just likes to flirt. She's told me several times that she can't see herself being married."

"Who says you have to be married?"

"Holy shit, Franceska! I would never do that."

"Why not? It wouldn't bother me. What is marriage anyway, but the formality of an emotional commitment? She will commit to you."

"How do you know?"

"We talk, Marc. I know."

"Wow." Marc thought for a moment, while Franceska folded laundry. "Can I help you with that?" He asked.

"No. I've seen how you fold laundry. I'd rather do it myself, I don't mind," she said with a smirk.

"I'm not trying to be worthless," he said.

"You're not worthless. You work very hard and I appreciate that."

"I'm not working now."

"I know. That's okay," she said. Then she added the weight of a proverb, "Even the mighty oak rests when it's cold."

"Franceska, you're too kind to me. I don't deserve you."

"I feel the same way about you," she said with a smile that would melt the mountainside. "So, what do you think about what I said?" She asked resuming the previous topic.

"I don't know. It seems like that would injure your trust in me."

"I told you that it's fine with me."

"Waiting until a formal, sanctioned marriage with you was one of the things that helped me through this experience with Lena. She had suspicions, but knowing that I had not done anything to violate her trust made me feel a lot better about what I was doing."

"So it's Lena. It's always Lena."

"What do you mean?"

"Lena is always... I don't know the word."

"Tell me what it means."

"She's like an insect, no I don't mean that. She's like a bird that flies around and around and around."

"Circling?"

"No. Like that, but I mean always there. Always circling around."

"Looming?"

"Yes. Looming. She's always looming over me, over you, over the kids, over everything."

"I'm sorry, Franceska. That's certainly not my intent. I didn't know you felt that way."

"Felt that way? You probably didn't even notice what she was doing that day."

"What day?"

"The day that she brought Kimmy and Travis."

"What didn't I notice?"

"She was rearranging things in the kitchen, Marc! Like I didn't exist."

"In the kitchen?" Marc started laughing.

"It's funny, is it?"

"No, it's not funny. As far as I'm concerned you can put anything in this kitchen anywhere you want. Besides, I don't remember seeing anything like that."

"Of course not. You were too busy dripping over her."

Marc laughed. "Do you mean *salivating* over her?"

"Yes! You didn't notice anything but her."

"I'm sorry that I made you feel that way. I thought we were all having a good time."

"We were, because I didn't let it get in the way, but that doesn't mean that I feel welcome here."

"What?" Marc yelled. "You're as welcome here as anyone. In fact you're more welcome than I am. Do you mind, Franceska, if I stay here? Is it okay with you if I sit here on this couch?"

"I see what you're saying, Marc, but that doesn't mean that she doesn't..."

"Loom?"

"Loom over me. For example, it's Lena that you don't want to hurt by having sex with Amy."

"It's not Lena," Marc said stressing her name. "I'd be just as concerned about hurting you."

"I already told you that it wouldn't hurt me." She waited for his response and received none, so she continued. "Marc, Lena is gone. I'm sorry. I didn't want it, but she's gone. She divorced you and she's hardly had anything to do with us for several months. She took you for everything she could. If it hadn't been for your stock in LogicStream, we wouldn't even have this house. We're almost out of reserves. You've got to move on, Marc. You've got to move on for all of us."

"I know," Marc said. He looked like a captain standing at the helm of a sinking ship, trying to decide whether to go down with it or swallow his pride and jump into a life raft. "I know, Franci. I know."

Marc said he'd like some Scotch and he asked Franceska for some ice and a glass. It wasn't that he was too lazy to get it for himself; he always asked someone else when he was being imprudent. It gave her a kind of power of veto, which he would respect. She asked him if he was really sure; after all he had barely finished coffee. He told her that he wasn't sure of anything, but he'd like some if she felt okay about a bum drinking in her living room. He said, "There is no guarantee, but it might help me to think."

As she left the glass and ice on the coffee table in front of him, she said, "Besides, if you would propose, Amy might change her mind about marriage."

Marc fetched the decanter and poured two fingers. Over the next several hours, he poured several more, but one tends to lose track of the tally at around ten.

"Well, that's it," Edberg said as he poured the last of the Scotch into his and Marc's glasses. Edberg had been drinking before Marc arrived. He wasn't slurring words, but he was acting unusually cheery.

"Are you sure this is okay? I thought you said you couldn't drink Scotch."

"I can *now*. It turns out that if nothing else gets you, cancer finally will."

Marc was stunned. He looked crushed, like a soda can heated in a campfire until it's glowing red and then suddenly immersed in icy water; it loses pressure on the inside and the pressure on the outside crumples it. "What?" he asked. Crushed ears don't hear too well.

"I have cancer."

"No. No way! You said you had diabetes."

"I do, but now I've been diagnosed with pancreatic cancer. I guess this pancreas of mine was determined to kill me one way or another. If it couldn't on the down side, it would on the flip side."

"So what are your treatment options?" Marc asked.

"I'm not seeking treatment."

"You've got to," Marc demanded.

"The doctor gave me six or eight months with treatment, but it wouldn't be the way I'd want…"

Marc cut him off, "How long without treatment?"

"A week, maybe two. It's quite advanced."

Marc crumpled again, but once a can has been creased, it crushes harder the second time. He finally regained his composure. "Thanks for telling me."

"You've been a good friend, Marc. One of the few I have. People like me don't have many. I wish that we could have associated longer."

"I wish so, too. You've really helped me; I've learned a lot from you."

"That's the other thing I wanted to talk to you about, Marc. I heard that you've been fired by Wesley."

"Yeah."

"Well, no matter. He had no imagination. I'll be quitting the project, too." Edberg laughed.

"It's not funny," Marc said.

"If I can't laugh, I'll die."

Marc glared at him.

Edberg continued. "You're gifted, Marc. It wasn't my lot to solve the big problems, but I have a lot of hope in you. You're standing on the edge of the greatest breakthrough in human thinking since…"

"Since what?" Marc asked.

"I don't know. Since, since… Well, there is nothing to compare it to," Edberg said. "It's *that* big!"

Marc said, "I hope that I don't let you down."

"You won't. But hey, no pressure, kid."

"No pressure. Right."

"Here, I'd like you to have this," Edberg said, handing his decanter to Marc. "You helped me finish my last drop; I won't be pouring any more. In fact, this will be the last time that we will likely see each other. The next few days won't be the sort of thing that… Well, let's just say, it's better to end on a high note."

"Thanks," Marc said quietly, taking the decanter. "Hey, Professor Edberg?"

"Yes?"

"Would you do me a favor?"

"Sure, anything."

"If you find a way to let me know that there's an afterlife, would you please?"

"Absolutely. But you know, as Hamlet says, death is "the undiscovered country, from whose bourn no traveler returns.' Nevertheless, if I can find a way, I will."

"If it helps, professor, every time I drink from this decanter, I'll be watching and listening for you."

"Are you going to get out of bed?" Franceska asked.

"I don't feel well," Marc said.

"I shouldn't have let you drink so much yesterday. You look really hungover."

"I'm sure it didn't help, but this isn't a hangover. I've caught something. The alcohol probably lowered my resistance. I think I have a fever. Do I feel hot?"

Franceska felt his head. "Yes, a little."

Marc spent the day in bed, and the next day, and the day after that. His fever was getting worse.

"Look at that," Marc said, pointing at the ceiling.

"Look at what?" Franceska asked.

"The ceiling," Marc said.

"I am looking at the ceiling," she said. "What are you pointing at?"

"The ceiling, silly girl. What do you see?"

"I don't see anything."

"You told me you were looking at the ceiling. Don't you see that little bastard grinning at me?"

"No. Where is it?"

"It doesn't matter," Marc said. "It's not really there. It's just goddamned texture. I should kick his ass. Who in hell does he think he is? What's the matter with me, Franci?"

"You're sick. You need to go to the hospital."

"No, I mean, why do I see bastards instead of friends? Life is nothing but an inkblot test. People see what they want to see, so why do I want to see that? Why can I find lies, but not the truth?"

Franceska sat still, listening to him with a concerned look.

"I found you, didn't I Franci? Do you know what that proves? It proves that I'm not all bad. No. No, it doesn't. No. I give myself more credit than I deserve. Maybe I didn't find you. No, I didn't find you. You found me, little angel. I didn't do anything at all. You did it all. You flew across the sea. You came to LogicStream. You wore that pretty little dress. You wrote those hearts on my mail. You found something in me that I couldn't see in myself. A capacity. A capacity that I'm still trying to live up to. You passed the inkblot test, Franci. Will you teach me how? I need you desperately. You're a good girl. You're a really good, good girl. Do you see good in me, Franci?"

"Yes, Marc. I married you, didn't I?"

"Yes, that's because you're good."

"You married me, so you must be good, too."

"No it doesn't work like that, dear. Little bastard doesn't think so, either. He's a little bastard, but that doesn't mean that he's wrong. He's calling me out on my shit. Franci, if you were not here, I'd tell him what I think."

"He's not real, Marc, so say what you want. It's just you and me."

"I know he's not real. He's an imaginary little bastard. Don't call 911; I know he's not real. Okay? I just don't want you to know what I really am... See? You're afraid to ask, because you're thinking, 'what if I don't like what I see?'"

"You don't know what I'm thinking."

"I know. I'm not a goddamned mind reader. I'm just saying you're afraid to ask."

"Okay, Marc. What are you?"

"I'm a goddamned piece of shit."

"No you're not."

"You have to say that."

"I don't have to say that."

"I mean that's the polite thing to say because you're so nice. Franci, you're the nicest person I've ever met."

"Okay, Marc, what have you done that's so bad?"

"I haven't done anything. Not one thing. It's not what I have done. It's what I see. Why can't I look into that ceiling and see the face of God? Why can't I look into that ceiling and see the next big thing? The earth shattering concept? The solution?"

"What solution?"

"THE SOLUTION. Whatever! There's world hunger. There's hate. There are little children suffering. Why can't I find the answer? Why can't I look into that ceiling and find you? I'll tell you why! It's because I am evil. Good things don't come to me."

"Thanks," Franceska said.

"That's not what I meant. I adore you. I already said that you're good. You're the best thing I have in my life. I don't have Lena in my life. She left me. She left me. Franci, she left me."

"It's Lena, Lena, Lena. Here we go again."

"No Lena, uh, I mean Franceska, I'm saying you're the best thing in my life."

"This is just like last night. It was 'Lena, Lena, Lena.'"

"Franceska. I'm sick. I'm really sick. I hope that I haven't hurt you. I don't think my mind is working right."

"It's not. Most of the time you don't make any sense. I'm calling emergency."

"No, Franci. I'll be alright. I just need to sleep. I'll sleep and everything will be alright."

A noise. A sight. What does a baby first see? Does he see a blinding light or does he close his eyes to some atrocity? What does a baby first hear? Does he hear his own cry or does he cry when he hears the world? There's a lot of speculation, but little certainty. Oh certainty, she's flying away. There are muffled sounds and a mingling of shadows and light. There's a voice, and another voice, unfamiliar voices. There's a condescending rattling of throats which belittle the child, as if he won't understand, but he'll understand far more than they. There are mechanical lungs and mechanical minds. They run on motors and beeps. Stop beeping! What are they to the wonder of human things? There are plans and deliberations. There are flowers. They won't last. They'll wither before he wakes. There are wishes. If wishes were fishes. Well, there's a sea, isn't there? Sounds run different in the sea. Faster. Now, the child can swim. Faster. Faster. He's older and muscular, like Hercules. He captures glances of sighing girls. They love his hands and pine to be held by them, but they can't hold a thing. His hands are too weak. The girls will be sad. His girl will cry. His girls will cry. Why is there so much crying? The world's a joyful place. Maybe not. Maybe it's as depressing as everyone makes it be. Not everyone makes it be. Some turn winter into spring. She always turned winter into spring.

"I can hear you. Why do you keep asking me?"

"I only asked once."

"Who is that?"

"Franceska. It's Franceska, Marc."

"Oh there you are. I feel much better, now."

"We're all here."

"Who's all here?"

"Your dad, your mom, and Laura, Chuck and Zack."

"Where am I?"

"In the hospital."

"What in the hell am I doing here?" Marc asked, looking around, somewhat frightened.

"You're very sick, son. But the doctors say you're doing a lot better."

"What happened?"

"You had a bad case of pneumonia," a woman said.

"Why are you in pajamas?" Marc asked.

"I'm in my nursing uniform."

"Oh, right. I'm sorry. Everything seems so foggy."

"No problem, Marc. We'll take good care of you."

"I know you will," he said to the nurse. He turned to Franceska. "Where are the kids?" He asked.

"They're with Amy. She's watching them so that I can be here with you. They'll see you tomorrow."

"Oh, that's nice of her," Marc said.

Everyone expressed his or her relief and gratitude that Marc made it through. Apparently it was really scary for a while there. He gathered that he had been in a medically induced coma for three weeks. The nurse told him that Franceska called the paramedics just in time. If he had waited any longer for treatment, it would have been much worse. He was a very lucky man to be alive. Eventually everyone left except Franceska and Marc's dad, Bradley.

"Where did everyone go?" Marc asked.

"The doctor didn't want us to crowd you too long. They left so that you could rest," Bradley said.

"Sorry I missed fishing with you, Dad."

"That's alright, son. Just focus on getting well. We'll go fishing soon."

Between naps, drinking juice, and the anesthesia wearing off, Marc gradually grew more alert. He started being more inquisitive. He wanted to know what happened, when it happened, and how long it happened. Bradley and Franceska did the best they could to answer his questions, but they were being reserved and even vague in their answers.

Finally Bradley said, "Son, we have something to tell you. There's no easy way to say this."

"Why are you looking at me like that?" Marc asked frightened and concerned. "Am I okay? Am I in one piece?"

Franceska started crying and Bradley quickly added, "You're fine. You're all in one piece. We're very grateful for that."

"Then why are you looking at me like that? Why is Franceska crying?"

"Son, there's been an accident. It was Lena, son. She didn't make it."

"What? What? No. What are you talking about?"

"I'm so sorry, son."

"What in the hell are you talking about, Dad? What in the name of God are you talking about? Lena? Are you sure?"

"Yes, son."

"No! No, goddamnit! No!"

"I'm sorry, son. She was hit by a big truck, head on collision. I don't know what to say. It's a cruel, senseless world. We debated whether to tell you or not, considering how sick you are, but we decided it'd be cruel to wait, too. I wish this hadn't happened."

"Was she here? Did she come to see me?" Marc asked.

"Yes, son. She came early on, a couple of days before her accident."

Marc started rocking back and forth. Bradley expressed his deepest condolences. Finally, Marc asked how the visit with Lena went. Bradley said that he wasn't present, but he would wait outside so that Marc and Franceska could discuss it privately. He would be there if they needed anything.

After Bradley left, Franceska described Lena's visit to see Marc in the hospital. "We talked for quite a while. She was really worried and I gave her a lot of details about your condition. Then we talked about the kids and their schooling. She told me how much she appreciated me for taking care of Kimmy and Travis when they came to visit. Eventually, I got up the nerve to ask her why she left. She told me that she didn't really know, but it didn't have anything to do with you or me. She said that there's a lot of prejudice against polygamy and she kind of fell into that, but she could see a lot of benefits, too. She was really nice about it. I told her that I never intended to drive her away, or replace her, and that I really missed her. She said that she believed me. Then she said something like, 'who knows what the future may hold.' I didn't really know how she meant that, but she said it with a gleam in her eye, so I felt like she was considering remarrying you." She paused to assess how that might affect Marc. His eyes responded deeply, but the rest of his face was almost expressionless, like he was conflicted between feeling joy or distress.

Franceska continued in a cautious tone. "Then I asked if she would like to have some time with you alone. She said that she would like that very much. While I waited outside, I could hear her reading to you. I couldn't tell what it was, but then it went quiet for about twenty minutes. When she came out, she had tears in her eyes. I'm incredibly sorry, Marc. I think she really loved you."

Marc started trembling. Franceska held him, cried with him, and tried to comfort him. She was salve to his sorrow and cotton to his wounds. Nevertheless, grief is a relentless dagger that keeps stabbing until the heart is completely minced. There are many hearts, all woven together. The kids, the poor kids, and the Brensetts, they were all grieving, too. Franceska was grieving. She said that she regretted telling Marc that he needed to move past Lena. If she had known that this would happen, she would have begged Lena to return.

When one layer of pain was completely felt, another kicked in. Sleep offered a temporary reprieve, but one must eventually wake and face it again. When the kids came the next day, Marc kissed them and clung to them. He told them how much he loved them and their mother, too. He never stopped loving her. He was indescribably sorry that things went the way they did. Kimberly was being big and Travis wiped his own tears. They told Marc about their mom's funeral. It was a week ago. They wished that he could have been there, but they were glad that they didn't lose him, too.

Two more weeks rolled on and everyone involved worked very hard to find their smiles again, but they were mostly pasted on. When the doctor gave Marc discharge instructions, he said that even though Marc had been engaged in physical therapy, he still wasn't strong enough to return to his regular activity. Marc thanked him for the information, because hardly being able to walk wasn't evidence enough. The doctor said that he was glad that Marc could laugh about it.

Marc said, "If I can't laugh, I'll die."

"Laughter is the best therapy," the doctor said and continued with his instructions. Marc needed to take it easy and not engage in strenuous activity until his body repaired. It may take months or even years. It was unlikely that he would ever regain his full fitness level. The doctor said, "You were in good shape when you got here. That's one of the things that saved your life. I think regaining 80 to 90% is an optimistic goal."

When Marc was finally settled at home, he saw Amy for the first time. She pulled up a chair and sat beside his bed.

"Hey, there," he said.

"Hey. It's good to see you. I've been worried."

"It's good to see you, too. Thanks for all of your help with the kids. I don't know how I can ever repay you."

"You don't need to, Marc. I did it because I wanted to help. Besides, Laura helped as much as I did."

"Well, I really appreciate it. Thanks."

"You're welcome. Marc, I have something to tell you. It's not easy."

Marc closed his eyes, took a deep breath, braced himself, and then looked at her.

She said, "Do you remember that test we ran on the software?" Marc nodded and she continued. "Well, I didn't leave it at that. I took our findings to Lena."

"You did what?"

"I wanted to know if she thought there was anything to it. I thought, 'worst case scenario, it would persuade her to...'"

"Persuade her to what?"

"Persuade her to reconsider you."

"How would exposing her family cause her to reconsider me?"

"Because she would see what you were sitting on, what you wouldn't use to your advantage because you were taking the high road."

"I *was* taking the high road," Marc exclaimed as much as his weak lungs would permit.

"I know, Marc. I'm sorry. I'm an investigator; it was driving me crazy not knowing."

"There was nothing to know. It was probably coincidental."

"Maybe it was, but now Lena's dead within a couple of weeks of finding out. I'm very sorry, Marc. I'm a thousand times sorrier if I caused it in any way."

"What are you saying, Amy?"

"Maybe working on this project has made me paranoid, but I'm saying that Lena started asking questions."

"I can't believe what you're saying. You're suggesting that she was murdered?"

"I don't know," Amy said.

"Her family would never do that," Marc insisted.

"Her family wouldn't, but it went pretty high up. The governor might."

"I can't talk about this right now," Marc said, visibly shaken.

"I can say this…"

Marc cut her off. "I said I can't talk about this."

"Okay. I'm very, very sorry." Amy stood up and moved the chair back. She stopped before opening the door and said, "Lena told me that she made a mistake, ya know, leaving you. I know that she loved you. It was obvious. This is probably the worst possible time to say this, but I love you, too."

It took another week or two, but as soon as Marc regained enough strength, he visited Lena's gravesite. He stood there for a good long time, saying nothing. It was cold but he didn't seem to mind. Perhaps he was punishing himself. Finally he began his lonesome monologue.

"I love you, Lena. God, how I love you. I said I always would, and I meant it, but I'm angry now. I know that I shouldn't be, but I am. I can't really be angry with you. It's not your fault. I'm angry with myself, for a thousand things that I did or didn't do. I admit that I'm a little angry with you, too, but mostly with myself, for not being more, for not being able to find my way through to you. I truly believed that I could reach you. I believed that my love would prevail. I put all of my stock in it. Now, I don't know what to believe. I don't know if there's anything *to* believe.

"I don't know if you can even hear me, but I'm sorry. I'm monumentally sorry, Lena. I know it doesn't do any good to place blame; it won't bring you back. I just don't know what I'm supposed to do anymore. I was focused when I had you, and I was focused on bringing you back. I didn't worry too much about the divorce, because I knew that I would win in the end; there was no doubt. I *knew* that if I kept loving you, and reaching out, that you would eventually love me, too. Amy and Franceska say that you still loved me. I hope that's true. It would mean an awful lot to me, but it's really hard to accept that I will never know for sure.

"I'm going to try to move on, Lena, but I don't think my heart will ever mend. I'm going to do my best with this gaping hole in my chest. I'll never forget you. I'll never stop loving you. I miss you, horribly. I ache for you. There will always be a void where you once stood. When I can, I'll visit here and other places, you know, places that were special to us, but I have people depending on me and I can't disappear. I have to be strong. If you're there and you're watching, I want you to know that I'm always thinking of you. It's with an ever-present pain that I'll be marching on.

"I'm going to visit our mining shaft, but I can't rappel today; I've got to save my strength for something else. I think about that day a lot, Lena, when we made love down there. I think we both felt that it was a permanent commitment. In my heart, my broken, smitten heart, I don't think you ever broke that. I hope you know that I never did. I'll treasure the moments that I spent with you—sunsets, walks, arguments and making up, the way you taught me to look at the world—our last kiss. I think you enjoyed it as much as I did. I saw it in your eyes. Maybe it frightened you. Maybe that's why you distanced yourself. I know that I asked for an awful lot from you, but that's because I…"

Marc paused. He fought off the deluge of tears, but they overwhelmed him. He choked on a phrase several times. He apparently decided to leave it buried inside because it eventually stopped lodging in his throat. After he managed to compose himself again, he continued. "Lena, I don't have a sufficient reason for it. My decisions seem so costly now. You wondered why I… Why Franceska? I promise you, I swear to God, it was never because you weren't enough; I was trying to become something more. Believe it or not, I wanted to impress you. I know you didn't understand, but I'm certain that you would have loved the man that I was growing into.

"I enjoy being a parent to all of our kids. I'm making decent progress with Benny and Kira. They enjoy their new school and they're making friends, too. Franceska is close to giving birth to our new baby girl. She wants to name the baby 'Lena.' I think that's a great idea." Marc paused while he battled his emotions. Finally, he proceeded, choking on his words. "Kimmy and Travis really miss you, babe, but they're trying to be brave. It's going to be hard, without you. You were a rock in our lives. I think Kimmy blames me. The hard part is that she isn't wrong. I'm going to work hard to repair my relationship with her; I don't know how, but I'll find a way. They're currently living with your parents, but I'm going to file for custody, soon. I suppose your parents will fight me, but don't worry, Darling, I'll take care of our little ones, no matter what. I'm going to visit your parents soon. I need to make peace with them.

"Well, I suppose you're getting tired of hearing from me," Marc said with a laugh that stung him. "It is with great sorrow, that I part from you. I don't know what comes after this, but I sincerely hope to see you again. For now, goodbye my love, my darling, eternal love. Goodbye."

Marc looked into the face of the cold, hard stone which marked her grave. He took off his right glove, touched his finger to it, and melted an icon of the sun into the frost. He set his jaw to the wind and drove to the mining shaft. He found the narrow opening to the consummation of their love covered with a large boulder. Apparently, park officials considered it dangerous to the public health. He placed his hand on the stone and said, "It's just as well, I suppose."

Then he drove to the canyon and laced on his hiking boots. His doctor certainly wouldn't approve. He flung the portable oxygen tank over his shoulder and started hiking to his temple in the snow, stopping often to regain his breath.

At this pace, it would take quite a while. Up ahead about forty paces, beside the trail Marc finally saw it—a big cat and it was saw him, too. The lion turned to face him and Marc stood perfectly still while they sized each other up. In Marc's weakened condition, he didn't stand a chance. It took a step toward him and Marc took a step toward it. It's best never to let one's enemies know how weak one truly is. Eventually, it turned and ran away. At that point prudence would dictate turning back, but Marc moved on, slowly on. Perhaps it felt like a victory.

He approached the ice covered alter and with all of his strength and with all of his lungs, he shouted, "Are you there?"

The trickle of water and the panting of lungs were the only sounds. The snow and the trees, the stone and the sand, they made no reply. He fell to his knees and wept until the tears flowed dry. He fell to his side onto the cold, wet sand along the stream. He looked to the clouds and asked, "Why? Why? Why?"

After many more clouds passed and the sun fell behind the cliffs, he picked himself up and knelt again. He said, "God, I will never forsake you. I don't understand. Perhaps I never will, but I love you still."

He hiked back to his vehicle and composed a text to Amy: "I love you, too. Let's build something new."

ACKNOWLEDGEMENTS

I'd like to thank my parents, all of them, for the wonderful upbringing that they provided. They sacrificed their own dreams to build mine. I'd like to thank my mother in particular. She very gently nudged me toward greatness, to learn, to grow, to be more open minded, and to love when prejudice was the rule. She worked very hard and, even while attending school, she managed to provide wonderful learning opportunities for us kids. I often argued with her and thereby I learned a great deal.

I'd like to thank my wives. It was their support and devotion, their confidence and faith that brought this book to completion. Thank-you for turning an ignorant little boy into a man. Thank-you for putting up with all of my shit. You have inspired me. I hope that I can serve you as generously and with as much love.

I'd like to thank my teachers. You were more than teachers; you were mentors and friends; you were mothers and fathers. This book is as much yours as mine. I'd also like to thank the great teachers whom I never knew personally. There is insufficient space to name them all, but I'd specifically like to acknowledge Jesus, the prince of peace.

I'd like to thank my reviewers whose suggestions and criticism improved this book. Thanks to my cover designer who saw the vision and responded. Thanks to the creators whom I quoted. I usually credited them directly within the text. The following are authors whom I quoted without direct credit within the text: the great Anonymous, Shakespeare, George Lucas, Joseph Smith, Jr., and the biblical authors of Genesis, Exodus, Psalms, Matthew, Luke, and John. Whenever possible, I tried to give clear clues as to who the author was. I also borrowed liberally from the book of Ruth.

Finally, thank you God! Volumes couldn't express how much I adore you and marvel at your greatness. I don't know how to show my appreciation sufficiently, but I'll keep searching. You give everything and ask nothing in return. You are my greatest inspiration and the cynosure of my life.